# BAIT

Book One in The Wake Series

by M. Mabie

***Bait: The Wake Series, Book One***
Copyright © 2014 M. Mabie

ALL RIGHTS RESERVED. This book contains material protected under International and Federal Copyright Laws and Treaties. Any unauthorized reprint or use of the material is prohibited. No part of this book may be reproduced or transmitted in any form or by any means, electronic or mechanical, including photocopying, recording, or by any information storage and retrieval system without express written permission from the author/publisher. The characters and events portrayed in this book are fictitious. Any similarity to real persons, alive or dead, is coincidental and not indented by the author.

LICENSE NOTICE. This book is licensed for your personal enjoyment only. This book man not be resold or given away to other people. If you wish to share this book with another person, please purchase an additional copy for each person you share it with. Thank you for respecting the hard work of this author.

DISCLAIMER. This is a work of adult fiction. Names, characters, businesses, places, events and incidents are either the products of the author's imagination or used in a fictitious manner. Any resemblance to actual persons, living or dead, or actual events is purely coincidental.
The author does not endorse or condone any behavior enclosed within. The subject matter is not appropriate for minors. Please note this novel contains profanity and explicit sexual situations.

Cover Design Copyright © 2014 by Arijana Karcic, Cover It! Designs
Book formatting by Stacey Blake, Champagne Formatting
Editing by Marion Making Manuscripts, Marion Archer, and Bare Naked Author Services, Claire Allmendinger

ISBN-10: 1502388472
ISBN-13: 978-1502388476

## ALSO BY THE AUTHOR

FADE IN

*For Danny, my hook*

# ONE

## Blake

**Friday, May 23, 2008**

IT RAINED BUCKETS the whole day. There wasn't much that could make me feel more disgusting than a plane ride coupled with that wet and dry moistness you get from being in and out of the rain. Moist. That word alone made me want to take a shower.

I'd flown into San Francisco to attend my dear friend, Micah's, graduation. We met when we were both attending culinary school at The Art Institute of California in San Francisco, when I was in my second year and she in her first. The ceremony wasn't until the next day, but I'd flown in early so I could go out with her and our friends.

After I graduated the previous May, I moved back home to Seattle. Most of my family lived there, so they appreciated my closer proximity. I loved being close to them, too. My mom and dad had been married forever. For someone my age, it was odd to have married parents who still liked each other. All around, we were a close family. I was the youngest of three and the only girl.

For a year, I'd been dating my boyfriend, Grant, and if my blabber-mouth parents were correct, he was soon to be my fiancé. Grant and I didn't live together. His choice, not mine. I lived in my mediocre apartment and he lived in his, four blocks apart. Even thinking about it drove me mad. But Grant was a great guy and insisted on not living together until we were married. I could only presume he'd insist on that sooner than later. That was the traditional thing to do.

He was traditional. A classic. The all-American guy.

But I didn't think of myself as the classic, all-American girl.

Opposites attract. Apparently.

We got along great and rarely fought. Well, until that morning, when we fought about him bailing on the trip last minute. That was the kind of day I'd had.

I finally made it—damp and all—to the Hook, Line and Sinker, or HLS if you were local, and my first beer was on its way. I should've probably ordered two. That first beer wouldn't last long.

Oh, yeah. The airport lost my luggage, too. Thankfully, I had my toiletries with me. It was almost a silver lining. Almost.

"Blake!" I heard Micah shout my name when she blew into the bar. I twisted in my stool to face the door where I saw her bouncing up to me. She looked the same as she had a year before. Micah had a messy, blonde pixie cut. She looked like a little fairy.

As soon as I stood, her short, petite body hugged me and I hugged her back in earnest.

"I've missed you so much," she said into my hair and squeezed me hard. She was a mighty little thing and her hold on me was more than I'd anticipated. As she pulled away I saw the two guys she came in with order beers.

I knew she had a boyfriend. I'd seen pictures of them together and she'd said that I met him before I left. I really couldn't tell you which one he was. I assumed the one closest to her.

Then I noticed they were the same damn dude. Well, two versions of the same dude anyway. I swore they were twins. They had to be.

Micah stepped closer to the one of them and introduced, "Blake, this is my handsome boyfriend, Cory Moore. Cory, this is my talented friend, Blake Warren." He offered me his hand and was happy to shake it.

He looked thoughtfully at her and asked, "What are you drinking, baby?" I already liked him. He seemed very sweet on her by the way his hand affectionately rubbed her side.

"I'll take a pint of whatever Bay they now have on tap." She crooked her head and smiled brightly at the replica of her boyfriend. He swiftly looked at her with a cool, knowing grin. "What are you drinking, Blake?" Micah lifted up on her toes to look around me on the bar where I had my glass. "She'll take one, too!" I never ordered the second one, so I didn't object.

Cory motioned to his brother, who'd taken a seat behind them at the bar, and said, "This is my brother, Casey." Casey didn't bother to look up. Instead, he fiddled with his phone, not paying any attention. Cory kicked him for being rude or maybe just to get a response.

I could unquestionably tell they were twins by then, but they weren't carbon copies, at least not anymore. Cory's hair was cut very short on the sides, a little longer on the top and neatly combed to one side. Casey's was full-on loose curls everywhere. Cory wore a crisp pair of gray tweed trousers, a white shirt and tie, complete with suspenders. Casey had on dark jeans, and a loose fitting, black V-neck T-shirt.

Cory was attractive and Casey was perfect. Simple as that. I could have stood there comparing the two all night. They were identical twin bodies, transformed into totally different men by their styles and personalities alone.

Casey finally looked up with a blank expression. Standing stock still, he said hello then went right back to his phone.

"Don't mind him." Cory smiled and then our drinks arrived. Only when I took a swig of my beer did Casey look my way again.

I smiled at him and mouthed "mmm, good."

I wondered what his problem was. He looked like an easy-going guy. He wore flip-flops with jeans for crying out loud. I decided that maybe he, too, had had a shitty day.

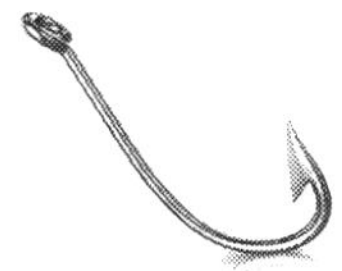

It wasn't too long before all of the old gang filled HLS. We chatted and played catch-up. It was fantastic seeing everyone. The cocktails flowed, my drowned appearance and lack of garments quickly forgotten.

Cory and Micah danced in the other room. They made a great couple. Since I needed another beer, I decided to belly up to the bar next to Casey, where he'd been most of the time. All night I'd wanted to walk over and talk to him and needing another drink was reason enough.

Leaning toward him a little to get his attention, I said, "What are you drinking? It's Casey, right?" I was, obviously, really smooth. It was evident he'd been drinking the same draught beer I had. Okay, so I didn't know what to say to him, but I really wanted him to talk to me.

"Right." He was tight-lipped. I didn't feel like being a pest, so I waited patiently for the bartender. I bounced and bobbed to the song playing that filtered in from the large, banquet-style room on the other side of the bar.

"And..." I coaxed.

Finally, he spoke more than just two words in a row, "I'm drinking a new Bay brew. It's pretty good." But he still refused to look at me straight in the eye.

"I think I'm drinking a Bay beer, too. It must be local."

"They're local," he said. "I'm a brewer. That's what I do." It finally seemed like he might be interested in small talk with me. I was relieved.

"That's cool. I'm a chef. A sous chef now, but I'll be head day chef soon. So..." I trailed off, and faked my impatience waiting for another pint.

"That's how you and Micah know each other then? You're friends from school? I think she mentioned that." I liked his voice. It sounded raspy and fallow. I definitely didn't want him to stop talking.

His eyes finally met mine and then he seemed to survey me from head to toe. It made me self-conscious, like my face had something on it, but I pretended to be unaffected. He was blatantly taking inventory of me, which worked in my favor because I wanted to do the same.

"Yeah, we lived together for a few years. Micah's amazing and she looks really happy with your brother."

He nodded his agreement. "I know. They make me nauseous sometimes, but yeah, they're good for each other." Casey finished his beer and motioned to the bartender to bring two instead of just mine. "If you cook as well as her, I bet you're pretty damn good." There was almost a grin hiding behind the beginnings of a beard he had going on.

"Thanks, I'm sure your beer is pretty damn good, too," I said in return. He was finally being friendly. I could be, too. He gave the bartender money for both our beers.

"Thank you." He turned in the stool facing me. I had his full attention. His eyes didn't look like they had when he walked in. He looked more at ease. More comfortable.

"Oh, you'd like my brew," he said and nodded confidently, with the first real smile he'd gifted me.

It was worth the wait. I felt like I'd truly earned it.

"How do you know that? I have a very particular palate." Cleary flirting, I arched an eyebrow.

It was true. My mouth had an uncanny ability to detect things. It worked well for me in my occupation. Chances were, if I liked a dish I could guess the ingredients from taste alone. It hadn't ever failed me.

"Because you've already had four of them. Going on five." His fresh smile broke clean through, teeth and all. He was charming me and he had me dangling on a line. I laughed in jest at the trap that I'd played right into. If it kept that look on his face, he could have tricked me all night.

When Casey smiled, his whole face was involved. His eyes, his cheeks, his mouth, those teeth, his chest puffed out, and his head tipped back. He looked pretty damn proud. His delight was contagious.

He had the most perfect set of teeth I had ever seen.

*I needed to leave him alone.*

That was probably why I felt the need to deflate his ever-growing ego. So, I told him, "I've had better."

"I doubt that."

I feigned offense. "That's awfully cocky. You're the cocky twin then?" I retorted in an attempt to knock his peg down a rung. I failed. Miserably.

"If you mean I have the better cock, then yeah. I'm the *cock* one."

"I said cocky." My mouth went dry and even though it played right into his hands, I took a long drink of my beer.

Casey leaned in and said, "See? You already can't get enough."

"You're trouble."

"Yeah, I am trouble. And you should go dance with your friends before you find out what kind." The mischievous gleam in his hazel eyes promised he could back up the threat.

That called for another long drink. Did I want trouble? I typically wasn't a trouble seeker. So why didn't I want to walk away? God, I probably looked like a fool standing there with my beer glass that hovered in front of my mouth while I stared at him. All I could think about was that mouth and those teeth all over me.

I broke my blatant stare and, instead, watched his lips move in the mirror behind the bar as he said, "I can tell you right now, that isn't a good idea."

"What? You don't know what I'm thinking." I blushed. *Did he?* No. But what had he assumed I'd thought?

I stole a glance at the dance floor and then my eyes went right back to him. Standing there flirting probably would get me in trouble.

I had a boyfriend.

I had an almost fiancé.

But he stayed in Seattle. He made his choice. A voice inside me said, *this might be a good time to sow some oats.* Surely, it had to be better to cheat on a boyfriend than a fiancé. I'd never once cheated before. It wasn't how I rolled. But Casey was too good to pass up.

What would one night hurt? I was drunk, right? This happened to people all the time. They made poor decisions after drinking too much. I hadn't drunk enough to completely sever myself from my better judgment, but I had drunk enough to pretend I had.

I was going to hate myself in the morning, but I did, in fact, want his trouble. I was too curious.

"Compromise?" I asked.

Casey's dark eyebrows shot up at my challenge. I'd caught him off-guard.

"I'll leave your trouble over here, like you advise. If you follow my trouble over there." The bass was thumping and it sounded like everyone was about to get their sexy back and that included me.

Acting so wanton was out of character; it must have been the beer.

Best-case scenario, we'd have a great time dancing and I'd make a new friend. Best *worst*-case scenario, I'd finally get those dirty clothes off.

He was clever man. I could tell. He asked no questions and simply picked up his beer, grabbed my free hand and started us in the direction of the dance floor. He turned around and walked backward with the sexiest sway to his shoulders. Then, he stopped short of the dance floor.

"I've already warned you. You won't be able to get enough. Now, here's your chance to stop this, while you still have the willpower." He was both menacing and tempting.

My warm cheeks tightened and I couldn't help but cackle out loud with a resounding, "Ha!" I pointed my finger straight at his face and bent over. He was kidding and flirting, but also I knew he spoke some truth. It didn't matter though, because I still followed that cocky man.

Playful and shamefaced, he admitted, "My moves are potent. You've been warned, honeybee." His hips began swaying in time to the beat. He danced right where he stood. He was joking, but as soon as his body touched mine I knew it wouldn't be enough.

*Honeybee? Could he be any more swoon-worthy?*

"What's with the honeybee thing? You have an insect fetish?" I asked. Praying to God that I was wrong. I mean, it was likely that I was way off base, but you never knew. People were weird.

"I don't know. Your eyes kind of look like honey and your name starts with a B. Plus, you sort of have this buzz about you." His eyebrows bunched together and he waited to see if I bought it, then added, "Maybe I do have a thing for bugs."

We both tried not to laugh, mouths puckered.

He said, "I don't know why I picked it, I just did. I can stop."

"No. Don't. I like it."

We made our way onto the dance floor in time for the end of the song and for another one to begin. There was that awkward silence in between songs. We looked at each other expectantly. That was about the time when I realized I was fucked. I knew the next song when it began. Casey's eyes lit up like he would have picked it himself. And then there was that smile again.

He took the beer from my hand and placed it on the nearby ledge and asked, "Okay, honeybee. You in?" I wasn't sure what he was asking me, but my answer was yes. He only waited for the start of my smile before he had his hands on my hips, pulling me into him.

He held me tight. His right hand circled all the way around my lower half and his left ran straight up the center of my back. My chest was pressed beneath his and I could feel how hard his pecs were.

Instinctively, I brought my hands around his neck and clasped them together. I felt shy and possibly guilty.

I had a boyfriend.

I had an almost fiancé.

I was a ho.

I was about to stop the whole charade; my arms began to slip from our embrace. But before I could retreat, he put his nose against my cheek and breathed into my ear. "Hold on to me, Blake."

Willingly, I tightened my hold on him. And then he moved us. His hips swayed our bodies side-to-side and back-and-forth and Led Zeppelin begged the girl, "Don't go."

Casey sang along immodestly the whole time. With every "Oh" and "Ay" I felt him vibrate. There was no turning back. I shouldn't have, but I wanted him. I should have stopped, but I also knew that I wouldn't. *I couldn't.* It felt too right.

The stubble on his cheek scratched against my forehead. Our bodies created friction everywhere. My hands were hot and had clenched fists full of Casey's shirt. I could not get close enough. I didn't know this man. He didn't know me, but hell if the two people dancing on that dance floor didn't fit in the most fundamental of ways.

The hand he had possessively resting on my spine trailed its way into my hair. His long fingers fanned across my skull which created a tingly sensation down to my toes. He clutched the hair at the nape of my neck and pulled my head away from his.

I smelled the delicious beer on his lips as he confessed, "I like your trouble."

My words failed. I didn't know if it was the beer, the music, or the man attached to me, but I felt pliant.

Anything could happen.

Anything at all.

Looking back, it was the first night of so many that I thought those exact words. Anything I could get from Casey Moore was better than nothing at all. I would take any scrap of this man I was offered. That's the night my heart split into two equal and separate pieces. That's the night I gave one to a perfect stranger, and the remaining piece felt fuller even being left in half.

We danced forever. Our bodies moved easily to the rhythms of songs, both fast and slow. I forgot where I was and who I was with. I especially forgot about who I *wasn't* with and, I should have paid so much more attention to that.

"Here come the lovebirds," Casey said looking over my shoulder. Weren't they dancing, too? I looked around and the bar was almost empty and we were the only couple on the floor.

"Blake, I think we are going to head out. I have a big day tomorrow with the family and everything. I'll see you at graduation?" Micah looked tired and she swayed. She'd had a belly full of beer, too.

"Sure, I bet you have a lot to do. I'm staying across the street. I'm fine. I'll go get my things from the bar." I separated myself from Casey, but I didn't miss the look Cory shot him.

"Do you want to share a cab?" Cory asked his brother, staring at him pointedly.

"No, I think I might meet some friends downtown," he answered looking at his watch. "I'll see you later. Call me if you need anything tomorrow." They did a one-handed, back-pat type of hug and Casey leaned in to kiss Micah on the cheek. "Congratulations and thanks for inviting me out tonight, Mic. You guys get some sleep." He winked and wagged suggestive eyebrows in their direction.

"Be good, Casey." She scolded and smacked his arm.

Cory gave me a hug and I accepted it. He told me it was a pleasure to meet me, but he needed to get Micah home since she had to be up bright and early.

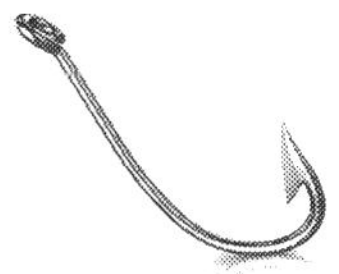

Casey and I walked to the bar where my things, thankfully, were still intact. How fucking dumb was I to walk off and leave the only belongings I still had?

"Night cap?" Casey asked eying me up. His smile alone could get me drunk.

"Sure, what time is it?" I looked for my phone in my over-sized travel bag and found that not only had I missed calls from both my mother and Grant, but also there were texts to accompany them.

The bartender looked busy, like he was tidying up. I noted the time at one-thirty and asked him, “What time do you close?”

“We close at two. You guys want last call?” The big barman came to stand in front of us and we shared a questioning glance between ourselves.

Casey ordered, “Yeah, we’ll have two Remy Martins. Neat.”

I choked. “Whoa, that’s a serious nightcap. You’re going out after this?” The drink would most likely put me, thoroughly, on my ass for the night.

“That depends.” He hunched over the bar, putting his head in his hand, and looked at me with a devilish grin. His fingers ran through his thick curls, almost boyishly. “I’m going to be honest with you. I saw you when we walked in and I tried to ignore you. I have a girlfriend. At least tonight I do.” Then he looked away and clarified, “I won’t by tomorrow night. I was breaking things off with her tonight and my plans got a bit...hijacked.” Casey’s hazel eyes studied me, trying to read what I thought of his statement.

“Okay.” I wasn’t sure where he was going with that, but I’d been having such a good time with him. I sort of hoped that he’d ask me to continue the night with him, and go somewhere else like he’d told Cory he might. I tried not to let my budding disappointment show.

The bartender placed both our cognacs on napkins and left us to them.

“I want you to know that I’m not some jerk or asshole that sleeps around on his girl. I know we’ll see each other tomorrow after I’ve talked to Aly, and you are bound to hear Cory or Micah ask about it.” He was very serious and didn’t break eye contact with me.

“We were just dancing. It really isn’t that big of a deal,” I said making light of our night. Sure, we were a wash of blurred lines on the dance floor, but after getting some distance it seemed like we were mutually fine. At least I hoped I looked like I was collected.

*I had a boyfriend.*

Why didn’t I just say it? Even *he* didn’t want to seem like some manwhore, so maybe he would have respected me if I told him about Grant.

Casey swiped both his hands through his brown mess and pulled it away from his face.

The bar stool rumbled across the wood floor as he turned sharply to face me. He grabbed the seat I was in and pulled it closer. My crossed legs were situated in between his and he handed me my tumbler while taking his own.

"Go ahead, Blake. Take a sip."

I hesitated and looked into his bright eyes. He nodded, telling me to do what I was told. So, I did. It was very warm and it slid like molasses down my throat. I felt the fire when it topped my stomach. Then he removed the glass from my hand and put it back on the shiny bar-top.

Casey leaned into my space and we were face to face. I watched as his blue-ish, green-ish, brown-ish, grey eyes circled my mouth. Then they went south, down my neck and returned to me directly.

"I want you tonight. You've got something I need. I don't know what it is. I'm probably crazy. Humor me though," he sighed, then said, "be with me." The warmth from the nightcap spread throughout my belly and his words heated everywhere else. I wanted him, too, but no one had ever just flat-out presented themselves like that to me. It was so daring.

It was also the sexiest, most confident request I'd ever heard. I felt desired in a new and foreign way.

"I don't, exactly, know what to say. I don't even know you. I don't live here. I have to leave on Sunday." *I have a soon-to-be fiancé.* I'd left out the only good reason there was. The only valid reason I had.

"Blake, I don't normally do this, and I don't know where all of this is coming from. But I just can't *not* tell you. I can't *not* try. I think if I did, then I might always wonder what you'd be like. What we'd be like, together. I know I don't know you. You don't know me, but shit!" The slap of his hand on the bar snapped at my ears and I straightened. Then he continued, the sensual timbre of his voice back to normal. "I want you."

I didn't know where it came from, but it felt instinctive. My hands went to his cheeks and pulled him to my mouth. I had to. The choice was made for me. My lips were thankful.

Casey reached for me and pulled me to him. I stood in between his legs, with my hands still framing his beautiful face.

I parted my lips and it was enough of an invitation for him to accept. Before I knew it, our mouths were swimming with each other, cognac and desire like I'd never tasted before.

But I had a boyfriend.

With that thought I begin to pull away.

"Stop it," Casey whispered around the kiss and smile on his busy lips. "We'll sort it all out tomorrow. Be with me tonight. Please?" Then he held me tighter and lifted his eyes to mine and repeated his plea, "Blake, please?"

I wasn't sure why he had such a strong pull, but I couldn't imagine he'd ever had to plead with a woman before. He had captivated me from the moment I set eyes on him. I knew he was dangerous, that he was trouble, but I lost myself there for a few long moments. The depth of yearning in his eyes coerced me.

*God, what was I doing?*

# TWO

## Casey

### Saturday, May 24, 2008

*GOD, WHAT WAS I doing?*

I hadn't even broken up with Aly. Yet.

I didn't care. I had to have that girl. And there she was looking at me like I had all the answers. I really laid it out there. She must have thought I was a pushy prick.

I still didn't care.

I know I'd kick my own ass if I let her walk out of there without saying something.

Fuck. The feeling of her, as she hung onto me while we were dancing, made me want to take her to the bathroom and strip her bare, right there in the bar. So, I supposed I kept hold of my control as best that I could.

*Say yes, Blake. Ask me up.*

I willed her to want it like I did. She was taking too long. I had to kiss her again, while I still had her there, just in case she said no. I reached down and picked her up. I put her back on her stool.

Thank God we were the only ones in the bar and Nate was leaving us alone. I wished the doors were locked and the shades drawn. I would have had her right there. As I sat her back down I shimmied my hips between her legs and I was only a little surprised when she wrapped a leg around to pull me closer. My lips crashed into hers and I couldn't slow down. She tasted like honey and cognac.

I was desperate to be everywhere, in her mouth or otherwise. I couldn't put my finger on why, but one look at her fucking knocked me in the gut when I walked in and saw her.

She was obviously all strung out from the rain. Her long, brown hair was messy. It was sexy as shit. Those pouty lips and, fucking hell, her big brown eyes. I couldn't even fucking look at her. I was totally screwed before she even knew my name. Blake wasn't dolled-up like most of the women from my past. Not requiring any tweaking, she was gorgeous, just as she was.

Jesus, I really needed to get a grip.

"Come up to my room with me?" she murmured around our kisses. That was all the answer I needed.

"Good choice, honeybee. Kick that drink back." I took the last half of mine and fished some cash out of my wallet to pay Nate.

"I'm staying across the street. Give me a few minutes to get situated in my room? Where's your cell?" She stood there looking at me like I wasn't moving quickly enough. "Come on, Cocky. Chop-chop."

I handed my phone over and in no time I heard Seven Nation Army playing from her purse. I thought that was kind of badass.

"I'll call you, in like, ten minutes with my room number. Is that okay?" She looked almost afraid I might say no. She was bat-shit crazy if she thought I'd change my mind.

"That's fine with me. I'll hang here until you call."

She didn't say anything. She smiled and it was refreshing. I watched her walk to the door and when she went to open it, she turned back around and caught me ogling her. Her petite hands came up in a "ten" and then she left.

I was screwed.

Still holding my phone, I looked down to the number she dialed. Normally, it wouldn't occur to me to save a girl's number in my phone.

Honeybee entered a lot more than my phone's contact list that night.

I waited. It felt like it took three fucking years. I couldn't get the initial image of her out of my head. I'd never looked at a chick before and immediately wanted to talk to her. Fuck her? Sure. Get my dick sucked? Lots of times. But she was so beautiful and *real* looking that I wanted to *talk* to her.

Then, I heard her voice and knew I needed to leave her alone. Her laughs, from across the room, made it torture for me to keep my ass on that barstool.

I had to fight going to her really fucking hard.

I texted Cory a 'thanks for not warning me' not long after we arrived. He knew I only came for a drink, or so, and then I was going to go break it off with Aly. That got shot all to shit when I saw Blake.

I wasn't going anywhere, until it was to one of our beds.

When you saw a girl like that, like Blake, you didn't approach. The dumb ones liked drinks; the aggressive ones liked a nice ass-grab as you walked past. It was the smart, out-of-your-league types that had to come to you.

And in my experience the only way to get a reaction from them was to leave them the fuck alone.

Just enough.

Be the ball. Or, rather, be the bat that they wanted to give a swing with later.

So, I had no choice but to wait and hope. If she approached me I wouldn't be able to resist her, and I was damn close to breaking my own rule before she came over.

Then she did and I was screwed. I was hers.

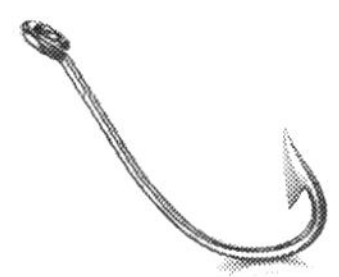

Then my phone vibrated and Honeybee was on the screen. I couldn't believe that she actually wanted me, too. I'd got hard just from the text message.

Even if it was for one night, I'd be the luckiest son-of-a-bitch on the planet.

I stood and yelled a good night at Nate. He was a good dude. I met him a few years before at a beer swap and we'd been buds ever since. It didn't hurt that HLS was his family's bar and I'd recently negotiated a deal where they kept my beer—well my boss's beer technically—on tap.

I walked across the street into the Ashcroft Hotel looking back at her text.

**Honeybee: Rm 315**

I didn't bother with the elevators and made my way for the staircase that led straight up to the second floor from the large, open lobby.

It didn't take me any time to find the second staircase and then, just as fast, I was on the third floor outside of her door. I felt weird knocking, so I text her back.

**Me: I'm here – Cocky**

I heard her phone chirp on the other side of the door and then I heard her laugh. A real no-one-can-hear-me laugh. It was so fucking hot and if I thought my cock couldn't get any harder, I was wrong. Blake opened the door and I almost died. She had on a hotel robe and her hair was freshly washed. She'd taken a shower.

She was fast. I liked that, too. Shit I liked everything about that girl.

"I know this looks pretty cliché, but the airport lost all of my luggage today and I felt so damn filthy from traveling and the rain..." she rambled.

Thank God for airports.

Thank God for rain.

Thank God for terrycloth hotel robes.

Thank God my knees didn't buckle.

I told you. Luckiest fucking bastard on the planet. That was me. I didn't know what to say. Every time I thought the rug was going to be pulled out, the night kept getting better.

"You're perfect." She was. She looked like she was probably twenty-three or -four and I tell you what, that body was out of control. A criminal ass. Perfect sized breasts. I wanted to get lost in her for the next few hours, at least.

"Can I come in?" I was the one who sounded cheesy and cliché, but my dick wasn't sharing any of my blood supply with my brain.

"Yes. If you still want to." Blake turned, walked to the bathroom and flicked off the light, not stopping before she got to the bed. "I thought about what you said earlier. The thing about always wondering what we'd be like? I'd wonder that, too."

Her voice sounded so confident, but her body read otherwise. One of her bare feet slid behind the calf of her other leg and methodically rubbed up and down. There was something like nervousness in her posture.

It was bittersweet. I liked watching her squirm but hated that she second-guessed herself. So, I did what felt only natural and went to her. I had every intention of rushing her body and knocking it straight to the bed, but when I got to her I couldn't.

Instead, I touched the damp hair that lay across her shoulder and pushed it out of the way. It was then I understood why women loved romantic, vampire shit. Because her neck was so goddamned sexy. Seeing her peach-colored velvet skin, that peeked out above the large robe, made me want to cover every inch of it with my mouth.

I looked at her one more time to be sure she wasn't too nervous. The tip of her nose was flushed pink and her big brown eyes showed her trepidation and desire. I registered it and it was the only sign I needed. No one wanted to be the guy the girl regretted. I wanted to be the guy she couldn't get enough of. The one she never forgot.

I wanted to raise the bar for which every other man was measured against.

As gently as I could I lowered my mouth to her neck. And as I softly as I kissed her lovely skin, she sighed and brought hands to my chest. That taste of her skin was my first hit of Blake. My mouth watered she was so good, but I wanted to know all her flavors, not just her neck.

I knew in those first seconds that I'd never have my fill or run out of places to taste.

I also knew if I didn't get a handle on myself and find some control, my hours with her could easily turn into minutes and I wasn't ready for that yet. I needed to take my time, for the both of us.

I whispered, "Lose the robe," into her ear, and her breath left her body in a wave. Then she dropped it. I had a hard time deciding if I wanted my mouth or my eyes on her.

My eyes won out. She was a feast. She moved her damp dark hair off her shoulders and offered her body to me. Through all of her nervousness, she never hesitated to do as I said.

I couldn't have stopped myself from staring if I'd had to. Her tinted alabaster chest grew pink under my gaze. But she stood there and waited patiently for me to...what? She would have done anything I said. I could see it in her eyes.

I did what any other man would. I got naked. My clothes were the only things in-between my body and her body getting acquainted. And I didn't want to wait another second.

I reached up behind my back and pulled my shirt over my head. I threw it to the other side of the room; I didn't care where it landed. As I unzipped my jeans and kicked off my shoes. When I looked back up at her and she was smiling. It was a beautiful smile.

"Something you like?" I asked her. Her smile was so big it almost looked like she was about to laugh. "What?" I looked down at myself. I wasn't a supermodel, but I worked out.

Well, I had worked out *before*.

"I like," was all she said. Not having any clothes on and both of us standing there naked, I wasn't really sure how to approach her. It was strange.

I was expecting a hot rush, hands and arms everywhere. Sweat. Screams. But in that moment, she seemed to want her own look. So I let her and when I couldn't wait a minute longer, I took a step towards her, meeting her smile with mine.

"Are you sure about this, honeybee?"

Only nodding, she looked to me with the biggest brown eyes, the colors in them shimmered like a dark amber lager.

"I need to hear you. Tell me."

"I'm sure." Her voice was quiet, but steady. "Please, kiss me?"

*Please, kiss me?*

She didn't need to *ask* me to kiss her. Why would she think she did? Her voice was like velvet, soft and smooth, and there is no way I could deny her anything. So, I kissed her.

The sound she made when I slid my tongue into her mouth was so erotic. Like all of the sounds she made, it was pure pleasure.

When I pulled her thigh up to my hip, I heard a whimper behind her lips that made my ears ring.

The purr she made when I positioned her body underneath mine for that first time added minutes to my life.

The way her moans were desperate and needy made me all the more eager to give. She was like my brand new instrument and I wasn't stopping until I heard every noise she'd make, including my name.

I kissed my way down her stomach, all the while watching her reactions. And when I got to her center, her whole body shivered. Blake responded to my every move. My lips found her wet flesh and my tongue outlined the ridge of her sex. Her hips bucked, and I found myself moaning with pleasure from the erotic show.

It was bewitching how the flick of my tongue, or a light graze of my teeth, in just the right spot, affected her.

Her body arched as I took one long, last delicious lick up the middle of her glistening pussy. With one finger curled inside her, she came in my mouth. Her orgasm was silent, but her hands clawed at the sheets and her body pulsed against me. It almost did me in and couldn't control myself any longer. I had to have her. I had to be inside her.

I couldn't help the way I went at her that first time. It was almost savage. My body did all the decision-making. I spread her legs and moved myself to her opening without a second thought.

The second I was barely an inch inside of her, she sunk her teeth into her lip. I waited for her to let me know she was all right, or maybe I was giving her a chance to tell me to stop.

She said, "Yes," and I continued. That first inch. That first time inside. It was fucking Heaven. I moved steadily deeper and paused again. Her eyes went wide and her mouth fell open as I made the final push. She was so tight around my aching cock. I watched as lust mired her features. Uninhibited and exquisite.

"Casey?"

At first it sounded like a question she was asking herself, but I held myself there one more second before grinding my hips against her clit and then pulling just shy of out of her. I said nothing. Blake's dark eyes dilated as she exhaled and she said, "Yes." Then, I lost myself. I couldn't get deep enough. I couldn't go fast enough.

She cried, "Casey," over and over. The harder I came at her the louder she got. I watched as she came, shaking her head side to side like she was telling herself no. Like she was fighting it.

I stilled her face with one hand and made her look at me. "Don't fight it. Let go." And she did. That sweet pussy gripped me and wrung me out. The feeling of her coming around me took me to the edge of my sanity.

I was aware if I kept going like that I could hurt her, but something in the back of my mind told me that in the long run, she'd hurt me much worse.

As I came, she leaned up and kissed my open mouth until I was empty.

I didn't even have the strength to roll over. I pretty much collapsed into her heaving chest as we both fought to catch our breath. I was still inside her and I was so satisfied that I couldn't move.

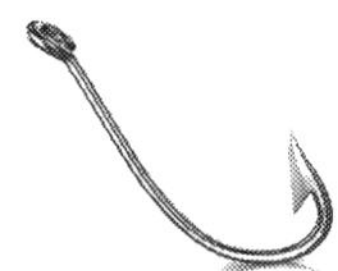

"Are you okay?" Blake finally asked me when I had lain there with my head in between her perfect breasts for minutes that felt like hours. It took everything for me to lift my head and smile at her.

"Hi," she purred.

"Hello."

"What's your name again?" The little minx was playful post-coital. I so dug that.

"Lou," I answered and watched her face light up.

"It's a real pleasure to meet you, Lou. Mind getting out of me? I need to use the lady's room." And she wiggled underneath me.

I rolled over to my side and watched her tiptoe to the bathroom. She didn't turn the light on or even shut the door all of the way. I couldn't see anything except her little feet tapping against the tile as she peed. Even that was fucking cute. I needed serious help.

"I'm sorry, I don't remember if I caught your name or not. I'm at a loss right now if you could help me out...?"

"Excuse me. How rude of me not to formally introduce myself. How un-ladylike," she mockingly chided herself in an *almost* believable faux, Southern accent. "I must have forgotten my name and my manners. My name is...Betty."

"Betty, is it then?" I wondered why Betty, but I went along.

"Yes. Betty," she admitted and sauntered back to the bed after flushing and washing her hands.

I rolled over onto my back and stretched my arm out to the side, she took it as an invitation to come to me and she was more than welcome there.

"Lou, I have to get up very early and go shopping to replace my lost luggage. You're welcome to stay if you like, but don't feel like you have to. I'm sure I'll be sleeping well tonight." She barely finished before giggling and curling into me.

My hand lazily ran up and down her side, up to her shoulder and down to that perfect ass. Over and over. I felt her get goose bumps, but I continued anyway.

I wanted to stay.

"Well, Betty. How early is early?" I asked trying to get a sense of what she'd prefer. I didn't want to seem like the guy who couldn't take a hint.

"Well, not too early." She rolled over and clicked off the light, staying on her side that faced away from me. "I'd be more than happy to wake you up before I go-go." She laughed at her stupid WHAM joke and I couldn't help it, I did too.

"How would you wake me up? Maybe I'm an awful morning person."

"I guess you'll have to stick around to find out."

"You really are trouble, aren't you?"

She only hummed a response. I fell asleep listening to her hum that stupid WHAM song until we both passed out.

I'd never slept so well.

# THREE

## Blake

### Saturday, May 24, 2008

I'D NEVER SLEPT SO well.

The first thing I thought to myself, when I woke with Casey naked in my bed, was *what in the hell was I thinking?* The second thing I thought was *this guy is sexy and fun and I can't resist him.*

So, before thoughts of my boyfriend totally saturated the last of my resistance, I ran my hand around the waist of the big warm body that lay comfortably next to mine.

Aside from the morning breath of which I probably suffered from, I couldn't think of any other good reasons why not to wake this glorious man up the best way I could think of. I slid my fingers gently around his front and down to find him already hard.

Morning wood.

Casey's morning wood.

I almost pulled away when he stirred, but decided to try staying perfectly still, as not to wake him completely. He moaned a bit and rolled onto his back nuzzling his head deep into the pillow.

His curly hair was a wreck. Big brown curls wound everywhere, sticking straight off his head. I brought the hand that was stashed under his pillow up to touch them. I lightly pulled a lock to see its reaction. Just as I pictured it would, it straightened out to about three times its curled length and bounced right back to its tightened spot after I let it go.

He was so handsome, his face calm and peaceful. Full, black eyelashes fanned across his cheeks. He was adorable, as he lay there looking like he was grinning in his sleep.

Getting back to my earlier mission, I set back to investigating his man parts that were currently tenting my crisp white hotel sheets. I slowly brought my hand around the base of him and was actually impressed.

I'd felt him, *all of him,* the night before, but I wondered if it had been my excitement and my overactive mind embellishing his size in my memory.

Nope.

My hands were small. Please, no jokes about carnies or smelling like cabbage. I've heard them all. But my fingers wouldn't touch around him, maybe if I squeezed, but squeezing isn't stealthy and I was curious. I wanted to check out this specimen. If only to figure out what it was about him that caused me to be so…so careless. If I could only pin point what it was about him that made me forget why I shouldn't have done what I did, then at least I'd have a good reason.

I didn't know the guy.

I had had a one-night stand, something I'd never done before. Even worse, I'd cheated on my boyfriend in the process. What in the hell was wrong with me? I didn't have an answer for that yet.

And even though it was true, and my morals and conscience would be all over me later, I found my hand stroking him and my leg crawling up his. It was crazy how touching him turned me on so much. I wondered how far I could go before he woke up and decided to do some other investigating first.

I abandoned his private parts for more conservative locations. I didn't want him to wake up to find me molesting him in his sleep. Who knows, the guy might have been really drunk last night and full of shit about breaking up with that girl. Maybe he just wanted some strange. Ewww. That made me the strange.

My curious fingers made an exploratory pilgrimage over his hipbone and up to his belly button. He had a happy trail and I ran a soft finger in a circle through it, swirling the hair as I watched his sleeping face.

His skin was smooth and hardly even a freckle blemished it. I pretended I was the only one who'd ever touched him, like I'd discovered this paradise in the form of a man. Even though the chances were, that a man who went home with strangers was most likely used to being touched. Probably a lot.

His stomach was flat and tight. He was no beefy muscle man. He was lean. Almost, skinny. His abdominals were visible, but not in a fitness model kind of way, more like a swimmer or runner. His pecks were much the same. The lines of those muscles stretched upward toward his shoulders and hosted nearly perfect right angles in the center before parting aside his breastbone. There, and only there, did I find a few more playful, and somewhat, curly hairs. They'd be easy to count.

I thought about naming them.

The ridge of his collarbone was sharp, and on one side there was a knot before it fell away into his muscle. My hand gingerly roamed over it and I was curious about what had happened there.

I look down our bodies and found his feet sticking out from under the sheets. They were huge. I guessed in his case, what they said about big feet was accurate.

Looking at him, studying him, I should have felt guilty and I noted, surprisingly, I wasn't. Well, not yet anyway. I was sure as soon as he wasn't lying naked beside me that I'd see the error of my ways. I moved my thumb over his nose and traced his eyebrows.

I was being seriously creepy.

And my phone was ringing.

*Shit. How long had it been ringing?*

I wrangled free, the arm that was trapped under Casey's head, and rolled off the bed toward the sound of Grant's ringtone. If I didn't answer it, he'd keep calling. I didn't answer him the night before. I didn't even text him when I got up here to let him know I'd made it okay. He was probably freaking out.

Bringing the phone to my face, I read that I'd missed seven calls and I had ten new text messages. It stopped ringing while I was on my way over, but only for a second. He didn't leave a message; he called again.

"Good morning," I said quietly, but somewhat chipper. But then again, I was chipper. I'd had a fantastic night and sex with a sinfully gorgeous man. The problem was that it wasn't with my boyfriend. My almost fiancé. It was with a stranger and he was still there.

"Jesus, Blake. It's about time. I almost called your parents. Are you okay?" His tone was harsh, but I would have been be worried, too. That was, if I'd been calling him all night without any response.

Would I have done that though? Called that much? Probably not. Especially, if he was merely spending time with friends who he hadn't seen in a long time.

Traditional.

Trying to keep my voice low, as not to wake up my guest—I didn't want to be inhospitable—I answered, "Sorry, I didn't hear my phone last night and fell asleep the second my head hit the pillow. I'm fine. How was your night?"

"I can hardly hear you. Why are you whispering? Hung-over?" He laughed a little, teasing me, but he was right. I shouldn't have been whispering. I wouldn't if I were alone.

Trying to compensate for my negligence, I spoke at a normal morning volume, "A little? It was fun though."

"Listen, I'm sorry. I shouldn't have ditched you. I thought that was why you weren't answering. I thought you were mad and you have every right to be. I should have come with you. I'm a stupid man. I'm sorry." Very stupid as it turned out. And I was easy to distract.

Apparently, we both sucked.

"You better be. Listen, my luggage got lost on the flight. I have to go buy some clothes and get some things. I'll call you later, all right?" All true. Oh and there was a naked surfer-type guy in my king-sized hotel bed sleeping.

"That sucks. Not a very good trip, huh?"

"Uh, actually it's been pretty great. A girl can always use more clothes. Right?"

I hated shopping. I'd rather saw my arm off.

"Right. Well, pick up something nice. I'm taking you out Monday." I heard the smile in his voice and I felt dread like I'd never felt before. What if he wanted to propose then?

I almost heaved. In my hotel room. With the very visible leftovers of my one-night stand still in my hotel bed. I spared a glance at a sleeping Casey. My conscience demanded explanations, but looking at him, I realized I would have a difficult time listing them all. *Who are you and what have you done with the real Blake?*

"Okay, I need a shower though. I have a lot to do. I'll call you later."

"All right, I love you. Have fun," he said sweetly and my vision blurred.

*What had I done?*

I turned away from the bed so I wasn't facing Casey. It didn't seem right to profess love to one man, while I lusted over another. Merely turning away from him didn't make him disappear though, not like I wanted him to or like it would offer any kind of privacy, but I did it anyway not wanting Casey to hear. "Love you, too. 'Bye." And I quickly hung up.

Before I turned back around, I heard a faint, "Lucky bastard," come from my messed-up sheets. I looked over my shoulder and smiled. I lifted my phone showing him that I had been talking to someone, "Grant. Boyfriend."

"Casey. Horny." I chuckled. I supposed there wasn't any point in hiding anything from him. He was in the same situation that I was.

"Blake. Slut." He frowned.

"You're a slut? Shit. I wish you would have told me that before." He patted the bed were I slept beside him all night and I went to him and sat. "Regrets?" he asked.

Regrets? I thought about it and picked at my thumbnail. Do I regret it? I searched myself for the regret and it wasn't there. "No, I don't regret it. Do you?"

"I can't really remember what happened." He bit his bottom lip. "You might have to refresh my memory." Then, his smile broke free. There he went again smiling and wiping clean away any trace of sensible thought I had. That toothy, lopsided smile equaled big trouble.

"Nope. If you can't remember it, then maybe I dreamt it. That makes more sense anyway." I replied to him facetiously as I thought about how I would very much enjoy to doing it again.

I inwardly chastised myself. But I had been drinking more than normal the night before, when I slept with a guy I had just met. I could explain it away with lots of excuses.

However, at that moment, I was sober. I had no excuses. Not his naked body. Not his pretty smile. Not his sexy, messed-up hair. Not the way his body pulled me to him. Nothing.

"As much fun as that sounds, I really need to be getting around. I have to find some clothes and I will perish if I don't get coffee soon."

"Perish? We don't need that." He sprung up and the sheet fell away from his body. He stood and looked around. It shocked me. He hadn't any modesty. It must have been written all over my face. I could feel my eyes about to bug out of my head.

"I know what you're thinking. How is he going to fit that big dick into those jeans, right? I get that a lot." He rocked his hips forward, unashamed of his obvious arousal, and made a face like he was thinking, "Yeah."

"Oh my god. Were you like this last night? Maybe I do have some regrets," I said, only trying to toy with him.

He huffed. "Ouch." He jumped up and down, getting his jeans on, all the while searching for his shirt, scanning my room. "There it is," he said as he walked past me to the place where his shirt was wadded up on the floor. That was when I realized I'd been naked the whole time.

Where the fuck was my brain? Here I was thinking how brazen he was and I was as naked as the day I was born. Newly aware of my exposure, I almost yelped and scrambled for the robe beside the bed.

I wrapped it around myself and fumbled for the fabric belt to tie around and hold it shut. Casey walked to me and found the two ends that I had been looking for. He held them apart. Then, he quickly opened both sides of the robe and said, "Damn," before tying the robe closed. He chastely kissed my forehead. "I had to have one last look."

The word "last" made my stomach roll. Last.

He motioned to the bathroom, silently asking if he could use it. I waved my hand showing I didn't care.

"How about I go downstairs and give you a few minutes and then I take you to coffee?" he offered from behind the closed bathroom door.

I should have stopped it right there. I bit at my thumb, in private, considering what to do.

I'd probably see him later that night and having coffee, and spending any more time with him than I already had, would be detrimental. To my relationship. To my life. To my sanity.

"I don't know. I think I'll grab a quick coffee and hit some shops. I really have a lot to do."

He came out of the bathroom and demanded, "Don't tell me no. I'll be downstairs." Then he left. It was obvious that I truthfully couldn't tell him no. So, again, I didn't fight it.

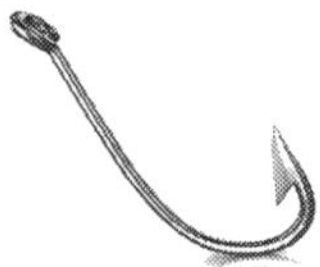

When I got downstairs, he was waiting for me near the door. He looked carefree and comfortable. I felt anything but. My legs moved me forward—my body on autopilot—and I went straight to him.

"'Bout time," he teased. It had only been about ten minutes. Hell, I was still wearing yesterday's clothes. Only running a comb through my hair before gathering it up into a messy knot on my head, and brushing my teeth, I looked like a hot mess. With my bag slung over my shoulder, I only answered with, "Coffee," as I slid my sunglasses over my eyes.

Casey ushered. "Right this way."

We walked down the sunny street and I was thankful we were in a part of town littered with shops. I didn't care for shopping. I hated malls. I hated feeling like a consumer on a conveyor belt. When I shopped, I preferred stores like the ones we were walking past. I mentally noted to hit a few of them after we got coffee.

"Stop, I'll be right back." Casey rushed into a store and glanced at me through the window, holding up his index finger. When he came out, about five minutes later, he had two big coffee mugs and wore a pair of lime green sunglasses. One mug was bright yellow and the other was black and white striped.

"I like the sunglasses. What are these for?" I asked pointing at the mugs.

"What do you think they're for?"

"Well, they're coffee cups, but I don't get it. We're going to a coffee shop, right? In my experience, they give you a container with which to drink your coffee from."

"Gross," he said and tugged at my arm to continue us down the street. "You're a chef, correct?"

"Yeah."

"Then you should get it." His voice was coated with something like annoyance. "Okay. Imagine the perfect steak. You eat meat, right? Otherwise this analogy won't work." He looks at me and lifted his glasses.

I lifted mine, too, and said, "I love meat." Then I gave him an exaggerated wink.

"Perfect." He continued and weaved us around a couple who were window-shopping. "Okay, so you have this steak. It's perfect. Just the right cut. Grilled to heavenly, juicy awesomeness. Shit, I need a steak. Anyway, there has never been, nor will there ever be, a better steak than this one. Now, picture eating it off of a paper plate. Yuck."

I laughed. "Oh, so you're crazy?"

"That's how I feel about drinking out of paper. This coffee shop," he stopped us in front of a beautiful brick building, with a chalkboard sign that read *The Best Sip* and their specials, "has exceptional coffee. Drinking it out of paper should be criminal. It's blasphemy." He was so animated and quite obviously very passionate about his beverages.

Casey Moore had so many moods. At the bar, he was closed off and reluctant to talk to me at all. Then when he did, he was cocky and bold. The morning had exposed yet another facet of his personality. He was playful and a little eccentric. I wondered if I'd enjoy them all, because so far I had.

Casey opened the door and I instantly thought he might be right. The smell of roasted coffee beans was heavenly as it infiltrated my nose. My tummy grumbled and suddenly I was a believer.

"But I like it when they write my name on the side," I implored. He looked at me like I had three heads. His eyebrows bunched together as if I'd told him that I liked ketchup on my ice cream. I giggled. "What?"

He rolled his eyes. "How do you like your coffee?"

"Surprise me. Your beer is really good. I'm sure whatever you choose will be, too. I want to know what you like. I'll find us a seat."

His smile spread across his face like a wild fire.

I found a little table off to the side that seated two. When he reached me he was carrying the two coffee mugs like the cargo was liquid gold. He bobbed and weaved around people trying his best not to spill a drop. I couldn't help my grin.

He offered me the hot mug and I was more than happy to take it.

I put it on the table and awaited further instruction. For some reason, I was compelled to wait for him. He sat across from me and unraveled his long legs out to the side of our table. His funny sunglasses, perched atop of his head, held back his hair like a headband. It was adorable and strangely sexy seeing him without the hair framing his face.

"Are you ready for this?" he asked.

"Probably not."

"Drink it, but be careful it's hot."

I grasped the handle and I turned it so I could lift it with my dominant left hand. Scribbled on the side was "Betty Is Trouble." My head swam. I stared at it. I read and reread it. Then, I looked over to Casey's cup. He turned it so I could read his, too.

"Lou Likes Trouble."

It was so weird and sweet and unexpected at the same time.

Where in the hell did this guy come from?

# FOUR

## Casey

**Saturday, May 24, 2008**

I DIDN'T KNOW WHERE in the fuck she came from. And I didn't give one shit. If I only had that day with her, and hopefully that night, I was going to take advantage of every single minute.

Boyfriends and girlfriends be damned.

"How do you like that coffee?" I asked, but I knew she loved it. She'd only taken about three drinks and her cup was almost empty.

"It's really good. Thank you."

"You're welcome. Now. This boyfriend..." I began.

She bared her teeth and inhaled a long breath. It made a whistle sound and she winced.

She stood. I thought she was about to leave. Instead, she slugged back the last drink in her cup and looked into mine, seeing it was empty, too.

"Another?" Blake asked.

"Yeah." She walked to the counter, and bought us each another cup. Walking back she looked worried. The subject of our significant others wasn't going to be a comfortable conversation, but it was necessary. I was breaking it off with Aly that day. I hoped she'd tell me that she and this other guy were on the downhill, too.

I didn't know why.

What difference would it have made? She didn't live in San Francisco. I did.

I thought she could do better than be with a guy who she could so easily forget, though. He couldn't have been that great and that was the part that got into my craw. I fully intended on being inside her again, and soon hopefully, but first I needed to know some things.

"So, what's up with this boyfriend?" She shifted in her chair and tapped her fingers on the tabletop. Seconds passed. Then minutes. I wasn't changing the subject. There wasn't any reason for us to not lay it all out there.

She finally relented after a stare off, "What do you want to know?"

"Oh, I don't know? Is it serious? How long have you been with each other?" *Was I better in bed? Did he make her come as hard as I did?*

"I don't know. I guess it's serious. Why do you want to know all of this? And forgive me if I'm wrong, but don't one-nighters usually end, you know, in the morning?" Her defensive tone didn't go unnoticed. Neither did the nervous bouncing of her legs or the little twitch in her lip.

"Hey, I'm not judging you. We both did what we did. I'm just curious if you did it because you're not really that into him, or if it was something else?"

She cleared her throat and looked around, like anyone gave a fuck about what we were talking about. "I don't mean to be rude, but I don't think that it's any of your business, Casey."

She wasn't my business. She was right.

"That's fair. I just thought we could be friends." Instantly her features softened. Her brow relaxed and she took another long sip of her coffee.

"Sorry. I…I've never done anything like, you know, what we did last night." Her cheeks flushed and I hoped she was thinking about how good it felt. I needed to stop thinking about it, too, before I had to adjust myself.

"Never?" I asked.

"Never. Have you?"

I wish I could have said that I'd never fucked around on a girl. Not that I was a prick or anything. I liked to think I was more of an opportunist. Sometimes opportunity climbed on your lap. Sometimes an opportunity bent over in front of you when you weren't wearing pants. Sometimes the back of an opportunity's throat itched and wanted me to scratch it with my cock.

*Maybe I was a prick.*

But I'd never strung a girl along. I'd never lied. Sure, I had hooked up with other women while I was with someone. Granted, it was at the end of the relationship every time. Call it a red flag for me. If I wanted to bang the shit out of one chick, while I was dating another one, it probably wasn't mean to be.

"The truth? Yeah," I admitted.

I could can tell by the way her eyes wouldn't land on mine that she was not impressed. After I'd thought about it, I wasn't that impressed either. Maybe I should have lied and said I was a saint, but she probably would have saw right through it though.

"Listen, Blake. It isn't nuclear physics. If you sleep around on someone, there are only a few reasons why." I held up a finger and she looked at it like the answer was written there. "One. He's a jerk."

"Grant's not really a jerk."

"Very convincing. Especially when you add 'really' in there like that. But for the sake of argument, we'll say he's not."

"Okay."

I had her full attention. As if I were about to tell her where the Holy Grail was, she leaned over the table and her boobs pushed up enough so that her cleavage was on display just for me. It was mag-fucking-nificent. I needed to slow down and come up with a few more reasons. "Two. You think he's unfaithful and you're doing a tit-for-tat thing." I wiggled my two fingers and then directed them at her for an answer.

"No, that's not like me. Even if I did think that, I'd just break it off with him. But he's not like that either." Damn. I had hoped it could have been that.

"Three. You are looking for a reason for him to break up with you." Something fired in her eyes and then she shook her head, but didn't verbally shoot it down. "Or four. He doesn't know how to get you off."

She had a filling in her back, bottom left-side tooth. I gained this bit of Blake data when her jaw unhinged itself there in the middle of the cafe.

"So. Number four then? That sucks." I leaned back in my chair and watched her. I would have loved to hear what she was thinking in that moment. It appeared she was having a conversation with herself, the way her head was nodding and her eyes squinted in deep thought.

Would she change the subject or fight back?

"He gets me off. All the time," she defended, a little louder than I expected her to.

*She was a fighter.*

Then her small-framed body slouched after she noticed how loud she'd spoken. It was one of those moments when you're somewhere full of sound and right when you speak the planet goes on mute. She was living that scenario.

I kept going. "Nope. That took you too long. I feel a little bad for you. Women as a whole, really. Half the men I know don't give a shit if a woman gets off or not. I think it's a testosterone thing. They can't be blamed." Her eyes glazed over in thought. I changed the subject, "Wanna go find some clothes?"

She was so cute. Still shaking her head. I knew she was trying to think of the last time her boyfriend curled her toes. If he did, in fact, get her off like she'd claimed, it was a long time ago.

"Come on, Betty. You need some duds."

She rose. We made for the door and then she froze, "Wait. We can't leave our mugs." She turned back for our abandoned table and grabbed a few napkins from the counter on her way. As she came back to me, she tried her best to wipe them out. "You bought these. I'm keeping mine."

"Sure. Keep it."

"You don't want yours?" She looked a little disappointed at the fact that I was going to leave it behind. Somehow that morning, two fifty-five cent coffee mugs from the resale shop down the street had become landmarks. Mementos.

I didn't think of myself as sentimental, by nature, but seeing how attached she grew to those inanimate objects made me consider them special, too.

Maybe it was her. She was awesomely different. Original.

And, thank God, she didn't shop like other women I knew. Certainly not like the women in my life. She walked into a store, looked, touched, and bought. Very decisive. When I thought we were going back to her hotel, she stopped us in front of a shop called The Flower. From the window I could tell it was a bra and underwear place.

"Casey? I need to buy some private things. Thanks for walking me around this morning, but I think I've got it from here." Her nose was again pink. She was being bashful.

"Right. Right. Right. I get it. Are you sure you don't want a man's opinion? I have an eye for these kinds of things." I smiled, but I didn't feel like smiling at all. I hadn't even thought of leaving her. I wanted to spend the whole day talking and laughing with her. I wanted to go back up to her hotel room and have her for lunch. I guessed that was shot all to hell.

"I'll be at the graduation party tonight. Are you going to be there?" She looked hopeful, like she wanted me there.

"Does a hobby horse have a wooden dick? Yeah, I'm going. I have stuff I need to do anyway. I'll see you there." Real smooth. I was bringing back some real zingers.

"Good. I was hoping you were still going. Besides, you said that you needed to break up with Aly, right?"

*Well, wasn't that interesting?*

"I do need to do that," I said in agreement.

"I know my way around down here pretty good. I lived here. Remember? So you don't have to hang around. Besides, I need to buy a bra and underwear. I'll see you tonight."

*I have to kiss her.*

That fast, the thought sprung to mind. I needed to kiss her. Mark her lips. Leave a taste of me on them to remind her. Not giving it any more thought, I closed the space between us. She didn't flinch or move, so I continued. I cupped her pretty face in my hands and rubbed my thumbs across her soft lips. Her tongue snaked out to lick where I'd touched and that's when I moved in, catching her tongue mid-swipe. She still tasted sweet from the coffee.

She wasn't going anywhere until I let her go, so I had an advantage. One I thought I'd make good use of.

It was when she dropped her bags and wrapped her arms around me, deepening the kiss, that all hope was lost. There on the sidewalk, outside of a ladies' under-thingy store, our first sober kiss pulled something tight inside my chest. I swallowed the taste of *her* in my mouth and I moaned.

There I was trying to make a mark on her, and she's successfully turned it around on me.

I really needed to break up with what's her name.

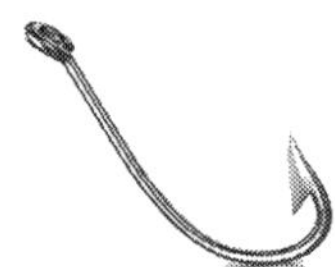

"You didn't do anything wrong. I think that we'd be better friends." That part always sucked. I didn't enjoy making girls sad. I heard Aly sniff on the other end of the line. "Are you okay? I'm sorry, Aly."

"I'm fine. I just wish I knew what I did wrong." She blew her nose. She was a sweet girl. There wasn't a damn thing wrong with her, but she was a yes girl. It's hard to explain. I wasn't looking for a girl who yelled at me constantly, or even bitched about everything. Call me crazy. Call me a masochist, but I liked a girl who had a backbone, a girl with a fire inside her. A spark. A fuse. A girl who had an opinion and wasn't afraid to give it.

Aly was sweet, yes. But she liked me more than I liked her. She agreed with me all the time. I'd even spouted off things that a sane person would dispute in a heartbeat and she would go right along with whatever it was I'd said.

I knew it was a terrible idea dating my boss's daughter. I really did. But what Aly had working for her had been her innocence. She wasn't a virgin, but she could play one on TV. I didn't know if that was really her, or the version of her she wanted me to see, but she gave off this vibe of purity that was appealing. She wasn't wild or aggressive, but she most certainly was willing.

But like her personality, her sexuality lacked an identity. She quickly learned what I liked and simply repeated that. That's a problem a lot of women have.

Sure, I loved that thing you did with your tits and my cock the first time, but every time? No, thank you. I liked it the first time because it was new, refreshing, a surprise. It's like opening up the same birthday gift every year when women find that special something and keep doing it. It became like a routine. And if there's one thing I didn't like, it was a routine.

"Aly, you're a good girl. You'll find a good guy and you'll be much happier. I promise. This wasn't going anywhere."

Harsh. I know. But, like I said, I didn't lie.

"Whatever, Casey. You'll change your mind," she bit back.

"We'll see. But I have to go. I'll see you Monday. Friends?" Even I winced. But shit. She was my boss's daughter and she worked there, too. I'd be able to avoid her for a few days, but I was sure to run into her eventually. It was not that big of a business.

"Fine. 'Bye."

"That was rough. Was she bawling?" said Cory as he straightened his tie.

"Yeah. You heard that?" I set the phone down and took a seat at our kitchen island.

"Sure did. What happened to breaking up with her in person?"

"Last night happened to breaking up with her in person. What did you want me to do? Break up with her at Micah's party? No, thanks."

I knew the look on his face; I'd seen it from my very own in the mirror. Being identical twins was a lot like that. Facial expressions are easy to read on someone when they're the same one's you make yourself. So, as he stood there with a look that begged for the details of last night, I tried to get out of it. "What? Nothing happened."

"So you're telling me that after we left, you and Blake didn't go back to her hotel and fuck like rabbits?"

I stalled. He noticed. Yeah, he knows the Jedi-twin-face trick, too.

"I knew it. I knew it the moment we walked in. You know she has a boyfriend, right? That he was supposed to come with her and then backed out last minute. Kind of a dick move if you ask me, but even so, what the hell are you thinking?" He sat on the arm of the leather couch in the apartment we shared. I said shared, but I meant that I lived there and he stored his belongings in it. He spent practically every night at Micah's, claiming it was closer to work.

"I don't know. It just sort of happened." I raised my hands in defeat.

I couldn't hide the pride last night gave me. I hooked up with the hottest, coolest chick at the bar. And made her scream my name. So, yeah. Who would want to deny that?

"Famous last words, bro. I saw you dancing with her. You should leave her alone. She's not available."

"She was available to me last night." I was defensive and, frankly, being a dick.

"You know what I mean. What would Mom say?"

"She isn't going to say anything, because I'm not going to tell her. Why would you say that? What the fuck, Cory? Mind your own business." Fuck him. I knew exactly what she'd say and what she'd think of Blake.

My dad cheated on her for years, with my stepmother, and that type of behavior didn't sit well with her. I guessed that she would probably say, "I bet your *dad* would like her."

Play-by-the-rules-Cory didn't know what he was talking about. Blake chose to be with me and I chose her just the same. I was sure she felt bad about it, too, but things happen. And as bad as it was, I'd hope it would happen again.

But even I knew she really wasn't a one-night-stand kind of girl.

# FIVE

## Blake

**Saturday, May 24, 2008**

I WASN'T A ONE-NIGHT-stand kind of girl.

That was a fluke.

He said he wanted to be friends, so that was exactly what I was going to do. I planned on being friends with him. Sure. Like ever there was a man who said it and meant it. I scrunched my eyes together and rubbed them as I admitted to myself, I hoped he wasn't just saying it. Really, if he didn't want to be friends with me then he would have simply got up and left me in my hotel room that morning. But he hadn't.

If he hadn't wanted to be friends with me he wouldn't have bought me the coffee mug, which was still in my bag.

If he hadn't wanted to be friends with me, then he wouldn't have kissed me like that on the street.

Okay, maybe that one was something else, but I liked him. He was interesting. The way he thought, the way he spoke. The way he watched me. Casey was captivating.

I shouldn't have wanted to see him again, but I did.

I needed to call Grant before it got too late. I'd been at Micah's for about an hour and people hadn't started showing up in hoards yet. I was sure that would all change fast.

"Micah, do you care if I use your room? I need to call Grant." She didn't know what happened the night before, I thought. She hadn't mentioned it, but the look she gave me certainly had something in it.

Dialing his number, I secretly hoped that it went to voice mail and I could leave a simple hello/goodnight message without a lengthy recount of my day.

"There you are," he answered sweetly and it made me smile.

"Here I am. What are you doing?" I asked, standing in front of a wall in Micah's bedroom that was host to framed pictures. I stopped when I found one of us from last year. Then directly next to it was a photo of Casey, Cory, and Micah. It looked like they were giving her some sort of hot-twin sandwich. *Lucky bitch.*

"I'm going to your parents' house. Shane is moving back in this weekend and I helped him with a few bigger things earlier. They're grilling out and invited me back." Shane, my oldest brother, was at the beginning of a separation from his wife of only three years, which was fine by me. Shane and Kari never made sense in my head anyway.

"That was nice of you." A twinge of guilt rolled itself in the pit of my stomach.

"Yeah, I'm a nice guy like that. I miss you, Blake. You fly back tomorrow, don't you?"

"Yeah. Wanna pick me up at the airport?"

"Sure. What time?"

"I should get in about seven tomorrow evening. Listen, I'm going to get back to Micah's party. I wanted to call you before it got late and/or loud. Tell Shane I said hey."

"Will do. Behave yourself. Have fun. I love you."

*Behave myself.* Right. Hearing him say that a day earlier would have sounded absurd, but right then it made me feel queasy. "I love you, too."

Ending the call, I was startled by Micah standing in her doorway clearing her throat.

"Oh, hey."

"What the hell happened last night?" Her voice was upbeat, but carried a hint of accusation. I didn't want to lie to her. I sat on the edge of her bed and faced the wall of pictures and Micah sat beside me, leaning a shoulder into mine as she began to talk.

"They're pretty close, you know," she said.

"Who?"

"Cory and Casey. They fight. God, do they fight, but they're close. How serious are you and Grant? I mean, it isn't my business, but last night wasn't like you." She walked the thin line of being nosey with being concerned like a pro.

Apparently, the brothers talked a lot, too. "Uh." I leaned forward and put my head in my hands. It was the moment I was dreading. But somehow my feelings were crossed. I didn't know how to explain it. I was more ashamed of myself for being with Casey, when I had a boyfriend, than I was for sleeping with another man when I was dating Grant.

I tried to explain, "I know. It just happened. It was spontaneous and…" looking for a word as I stood and began a short pace in front of my friend, "he's just so sexy and fun and interesting, Micah. Of course I feel shitty for doing that to Grant. Don't you think I feel bad? And you're right. It isn't like me at all." I looked down at my hands and picked at a hangnail that I could only imagine getting worse and worse now that I'd honed in on it. "It was a mistake."

"A mistake?" I heard a familiar male's voice say from across the room. Didn't anyone knock around there? "It was a mistake?" he repeated.

Casey was standing in the doorway. He wasn't pleased. Quickly, I looked to Micah for reinforcement. She didn't meet my eyes when she said, "You guys need a minute. It's okay if you stay in here." Then, like she realized that she'd offered her bedroom to two people who clearly had no self-control, she added, "Just...just behave." There it was again. *Behave.*

I watched my little friend walk around the man who danced his way into my hotel bed the night before. She patted his hard chest as she made her way past.

"That didn't come out right," I said.

"It sounded like it did." His big hands were in his hair, holding it while he continued, "Listen, I know you have a boyfriend, but you don't like him that much. Do you? I mean, how could you?"

*How could I?* The million-dollar question. Of course I loved Grant.

He was kind and sweet. He was my boyfriend. "I do like him. I love him. I don't know what happened last night."

"And this morning? Today?" He stepped closer, shrinking the space between us. "I thought we had a good time." His eyes burned into mine. His voice was almost pleading.

"What do you want me to say? I don't even live here." Feelings of frustration and confusion fogged my head. What did he want from me? "I don't know how to explain it."

"It's simple. I want you to say that you had a good time. You, obviously, don't like your stupid boyfriend and that you want to have a good time tonight before you go home." That didn't seem like too much to ask. Well, all except for the part about Grant, my stupid boyfriend.

"He isn't stupid."

"He's not?" A boom of laughter flew straight out of his chest. "Okay, then where is he?"

"He had something come up. He couldn't make it."

"That's lame. Micah said he was going to be there last night and told us how happy she was to finally meet him. She said that you were excited to show him around and introduce him to your old friends."

"So?" I fidgeted with the errant skin on my finger and pulled the flesh to the quick. I couldn't look at him. I felt like I needed to defend myself, and my relationship to someone who couldn't possibly care about it.

"So, if he was so great, then he would have been there." He kept advancing on me and I didn't know whether to fight or flee.

"I don't know why you care, really. It was one night."

"Yeah, it was one night. One night where you called my name, not his. One night where your beautiful lips begged for mine, not his. One night where you slept in my arms, not his."

My finger ripped apart the piece of skin and it smarted. I looked at my hand, it was bleeding. Absentmindedly, I brought it to my face for closer inspection. I had done a number on it. Without saying another word, Casey took hold of my hand and pushed the wounded digit into his warm mouth.

At first I was shocked that he'd do that. It was such an oddly intimate thing, putting someone's bloody finger into your mouth without thinking about it. It burned as his tongue ran over the sore spot, but it soothed, too.

Finally, I had the willpower to look him in the eyes and all I saw was concern. "What do you care anyway? Don't guys have one-night stands with women all the time?"

My finger left his warm mouth with a plop and he smiled. "I think you deserve better. That's all."

"You've known me for one day. You don't even really know me at all. As far as you know I'm a cheating whore." As soon as the words left my mouth, I was embarrassed and ashamed.

I hung my head on those words. I couldn't look at him and see my words reflected back in his eyes. But he tilted my chin back up and said, "Don't say that, Blake. You're not like that. Even *I* know you're not."

"Well, from what you know I sleep around on my boyfriend. I don't see how that makes you think I deserve more. Maybe I deserve what I get."

"That's stupid. He's just the wrong guy."

"And you're the right one?" I pulled my hand away. The closeness was raising my temperature and clouding my already terrible judgment.

Leaning down to whisper in my ear, he softly said, "Do you really think what we had last night was a mistake? Do you regret it?"

The moment of truth. Hell, no. I didn't regret it, but I couldn't say that it wasn't a mistake. The mistake was knowing what he tasted like. The mistake was wanting more. But I doubted I'd ever regret Casey Moore.

"Yes," was all I could manage. It was the easiest way.

The word no sooner left my lips before he straightened. His lean body tensed and he quietly chuckled and wiped his lips with his thumb. "Then you *are* a liar." And he left.

I stayed in Micah's room for a few more minutes and used her bathroom to freshen up. Looking at myself in the mirror I realized that lying to him felt worse than lying to Grant and I didn't know why.

When I left the comfort and privacy of the bedroom I was instantly assaulted with music and people. Lots of classmates, and I guessed, family and friends were there drinking and dancing. But I didn't feel like partying anymore.

The party was going stale on me and I knew I couldn't stay much longer. I found Micah and Cory and talked to them for a little while.

They were on the back porch waiting for their turn in a beer-pong match, and as a guy in an "Eat Me" T-shirt yelled to them, "You're up," I kissed my friend goodbye and told her I'd call her.

"Are you okay?" Micah asked into my ear as we hugged.

"Yeah, hey, I have an early flight." Another lie. "Congratulations. I'm so happy for you."

When I hugged Cory goodbye, I saw Casey through the French doors. A petite girl with long blonde hair was already on his hip.

First, I thought how appropriate it was. He wasted no time lining his night out the same way he did the night before. Cory followed my gaze and said, "They broke up," as if he'd read my mind. I hated that I was so transparent. But it was certainly the cue I needed to propel myself toward the door.

I reiterated to them, "I don't care. I have a boyfriend. It was nice meeting you, Cory. Take care of our girl."

"You, too. And I will." He kissed her head and then walked toward their side of the white folding table.

As I walked back inside, I realized my purse was on the counter next to where Casey and his not-so-ex-girlfriend were leaning. With my head held high, I reached for it around him. "She could do better, too," I said for only him to hear.

*There take that, Mr. Know-it-all.*

I walked to the door as fast as I could, hailed a cab and decided to cash out my hotel mini-bar.

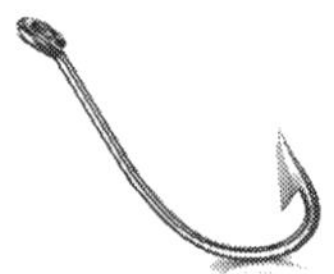

I didn't even turn the TV on. I went straight to the small two-person balcony that overlooked the street and proceeded to drink mini-bottle after mini-bottle of nine-dollar booze I had at my disposal. It burned going down and warmed my stomach. I considered what I'd done and tried my damnedest to reason the why of it all.

Didn't most people who had one-night stands just do it and move on? Didn't most people who threw caution to the wind not look back? Shouldn't I be focused on pretending like it didn't happen? Instead, there I sat thinking over every second of last night.

Every touch. Every playful bite at my skin. The way his voice still rang in my ears as he moaned his release into me.

I was so careless. Thinking back on it, neither one of us even broached the topic of protection. I wasn't worried, though. I'd had my shot a few weeks before. Pregnancy wasn't a worry that came to mind. What if he really *was* promiscuous? He could have given me something and I was so careless that I didn't even bring up using a condom. How could I have been so stupid and reckless?

I downed another bottle, but this time I chased it with a soda. I had lied when I said that my flight was early, but I still didn't want to be hung-over while traveling.

My body would be intact.

My conscience and heart would not.

Funny how a little drink can make you rewrite history fictionally in your head. I thought back to my senior year, last year, and played dress-up with my memories. I fantasized what now would look like had I met Casey while I still lived in San Francisco. I fantasized and pretended that we'd met when Cory and Micah did. That we'd fell in love.

We were still in love and he was just out for a while. I let my imagination wander into a parallel time where the night before wasn't an exception, but the norm. Where my body was more than satisfied and my heart was legitimately branded with his name, and it was his hand I held walking down the street every day to coffee. His jacket I wore when the night air got too crisp. And it was him who was about to propose.

Why was it I didn't dream of those things with Grant? Why was it my heart didn't beat erratically at the thought of being touched by him, being made love to by him? And if everything that I'd done was purely physical, then why wasn't the guilt for what I'd done to Grant louder than my fantasies of Casey?

I thought, if I could have him one more time maybe I'd be sated. I could rid myself of those thoughts.

If he were there with me, I'd pretend my fantasies were real and that we shared them. If he were here I'd prove they were real until they were.

If I could just touch those lips one more time.

# SIX

## Casey

**Sunday, May 25, 2008**

I HAD TO TOUCH those lips one more time.

I didn't care if she told me to leave. I didn't really give a fuck if she slapped me. She was there, in my town, and I had to give it a shot. It might be the only one I ever got.

As I walked down the street toward her hotel, I stopped and looked up at the brick front of the old building. The balconies peppered its façade and I saw her. Her hair blew gently in the light breeze. I watched as she poured a little bottle down her throat and then brought a can to her mouth.

She looked weary. She looked lost. She looked beautiful.

She'd go back home the next day and probably try to forget me. Probably try to forget we met at all.

Well, fuck that. If I had anything to say about it, she wouldn't ever forget me. If I had anything to say about it, she'd think of me each time someone else touched her perfect skin for weeks. Months. Years. Forever, I prayed. If I had anything to say about it, she'd have to bite her lip from calling my name if the lucky bastard actually did make her come.

There wasn't a winning side in this game. I would likely lose. But not that night. The next day I'd walk home with my tail between my legs and I'd pretend like it never happened. I'd be the one thinking of her when someone touched me. When I pushed toward a climax, with whoever it may be, Blake's name would be the one on my tongue. And when I'd stroke myself off, it would be her I was picturing for months to come.

But that night, I was going to make her mine one more time. One touch. One kiss. One lick at a time.

I watched her for a few more minutes from down the street. I saw her warring with herself, or me, or him, or life in general. When I got to the doors of the hotel, I decided not to run up the stairs like I had before. I rode the elevator and tried to come up with a good reason for her to let me in.

The shit of it was, I didn't have one. There was no rational reason for any of this. Even I knew that. But I wanted her. That was a fact.

At her door, my hand knocked on it before I told it to.

Tap. Tap. Tap.

I shook my hands out and steadied my nerves. She might have told me to fuck off and I'd have no choice but to do just that.

I heard her lean on the door and it creaked as she pressed to look out the peep-hole.

"Casey?" she asked. Then I heard the thump of her head against the wood. "What are you doing here?"

"Please, let me in." I wasn't messing around. I wanted in and I saw no point in fucking around about it.

She said through the door to me, "It's late."

"I know what time it is. Let me in."

"Casey, this is a bad idea."

"You leave tomorrow. Don't you?"

"See? This isn't right. I have a boyfriend and you clearly still have a girlfriend. Last night was—" Then she stopped.

"I don't still have a girlfriend. I don't know why she showed up. And honestly, right now, I don't give a shit about your boyfriend. Open. The. Door." I walked a thin line. I never talked to women like that usually. To tell you the truth, I'd never had a reason to. None of the chicks I'd dated ever had this effect on me.

I lightened the mood and clawed my way toward a miracle, I pulled out what I hoped were the big guns. "Betty, please?"

I heard her laugh a little and hiccup. Her fingers fumbled around with the lock. It rattled the door as she tried to get the mechanisms to unlatch. When she got all the way to the top, she huffed and kicked the door.

She was frustrated. I knew the feeling.

"Almost there, Lou," she sang. When the last lock slid from that bally thing and met the face of the wooden door, I reached and turned the knob myself.

She swayed, stepping backward at the same time. The back of her knees hit the luggage stand and she stopped, flinging her arms out to her sides and carpet surfed the whole way back to her equilibrium.

"Are you okay?" I shut the door gently, not wanting to startle her when she was already having a difficult time standing.

Her flimsy hand washed past her face, narrowly missing her bright red nose. It was so cute. It had gotten like that when she was flushed from sex, but I didn't notice it when she was drinking. A sane person's brain would say, "Oh, it probably does that when she's drunk." But I wasn't sane at the moment. I was looking for any reason that I was doing the right thing. I stood there internally debating why the fucking perfectly pink nose glowed like Rudolph.

"I'm fine," she said, pinching her lips together like a duck.

A conniving voice in my head said it was pink for another reason.

"Are you drunk?" I walked around her, straight to the couch. I wanted her to come to me. Sure, my intentions weren't the purest when I'd decided to come back to her hotel. But being there, I wasn't as interested in sex as much as I was about getting information out of that mind of hers.

*And maybe some sex, too. Sex with her was dynamite. Who wouldn't want more of that? But that wasn't what this was about.*

"Yes. I am. We should sleep together. At least I could blame this time on the booze." She laughed at what she was trying to pass off as a joke, but it went flat.

I didn't think it was funny.

"Is that what last night was? Your drunk mistake?"

Again, she picked at her fucking nails and I fought the impulse to slap them away from her and make her look at me. "Come sit by me,

Blake. I won't bite."

She looked at me and then her face flushed, coloring her grin.

*Dirty girl, I'm on to you.*

She relaxed a little and padded over to the couch, around the coffee table, and sat as far away from me as she could. She was still wearing the skirt from earlier, but since returning to her hotel room and her own personal bar, she'd taken her bra off and changed into a tank top. She folded a porcelain white leg under herself and leaned away from me onto the arm of the couch.

"I don't know why I did that last night," she said as she stared off into the room, still avoiding me. "I had a little to drink, but I wasn't that drunk. I was a little mad at Grant, but I wasn't trying to get back at him. You know?"

She finally looked at me, genuinely bothered by her admissions.

She added, "Even before you would talk to me, I knew what I wanted. I waited for you to talk to me. I thought about it," her face grew serious as she paused to collect her thoughts, putting a stop to her rambling. She sucked in a lungful of air. "I made a decision to try...to try to be with you. I didn't think it would go that far, but I thought about that, too. I wanted last night. I wouldn't change a second of it."

I smiled wide, I probably looked like a fucking dope, but I couldn't care less. Those words were the coolest words I'd ever heard. She was totally honest. Her nose returned to its creamy natural state and she continued, "That's the part I regret. You know?"

That's where she lost me. Didn't she just tell me she was into me? *Stop there. Please, stop there*. She saw the puzzle polluting my face.

"What part?" I pulled her hand to make her face me completely and I turned on the cushion to meet her halfway.

"I regret that I don't regret it at all. That's the part that's kicking my ass." She blew out a silent whistle of air and it went right in my face. She'd drunk tequila. I think I smelled the worm.

"I don't know what to say," I told her.

"Just say whatever your thinking. One. Two. Three. Say it." She roughly pointed into my chest.

"Ouch. I think you're pretty and smart and cool. And I know about that feeling last night. I think I know what that's called."

Like I'd witnessed her do before when I had her full attention, she leaned forward eager for more information.

"It's a hook and a fish," I said.

Her laugh bellowed and she quickly shut it off, re-masking her face with rapt interest.

I said, "See a fish doesn't want a hook. They'd probably rather not meet one and they're a bitch to get rid of. You follow?"

She bobbed her head with rapt attention. "And a hook, well it's only a hunk of metal. It doesn't know anything. Right?"

"Yeah."

"You have to add something special to these two to bring them together. Something that one can't shake and the other can't resist." I wrapped my hands around her low on her hips so I could pull her to me. I wanted her closer. "It's the bait, Blake. The bait is this outside force that brings these two totally different, foreign, objects together. Neither the hook nor the fish have a choice. We have something like that. We have the bait."

"The bait," she repeated, almost in a daze. Her brow furrowed. "So am I the hook or the fish? Or am I the bait? Sorry, I'm a little drunk, remember?"

She was adorably lost and I chuckled at her confused expression. "You're the fish."

"I'm the fish? *I'm the fish.*" I saw a little light pop on behind her eyes. "I couldn't resist you because of the bait," she said slowly.

"Right. And I didn't have a choice in the whole fucking thing because I'm just scrap metal." I wasn't sure where it was coming from, but it was true. I had never felt the lesser in a relationship, but with Blake, I was simply the hook. Not in control, and certainly dependent on the bait, or whatever the fuck it was, to attract the alluring woman before me.

She laughed and for some reason, I felt better.

"Okay. I'll buy some of that, but the hook doesn't want the fish or the bait."

"See that's where you're wrong." I pulled her even closer, placing them over mine, and she wrapped her arms around my shoulders, like we'd sat that way all the time. "The hook's sole purpose is to get the fish. That's what it was meant to do."

"Okay. That's a little weak, but I'll let it slide because you're cute."

I liked drunk Blake.

"What were you doing up here all by yourself drinking?" In her honey-brown eyes, I saw the sweetness and playfulness I couldn't get enough of.

"I was just thinking. And drinking." Her eyes darted away and something magical happened. Her nose flushed again, the tip blushing that same pink as it was when I came in.

"What were you thinking about?" She gave me a stubborn look that said *ain't going to happen*. "You can tell me. It doesn't matter anyway. You're leaving tomorrow and you'll forget all of this happened. So, spill it. What's got your nose all pink?"

"My nose is pink?" She quickly covered it with a small, cupped hand. "Mo mits mot."

I couldn't fight the chuckle that came from deep within my gut. "Yeah it is and it looked like that last night, too."

"Whem?" The palm of her hand muffled her embarrassed denial.

"It was a little rosy when I kissed you in the bar, and it was full on red after we—" I stopped as her eyes widened. I moved her hand away from her face. "Stop. Don't ever hide yourself, it's you"

"Oh." Her eyes still eluded mine, until I swerved my head to meet up with them.

"What were you thinking?" I asked.

Her small, pebbled nipples pulled against her shirt as she drew in a lung full of air and released it.

"I think I was tired."

Tired? *Not quite, honeybee.* "So you're tired now?"

She shrugged a weak yes. I moved her small body off mine and stood. "Stay right there." Quickly, grabbing the trashcan on the way, I went to the balcony. Just as I had expected, mini Tequila, Whiskey, and Vodka bottles lined the rim of the small table. I threw them away and straightened up the seats. I returned the receptacle under the desk and headed for the fridge to get two waters and I brought the blanket from the bed back with me.

I planted my ass down on the end of the couch and pulled her down to rest on my lap, throwing the thick white comforter over her legs and bare feet. She lay on her back and gazed up at me.

"Is this what you came here for, Casey?" she asked in the sweetest voice.

"Yep." And as I ran my fingers through her hair and watched her heavy eyelids battle to stay open, I realized I didn't have it in me to tell her goodbye.

I couldn't evade it. I didn't fully understand it. But it sucked.

"You wanted to come up to my room and talk to me while I am drunk and make fun of my nose and call me a fish." She brought her hands back to her face, standing as a barrier between her eyes and mine. "You men are *all* the same." She was funnier when she wasn't funny at all. She tried to joke again, pretending like she'd heard this song and dance. But this was a brand new song, and I didn't think either of us had enough footing yet to dance to it.

"Uh-huh, this must happen to you all of the time," I said sarcastically.

"It does. It's so unoriginal." Finally, her smile crept across her face and I took one of her hands so she wouldn't eat it whole. I laced my fingers with hers and she placed our joined hands on her chest, right in between her perfect breasts.

Before I could filter my words, I asked, "Is that how what's-his-face got you?" I heard the bitterness and quickly growing jealousy, over someone who didn't even belong to me, saturate my voice.

"Yep. Well, everything but the pink nose thing. He wouldn't notice that."

I thought about how I couldn't wait until she dumped that poor bastard. Then I realized that I wouldn't even know.

"So we're going to be friends then, honeybee?" The flame faded fast in her eyes as they took long blinks.

"Mmm. Hmm."

I watched her fall fast asleep and I wished I had had a drink. I would sip it and savor every second of both the liquor and the view. Her hair was soft and I threaded my fingers through it, over and over. Combing them clean through without a knot to yield me.

After what seemed like minutes, and light years alike, my legs gently slid out from under her head and I moved silently away from her. Crouching down by the couch to get one last look at her, I tasted her lips one more time.

She must have settled into a dream, because heard a soft hum come from her. I pretended it was me she was dreaming about as I kissed her. She hummed again and I considered many things, like moving and kidnapping, but settled on missing.

As I shut the door to a room, where only the night before was full of panting and sweating, I wondered if I'd ever see her again.

And I missed her already.

# SEVEN

## Blake

**Sunday, May 25, 2008**

I MISSED HIM THE moment I realized he was gone.

My flight was on time and the afternoon plane ride was clear all the way north up the coast. I didn't feel like I was going home though. I couldn't shake the feeling that every step I took was wrong. The closer I got to the airport, the more it felt like leaving was the real mistake.

My conscience was probably just getting to me. The angel on my shoulder sat with her head draped forward, haloed head in her hands.

Hang-overs sucked.

Hang-overs and shoulder angels were real drags when you were flying home after a massive alcohol and tempting-man binge.

*Casey.*

He was gone when I woke up that morning. I remembered him covering me with the blanket. I had lain there fantasizing about him kissing me and making me forget how bad I was. But fantasizing in the face of opportunity only equaled disappointment. I fell asleep before ever getting my second chance.

My last chance.

At about thirty thousand feet up I decided I wasn't going to think about Casey Moore again. I wasn't going to scan my memory counting his different smiles. I wasn't going to remember his hands digging into my hips. And I definitely wasn't going to close my eyes and beg my conscious thoughts to replay every second I spent with him.

But that decision was wasted, because I did all of those things.

The plane landed uneventfully. I departed the recycled air and the only thing I wanted was the sanctuary of my bed. Alone.

Knowing I'd lost my luggage, Grant waited for me at the ramp leading to the bag conveyor. I returned his smile as brightly as I could, but it was forced.

Wasn't he everything I wanted? I must have left my love for him in my AWOL suitcase, because I wasn't feeling it.

He was so smart and ambitious. Kind and gentle. My family loved him, mostly. My brother Reggie never really paid him any attention, but Reggie was much different than the rest of us.

In the offspring hierarchy of my family, Reggie, Reagan Ashley Warren, was the middle. Shane was the eldest and I was the baby. He couldn't have been more opposite from our oldest brother, Shane. Reggie lived in a high-rise in Chicago, Shane currently lived with our parents again. Reggie was adventurous, flying to Europe on a whim, sending me pictures of himself in front of global landmarks. The pyramids. The Eiffel Tower. The Taj Mahal.

The most adventurous thing Shane ever did was run off to Vegas and marry Kari. Sharing his current address with our mom and dad said a lot about how *that* marriage was doing.

But everyone else thought that the sun rose and set in Grant's ass. Up until recently, I had too. I still did. I still wanted to anyway.

"Welcome home," he said and placed a chaste kiss on my mouth. My thoughts went to Casey. I was wicked. I was wrong and I hated that I felt like my boyfriend was kissing away the last remnants of the stranger I'd just met.

"Thanks for picking me up."

"No problem. How was your flight?"

How was my flight? Was I on a plane? My body was, but my mind was somewhere completely different. Somewhere with *him*.

"It was good. I'm really tired though. I think I'd like to go home.

Can you just drop me off? I have work early in the morning. And honestly, I just want to take a shower and go to bed."

I wasn't an idiot, I saw the confusion and disappointment on his face. In fact, I deserved it.

"Yeah, sure. Do you want to grab some food on the way or...?" His voice trailed off. I wasn't sure if I should or not. I didn't think I could be around him.

"No. I'm not that hungry. I'm really worn out." He slipped the big bag off my shoulder and rested the strap on his, then grabbed my hand to walk me out of the airport.

"Did you have a good time then? I'm sure it was nice spending all that extra time with Micah, since I wasn't there cutting in on your girl time." His face was hopeful and the attempt at making his absence a blessing, didn't go unnoticed.

"Yeah, it was great. I miss her." I really did, too. I didn't get to spend nearly enough time with her. I'd wasted it. But that wasn't the right word. It wasn't wasted; it was just misgiven.

The drive to my place was quiet. Uncomfortably so. It wasn't him; it was me. I was edgy. The seat in his truck didn't feel right. The temperature was all wrong. I hated the song that played. I felt locked up and caged.

I was never so happy to be home.

"Thanks for the ride, Grant. I'll call you later. Okay?" I said, before I leaned over and gave him a kiss with all the warmth of day-old dishwater.

"I'm glad you're home. I love you. Call if you need anything and get some rest." He smiled weakly at me. I was behaving strangely.

Warily, I got out of the cab of his truck and walked to my apartment door. I set my bag on the ground to dig for my keys and prayed that I didn't slip them into my missing suitcase. I willed them to be there. And they were. Right inside the mug that said, "Lou Likes Trouble."

*Ain't this a bitch?*

I pulled the yellow coffee mug out of my bag and dumped the keys into my sweaty palm. I'd forgotten that I'd put it in there. As if I needed any more reminders.

After getting inside and picking my mail up off the floor, I went directly to my bathroom. I stripped my clothes off and walked over to the big soaker tub—the real reason I signed the lease on that place—and turned the water to just the right temperature. I walked naked back into the kitchen, grabbed my phone, a cold bottle of wine and the mug.

I climbed into the scalding hot water, sunk down low and tried to wash the memories off me. I needed to wipe all of it clean away and rid myself of my foolish behavior and silly thoughts of a guy, who I had no right to be thinking about.

None of that happened.

Instead, I soaked in the tub, drank two Lou mugs of wine. I begged myself not to call him and compromised, that if I didn't call his number it could remain in my phone. Knowing it was there was enough.

## Sunday, June 22, 2008

As the days went by it got easier to not think about Casey. Although, he was always there at the back of my mind. I began working extra shifts at the restaurant and unintentionally avoiding Grant. I was avoiding everything but time. I needed time. Time to sort it all out. Time to get my head back into reality.

It was no surprise that Grant didn't propose right away after I returned from San Francisco. I was barely there at all. I was in a daze. I'd tell myself, *Self, he isn't thinking about you. It was a fling. You have a real boyfriend here who loves and wants to marry you. Get your shit together.*

But Self was a hussy with a damn good memory.

I dreamed of him. Almost nightly. I was even a little paranoid that if I slept in the same bed as Grant I would say his name in my sleep. So I avoided that, too. Every reason turned into an excuse, all the while, Grant was patient. It was a paradox. Grant's patience and Casey's insistence. And just like that, thoughts of him invaded my mind.

Working as many shifts as I was, I was tired and so that excuse usually went undisputed. Others didn't have the same effect.

"Laundry again? Blake, you said you had to do laundry the other night, too. Are you mad at me? What did I do?" Grant said as we sat on my parents' back patio. My mom and dad were cleaning up the dinner mess and Shane, my oldest brother, was in the yard tossing a ball for

Randy, my parents' eight-year-old Saint Bernard.

"I'm not mad. I'm sorry. I've just been stressed out at work and thinking about this new job thing. I don't know. I'm sorry." I wasn't being fair to Grant and it was time I put the past behind me. The past, as if it were some long tumultuous affair.

It was one weekend and one crazy night, and there I was letting it affect my life so much. I needed to get him out of my system.

"Listen, I don't have to work tomorrow. I'm going to that interview. What about I cook you dinner and you stay over tomorrow night? I'll make that thing you like." And for the first time in the past few weeks I put a smile on his face. We hadn't had sex since I'd left. "And I'll wear that thing you like, too."

He scooted closer to me on the back seat we shared. "What about tonight?" he said leaning into my neck and placing a soft kiss under my ear. "I can't wait until tomorrow. Please?"

His kiss felt warm and welcome. Which made me happy. I'd been so closed off since I got back. Our relationship was great before I left. It wasn't knock-your-socks-off crazy, we weren't pawing at each other in public, but it was good. Comfortable. Secure. *Traditional.*

"No. I owe you. I want to do something special for you. Let me get this interview out of the way and I'll be able to focus. Can you do that? Can you wait one more night?"

"No, but I will." He pulled my mouth to his with a gentle hand on my cheek. "You're worth a little wait. Besides, I might have a surprise for you, too."

I had a feeling I knew what it would be. In forty-eight hours I'd probably be engaged. I'd give myself this one last night. One last night to replay those few hours I'd had with Casey then, I'd be Grant's for good.

We sat there for a few more minutes and chatted with my family. I saw Grant wink at my dad when he told him about how I planned on cooking him his favorite chicken marsala. My dad nodded and gave me a quick smile.

"Thanks for coming over, sweetheart," my mom said a little later as she hugged us in the driveway. "Good luck at your interview tomorrow. Call me when you finish up. I want to hear all about it. And see you later, Grant."

Then my dad hugged me, which wasn't uncommon, but this hug was tight. He whispered into my ear, "Cheer up, you look like it's the last day of summer." He gave me another squeeze and rocked me side to side. "Good luck tomorrow, baby girl."

I said into his shoulder, "The interview will go fine, it isn't like I'm unemployed."

"I'm not talking about that." And he kissed my head. "Be happy." I knew his simple words were meant two ways. My dad could see through my bullshit. He never told me what to do, but knew how to comfort me regardless.

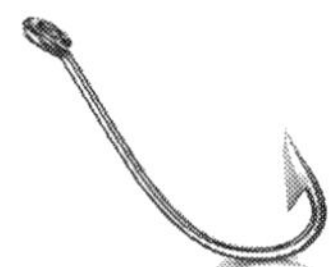

Like I requested, Grant took me home and didn't even attempt at coming in. I'd been carrying this weight around with me the last few weeks and even though he didn't know what it was, he knew well enough to give me some space.

I couldn't put a name to my feelings. I'm not sure there even was one. All I knew was this other man had crept his way into my head and he didn't want to leave. I needed an exorcism. A Casey-cism. And that night was as good of a night as any to try my best at making that happen.

I looked through pictures of Grant and me.

I played Grant's favorite music.

I even made myself a rum and Coke—his favorite drink—and I did everything to put my head back into Grant-mode. And it was working. I flipped through my phone at the pictures I'd taken of him and us and played our best hits, memory-flashback style, in my mind.

We'd met when I was home on Christmas break my senior year of culinary school. We were pumping gas at pumps that faced each other. He peeked around a few times and smiled. He was cute, a clean-cut, all-American boy. It was cold and he had a scarf wrapped around his neck. When I caught him smiling at me he slunk his neck down into the argyle to hide his grin.

Our gas pumps went off at the same time. We walked into the station to pay. He held the door open for me and let me go first in line at the register. I paid. He paid. We both walked out. As I was starting my car, I watched him do the same, he gave me another look and didn't hide his smile from me that time. Then he started to pull away. It was then that I noticed he'd left his gas cap and flippy-door open. I sprang from my car and ran after him, waving my arms, "Wait! Your gas thing is open."

He slammed on the brakes and shifted into park. Jumping from the vehicle, he ran back at me.

"What? What's wrong?" he asked huffing.

"I'm fine. It's your gas cap. You left it open."

Grant turned behind him to see what I was talking about and then embarrassment covered his face, he looked back at me. "God, I thought you wanted something else." He ran his gloved hands over his short hair. Then out of the blue he said, "Let me buy you dinner."

His statement shocked me, as I wasn't expecting a date out of the whole ordeal, but I simply said, "Okay."

He pulled his phone from his coat pocket and asked, "Can I have your number?" I gave it to him and he promised to call. I knew that he would. I never doubted I'd get a call from him and I had looked forward to it.

"What's your name?"

"Grant Kelly. What's yours?"

"Blake Warren."

"I like it. I've never known a female Blake before."

"Well, you do now."

"Yes. I guess I do." He shuffled his feet like he didn't want to leave, but had somewhere to be. "I'll call you, Blake, the female, and we'll work out our date." With that he beamed.

"Sounds good. Merry Christmas."

"It is now." He walked back to his truck and closed the gas thing. He looked at me, no short of three more times, before he shook his phone in the air and he stepped inside the cab of his truck.

I let those memories wash over my consciousness, I felt better than I had in the weeks since I'd returned. Grant was a great guy and come the next night he'd be my fiancé, for real.

I had needed that.

I needed to get my head clear of *him* and focus on what I had. A man that loved me. A man that would take care of me. When my phone buzzed, I assumed it was Grant telling me good night, as I lay in my bed ready for a peaceful night's sleep. But when I read the name on the screen, I knew it was a lost cause. My dreams would be hijacked. Again.

**Casey: Good luck at the interview tomorrow.**

*What the hell?*

My stomach knotted with a need. A need to reply. I didn't want to text him. I didn't want to think about him. Sometimes you don't get what you want or need, but sometimes you just can't tell the damn difference.

So much for pretending I didn't have his number.

# EIGHT

## Casey

### Sunday, June 22, 2008

I COULDN'T KEEP PRETENDING I didn't have her number. It had been almost a month and she was all I thought about. If she didn't reply, or told me to fuck off, I would have left her alone. Probably. But what I couldn't do was have her number in my phone and act like I didn't skate past it ten times a day anymore.

**Honeybee: Thanks. How did you know about that?**

**Me: Micah. I overheard her talking to Cory about it. She said that she'd wanted it, but didn't want to travel. So she recommended you. Do you want to be away from home that much?**

**Honeybee: I like to travel.**

**ME: Me too. I've been doing a lot more of it for my job. I'm in Phoenix now.**

There was radio silence for a while. This wasn't as easy as it was when we were together. Maybe, hopefully, this will work her out of my system and I wouldn't have to jerk thoughts of her out of my dick in the shower every morning.

Probably ten minutes went by before another message came through.

**Honeybee: Well, thanks for the well wishes.**

**Me: I can't stop thinking about you.**

*Delete.*

**Me: It's nothing.**

**Honeybee: It's something. I almost erased your number. Like every day.**

Now, that *was* something. These past few weeks I'd been going to trade shows, trying to get Bay's brand and name out there and into restaurants and bars outside San Francisco. It was nice being away. But every night I stood outside of my hotel room imagining what it would be like if she was on the other side of the door again. Wishing that she'd be there. It was getting pathetic.

**Me: Why didn't you?**

**Honeybee: I don't know.**

**Me: I know the feeling.**

And, fuck, did I. Every time my phone rang I wanted it to be her. It never was.

**Me: So are you married yet?**

*Delete.*

**Me: How are things going with the guy?**

Another long pause. I should have stopped while I was ahead.

**Honeybee: Fine.**

*Fine? That sounds really fucking fun.*

Her response didn't really convince me that she was all too ga-ga over the dude. Not that I thought we had a shot. We lived nowhere close to what would be deemed remotely proximal to one another, but morbidly, I liked the idea of her out there being just *fine* with him when she was way more than that with me.

**Me: So you think about me every day, huh?**

**Honeybee: The truth?**

I had been joking. Okay. Maybe not. Maybe I wanted to know if she was thinking about me. I sure as hell was thinking about her. It was getting tiresome and I needed to either make a move or let it go.

Ah, let it go. I love when people tell you to, "Let it go." What bullshit. It's usually them who bring up the sensitive topic anyway. And you of all people know how bad you should just let it go, and you're trying your damnedest. Then, some know-it-all prick reminds you that you should, in fact, forget about it.

Let it go. Bullshit.

I say do the opposite. If someone can tell that you're thinking about something so much that they tell you to let it go. That's the fucking thing you shouldn't. That's what's got you worked up.

That's the girl you should chase...hypothetically.

It's just, if one gets one's self in such a position where something is commandeering every waking thought that skirts around one's poor lonesome head, then you aren't working hard enough. Go get it.

Don't. Let. It. Go.

I realized this, about three minutes before I sent Blake that first message. I realized I had two options: Either be a chump and think about a girl who is with another man or be the other fucking man.

**Me: Good or bad. The truth.**

**Honeybee: I don't know why, but I can't let it go.**

If I had been a person waiting for a sign, I would have just got it.

The bait.

I'd fight. I might lose. I might wish I'd let it go. But I wasn't going to be the old man with the regrets. I'd definitely be the old man. Maybe I'd even be alone. Maybe I'd be with someone else, but maybe, just maybe, I'd be with her a little more first.

**Honeybee: You left before I woke up. You should have stayed.**

**Me: Nah. If you think it's rough now, think about how bad it would be if I had stayed.**

There would have been no leaving. Not me. And there was no way in hell I'd let her leave either. I had to go that night. My sanity could only take so much.

*What am I getting myself into? This is going to get way worse.*

**Honeybee: Guess you're right.**

**Me: I think we should be friends. Real friends.**

I knew my terminology was all wrong; by friends I meant lovers. I wanted to be more, but I had to see where her head was. I couldn't go balls-in if she was only looking for a fling on the side. My gut said that wasn't it, but I barely knew her. She had a boyfriend.

Still did.

**Honeybee: I don't know.**

**Me: Well you can't stop me. You're my friend now. You'll have to block my number or something. I'm hanging around.**

I thought while the silence screamed at me how big of a fool I was being. I sounded like some lame fifteen-year-old sending letters through neighboring classmates in homeroom. Do you like me? Yes or no. It felt like my only in. My only way to be near her. For now.

**Me: Let's go back to where you couldn't stop thinking about me.**

**Honeybee: See!!! Friends don't say that.**

**Me: What do they say?**

**Honeybee: They say pleasant things like. Have a good day. What did you have for lunch? Things like that.**

**Me: It would have been a real good day if I'd had you for lunch.**

I sent that one before I had the better sense to delete it. It was too easy and fun riling her up.

**Honeybee: I might block you.**

**Me: No you won't. You can't get enough of me**

**Honeybee: Neither can what's her name.**

She sounded jealous. A rational person would pacify her. A rational person would want to make her feel better and reassure her. But her having a boyfriend made me irrational and misery loves company.

**Me: Who? Aly? I know. She's called twice already in the past twenty minutes.**

**Honeybee: I'm sure she has. Listen, friend, I have to get up early. I'll let you know how it goes. Tell Aly hi for me. Goodnight.**

For a girl with a steady boyfriend, she sure did like the chase. Maybe I'd let her chase me for a little while. It was my best option. After all, I opened the door by texting her. And as much fun as it sounds grabbing her by the hair and dragging her through it, it would feel much more rewarding when she crawled through on her own. I just had to play the game she wanted to play.

Being forward didn't get her attention, but being cool did.

I'd be the coolest motherfucker around.

**Me: Nite, Betty.**

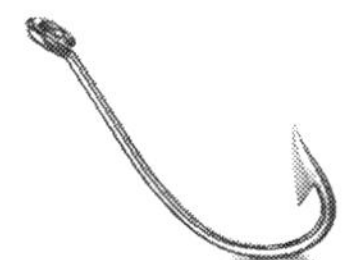

She didn't respond after that, I didn't think she would. I hoped she was stewing over it. I hoped she was uncomfortable and irritated. That's how I felt.

I put my phone on the charger and turned it off, ensuring I wouldn't keep stoking a fire I hoped I'd set. I didn't want to be a flash flame. I wanted to be a slow burn. I wanted to heat her from the inside out. And as I stood there alone in my hotel room, I thought about that night.

With my hands on the bathroom counter and my head hanging, I closed my eyes and remembered what it was like being between her legs. The way she smelled like jasmine and a fresh shower. Her lips were minty, but I could still taste the lingering bourbon on her silky tongue.

I didn't have to look. I knew I was as hard as the granite holding me up. So, I did what I did nearly every night since the one at Hook Line and Sinker, ripped off my clothes, set the shower to cold and climbed in.

I wasn't proud of the fact that I'd had plenty of opportunities to get laid and passed them up for yanking myself in a cold shower. But there I was. Again. One arm up on the wall and a fist around my stupid cock. Every pull I fought for the feeling of her wrapped around me. With every flex of my grip, I pictured her head thrown back against the pillow. I could hear her moans; I could see the flash of honest passion in her eyes.

Then I'd come and felt no better for having done it. Sometimes I'd go at myself again and others, like that night, I'd let my dick suffer for making me victim to reliving the night I couldn't forget.

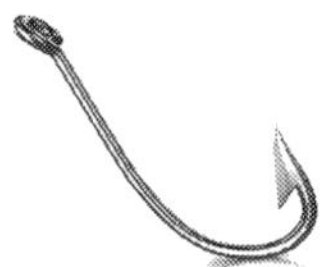

My flight home was early the next morning, I didn't sleep well but that was nothing new. I decided that since my mom lived so close to the airport it would be a good time to pop in and say hello. Yeah, I was a momma's boy.

My feet shuffled up her driveway after stopping at her mailbox and getting her mail. I read her name, Deb Moore, and wondered why she never changed it after my father and her divorced. If I were a woman, the second my marital status changed my name would, too. Especially if the jerk ran off with a woman ten years younger, like my dad had.

Don't get me wrong, I was well past over that by then. People get divorced and remarry. But he did it in a hurry. My dad and Carmen married after a three-month engagement, then they gave Cory and me a little sister, Audrey, about eleven months later. They gave us two actually, Audrey and Morgan. Audrey was seventeen and wild, where Morgan was sixteen, shy and quiet. They were both good girls and I loved them as much as I loved Cory, even if we didn't share the same mom. It's funny how things like that work out.

I opened the door to my mom's house with the key I'd never part with and yelled, "Mom!? It's your favorite son and I'm hungry."

"Cory is that you?" she yelled back as I saw her round the hall into the foyer where I was standing. We're twins, but she knew my voice. She just liked teasing me. "Cory, you look like hell," she said sheepishly, laughed, then complimented herself. "That was a good one."

"How long have you been waiting to use that?" I pretended to be wounded and placed my hand over my heart. "That hurts, Mom."

"Oh you poor baby. If you visited your old mom more, I wouldn't forget what you looked like. Come here." My mom was the picture of graceful aging. She was about five foot five and in great shape. That day, she wore cargo shorts and a tank top covered in dirt. Her tan made her long, wavy, silver hair seem even more polished. Her blue eyes sparkled as she leaned up to kiss me on the cheek. "I'd hug you but I'm mucky. I've been out back harassing the plants."

I wrapped both of my arms around her anyway and picked her up. She protested and hit my shoulders telling me to put her down. "Casey, you'll get dirty. Knock it off," she scolded through her contradicting giggles. I placed a kiss on her head when I put her back on her feet. She was the mom to twin boys and used to being manhandled by us.

"I flew in this morning and decided to stop by before I headed home," I told her as we walked into the kitchen where she immediately started washing her hands to make me something to eat. I didn't expect her to, but telling her not to was a losing battle.

"Well, I'm glad you did. I've missed you. You're a busy man these days. I'll probably never get that shed painted now." She opened the fridge, knowing exactly what I was after. She didn't like pastrami, but it was always in there. I wondered how much she threw away when I didn't show up for a few weeks. "Provolone and mustard? You want me to slice a tomato?"

"No tomato. That's fine."

"I just brought one in. It's no trouble." She looked expectantly at me, proud of her garden and wanting me to eat something she'd harvested. I was like that with my brews. The look in her eyes was easy to read. It said, *"Eat the tomato, I grew it just for you."*

"Actually, that sounds really good." She smiled, prideful.

"So what's new, baby boy? Where did you fly in from again?" She busied herself with making the sandwich and I waited patiently on the barstool opposite her.

"Phoenix. Marc has me traveling a lot more since we've been so busy. We're actually buying the warehouse across from our building now. It's crazy."

"How exciting."

"Yeah, it's pretty awesome. He said that we're hiring a few more people, too. Ten, I think, for now." She nodded, listening.

Marc's dad started Bay Beer Brewing Co. about fifteen years earlier, and had been slowly gaining clout. I didn't know what would happen to it if—when—Marc decided to retire. I was sure he'd leave it to Aly, but she wouldn't know what to do with it. I'd been thinking of talking to him about possibly buying into it somehow. I just needed to do it the right way since I wasn't family, and wasn't planning on becoming family either. Marc and I were pretty close, though, and he knew how much I loved it.

"That's great news," she said and took a plate from the cupboard and sliced the sandwich in half, then passed it across the bar.

"So, I've been doing a lot of the traveling over the past couple of weeks. I'm actually doing a pretty good job selling."

"Of course you are. Look at you. That face. Your charisma. You know everything there is to know about that brewery. I'm excited for you."

"I kind of want to own it. Or part of it. Someday. I don't know. I need to talk to him about it more." I bit into the pastrami sandwich and closed my eyes. There's nothing like a sandwich made by your mom. She had a secret to making them taste better than I did and we used the same shit. *Moms*.

"You should do it. You've worked your way up this far."

It was true. I'd worked in the brewery, the docks, and recently moved into sales. I loved hearing her say she thought I could manage it. It was reassuring, even though she was my mom and she thought I could do anything.

"We'll see," I told her while chewing. My phone beeped and I pulled it out hoping it was Blake. She must have seen my face change from excited to something else.

"Not who you were hoping for?" she asked.

I said, "Not really." It was Aly. Again. Yeah, I'd broken up with her a month earlier, but working for her father's company sort of kept us in close proximity. Especially that she was doing a lot more in the office. She knew where I was almost every fucking hour of the day. Don't get me wrong. I cared about her, but fuck. The spark—the bait—wasn't there with us. Not like it was with Blake.

"Hey, I was thinking," she said. "You know how you have all of that brewing stuff in the basement?" she asked tentatively as she cleaned up the mess from sandwich making. "Can you show me how to use it? I think I want to make my own."

I laughed and almost choked on my last bite. "You want to make beer?"

"Ale, Casey. I want to make ale. Will the stuff you have downstairs work for that?" She looked hopeful, like she'd already thought it through.

"It will. What kind of ale, Momma? Are you trying to run me out of business?" I joked.

She sat beside me on the barstool to my left and slapped my arm with the wet rag she was had. "No, don't be stupid. I just want to see if I can make it. I have lots of things I can use in the garden and I thought it would be fun for you to show me how." She nudged me. "You'd have to come over a little more than you do, and I know you're busy now, but I think if you showed me I could do it."

She was the coolest mom in the world. Not that Carmen was awful or anything, but I wish my mom were Audrey and Morgan's mom, too. They were totally missing out.

"You're damn right you could. You have a brewing prodigy for a son."

After we talked a little more, she prodded for more information on the person who I wanted to be calling me.

We went downstairs and I showed her how to set up the siphons, fermenters and carboys. She wrote everything down.

I had fun and she said it sounded easy enough. I told her to stop by Bay the next day and I'd make her up a little starter kit with a few other things she'd need. She agreed and told me she'd buy me lunch for my help and instruction.

To be honest, it made me proud to see her interested in doing it. That was the first brewing kit I'd used and it was how I made beer for all of my friends back in high school. I couldn't buy beer when I was underage, but I made a shit ton of money making it. My dad had left that set up when he left my mom. Cory and I found it in the storage room down there when we were about fourteen. It was amazing what a little research and juvenile mischief led to.

She'd immediately caught me on my first batch, but she'd just laughed and said that at least I was smart enough to get around the system. She'd stored my yields in a refrigerator that she locked so that I couldn't get into it whenever I wanted. I eventually found the key, but was quick to replace what I took. I think she drank more of it than we did, so she never got on our asses about it.

Being there with my mom that day took my mind off Blake for a while, but it all came back when I got to the apartment and heard Micah on the phone with her.

Micah said, "That's great, I knew you'd get the job. Congratulations!" Then she covered the receiver, which never fooled anyone, and said "Hi, Casey," to me as she watched me walk in. There was no way for her to know that I'd sent Blake a text the day before, so I didn't let my true excitement show.

But she got the job.

She'd be traveling.

She'd be away from her boyfriend and he might not like that. They, sadly, might not work out. What a shame.

And I'd be traveling too. She might not text me that day, but she would soon. I'd wait.

The possibilities were endless.

# NINE

## Blake

**Monday, June 23, 2008**

"THE POSSIBILITIES ARE ENDLESS, Micah." And for the first time, in I didn't know how long, I felt like things were going in the right direction. I pretended I didn't hear her say hello to Casey and focused on our conversation. "They said they liked my ideas and offered me the position on the spot. I can't believe it."

"I can. You're awesome. When do you start?" I could hear the excitement in her voice. One of the best parts about the job was that they had two main offices, one in San Francisco and one in Seattle. Couture Dining Incorporated specialized in the hospitality industry. They designed restaurant themes and menus for hotels all over the world. They were the benchmark in hospitality dining and, branching out, a new part of their company would focus on the invention of new restaurants and another other part on revamping already established ones with fresh menus and systems.

That morning, when I woke up after getting some of the best sleep I'd had in ages, I was excited. But after going to the interview and then out to lunch with Bridgett and Lance, the owners of CDI, I was having a hard time not coming out of my skin. It felt so right.

"I start next week. They have a trade show in a week or so in Chicago and invited me to go. Ahhh," I screamed. "I need to call Reggie. I might just stay with him. Ah, he's going to love this."

"That sounds fun. I'm so happy for you." I was so happy that I might get to see her more. "Call me when you find out when you'll be in town. You can stay with me if you want, it'll be like we're roommates again."

"I will. Micah, I'll never be able to thank you enough for recommending me. Ahhh. I love you."

"I love you, too. Talk soon. 'Bye, B."

When we disconnected, I immediately called my brother Reggie and waited for him to pick up. But then I realized it was almost two in the afternoon and he'd still be working. I heard his voicemail message, "Hello, this is a Reagan Warren, I'm not available. Leave your message and I'll return your call as promptly as possible." My brother was becoming such a stiff.

"Hey smear, it's your baby sister and I've got great news. You're going to love it and that's all I'm going to say. You'll just have to call me back to find out. Don't make me wait," I rambled and then I hung-up.

I called my parents next. My dad was a professor and my mom a grade school teacher, so I knew they'd be home at that time of day in the summer. They were so excited for me. They invited Grant and me out to dinner to celebrate. I shouldn't have accepted, because of the special night I had planned with him, but the job trumped that. It was major. We could do dinner some other night that week. I placated my real thoughts with these reasons for re-nigging on my night with Grant; deep down I knew it was because I chatted via text with Casey the night before and I was back at square one, feeling neutral towards Grant and the promise of his proposal.

My fingers itched to text Casey my news, but I didn't. Doing what my brain told me was the right thing, I sent Grant one instead.

**Me: I got the job. It's much more that I thought it was going to be. I can't wait to tell you about it. Rain check on our night in. The parents are taking us out to celebrate.**

I didn't expect him to text back in quick fashion. Grant worked for his father's real estate company and he was often with clients or on the phone during working hours. I tried not to bother him much. He'd reply when he could.

I needed to tell my boss at the restaurant about my new job, but that could wait until the next day. I had a feeling he wasn't going to like it.

I'd been working my way up and they relied on me a lot. It would come as a shock, but sometimes opportunities happened when you least expected them. I hoped they saw it that way, too.

My luggage found its way back to me about a week after I got home from San Francisco, but it would never be the same. It was really wrecked. I decided to make use of the rest of my day off and shop for new travel gear.

I found the perfect charcoal-gray luggage set right as I walked into the department store. It was the least painless shopping experience ever.

As I walked my bags to the car, I noticed a sign at the salon across the mall parking lot. It was a photo of a woman with a cute haircut and it compelled me to walk my happy ass over.

I felt impulsive and spontaneous. It was becoming a habit, I guessed.

I walked in and signed my name to the list and noticed there was only one other lady before me. I sat down on the row of plush chairs facing her and grabbed the magazine she'd discarded. I thumbed through it reading celebrity gossip and fodder. I looked at the pictures mindlessly.

"I hate waiting before a haircut," she said.

"Yeah, I know. I just decided to do it, so I suppose I can wait a few minutes," I admitted. She looked older than me by a few years and she dangled her sandal off the end of her foot nervously. I politely smiled and looked back down at the magazine.

She asked quizzically, "Are you cutting a lot off? Your hair is sort of long." I ran my hand over the braid on my shoulder and considered it.

"I don't know. I want to cut it. I think I need a change."

"I hear you," she said, "but every time I cut it too short I always regret it. Then it grows back and I do it again."

"I know the feeling."

She grinned a small smile. "Right?"

"Maybe I'll get bangs." I'd always wanted to try them and hopefully they would be enough to pacify the urge I had. It was decided. A trim and bangs.

"I think they'd look nice on you. You have a good forehead for it," she complimented and then was embarrassed again. It was a weird thing to say to a perfect stranger.

"Thank you," I said to reassure her and I laughed. "I think that's what I'll do. How about you?"

"Oh no. I'm only getting a trim. My husband would kill me. He likes it longer."

I nodded. But something about that sentence irritated me. Sure. Her husband's allowed to have an opinion on what he likes, but the way she was so quick to shoot it down was a little sad.

"If he didn't have a preference, then would you get it shorter?" I asked. I continued to smile, humoring her. I didn't want her to get defensive, I was only curious.

She looked up at the large poster behind me, which showed the nail polish colors that were available, as she squinted in contemplation. "I don't know. He's never told me to *not* cut it, but he always reminds me of how much he likes the length when he knows I'm coming in." She smiled thoughtfully and it eased my unnecessary concern. "I don't know what he'd do." She continued to look off into space, probably imagining the conversation they'd have if she came home with a short cut. "Is it strange that I like that he likes my hair a certain way? I'm sorry, my name is Annie."

She leaned forward and offered me her hand to shake, making our acquaintance official. "Blake. And no. On the basis that he does things that you like. Does he?" If it was a mutual thing for them to please each other, like that, then I thought it was great. If it wasn't, then I thought it sucked. "It's none of my business. I'm just curious."

"Oh. You're not married?" she asked and looked at my ring finger.

"No. I'm not. God, no." My reaction surprised me. I could have left God out of it. I'd have to think about that more later.

"It's okay. Let me think. Does he do things like this for me?" She swung her foot at a more rapid pace, almost like she was shuffling through memories with her shoe. After a minute or so went by, she said, "Ah, ha! He cleans the toilet for me, because he knows I don't like it. I know he doesn't like it either, but he does it anyway. Does that count?"

"I think so." Even though it wasn't the same thing, I thought that was a compromise.

We went back to our comfortable silence and she just sat there staring at the same nail polish poster. A woman with bright blonde, shaggy hair came out to the desk and looked at her list. "Annie?" and then she looked from me to Annie to decipher which one of us she was attending to next.

Annie lifted her hand, but didn't say anything.

"Hi there. As soon as I finish ringing her up," the blonde stylist said, "I'll take you back and get you shampooed."

She straightened a few magazines and collected her things. She took out her phone and, presumably, sent a message. Then she pocketed it again.

Annie walked over to me and said, "It was nice chatting with you, Blake, I'm sure your bangs will look great."

The stylist, upon finishing with her last client, walked around the counter and ushered Annie to the back saying, "So what are we doing today?"

I heard Annie say, "Cut it all off." And then she laughed. "I can get used to cleaning toilets."

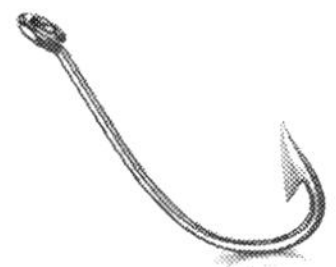

I had the stylist cut my bangs thick and not too short. She said the part that I normally wore would train to lay flat, but the way she fixed it, after she gave me the trim and some new face fringe, I didn't see that there would be any problem with me styling it on my own.

When I got home, I put on a little more makeup and slipped into an amber sheath dress and paired it with nude pumps. I was a little overdressed for Michael's, the restaurant my parents were taking us to, but I didn't care. I felt great.

On the way over, the conversation between Grant and I mostly centered on my new job. I told him that I didn't want to tell him everything in the truck, because he'd just be bored at dinner, hearing everything twice. But honestly, it was because when I told him I would be traveling a few times a month, he didn't share my enthusiasm like I'd hoped.

I said, “I’m excited. I’ll be going places I’ve never been. I’ll be meeting so many awesome chefs.”

He only answered with, “Your hair looks different,” and kept looking at me oddly. It wasn’t the most comfortable drive.

My mom, dad, and Shane met us there and were already at a table waiting when we arrived. Mom stood up to hug me when we approached the table on the restaurant’s outdoor dining deck. They knew I loved that place. It had decadent food and I loved eating outside. The weather was perfect for dinner on the patio.

I didn’t miss the look my dad gave Grant or the slight head shake with which he returned it. My intuition said it had something to do with my ring finger, but I put it out of my mind.

“Blake, honey, tell us all about it.” My mom’s enthusiasm was exactly what I needed. Even Shane looked like he wanted to know all about my new job.

“Well, it’s a growing business and I’ll be working with the owners on big idea things. At first, I’ll accompanying them to trade shows where other industry people will be, as well as potential clients, and I’ll go with them when they work on projects to get the feel of what my position will be. If everything goes well, I’ll start going to shows on my own. They said they’d eventually want me to take on entire projects.”

She quietly clapped her hands together in front of her mouth, like a thank you prayer, and smiled from ear to ear.

Shane said, “That sounds cool, so will you be cooking then, or what?”

“I’ll do some cooking. Part of the job is revamping tired menus and coming up with new ones. So, there will be some cooking, but not like I was doing every day. It’s more creative, and I love that,” I said answering him, and looking at my mom to show her that was the part I was most excited about.

“And I’ll get to travel all over the place. They don’t have many existing customers outside of the U.S., but there are some. I think they said mostly touristy locations like Jamaica, St. Bart’s, places like that. And they also have clients in Alaska, which I think is cool. Oh, and they have two offices, one here and one in San Francisco. So, I’ll get to see Micah more. I’m so excited.”

“Wow. That’s a lot of traveling. Take me with you,” my dad joked.

"Your brother is already driving me nuts."

"Phillip, he is not." My dad grimaced from what I bet was a pretty firm kick under the table, compliments of my mother.

When I looked at Shane to see if he took the teasing well, he was scratching the side of his nose with his middle finger. No hurt feelings there.

We ordered every appetizer on the menu; it's how my family always ate dinner when we went out. I loved it. We talked about everything and shared. It was the only way to dine with your loved ones. I caught a few more loaded glances between my dad and Grant, but even Grant was laughing and seemed to enjoy himself.

Only Shane teased me about my new bangs, but I didn't care. I loved them, too.

Grant's phone rang quietly in his pocket. He looked at me apologetically, but said, "I'm sorry, Blake. It's probably the Jensens. They put in an offer and are probably calling to get an update." It wasn't strange for him to get calls at dinner, or anytime really, and I understood that it was just part of his job.

"Don't worry about it. Take the call." I gave him a sincere smile and he appeared grateful as he retrieved his cell and stood to excuse himself. He walked over by the edge of the outdoor dining area, closer to the pristine view of the water.

My dad threw his napkin at me and said, "I have an extra ticket to tomorrow's ballgame. Or are you working? Did you quit?"

"I'm talking to them tomorrow. So, I'll let you know about the game." I wasn't looking forward to talking to my current employer, but it had to be done. At least if it didn't go well, my dad would get me drunk at the game.

## Tuesday, June 24th, 2008

They let me go. Let's just say it wasn't a congratulatory goodbye.

"Well, congratulations," my boss said shortly. Then he said, "Fuck," and walked out.

I left with a small plastic bag containing the few personal belongings I'd had in the break room and at my station. I told a few people goodbye and then I left. I liked that job, but the feeling of new and exciting possibilities overshadowed any disappointment I may have felt.

I was eager to travel and excited with not being nailed down to one city, at least for now.

When I got into my car, I called my dad. He was happy I could go to the game with him and he told me that he'd pick me up around two.

The ballpark was bustling. We found our seats while the bleachers filled with Mariners fans. My Dad sat next to me and we had beers and hot dogs.

"God, these are good," I told him as I ate my ballpark frank.

"We haven't been to a game together in a long time, sis. I'm glad you could go," he said and bumped his shoulder with mine.

"Me, too."

I loved my dad. My mother and I were close, but not like my old man and me. We were a lot alike. We shared the same sense of humor. Ours was a relationship that was easy and strong.

"So, tell me about this new job. Are you nervous?" he asked as he washed down the last of his lunch with his beer.

I was chewing, but with him I wouldn't be scolded for talking with my mouthful. I covered my lips with my hand and said, "Yeah. I think it's going to be really fun, you know? I love traveling and getting to work in different places sounds ideal."

Thinking about all of the different cities that Bridgett and Lance told me about yesterday made me think of Casey. They'd mentioned a place in Phoenix and of course their other office was located in San Francisco.

"Good. I'm going to go get another beer. You ready for another?" he offered. I didn't have to work tomorrow, so I thought, why not?

"Yeah, a big one. Hurry though, game's about to start."

He sat on the end of the aisle, so a quick dash out and back wasn't much of a hassle.

Still thinking about Casey, I decided I should text him. I'd said I would and that was two days ago.

I opened up our message thread and smiled.

**Me: I got the job. Cheers!**

Then before I thought too much about it, I snapped a quick selfie with my beer and sent it.

I watched my phone and waited, hoping that he'd reply quickly. Nothing happened and then my dad was handing me my second draught.

"Thanks," I said.

"You're welcome."

We watched the game, cheering on my dad's beloved Mariners. They had been in a bit of a slump that season, but seemed to be pulling it together that afternoon.

"Go! Go home!" he yelled as Beltre rounded the last base and continued down the home baseline. My dad had stopped drinking, but I continued.

I felt the vibration in my lap and looked down to see a reply from Casey.

**Casey: That's great. Where are you? Beer looks cold.**

**Me: Ballgame with my Dad. It is cold.**

My cell alerted me to an incoming picture message. I tapped it to download what he'd sent. It was Casey holding up a bottle of water, an awesome view of the Golden Gate Bridge behind him.

**Casey: Cheers. No beer with me right now or I'd have one with you. I'm with my sisters.**

**Me: Where are you?**

**Casey: Bike ride.**

**Me: No helmet? Couldn't find one big enough to cover that hair?**

**Casey: ha ha You ride?**

**Me: No. I was terrible at riding bikes when we were kids. Haven't been on one since I was little.**

**Casey: You never forget how. Like blow jobs.**

I shouted, "Ahhh!" after reading the message and laughed really hard.

My dad noticed and asked, "What's so funny? Let me see?" When he leaned over my shoulder to look, I flipped it face-down and placed my hand on it.

"No."

"Well, well. Okay. I won't look." He chuckled. "I'm old. I get it." He played hurt.

"No, it's not that. It's just…you won't think it was funny, is all."

"Is that Grant? I'll get it out of him later." He popped his collar. "I'm still pretty cool, you know."

I had a great buzz and my dad really was cool, but I was confident he didn't want to see a text to his little girl referencing oral sex.

I didn't want him to mention it to Grant though. He wouldn't know what my crazy dad was talking about. I actually hadn't heard anything out of Grant that day.

"It's not Grant. It's just a friend."

His face looked curiously at me. "A friend?"

"Yeah, you should know about those. You're so cool, remember?" I said playfully and knocked into him.

"A guy friend?" he asked diverting his eyes back to the game and taking a drink from his lemonade.

I'd never lied to my dad. I didn't think any of us ever had. Sure, with mom we'd bend the truth, but Shane, Reggie and I could always talk to our father. He wasn't a judging man. He had a vastly open mind when it came to most things. When we were teenagers, he'd spoken candidly about his own life experiences, both good ones and not so good ones. I think it made us feel like we could tell him the truth about anything.

"Yeah. It's a guy friend."

"Hmm. Good guy?" he asked still not meeting my eyes. Pretending to watch the game, he leaned back into his seat to hear me as best as he could with Mariners' fans whooping and hollering around us.

"I don't really know. I don't know him that well. We met at Micah's graduation. Well, the night before."

He thought for a while, quietly.

I couldn't resist looking back at my phone. It had buzzed twice while I was talking to Dad.

**Casey: Hey. Where'd ya go?**

**Casey: Are you trying to remember bike riding or blow jobs? Send another picture.**

I quickly thumbed back.

**Me: I'm with my dad. No blow job texts. No more pictures for you.**

**Me: I'll text you later. Have a fun ride.**

I pocketed my phone and decided that the combination of beer, my dad, *and* Casey were not good. The three were a little difficult to manage at once. I settled for beer and Dad at the moment. Casey later.

"So what's—" my dad paused, waiting for me to fill in the blank with Casey's name.

"My friend." He cocked his head at me and gave me a cut-the-shit look. "All right, Casey. His name is Casey."

"Casey. So what's this Casey-friend like?"

I puckered my lips off to one side in contemplation. I didn't know a lot of things about him, just the basics.

"He's a twin. Micah's boyfriend Cory's twin actually. It's weird. Their identical, but they don't look that much alike."

He didn't understand what I was saying.

"They look different. They have different styles and hair. He has crazy hair. It's all over the place. Big curls. Messy." I considered showing him the picture. Then, decided what the hell.

I fished my phone back out and tapped the picture from the text so that only the picture could be viewed.

"See?"

My dad studied it and then smiled. "That's some hair."

I took my phone back, taking a minute to look at the picture of him smiling brightly. His bicep was flexed holding the water slightly above his head. He was wearing a sleeveless T-shirt and the lime green aviator sunglasses he'd bought when I was with him. He was hot.

"He's fun to talk to," I said shrugging as I leaned over toward my dad and returned my phone to my pocket.

"What does he do for a living?" What a dad question to ask.

"He's a brewer. He works for Bay Brewing Company. He actually just got promoted or something and he's doing sales for them. I think he's worked there a long time." I tried to remember more of our conversation from the night at HLS, when he told me I was drinking his beer, but I wasn't paying close enough attention to what he was telling me.

I was too busy watching his lips move and imagining what they'd feel like flush against my…well, everything.

The sun started to make its way to the opposite side of the field and I had to pull my sunglasses down from my hair and wear them.

Finally my dad said, "I *always* wanted to brew my own beer." He smiled. He didn't push or pry, but I could see so many unasked questions in his expression. "Sounds like a cool guy."

"Very cool," I said before I thought better of it.

His head snapped to me and I gave a terrible fake impression of a smile.

"Not cooler than me, though."

"No. Of course. You're the coolest man I know."

"Good. You're the coolest girl I know."

My faux-smile transformed into the real thing. I swelled with pride. "You think I'm cool?" I laughed and leaned forward to grab the beer I'd set on the cement between my feet.

He winked. "As far as women go, yeah. You're cool."

"Cooler than Mom?"

A mischievous smile crept across his face. He adored my mom, but I was his baby girl. This was a true test.

"Let's just say you have more cool than her on account of your genetics. It's only logical that you're doubly cool because of your parents. I guess that makes you lucky, too." *My dad, so witty.*

He leaned over and gave me a kiss in my hair and said, "Be good, Blake."

He said it at the right time for it to imply he didn't want me trying to throw my mom under the bus, but I know he meant be a good girl and not a cheater or I'd lose my cool card.

Oh. Wait. I already had. In that moment I felt like telling him everything. The whole story, but I didn't have the nerve. The feeling like I'd lied to my dad for the first time burdened me.

It was the *friends* terminology that made it false, deep down I realized that we weren't just friends.

# TEN

## Casey

### Sunday, June 29, 2008

THERE WAS NO FUCKING way we were going to be *just* friends. Number one, my dick didn't get hard when I text my friends. Number two, my dick didn't get hard when I simply thought about texts with my friends. Number three, I rarely asked my friends for naked pictures. *Especially* when they were in a relationship.

**Me: Just one?**

**Honeybee: You're out of your goddamned mind!**

**Me: LOL You're right.**

**Me: If you're going to send one, then you might as well send two. What was I thinking? I'm a silly man.**

**Honeybee: I'm not sending you a picture of my underwear drawer.**

**Me: Prude. I bet it's so organized. You're a freak aren't you?**

**Honeybee: If preferring perfect rows for my G-string, satin**

**thongs makes me a freak then...**

Okay. Our texts had escalated.

She was so funny. Seriously, the weirdest person I'd ever had the pleasure of meeting, but I couldn't get enough. She ate mustard on her tacos. She didn't like her look. Her term was geek-chic. She couldn't sleep with socks on. Actually, she'd prefer to never wear them. She never remembered to charge her damn phone. She had both terrible and also a generous amount of self-esteem, it just depended on the subject. On the flip side, she was more competitive than any man I'd ever met and was convinced that she could beat anyone at anything. She was a walking, talking contradiction.

**Me: That wasn't fair. We were texting about your tidiness. Don't change the subject. Your brain is always in the gutter.**

**Me: Am I gonna have to block you?**

Oh, and she wound up like a clock. She was stubborn and her temper was fascinating. The strangest things got her feathers ruffled.

We were texting about ketchup and she swore and pulled the "I'm a trained fucking chef card" when she argued that it had to be refrigerated. I think she almost blocked me for real when I made her send me a picture of where it said that it needed to be refrigerated after opening. She couldn't and she was pissed about it. I had to remind her that I didn't invent ketchup and that she needed to contact them. In reality, some ketchup said it and some didn't.

But she would back down eventually. That was my favorite part.

**Honeybee: I have to go to sleep. I'm going into the office tomorrow. It's my first day. I want to be coherent. I'm not staying up late texting with you again tonight. Don't you sleep?**

**Me: You don't have to text. I told you. Send me pictures.**

**Me: Or call.**

I'd asked her to call me almost every night, but she never would. She said that friends didn't talk in bed. I had to, of course, remind her of the friendly things we'd already done in a bed and that talking on the telephone was a much lesser offense.

She got mad. Went radio silent. Then text me the next day that her phone had died. It was quite predictable.

**Honeybee: Goodnight, Casey.**

**Me: It was. Anything else?**

The incoming picture was of her underwear drawer. It wasn't exactly as neat as I'd thought, and there weren't as many satin, G-string thongs as she'd said, but I did see one pair I'd like to see more of in person. Or in a perfect world, they would be lying next to a bed she was naked in.

I quickly went to my dresser and snapped a picture of mine and sent it. Turnabout was fair play. At least that was a courtesy I hoped to implement. *You send me one. I'll send you one.* Sure, at the moment, it was underwear drawers, but I'd hoped it wouldn't be long before it was a lot more personal.

**Honeybee: A man who likes variety.**

**Me: Maybe, I just haven't found the right underwear yet. I like to keep my options open. Thank you very much.**

**Me: Go to bed.**

**Honeybee: Ok. Bossy.**

I wouldn't want to admit how much time we'd spend sending messages and random, nonsensical things. But it was a lot. It started to feel like a new hobby.

I'd been home for a week, and I spent some time with Cory and our sisters. It'd been nice. Mom was on me about that damn shed, but then Marc needed me at work, so I'd put some hours in on the floor in the brewery. It was nothing to complain about. I'd much rather make beer than paint a shed any day.

Blake and I had texted every day, sometimes all day. She was really excited about her new job and the opportunity to travel. I knew she had a trip coming up, but I didn't know where.

I was leaving in a few days, too. Unfortunately, I didn't get to take our friend Troy with me since it wasn't a trade show situation, which he sometimes came along for to help with. It was much more fun when he came. Instead, Aly was coming along. Her dad, Marc, wanted her to get a feel for talking to customers, or at least potential ones. He wanted her to listen to the questions I asked and how I answered theirs.

I'm not arrogant, but I'm smart and I work hard. Plus, I know everything there is to know about *her* company. It was no wonder Aly's dad wanted her to know how and what I did. I think deep down he wanted her to be out there doing it, too. In the past few months since I'd been out on the road we'd got a lot more attention and that had meant dollars for her and her old man. I guessed me, too.

I wasn't looking forward to being on the road with Aly. She was a cool girl and all, but she didn't do it for me. She felt differently, but I knew how to be professional. I hoped she did, too.

## Tuesday, July 1st, 2008

Aly and I flew from San Francisco to Austin that week. They loved our beer, but the distributor was lax. He might call, then again he might not. They liked our product, our packaging and our business model. All good things. They didn't like it when Aly said no thank you to her own beer because she was full after lunch. And when they told us they'd call she asked, "When?"

Aly wasn't cut out for sales. She didn't have that easy-going, everybody's friend thing that sales people needed. She was more of a numbers girl.

*These are our gross sales for the year. This is our turnaround on orders. These are the awards we've won for excellent brewing. And how many cases would you like monthly?*

But she tried.

She was quiet on our flight that day to Chicago. I let her think about it. When she was ready, she would ask. If she didn't, then I'd simply tell Marc he needed to hire another sales person. When we touched down at O'Hare and we were allowed to turn our devices back on, I was stoked to see an influx of texts from Blake.

**Honeybee: What was that band you were talking about the other day?**

**Honeybee: Oh, never mind. I'll scroll up.**

**Honeybee: They're pretty good. You said they're from San Francisco?**

**Honeybee: Mayday Maggie. I like that band name. What are you doing?**

**Honeybee: Are you ignoring me? Is this about the steak? I said I'd eat it rare, but only if I cooked it.**

**Honeybee: I wish you'd text me back.**

I couldn't contain my smile. In fact, the damn thing stayed with me all the way off the plane, through baggage claim and out the doors into a cab.

"I don't know why you think this is so funny. I suck at this." Aly admonished when she climbed into the seat next to me in the taxi. She thought I was laughing at her. I wasn't.

I was smiling because the girl who I wanted was showing signs of wanting me back. And it had nothing to do with our physical chemistry, which we had in spades.

I thought about texting her and letting her off the hook, but I sort of wanted her to dangle there a little longer. On my hook. Waiting for me.

It felt amazing.

"I'm not making fun of you. I got a funny text. That's all," I finally admitted to Aly on the ride to the hotel. She only rolled her eyes not believing me.

The next day we were meeting with the owner of a string of restaurants in the Metro-Chicago area. It was a pretty big deal. We were going to need our A-game. And by A-game, I meant Aly should probably sit this one out.

"Hey, you don't have to go tomorrow if you don't want to. I can go. Then tomorrow night you can meet up with us for dinner," I said after we were checked into the hotel and walking toward the elevators. "You'll get the hang of it."

"Okay, you do the meeting part and then I'll catch up with you, but I need to learn how you do this. You need to tell me what I'm doing wrong." She huffed as she wielded her luggage into the elevator car. "Let me have it."

I looked at her and thought that if it were Blake telling me to let her have it, I'd give it to her right here in the elevator. Instead, I just looked at Aly like...like a friend. Or a cousin, although that was gross considering I'd already slept with her. The feeling of attraction, that I sort of got when she first started coming around, wasn't there.

She was still pretty, with her long, blonde, wavy hair and green eyes, and she was fun to be around. She had an amazing body and took very good care of herself, but I didn't crave her.

I craved Blake. I snapped myself out of my thoughts and bucked up. If she wanted the truth—no bullshit—then I was going to let her have it.

"You're stiff in front of people you don't know. You need to act like you've been friends with them for years. You know, like you relate to your friends or me. Just be yourself. I can see you're only trying to be professional and that's great. But, Aly, no one is going to listen to you rattle on about numbers and spreadsheets if they don't already like you. That's sales."

I watched her take it all in. A crinkle across her brow told me that she was deciding whether or not I'd insulted her.

So I added, "You just have to sell yourself first and then sell the beer second. I swear. That's it."

The door dinged as we arrived on our floor. Our rooms were next to each other. She wanted to share last week when we were making arrangements, but I shut that down quickly. I wasn't about to toy with her, even if it would have been as easy as shooting fish in a barrel.

We stopped at 811 and 813, and she held both of the cards. Handing me one, she asked, "Do you want to get dinner in a little bit? I'm hungry, but I think I'm going to take a nap first."

"Sure. Knock when you're ready."

"Okay," she said as she lugged her bags inside her room.

The room was nice. The customary king-sized bed, a nice wet bar, and a sitting area. That was more than what I needed, but I was happy to have a little space. Staying in hotels night after night was great, but sometimes they felt a little tight.

The beds were sometimes too close to the walls. The showers were often too short for my body. I'm not a giant, but six-foot-two guy like me should be able to fit under the showerhead. I've got a lot of hair. It's a pain in the ass to get the soap out.

I don't mind living out of a suitcase, but I liked my space, too.

After I took out my clothes for the next day and hung them in the closet, and made the hotel room my home for the next forty-eight hours, I found myself on the couch looking at my phone. Reading and rereading the messages Blake sent. I wondered what she was doing. I did the math. What time zone was she in? What time zone was I in? This was becoming commonplace. This new me versus Blake time equation. Should I make her wait? Should I see if she'd give up or if she'd keep messaging me?

Then my mind would go somewhere else. It would wander to a place where she was with her boyfriend and they were happy. My conscience would tell me, "Drop it. She's already taken." But the biggest part of me said, "You want her. Make her yours."

Was that an alpha male thing to think? I didn't think of myself like an alpha male. Pissing on everything I liked. Claiming everything that I conquered as my own. But when it came to her, my instincts told me to act. To claim. To take.

That part of me said, *get her*.

Then, like I did almost every day, I sent her a message because I couldn't wait to see what she'd say back.

**Me: I just got off a plane and into a hotel. What are you doing?**

Was she with him? What did she tell him when she got messages from me when he was around? Maybe she hid it. Maybe she just didn't answer her phone. There were so many things that I didn't know.

Sure. We'd had a one-night stand, but we didn't really mention it. For the most part our messages were strictly on the friendly side. Not that there wasn't flirting. There was and it was quickly becoming not enough for me.

Still, I'd played it cool. I sent her the reply and then decided to flick through the channels and find something on TV. I turned up the volume and drowned out my crazy mind with the Food Network.

That was also becoming a habit.

I watched mindlessly as the chefs battled it out for some top prize if they could make whatever the hell food out of these random ingredients. I both hated it and was hooked at the same time.

**Honeybee: Just got back home.**

When she would finally answer I always thought I should try to ignore her, but I never could.

**Me: I thought you were ignoring me. LOL**

**Honeybee: You're not funny.**

**Me: How was your day? So you like Mayday Maggie?**

**Honeybee: My mother is driving me nuts, but other than that it was good. Yeah. That band is really good.**

**Me: We should go see them sometime.**

*Delete.*

**Me: I think I'm going to go see them. Cory and our friend Troy know their bassist.**

**Honeybee: Small world. How was your day?**

It was six in Chicago, so it was four in Seattle. This time of the night was usually radio silent from her end. It made me curious.

**Me: Good. Traveled most the day. Lost a few hours in the process. I've got a meeting in the morning. I'll probably call it a night early. You know. Beauty sleep. LOL.**

**Honeybee: You need it. From what little I remember of you, you look pretty haggard in general.**

That was how she flirted. She insulted me. It was her way. She was becoming easy to read. If she thought things one way, then she'd admit to the complete opposite. It was her tell. At least via text. The other night when I told her I was going to brush my teeth and go to bed she told me she could still smell my dragon breath and that I better floss and rinse while I was at it. Since I'd already caught on to her exaggerations, I interpreted this as she thought about my mouth and liked it.

**Me: Haggard by way of ruggedly handsome? I agree.**

**Honeybee: Something like that.**

We bantered back and forth for over an hour. We covered random topics, it was becoming a ritual for me.

Eating. Drinking. Breathing. Blake.

I acquired the ability to time how long it would take her to be *my* Blake—well the Blake I knew anyway—through our messages. They would typically start in a very platonic tone, but before the end of the night, I'd get her flirting back with me and it was like I was chatting with the fun girl in the coffee shop, the girl she called Betty. I could almost hear her reading her text messages to me with that ridiculous pretend Southern accent.

She was *my* Blake a little quicker than normal that night. I regretted having to go to dinner with Aly, but I also knew I should. The better she got at this travel thing, the better for the brewery. The better the brewery did, the more money I'd make.

The more money I made, the better chances I had at showing up this guy who was fast becoming my arch nemesis. I really had nothing too negative to dwell on about him though. We didn't talk about him. Ever. Sometimes because I didn't want to bring him up and turn her back into *his* Blake and in part because for some reason, she didn't seem keen on bringing him up either.

But in my mind, I was the good guy and he was the bad guy. However, my mind wasn't really the picture of reality. He was her boyfriend and I was a guy trying to steal her attention and…and what? Make her my girlfriend? Did I want a girlfriend? I might have if it were her.

But hell, what did I really have to offer her? I was working damn hard to get ahead in my career. Would I even have time to be the kind of boyfriend she deserved? Not that anything in my made-up scenario was close to likely.

*What if? What if? What the fuck if?*

For now, it was flirty text messages and hopefully crossing paths in a hotel again sometime.

Oh, we were going to cross paths. I'd make sure of it.

But that night, I just wanted to come while I listened to her voice, or at least while I was imagining her voice while she sent me dirty pictures.

I had a big to-do list for my plans later on.

Keep *my* Blake chatting.

Get some much-needed visuals in the form of another picture. The ball game one was great, but I wanted to see more of her.

Possibly call her on the phone.

Then have phone sex.

It was a tall order, but I aimed high.

So while she was still being playful and sweet, I needed to solidify my pseudo-date for later.

**Me: You're fun.**

**Honeybee: I know.**

**Me: You're pretty.**

**Honeybee: You are, too.**

I wasn't expecting that. She was *really* sweet that afternoon.

**Me: I'm going to get a shower and go get something to eat. Will you be up later?**

*I'm going to take a shower and cum all over the wall like it's your mouth and then go to dinner with a woman who isn't fun like you.*

**Honeybee: What time?**

**Me: I don't know 10 here, 8 there?**

**Honeybee: Okay. Let me text you first.**

Let me text you first, I learned, was code for I'm going to be with *him*. I hated *let me text you first*. It hated every second of waiting for her, as minutes ballooned into twice their actual span of time waiting for Blake to *text me first*.

**Me: I'll wait. You could call.**

**Honeybee: I might.**

**Me: All right. Later, then.**

I thought about turning my phone off, but I couldn't. I threw it on the bed, stripped down to my boxers, and walked into the bathroom for a shower.

The water was hot. My hand was slow. My eyes were screwed shut. My mind was with her.

# ELEVEN

## Blake

**Wednesday, July 2, 2008**

MY MIND WAS WITH him. He was taking a shower.

I needed a shower. In some small way, I wanted to get into the shower because it made me feel like I was closer to him. We'd just finished sending messages back and forth like telephonic Ping-Pong. I could hear his chuckling at some of them. That was weird, right? That I could hear him laugh at my texts?

Well, I could.

Every time he replied with an LOL I let my mind hear it. The best part about my memory was it did this funny thing with his laugh. It wasn't the same laugh every time. My imagination would invent laughing sequences for a guy who I'd only met briefly. It was the strangest and most wonderful thing.

I stood there running the hot water about to get in, when I thought about Grant. Which I did a lot when I was thinking about Casey.

I'd become accustomed to comparing the two.

Casey was devilishly playful and crass. Grant was sweet and smart and thoughtful. But both were genuine.

Casey was low maintenance. We could text, stop for a while and then hours later pick up our conversation. Or we'd start a new one. It didn't matter. He was easy.

Grant was higher maintenance. He liked a schedule. He'd admitted that me taking the new job was awesome and that he was proud, but he was so minute-to-minute. He wanted to know where I was going, what I was doing, and did I like it so far? All things a boyfriend should. And even though I was excited about all the things he'd asked me about, everything always fell flat when he asked. It felt a little suffocating at times. It was probably just me, though, right?

Every girl wants the man with a steady job and a huge heart. Everyone wants the man who would spend time with your parents and—to the best of your knowledge—enjoy doing it. Grant wanted a family and home, a good life, which I was sure I'd have with him. The perfect, traditional life.

Casey lived out of a suitcase and hadn't slept in his own bed for days. He sold beer and needed a haircut. *All right, I liked the hair.* He was two years older than Grant and me, yet he acted like he was twenty-one, I thought, but I didn't know him that well.

I stepped up to the mirror and wiped away the steam from the water, which was hot enough to distract me and clear my head for an evening with Grant.

I noticed my bangs were growing out fast. They needed trimming already. I made a snap decision to get the kitchen scissors and trim them myself.

After rifling through drawer after drawer, I finally found them in the dishwasher. I shut the dishwasher door and I saw my phone light up and heard it vibrate. Maybe it was him, but I told him I'd text first and so far he'd always waited. I hadn't wanted to be rude to Grant and text Casey back right in front of him. Grant wouldn't think anything of it. I text my family and friends all the time. He'd never acted the slightest bit jealous or suspicious.

Why would he then? And I'd be guilty, because I'd answer him. I just knew I would. I couldn't help myself.

The screen said I'd got a text, but the number didn't jive with my contacts.

**Unknown Number: Why are you texting my boyfriend?**

I read. Blinked. Read it again. My heart raced.

Casey told me he was going to get a shower and something to eat. Then he'd be around later. I couldn't understand. I didn't know what to say. I wanted to delete it and block the number. I didn't want to respond.

I needed to take a shower. I needed to get ready for Grant.

*Casey was someone's boyfriend. What the fuck?* I felt ill.

I'd known what we'd been doing was wrong on some level. All right. On every level. I'd been unfaithful to Grant, but I honestly hadn't thought about the girl Casey was with at Micah's since he'd said they'd broken up that night in my hotel room, when I was drunk.

I supposed things changed.

Maybe they'd gotten back together.

Maybe that was a different girl.

Maybe he lied about all of it. I felt a cold sweat break over my chest and back. I felt lightheaded. My clammy and nervous hands held the phone out in front of me and every time the light on the screen timed out, I'd press the button and swipe it open to re-read it over again. Minutes passed and I did it over and over.

It wasn't like I'd thought Casey and I would ever have a chance or that we'd even see each other again. Although, in the back of my mind, I thought it was possible if Micah and Cory ever got married. But that wouldn't be for a while.

I hadn't spent a whole night with Grant since we started texting. Not that I was afraid of getting caught. Honestly, I wasn't. It was that I liked being alone and with Casey at the same time. I didn't want to be around anyone when he was giving me his warped brand of attention. It felt all my own. My crazy secret.

I loved talking, well texting him. Lately, it was the highlight of my day. Where I never wanted to talk to Grant when he asked me about anything and everything, Casey not asking made me want to tell him every minute detail. Having that small connection with him had been awesome. Every night I looked forward to hearing my phone buzz. I anticipated what he would text; he always told me the strangest things. Things I didn't even know I cared to know.

Some of his weird messages ran through my head.

**Casey: Did you know that you can use semen for invisible ink?**

**Casey: I read that the inside of a female's nose plumps up when she's aroused. Like a nose boner. LOL**

**Casey: Bees have five eyeballs. Gross.**

**Casey: Only one state has one syllable. Maine. Boom. Betcha didn't know that.**

I went to sleep happy every night.

Now seeing this message, although I had absolutely no right to be angry, I felt like I was the one who'd been cheated on.

How fucked up was that?

A surge of some type of territorial feeling flooded me.

**Me: I am texting your boyfriend because he sold me some line about Bait, and I think he's right.**

*Delete.*

**Me: Who is this? I think you have the wrong number.**

**Her: He calls you honeybee.**

It wasn't a question. He called me honeybee in San Francisco and sometimes in our messages. She'd read our messages. She wasn't asking. Thank God for the most part they were harmless.

Thank God? What was I hoping? That he didn't get caught?

I don't know what I was thinking. I was so damn confused.

When I'd been typing the messages, I felt like I'd been good at staying in a friendly zone. But now thinking about them through this *girlfriend* person's eyes, they'd seemed anything but.

Unease moved straight into anger, then it turned around and headed to denial.

**Me: We are only friends.**

**Her: Leave him alone.**

**Me: I told you we were just friends. I think he can decide on his own if I should leave him alone.**

*Girlfriend.*

Yes, from that point forward that would be her official name. Not like *his* girlfriend. In my mind it sounded a lot more like *bitch.*

**Her: He said you were nobody when I asked. That doesn't seem too friendly.**

*Bitch. Girlfriend.* Girlfriend. His girlfriend. Who obviously cared about him enough to stand up for herself and their relationship.

Who does that make me?

*Nobody? Casey's nobody? I'm nobody's nobody.* I'm Grant's somebody.

My mind struggled with what she'd told me. Did I believe her? If I were her I would have said the same thing. Hell, I'd say anything to make me leave *him* alone.

**Her: He was with me today when you sent so many messages. Maybe you should have taken the hint. He said you won't leave him alone. In fact, he gave me your number. Don't call him later.**

**Her: Leave.**

**Her: Casey.**

**Her: Alone.**

If only it were that easy.

It had to be. I was with Grant and Casey was with this girl, *Girlfriend Bitch,* who seemed to be ready to throw down if I got in their way.

I felt another rush of that cold hotness spring to the surface of my skin.

I needed a shower. Grant was going to be there in a little while and I needed to wash the grossness away. I needed to get my shit together. I needed to grow up.

Casey wasn't *my* cheater and I wasn't *his* hypocrite. Or maybe it was the other way around.

I turned off my phone. I couldn't allow myself to think about it anymore. That was it. It was done. I could finally move on. I needed to focus on the man who I had. A man who would never text another man's *girlfriend* behind my back. A man who was faithful and in love with me.

It was time I let this thing with my perfect stranger go. Let the secret become a memory. I didn't want to though, I only told myself I did.

I'd miss him. Even only spending one weekend with Casey, and barely a dozen days texting, I'd come to rely on him for something. Friendship, I guessed.

Maybe we were friends after all. I guessed I'd never really know.

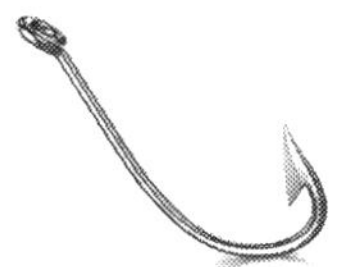

Grant was a little late, a bit unlike him, but it was good. It gave me more time to regroup, get my game face on, and prepare myself.

I'd known for a while now that he was waiting for the right time to propose and I'd given him some pretty obvious "not now signals" in my Casey fog.

I was just angry enough to make a decision. That's the thing about anger. It makes you decisive.

I wasn't taking what I had with Grant for granted anymore. Not after *Girlfriend's* messages.

When he came to my door with flowers, I looked at him like I hadn't seen him in weeks. Then I realized I probably hadn't.

He looked nice. He was still wearing his work clothes, brown pants and a blue shirt. He'd even had a haircut. He handed me the roses and I took them, feeling a little shy and unworthy.

"Thank you, they're really pretty." I turned back around then glanced back at him. "Come in for a minute? I'll put these in water."

"All right," he said. "Then I'm taking you somewhere." He walked into my foyer, sure and calm.

I busied myself with the flowers, looking at my phone on the kitchen counter next to me, the entire time. I wasn't even going to take it with us.

After sorting the flowers and putting them in a tall vase, I grabbed my purse.

He didn't say much, but he held my hand on the way to the car and it felt nice. After the afternoon I'd had, it was reassuring. That was what our love and relationship was, comforting and familiar.

No bullshit. No worries. *No girlfriend.*

He kissed the tops of my fingers before he dropped my hand to walk around the truck.

I didn't know where we were going, but I didn't really think it mattered. I was where I was supposed to be if I *was* with Grant. Even my parents thought so. Even Shane.

Before I realized where we were, he was putting the car into park. We were in the parking lot of the gas station where we'd met.

Tonight was the night.

"Blake, I love you. We met here at a gas station on Christmas Eve. I think I might have fallen in love with you that day." He turned and faced me, his freshly shaven skin looked so smooth. "I know that there's been something on your mind lately. I can tell. But I don't want to wait any longer."

I didn't know what to say. I was rotten.

He said, "I want to talk to you tonight about our future. Do you want to talk about it? The future? Our future, maybe?" He smiled and it was endearing, full of hope and love and goodness.

"I'd love to talk about it." I gave him the best smile I had.

"Do you see me in your future?" he asked. Cars drove around us and looked into our windows since he parked in the middle of the lot. Almost the exact same place we'd been standing when he got my number.

I thought about my future. I saw him there. It was peaceful and happy and predictable. In that moment, it felt good. Then, as I did, I put Casey in my future to see what it would look like. My evil imagination tried these men on like jeans in a department store.

In my alternate Casey-future, he would always be gone on business. I'd be stuck at home. And he would cheat on *me*.

After all, he did admit to cheating on other girlfriends and not just Aly, which created a mental image of flashing red warning lights reading "Danger!"

I didn't know. Casey's version was unpredictable, but the future with Grant looked nice, safe, and comfortable.

"I see you in my future," I said looking at my hands in the streetlight that poured through my side of the vehicle. I wanted to bite my nails badly. When I peeked up at him his face was alight.

"I see you in mine, too. Ours. If you want that."

"I think I want that." I didn't want to feel like I had earlier that day. I knew *that* for sure. "I *know* I want that."

"Good, then I have a surprise." He put the car in drive and we left the gas station where it turned out Grant and I made all of our major plans. First to see each other, now to be together in the future.

We drove through side streets close to where my parents lived. They'd been in the same house since I was small. The neighborhood was familiar and I'd always liked it. I scrolled through my mental map trying to figure out which restaurant we were going to. I came up short. There wasn't a restaurant in that area.

Grant pulled over to the curb and got out. Walking around to my door, he opened it for me. I didn't know what we were doing there. Maybe we knew the people who lived in the house. He grabbed my hand and walked me toward the bungalow's porch. It was a brick house and it had a porch swing, a holstered flag swayed over the front steps and big ferns hung on hooks between the four squared-off, white pillars.

There were a few lights on inside, but looking through the windows it didn't appear there was anyone home.

There on that porch Grant got down on one knee.

He produced a white, velvet box from his pocket and offered it to me for inspection with one hand.

"Blake, I love you. I love everything about you. I always have. I know I didn't discuss it with you and we don't have to stay here long if you don't like it, but I bought this house for us. I want this to be our home. I want you to be my wife and I want to be your husband. Will you please, please say yes and marry me?" He swallowed back some of the nervousness that must have risen to the surface of his throat.

Kneeling on the wooden plank porch, he looked so right. Everything did. The house. The ring. The man. It all seemed the way it should be.

It had been coming, but the house was a true surprise. It had a porch swing. And I loved porch swings.

It all felt surreal. I looked around. The bushes were perfectly trimmed. The windows were clean. The grass had been mowed and he was offering it to me. He was proposing a life, not just a marriage. A life I could be proud of. He would love me and care for me.

He wouldn't hurt me. He wouldn't leave me. He didn't have a *girlfriend.*

"Yes." I let a relieved smile melt across my lips. "Yes to all of it. I love it!"

He stood up quickly and kissed me. His lips were warm and soft and like always, his kiss was measured. Even in this emotional life-changing moment, he kept his control and his emotions at bay. So I did, too.

I always pictured that I'd cry when I was proposed to. But I didn't. There wasn't anything to cry about.

Breaking our sweet kiss he asked, "Do you want to go in?"

"Yeah. Let's see this house you bought." Maybe it was the terrible emotions from earlier colliding with the elation I was supposed to be feeling, I didn't know, but walking into my new house for the first time with my fiancé felt okay. Just okay.

I'm sure it would hit me later and the sense of excitement would fill me. I'd just have to wait for it all to sink in.

"We have some work to do, but I think it's going to be a great first home." He looked almost more apprehensive about the bungalow than he had about the proposal. "I know the floors need refinishing and the carpet needs replacing, new paint, new kitchen—you can do whatever you'd like in there—and a lot of other things, too. But it's ours."

"What's the address?" I asked.

"9335 Aloha Street."

I thought it was funny. Aloha meant hello and goodbye at the same time. Even the street name felt appropriate.

He showed me around and we had pizza delivered our new house. He walked me through every room and described every idea he had for the future of our home and he had lots of them.

We ate the pizza on the floor of the empty dining room and drank champagne, which he'd dropped by earlier, out of plastic cups.

"Do you want to come back to my place?" I wanted so badly to connect with him. To feel him. To get swept away by him. If ever there was a night to do that, it was the night he'd asked me to marry him.

When we got back to my apartment, I felt anxious, like it was about to be our first time all over again. Grant and I had a pretty decent sex life, until I got back from San Francisco. But lately we'd been busy. I'd had my period. He had been working a lot of extra hours—only then obvious to me—to save for both the ring and the house.

So we hadn't been together much lately.

Grant was a gentle lover. He was generous and sweet. He kissed my neck and caressed my skin. He looked deep into my eyes.

I'd asked him to stay over, and that wasn't anything new for us pre-San Francisco. He followed me into the bedroom. I didn't turn on any lights on my way, walking through the small apartment through the moonlight that spilled in through my windows.

When we got to my bedroom, we both sort of stood there. It had been a little while and it was taking a few minutes for us to find our rhythm again. Then he walked over to the bed and sat down. He took off his shoes and socks methodically in the dark, making sure not to make a mess. Not that I would have minded. That behavior wasn't anything strange for him though.

I had been in the same room, doing that same thing many times with him. It was only then I'd ever noticed how he took his clothes off himself and I found myself walking around to my side of the bed. I took my sandals off, followed by my pants and shirt. I left my bra and panties on, wanting him to take them off me. But when I saw him stripped bare, I followed suit and took them off myself.

He lay back on the bed and faced me. I mirrored his actions rolling on my side to the center to meet him.

"Thank you for saying yes," he said as he ran a soft hand down my cheek. I leaned back and he moved over me.

I only nodded.

*I shouldn't be doing this.*

His other hand found my waist and then moved south. I rose to kiss him, trying to shake this weird feeling that was blooming in my stomach. My mouth met his and I kissed him with fervor. My mind pleaded with my body to get on board.

His hand found my center. His fingers found all of the places he knew I liked. His touches weren't urgent or desperate; they were calculated with over a year's worth of history guiding their ministrations.

Grant took his time, not rushing through foreplay. He kissed me where he should. He stroked and caressed me in all of the right spots.

I touched him and worked his erection with one hand. He was hard and his tip was slick with readiness. I shifted, as a sign I was ready and that I wanted him inside me. I wanted to feel that rush of love and adoration that came with an orgasm. I needed it. I needed it for us.

He made love to me. He told me how beautiful I was. How he couldn't wait for our future. That I was the only girl for him. It was quiet, except for our breathing and the occasional moan. I didn't feel the usual build. I wasn't climbing like I could tell he was.

I looked at the clock, something I couldn't remember ever doing before in my life during sex. It read ten thirty-seven.

*I should be texting Casey.*

*Casey had a girlfriend.*

*I had a fiancé.*

*I wondered if he'd tried to call.*

*I'd told him to wait.*

*Did he know she messaged me?*

Grant's body language was such that I recognized him nearing his end.

"Are you getting close?" he asked in my ear, the closeness made my body shiver as his voice vibrated the little hairs inside of my ear. My body gave a little shake. Grant took the movement as my answer.

"Good. I'm about to, too." He leaned up on his elbows and slid his hands behind me under my pillow. His hips pushed in and out of me in a synchronized tempo. In and out. In and out. I almost looked at the clock again to work out how much longer he would take.

He thought that the tickle I'd had from his breath touching my ear was the beginning of my orgasm. I knew I wasn't going to get there and that his was knocking at the door.

He wouldn't be angry if I didn't come. He might have been concerned; it was a special night and all. I'd hate to make him feel bad after how wonderful he'd been.

So I began an act that I didn't know I'd prepared. I pushed my head back into the soft satin pillowcase under my head and my hands went to his ass. I began panting and moaning, meeting his thrusts with new energy. I threw my whole entire body into a performance.

"Yes," I purred leaning up to pair our lips. "Yes."

Grant wasn't a very vocal or loud man in bed. He told me how good he felt, or how beautiful I was, he would say my name and things like that. I could tell that my actions were ringing true to him, because his brow cinched and his mouth hung open and a long, "Ahhh," came out as he did.

He stilled and throbbed, slowing his movements inside me, collapsing on my chest. I squeezed my inner muscles in reflex to the sensation. He coated the tops of my breasts with pecking kisses.

"I love you, Blake," he said, stretching to my mouth and kissing me one last time before gently pulling himself out of me.

"I love you, too," I whispered loud enough for him to hear. "I'm going to get some water. Do you need anything?"

I had to get out of that bed. I had to be alone for a minute.

"No, thanks. I'm going to sleep." He rolled over and pulled the sheets up the length of himself.

I thought about another man while I was having sex with my boyfriend. *Fiancé*. They weren't erotic thoughts, thank God, but they were a distraction when my focus should have been on the man I'd confessed my love to.

An unsettling feeling once again festered inside me. It felt like shame. Like I didn't want anyone to ever know what had happened. Like I'd been unfaithful just now, when I hadn't. I was with the man I was supposed to be with.

Then my mind meandered to a place that turned my mild uneasiness into full-blown panic. What if he's with her right now? Irrational as it was, my thoughts were uncoordinated and didn't make sense.

I grabbed a tank top and put a pair of pajama pants on and walked down the hall to the kitchen in the dark. My phone still sat on the counter. I stared at it all the way to the refrigerator. I stopped, just before opening the door to grab a bottle of water.

I couldn't stop myself. Compulsion controlled my hand.

I powered on the device. It went through all of the startup screens and it felt like it was taking forever. Then nothing.

He'd only done what I'd asked, but I was hoping he hadn't. It was depressing.

My heart should be excited, in awe, but it felt as though it was slowly breaking.

No Casey. No missed calls. No messages.

No falling asleep happy.

# TWELVE

## Casey

**Thursday, July 3, 2008**

NO CALLS. NO MESSAGES. No Blake. *What a shitty night.*

Earlier when I'd come out of the shower, I found Aly watching TV and messing with her phone. I was thankful that I'd had the good sense to put on a towel. It turned out she had my other room key. She looked focused on what she was doing, so I didn't say anything.

I grabbed my clothes and went back into the bathroom to dress. I looked at myself in the mirror. I'd trim my face in the morning. My hair would behave for a while since it was damp. I brushed my teeth and I was ready to go.

I was so excited to get back and finish the night messaging with Blake, or even better—maybe talk to her. She said she *might* call. I'd hoped that she would.

"Are you ready? I'm hungry," Aly said already standing and holding her purse as I came back out.

"Yeah, let me grab my phone." I looked to the bed, then found it on the side table. I pocketed it and my wallet. It was nice to be a man. I had two things I needed and I was ready. Aly stood there with a bag full of shit. It never made any sense to me, the stuff women carried around with them.

We ate at an Italian place down from our hotel and ordered a deep-dish pizza to share. We both had beers and we talked about the next day. We solidified the plan of me going to the meeting and her catching up with us for dinner.

"I think I'll go shopping while you're working. Might as well do something useful," she joked. "Want me to wear anything special tomorrow night?" I recognized the tone of her voice. So far on the trip, she'd kept everything professional, but now after three beers in, her filter was clogging her real intentions for agreeing to come along on the trip.

"Something business-dinner appropriate. Whatever is fine," I said, trying not to play into her hand, taking a drink of my beer. I wasn't going to give her the wrong impression. I wasn't interested anymore.

The whole situation was pretty awkward. Dating your co-worker, and boss's daughter, no matter for how short of time, only led to a pain in the ass afterward.

Marc was cool, because he knew I'd been honest with her. I'd been upfront with him about everything.

We finished our dinner and walked back to the Omni. As we passed the bar, Aly looked up at me. She'd been quiet all the way back to the hotel. She asked, "Do you want to get a nightcap before we go up."

*Nightcap.* Honeybee.

"No. I better turn in," I told her. She looked disappointed but kept walking alongside me to the elevators.

"I wish you'd tell me what you want, Casey." She stared at the doors while we waited for the lift to pick us up. "I'll do anything," she said. The doors opened. We walked inside and she backed up against the far wall, opposite the doors and faced me.

I met her eyes and saw need in them. I only took a few steps inside and turned to press the buttons, giving her my back. I didn't want to face her. I liked Aly, as a friend, and I didn't gain anything from seeing her want me. Those watery green-eyes begging me to kiss her would be too much to say no to. I *am* a man. And she was a beautiful woman who only wanted to be with me.

All I'd thought about the whole evening was racing back to my room, to have a QWERTY conversation with a girl who wasn't available. Yet, right there stood a woman throwing herself at me and I wasn't interested.

Maybe I wasn't a man.

The doors opened and I left the elevator with Aly close behind. I could hear her heels click against the floor behind me. I still hadn't said anything to her. What was I supposed to say? There wasn't an argument to be had.

She said what she needed and I didn't need to reply. I walked past her door and stopped at mine to insert the key card. I slipped it in and pulled it out.

Red light.

I did it again and got the same result. The fucker wouldn't work.

I felt her arms wrap around me from behind and her hands wandered down to the crotch of my pants, her fingers wrapping as far around me as she could through the fabric. She pressed her tits into my back and said, "You can have me, Casey. I know that you don't want a relationship, but that doesn't have to be what this is. I can fuck you without the label. I don't have to be your girlfriend."

I pushed my forehead against the door and thought. What was I to do? I wanted to talk to Blake, but there was a woman all but jerking me off through my jeans right there. That second.

I tried the key again. Still, it didn't work.

She removed one hand from me and produced a key from somewhere. She held it between two fingers in front of my face, and I rolled my head across the wooden door to look at it. She pressed her chest harder against my back.

"You'll need this," she said.

"I have the same key. The lock isn't working." I really wanted to go inside.

"I changed the keys. I told them we lost yours and these are new. Let me come in."

"Open the door, please." I hadn't made a move to encourage her, well—my cock got hard, but I didn't have any control over that—I just wanted in the room. I shifted on my feet and felt my erection move in her hand. It felt good.

I hated that it felt so good.

She unlocked the door herself and let it swing open. I walked in and turned around to see her, standing in the doorway, she looked like a starved puppy. I wanted to feed her, but she wasn't my dog.

I looked at her head on. "You should go to your room."

"Just tell me what you want. I'll do whatever you like."

"I want you to leave. I'd like to go to bed." I walked toward her, growing sick of the situation.

If a woman was followed to her room, and groped, and then the man came into her room uninvited, then that would be grounds for arrest. When a woman did the same thing to a man, well, the man still got to play the part of the asshole. Double-fucking-standard.

I didn't care though. I'd been honest with her and now she was getting on my nerves. She was acting pathetically, which was the biggest turn off of all.

I opened the door behind her and stood there, waiting for her to take the hint and go. She loomed there for a second, let out a little laugh and turned to me. Her hair swinging around to her shoulder. She had a totally different look in her eyes. She looked angry.

She came forward, leaving like I'd requested. She stopped in front of me and whispered, "I'd let you call me Honeybee."

My balls hit the floor. *Honeybee*. What did she know about Blake? My mind raced, and my adrenaline spiked. Maybe I heard her wrong. My mind was playing tricks on me.

"What did you say?"

"Honeybee. That's what you call your friends, right? You can call me that, too."

"You don't know what you're talking about." I made sure not to grab her arm too hard, even though I wanted to squeeze the shit out of it. I guided her out of the room. I didn't even let my fingers wrap around it. I only let my palm push her through the doorway.

As soon as she was past the frame, I shut the door. She still had my key. I'd need to call the desk in the morning and get another one. But first, I needed to figure out how in the fuck Aly knew about Blake.

She saw her at the party, but I don't think I even mentioned her. I doubt that Micah or Cory said anything to her that night. Besides, that was weeks ago. Why would she choose then to bring it up?

And I never called Blake honeybee to anyone else. It was only in my phone.

My phone.

Aly went through my phone.

Aly switched my room keys.

Maybe she wasn't the pushover I thought she was. She certainly didn't act that way that night. I'd needed to talk to her. That kind of shit was crazy. She was nuts.

She saw what we'd written to each other.

I read through the messages from earlier that day. There wasn't anything to worry about, except for toward the end, it wasn't even *that* flirty.

I fell asleep that night with an uneasy feeling. Blake hadn't called. On one hand, I hoped Aly had something to do with it, because on the other hand was a possibility it had something to do with Grant. She could still be with him.

I hated that hand most of all.

## Thursday, July 3rd, 2008

I killed it at my meetings. Brewster's loved the beer that we'd sent them and was pretty much ready to place orders and get a regular delivery scheduled, as soon as possible. They committed to stocking Bay at their top three locations to see how it went over. Saying that if all went well, they'd be happy to make it a house brew at each of their many establishments. We finished early and had a long lunch at their flagship location downtown.

Bruce and Tom were cool guys. They would be fun clients.

It worked out well. We closed up everything that I'd wanted to accomplish in a day and a half in the sum of a few hours. There would be no dinner.

By the time I'd returned to the hotel, I'd already changed our plane tickets. We were leaving this afternoon. I just needed to let her know. It was probably passive aggressive, but I called Marc anyway.

I'd let him tell her that we were coming back early. I dialed him the minute I got back to my room, and into it with my third room key in two days.

"Hey, Case. How's Chicago?" He laughed over the line. "Did she tank another one?" He continued to chuckle. To this man a spade was a spade. I'd informed him about our Austin meeting and I was sure he'd spoken to Aly, so there wasn't any point in sugarcoating it. We both knew she probably wasn't cut out for sales.

"No. She didn't go this morning, and we actually wrapped up everything. They gave a verbal go ahead and I'll have the office send over the paperwork for their billing when I get back." The meeting went great, and the deal was well worth the trip, but at that point there was no need for another night in Chicago.

I didn't want to spend another night there like the previous one. I could use a long weekend.

"That's my boy. You're doing great out there. I'm glad we bought the building across the street and went ahead with ordering the new machinery. All these new orders already have us working at maximum capacity. I never thought I'd say that, kid. Hell, I might even get to retire," he added with a laugh.

"Yeah, you will. Hey, I changed our flights to head home today. Since the deal is already wrapped up, there really isn't a good reason to stick around here."

"Yeah, that sounds great. You gonna come in or are you taking tomorrow off?"

"I think I'm going to take it off. I've got a big week coming up. Is that okay?"

"No problem. Aly coming back, too?"

"I changed her ticket, but…" I didn't know how to say this, other than to just lay it out there, "I think you should call her and tell her."

He sounded concerned when he said, "Everything all right?" I didn't want him to worry. Everything was all right. She probably felt pretty dumb about it. I still needed to talk to her about my phone, but I'd have plenty of time on the plane. That conversation wasn't going to be the easiest, so I was thankful we'd be parting ways for a few days afterward.

"It's all good. Aly and I had a disagreement last night. I'd rather you call, if that's okay." If he called, she wouldn't be able to argue. She switched my key without feeling too bad about it, I supposed I could change our flights and she'd just have to deal with it. Fair was fair.

"Yeah, what time do you fly out?" he asked, thankfully not inquiring for more details.

"Have her meet me downstairs at five thirty, please. That will give us plenty of time."

He said that he'd tell her and asked again if everything was okay. I hated not telling him the whole story; it probably made it seem much worse than it really was. But I did care about Aly and I didn't want to embarrass her.

I had to get to the bottom of the phone thing though. I almost had myself convinced that she'd contacted her and that that was the reason Blake never called. I still hadn't heard from her. I needed to know if Aly knew why. But I wasn't confident, if she had done anything, that she'd even tell me.

After my call with Marc, I took my time, cleaned up my things and packed them away, readied myself to go home. I brought my bags down to the lobby. I'd planned on having a drink at the bar until it was time to leave. When I saw that Aly's bags were already sitting on a cart by the reception desk I knew I'd find her doing the same.

She was facing the bar, away from me, when I walked in. I caught her reflection in the mirror that hung behind the glass bottles. She lifted her glass to me when she saw me, too. The bartender, who'd seen me come in, headed in my direction as I sat next to her.

"What are you drinking, Aly?" I said as I perched on the stool to her left.

"Vodka martini. Three olives." She sounded like she'd already had a few, but it wasn't my business. It might actually work out well for me that she was a little buzzed. Maybe she'd tell me what the fuck happened.

"Vodka martini with three olives and a Gin and Tonic." He nodded and busied himself with making the drinks.

"Thanks," she said, finishing down the last of her current cocktail.

"What happened yesterday?" I went out on a limb with what my gut had been telling me. "What did you say to her?" She audibly exhaled and stretched on her stool.

"So she can't leave you alone either, then? I guess you two talked?" she asked guiltily, looking at me from out of the corner of her eyes. I watched her in the mirror looking straight ahead.

I didn't answer, only thanked the bartender when he placed our drinks in front of us on napkins.

"I didn't think she'd call you back. And I kind of thought that if she did we'd be...you know," she admitted, catching my gaze in the reflection. I shook my head at her, and gave her a friendly smile. If I wanted to get the *real* truth out of her, she needed to feel like she could talk. I wasn't about to show her my real feelings. I wasn't about to throw my glass at the wall and scream, because that is what I wanted to do with all my might.

"She said you were just friends and that you could pick who your friends were."

*Atta girl.* She didn't take any shit.

"What else?" I quirked a serious eyebrow at her refection.

"Nothing else. I told her to leave you alone." My mind screamed, *She's already leaving me alone!* I was angry, I wanted to argue with her, but again, there wasn't anything to argue *for*.

Then, my fury was doused with relief, I had no claim to Blake, but hopefully, Aly was the reason she didn't call. Maybe she wasn't with Grant doing things that my mind envisioned for those long hours that I couldn't sleep the night before.

My fingers itched to grab my phone and send her something, but I had to wait. It wasn't the right time.

At that moment, I needed to have a come-to-Jesus meeting with the girl hammering back Vodka martinis.

"Aly, don't do that again," I told her. "We're friends. We're co-workers. Hell, we're kind of partners. You're smart. You're beautiful." I turned in my seat, choosing to look at her for real, instead of in the mirror. I wanted to make sure she got the final point. "We're *not* going to be together like we were ever again. Find a nice guy and be happy, if that's what you want. But don't *ever* call her again." Her eyes looked red and she bit her lip. I prayed she'd got the message. I continued, "We don't need to talk about this anymore. Do you want another drink? We have about an hour before the cab comes." And that's where I left it. That was all I needed to say about it.

"I'm sorry, Casey," she said, and I let her pay for the next round.

The air felt a lot clearer in the car on the way to the airport. Aly seemed to understand what I'd been trying to tell her. At least I'd hoped she did. We talked about the sale and she was genuinely happy about the deal. She was a little more than buzzed, so she whooped and hollered, even asking the driver for a high-five.

She was feeling no pain for our flight back. I had to make sure they'd let her on the plane first. We'd be making a coffee stop before we went through security. Our cab pulled up to the curb behind a black town car. There was a guy leaning against it wearing a nice suit.

I hopped out of the cab and rounded the back as it popped open to get our luggage out. As I was closing the trunk, I saw a flash of the most perfect color of brown and I looked up.

It was her. It was Blake. I forced the lid down until it latched and moved our bags to the sidewalk. The whole time looking at her as she bounded up to this man. She threw her arms around him and he rocked her side-to-side, embracing her back.

Surely my mind was playing tricks. What would she be doing in Chicago? Who in the fuck was that guy? Was it *him*? Wasn't she with him last night? I opened the door of my car, glancing back and forth between my drunk-ish travel companion and what was happening no more than twenty feet away.

I took Aly's hand to get her out of the taxi, then I leaned into the window to pay the driver and Aly slipped on the curb falling into my side.

"Sorry, Casey." She laughed with her hand over her mouth.

I righted her and pulled her to the sidewalk next to our bags. I was still holding her hand when I glanced over to see if my brain really had short-circuited or if it really was Blake, as people passed by on the walkway.

When my gaze fell back on them, they were closer. She stared at Aly and me. I saw realization coat her face and then what looked like disappointment.

I was there with Aly. I knew what she was thinking.

"Hi," I said.

Aly pulled on my arm. "Come on, I need coffee," She tugged at me not realizing what else was going on around her. She grabbed her bag with her free hand and pulled me again toward the door.

"Hey," I said to Blake again, trying to get her to speak. She only looked at me, then to Aly and back. Stone faced.

"Aly, hold on!" I barked.

My shout caused Blake to jump. The man next to her wrapped a possessive arm around her shoulders and she walked backward toward their car.

"Wait," I said. "Just a second."

The man said into her ear, "Who is that?" I heard him, they were only a few feet away. So close that I also heard when she said, "Nobody."

The guy opened the passenger door and she got in. He rounded the car to the driver's side and I took off, my feet propelling me toward her before she was gone. I crouched, looking into the windows to see her, but I couldn't get sight of her through the tint. The guy pointed a sharp finger at me from over the roof of the car as he was paused getting in. He gave me a look that could kill.

As my hand went to slap the glass, to see if she'd roll it down, he said, "I wouldn't do that." I took his warning. Something about him told me that he was ten seconds from kicking my ass. And that guy was big enough to do it. Then he said before getting in, "Stay away from my sister."

His *sister*. The dude was one of her brothers.

I bent down so that she could see me. I only had seconds until they'd pull away.

"Please. Stop. Get out and talk to me. Please."

That didn't work. The window didn't budge.

Fuck it. She wasn't with *him,* I'd text her.

**Me: I'm still waiting.**

**Honeybee: Is she really your girlfriend?**

Her reply came faster than I'd expected.

**Me: No.**

**Honeybee: Then who is she?**

**Me: Someone who wants what she can't have.**

**Honeybee: Don't we all?**

**Honeybee: Leave me alone.**

Like hell I would. I mean, what were the odds of running into her like that? If I believed in signs, I would have admitted to just witnessing one.

# THIRTEEN

## Blake

**Thursday, July 3, 2008**

IF THAT WASN'T A sign from the universe, then I was losing my mind.

After my freak out the night before, and saying yes to Grant, I needed to get away for a minute. The beauty of my new job was that, with my laptop and a kitchen, I could do it anywhere. So I decided to go to Chicago early, to spend a few days with Reggie, before my first trade show on Saturday.

My bosses had given me a few menus to review and I was already starting to work up some ideas for the clients. Not only did I feel like I could do the job well, after only a few days, I also loved it. The freedom. Bridgett and Lance were incredibly laid back. It was a great environment for creativity.

So, I flew to Chicago.

"Does Nobody have a name?" my brother asked as we drove through the busy rush-hour traffic. I knew he was going to ask.

"I don't know," I said. All I could think was that she *had* told the truth. That was the girl he'd been with at the party. They were in Chicago together.

"You don't know or you don't want to talk about it?" Reggie and I were close in age. He was only about eighteen months older than me in reality. In life, though, he was years older. He graduated early from high school, went straight into college, finished in three years, and then got his MBA. He was the brains of our little family and he'd done really well for himself.

He'd looked so different when I first saw him through the airport doors. He was bigger than the last time I'd seen him, he looked like a full-on man. He certainly wasn't my nerdy older brother who I'd seen months ago over the holidays.

"I don't want to talk about it. You look good. You're bigger. Like buff," I said, changing the subject and trying to get out of my head for the first time in the past twenty-four hours.

"My building has a gym. So you're going to marry the robot, huh?" he teased, looking behind himself as he changed lanes with ease.

"He's not a robot."

"He acts like a robot. Tell me who that other guy was." So much for changing the subject.

So I stuck to my story and answered, "He's a friend."

"Okay then we'll do this my way. Since you don't want to talk now, we're going back to my place. You're going to cook for me. And then you're going to tell me what the fuck is going on. You look like shit. You got engaged and then came to visit—for the first time in over a year—the day after, the some *Nobody* sees you at the airport and you don't want to talk about it. There's no way I'm letting this go. So figure out how you want the story to sound, because you're telling me everything."

"Did you go to the store already?" I knew what he wanted. My lasagna.

"Yeah, I ordered groceries from work after you called. My doorman let them up a little while ago."

His new building was nice, I-wasn't-dressed-well-enough-nice. He parked us in the garage attached to the side of the high-rise that housed his place.

He got my luggage out and we took an elevator straight up to his floor. There were only five doors down his hall, and his was the one on the very end. Inside, it was clean and minimalistic. He had a view of the Chicago skyline on one side and a view of the lake on the other. I walked straight to the window to look out.

"It's a pretty spectacular view, huh?" I heard him walk up behind me. "I put your bags in the spare room. Want a drink?"

"Wine. I'll take wine," I said and laughed.

"Good, you'll spill your guts faster."

I cooked and he told me about his new job and the building. He had been made junior partner already at Price-McClellan, the firm he worked for as a venture capital consultant. I didn't really understand what he did, only that he was good at it and that he loved it, which made me happy. He was living life exactly the way he wanted.

I didn't hold back anything after glass three.

"What the hell am I doing?" I asked as I sat down with Reggie at his bar to eat.

"I don't know. I need to think about this," he said with his mouth already full.

There was a knock at his door, which I thought was weird because he had a door guy and no one buzzed. He wiped his mouth and got up to answer it.

"Just a second," he said, as he made his way across the open living room and up the three stairs to the foyer. He looked out the peephole and then wiped his hands on his pants one more time before opening the door part of the way.

He talked in a very hushed tone, but I saw a woman's head pop around him. She smiled and waved.

"Hello," I said. She looked really nice. Very pretty. I didn't know what they were walking about, but she bound past him and walked directly toward me.

"Hi, I'm Nora. I live down the hall from your brother. You're Blake, right?" She held out her hand for me to shake. I swiped the breadcrumbs off my hands and took it; her grip was quick and firm.

"It's nice to meet you. Have you eaten? I made plenty." Reggie ran his hand over his jaw, looking perplexed.

She looked to him and smiled really big. She had a cool smile. It was very different. Her teeth were white, but imperfect. Her eyetooth, just barely, overlapped her front tooth. It was a small thing, but I liked it. She was dressed in a fitted tan dress and had on the most audacious heels I'd ever seen. They had to be five-inches high.

"It smells so good. I don't mind if I do. Reagan told me before that you're a chef," she said, then looked like she wasn't so sure. She turned to my brother and asked, "Right?"

All I could think was *Reagan?*

Then he nodded and took his seat next to me again, totally at ease with her in his space. Her focus shifted back to me, "So, I'd be a fool to pass up this cooking." She made herself at home already grabbing a plate from the cabinet and snagging a wine glass from the rack.

They looked at each other for a long minute and then her eyes grew wide. They were having a silent conversation. She sipped her wine, which he'd poured for her. My mind reeled at the sight of them.

"So," she said, "What are we talking about?"

Reggie answered her, "Well, this is right up your alley." He looked at me for approval and then asked, "Do you mind if I tell her?"

I said, "No," because it was fine. I didn't know her and she didn't know anyone involved. Who could it hurt?

"My little sister here is in a situation. She's been dating the same robot—sorry, Blake, excuse me—guy for over a year. He's a decent guy. He's good to her and they love each other. A few months ago she ran into a man—we're still calling him Nobody—when she was out of town and they had a one-night stand," he paused.

Nora looked to me for confirmation that he'd told the story correctly.

"It's true. I'm a terrible person."

Reggie took a drink, then we all took drinks, and then he continued, "So, according to her description, it was pretty fucking good, without her going into too much detail. I'm her brother and I don't want or need the particulars."

Nora's eyes lit up and she smiled that big, not-quite-perfect smile of hers at me.

"Good, huh? Better than the robot?" she asked Reggie. Not me.

Reggie said, "I think so." They both looked my way and I conceded, bowing my head in agreement and defeat.

"Keep going," Nora implored my brother smacking his arm from across the bar.

"You're loving this, aren't you?" he asked her.

"Oh, you bet I am. Now talk."

"Okay," he continued. "They've been sending each other messages—"

I interrupted, "Clean messages."

His disbelieving eyebrow rose at me.

"—So they text back and forth every day. She feels bad, but she still doesn't stop doing it. Then yesterday, a woman who claims to be Casey's girlfriend—which Blake didn't know about—sends her messages telling her to, pretty much, fuck off."

It sounded so childish hearing it through my brother's recollection. It made me feel stupid and I bit my thumbnail down to the quick. It bled. As usual.

I quietly added, looking at Reggie, "She called *me* Nobody."

Realization dawned on him. "So that's where *Nobody* got his name. Gotcha," he said knowingly and made a sympathetic face. "You're not Nobody," then he kissed me on my forehead. "What a bitch," he added.

"So then..." Nora interjected, trying to keep the story going.

I decided to finish it myself. "Grant, the robot, proposed yesterday and I said yes. Then I panicked. Then I flew here. Then this afternoon, we saw Casey and the *bitch* at the airport. She was woman I recognized from when we were at a party the weekend we met. He tried to talk to me, but we got in the car and left." I buried my head in my arms on the counter. "That's it," I said.

It was quiet for a few seconds. I could only imagine the silently mouthed words and lip readings going on above my down-turned head between the two of them.

Finally, Nora said, "Wow. Reagan, do you have more red? We need another bottle."

*Reagan.*

He stood and rounded the bar to her side and pulled another bottle from his wine cooler.

He laughed. "Do you want to open it, Nora?"

"Very funny," she said sarcastically. These two must have spent a lot of time together. I wondered if they were... No. He would have just came out with it when he introduced her. Reggie didn't suffer fools, and I'd never heard him lie.

Nora stole my brother's chair and put a comforting arm around me and rubbed my back. She was kind. I hoped they were messing around. She'd be good for him.

She began, "Okay, I'm know that I'm going to be the minority, but this is what I think. How do I put this...?" I tried to read her face as she thought of how to say whatever it was delicately.

Stealing my attention away from the nice Nora, Reggie—or Reagan—added, "Nora is polyamorous. She doesn't believe in monogamy." But he said it to her, leaning over the bar in her direction, then filled her glass of red all the way to the top. "Isn't that right?"

"I love how you pour my glass, thank you," she said to him with her full smile on view. Then she faced me again, squared my shoulders with hers, and placed her hands on my legs.

"Blake, I understand what you are feeling. Do you love the robot?" Then her straight face cracked, and she giggled a little, then corrected herself with a cough. "What was his name?"

"Grant," Reggie and I said in unison, neither with much enthusiasm. It spoke volumes about what we thought of him.

"Right. Do you love Grant?"

"Yes. I really do." She pulled my chewed up hand away from my mouth and placed it under the palm she returned to my leg.

"And are you curious about your feelings for *Nobody*?" She smiled again, but didn't try to hide it this time.

"Yes," I admitted. She did understand. "Now what does that mean? Tell me what to do." I pleaded with them. "When he sent me a message earlier, he said they weren't together. What should it matter? I'm engaged. I'm so fucked up."

"People can be in love with more than one person at the same time, Blake," Nora said in a soothing, almost motherly tone.

Reggie chimed in, "Some people can."

"Yes, some people," she corrected. "But you have to be very honest. About everything."

"Tell Grant? No way. It would kill him."

"Then tell *Nobody* how you feel. You need to own up to it, for yourself...with someone."

I thought about what she'd said. "So do you think I'm polyamorous?" I asked, praying that they'd say yeah and that it was not my fault. That it was just my nature.

Reggie said no immediately. Nora said no, too, but only after a few seconds.

"Why? I'm thinking about two men?" I looked between them. They were sharing some sort of glance.

Nora asked, "Can you picture either one of them with another person and be happy for them?"

It would have been difficult picturing Grant with another woman, but if he was happy, then I guess I could be happy for him. Then I thought of Casey and seeing him with that girl. It made me feel violent and nauseous. I didn't want to go into all of that with them though. That would make me look even worse than I already did.

"No," I confessed.

Nora said, "Then you aren't polyamorous. It makes me happy to see my lovers with other people who make them feel good, both emotionally and physically. So, I side with your body, not your brain."

I was back at square one. "Reggie, what do you think?"

"*Reggie?*" Nora choked. He gave her a look and she said no more.

"Honestly, I don't think that Grant would ever run after you like I saw—" He stopped. I had to tell him his name.

"Casey."

"Casey run after you. Did he know who I was?"

"No." I hadn't thought about that.

"And if that was his girlfriend and you didn't mean anything to him, he'd be getting the hell out of there when you spotted him. I saw the look he gave me. He saw how buff, as you said, I am, but it didn't deter him in the slightest. In fact, when I mentioned the word, sister, he seemed relieved. I think you should give him the benefit of the doubt. *He's* not a robot."

I really wanted to call him. I wanted to hear, from him, what happened. I finished my glass of wine, poured myself another, and went to the guest room where I'd be staying.

It was getting late, but it would still be pretty early in San Francisco. If that was where he was even going. I considered texting, but I wanted to hear his voice. I wanted to *hear* his voice when he told me what was going on.

I dialed his number.

He picked up on the second ring.

"Finally," he said, then sighed on the other end of the line. Texting was fun, but actually calling on the phone felt so much more intimate. Faintly hearing him breathe healed something that was wounded in me.

"Hi."

"I was hoping you'd call." I heard his relief over the line.

"We need to talk and I thought this was better than sending messages back and forth." The day before I'd been excited to actually hear him and I'd planned to call him for that reason. That was before *her*. That was before I said yes to Grant. But, my want for Casey hadn't changed.

"Are you staying with your brother?" he asked.

"Yeah, how was your flight back? Are you in San Francisco?"

He had to sit next her on the flight to California and it must have been awkward. Clearly, she wasn't a very big fan of mine.

"I didn't go back."

*He didn't go back?* He didn't go back.

"Where are you?" My heart raced.

"All depends. Do you want to see me?" he asked.

Of course I wanted to see him. I wanted to talk to him. I needed to tell him how I felt. I needed to get things off my chest even if I was clearing the air with the wrong man. Nora and Reggie were right. I had to know.

"Yes," I told him, "I really do."

"I came back to the Omni, but it's pretty late," he said.

"I don't care."

He laughed and it sounded exponentially better than my imaginary Casey-laughs, causing the thick sludge that coated my gut over the past day to clear away.

"Send me your brother's address and I'll come get you."

Did I really want to do that? I needed advice.

"Okay. I'll text you." Then I hung up, not waiting to see what he'd say.

When I walked into the living room I heard Reggie speaking. Nora was by the door and he was standing close to her. It appeared like either they'd just been kissing or I interrupted them right before.

"I called him," I announced. "He didn't leave Chicago. He wants to meet with me. To talk. What should I do?"

They looked at me and Reggie took a step away from her. She

straightened her dress, flattening the front with her long, slender fingers.

My brother walked to the back of a chair not far from where they stood.

"Do you want to talk to him?" he asked, but his face didn't indicate his preference. Perhaps he didn't have one. Maybe his preference was the same as mine.

"I really do," I said. I stuck a fingernail in my mouth again, but I didn't have anything left to bite. My fingers were puffy and sore from worrying on them. "I think I'm going to see him. What's your address?"

"750 Lake Shore Drive. Is he driving or sending someone for you?" Reggie asked.

"He's riding over in a cab to get me. We're going back to his hotel. The Omni." My voice sounded sure and confident. I wanted to go and so I was. There wasn't anything complex about it.

"After you send him the message you'll have about twenty minutes. I'll meet you at the elevator in a few. I'm going to walk Nora to her place down the hall."

She was already standing in the open doorway and we smiled as we waved goodbye.

I needed to clean up. Brush my teeth. I did a quick wash in the spare room's bathroom and decided it would just have to do.

When I came out of my brother's apartment, I saw him standing at the end of the hall leaning against the wall waiting for me.

He looked flushed and tense. There was definitely something going on with them. I didn't want to be nosy, but I liked the idea of them as a couple.

As we rode down together I told him, "I like Nora."

He did this huff thing, something that my dad often did. It was funny seeing him do it and made him seem so much older, more grown up.

"I like Nora, too," he said as we walked through the marble lobby.

We stopped in entrance way and watched a cab pull up.

"He's a good guy, right?" he asked. *Brothers.*

"I think so," I said.

My skin was tingling with anticipation. We had only agreed to talk. We were only going to talk.

"I'm not this kind of girl, Reggie. I don't do stuff like this," I said softly.

"I know." He looked at me. "That's what makes me kind of like him, too." Then he nodded at the street. My eyes followed his to the man who made my skin prickle with anticipation.

I'd felt it earlier, but with everything going on, all I could see was *them* together. He stepped away from the taxi, wearing a loose green T-shirt and cargo shorts. He looked like a wild mess, but it was all him.

His hair was crazy and he had a few days' worth of stubble. Yet, at the same time, he looked as new and fresh as could be. When he saw me standing inside the door, he gave the most gorgeous full-faced smile. In my mind, Christmas trees lit, kittens played with yarn, and I was polyamorous. Everything was right.

He held my gaze for a few seconds and when he noticed Reggie he made the strangest face at him. Casey's grinning lips went off to the side in a boyish, this-is-a-little-awkward sort of way.

Reggie chuckled and we stood there while Casey made his way inside.

Reggie teased, "You're blushing. You don't blush for the robot."

"No. I'm not," I said, but I could feel that he wasn't just blowing me shit. My face felt like it was on fire.

Casey walked up to my brother, like he'd known him forever, and shook his hand. "It's nice to meet you," he greeted. Then, as smoothly as he leaned in and kissed me on the cheek, he whispered, "You look pretty," in my ear.

*Men don't say things like that to nobodies.*

Reggie said, "I'll see you later. Be careful." He looked at Casey and said, "You be careful, too," and walked away.

His eyes were shining brighter than bluish-green gems under a jewelry case. It could have been the lighting in the grand entrance of my brother's building, but I told myself it was something else. He tried to subdue his huge smile, but he couldn't hide the expression in his eyes.

"We have a lot to talk about," he said. "Come on."

Casey held my hand in both of his and walked backward out the hotel doors and to the waiting cab like he couldn't take his eyes off me.

In the cab he'd look at my lips, then steal himself away grinning, just to do it all over again.

Lips. Grin. Repeat.

He was blissful and easy going, none of the stress in his face like earlier at the airport. His contented energy was contagious and put me at ease.

I had a suspicious feeling I'd be falling asleep happy that night.

# FOURTEEN

## Casey

**Thursday, July 3, 2008**

SOMETHING TOLD ME IT would be a good night. I'd had a feeling she'd call.

I couldn't get on the plane earlier. I'd made sure Aly had coffee and was all right. She actually gave me the hotel keys, and since we hadn't officially checked out, I still had two rooms.

After the day I'd had, the fantastic sale, dealing with Aly, and then the airport, I played it cool, but I was wired like someone cranked up the voltage in my spine. Blake and I didn't say much, but it was incredible having her next to me.

She was fidgety on the way to the room and wasn't quite *my* Blake yet. She hadn't let her guard all the way down.

I shut the door gently as we entered the suite. She paused in front of me just inside. We were only inches apart and her essence arrested me.

"Why do I want you so goddamned bad?" I asked.

She faced me. "I want you, too," she replied vehemently. "I can't stop thinking about you," she stepped closer, "like this."

"I crave you." My words tumbled out like apples off a poorly stocked produce shelf. Knowing she was affected, and wanted this like

I did, made me bold. Made me feel gratified.

So I did what I wanted. I picked her up and pressed her against the wall. Her legs wrapped around me and held on. She pulled my hair back and ran her fingers through it and along the top of my scalp.

"We were just talking on the phone and texting," she panted. Who was she trying to convince? I didn't believe her for a second, but I went along.

I dragged my nose up her neck, but our mouths still hadn't touched. She was intoxicating. "I know. We're friends."

"We're friends."

It had been too damn long since I'd seen her. I'd made too many deals with the Devil for this exact moment to pretend it didn't mean everything that it did to me. "You know what?" I asked daringly. "Honestly, I don't really care what you call it. I want you. Text. Call. In the flesh. I can't tell you what you *think* you want to hear. So I won't, but I'll tell you everything else. Everything I *know* you want to hear. How badly I want you. Now. Up against this wall," my hips flexed into hers, "and we'll sort our *friendship* out in the bathroom in twenty minutes. Because right now, I want inside of you. It's been a long day."

I didn't need her to tell me she wanted it, too. It was written in pink on her nose.

"Put me down," she panted. I let her slide down the wall, but I held her tight around the hips. "Now take my clothes off," she instructed.

"With pleasure." She didn't have to ask me twice. I pulled her shirt over her head and had her bra off in seconds. She lifted my shirt off while I undid her button fly. I had to stop to wrestle my arms through my shirt as she pulled it away from me.

We were hands and legs and arms and stomachs and knees, and all of them were frantically knocking into each other.

When there were no more pants, no more shirts, and no more barriers between us she said, "Okay, now do whatever you want."

That was a tall fucking order.

First, I really wanted to kiss her. I cupped her cheeks and brought our mouths together.

She tasted like toothpaste and Blake. Her tongue found mine, and a moan escaped from her mouth into me. "So help me, God, that sound drives me crazy," I said with what little breath I had. Then she did it again and I smiled through our kiss.

I hoisted her up like we were before. I held her in my arms. Her legs circled my middle. I pushed her flat against the wall, with only my hands acting as a barrier to ensure the wall didn't hurt her beautiful skin. Her hands touched me feverishly. They were in my hair and on my back. They roamed my chest and held my face as we reconnected.

When my hand found her already wet she moaned again and that was all she wrote.

I lifted her up a little higher, and then set her down on top of my greedy cock. I moved into her against the wall like I was trying to push us through it. It wasn't gentle. It wasn't slow. Not this time. I couldn't wait any longer to hear her say my name, to feel her tighten around me.

She moved with me and it only stood to encourage my pace. Every inhale and exhale matched time with my thrusts, until I felt her beginning to grind down harder on my upstrokes.

"Ahhh," she panted into my neck. "Yes."

"It feels good. Doesn't it?" She didn't have to answer by saying anything, her body agreed for her. Her hold on me tightened and she arched her back. Her pretty brown hair fell off her shoulders as she let her pleasure overcome her.

She shouted, "Casey. Oh. Casey."

As soon as I felt her milking me for every drop I had, I couldn't hold back any longer. Simply said, there wasn't anything in the world that felt like Blake coming on my dick. It's the type of feeling that men start wars and write songs about.

"Blake, fuck. Fuck!" I moaned and my climax shot through me in powerful hot bursts.

She kissed my neck as I stood there holding her for minutes, still buried as deep inside of her as I could possibly be.

She laughed. It was a most-satisfying sond.

"Shit." I breathed, with my head resting on the wall to her side.

She giggled again. "I know." Then she bit me.

I forgot that Betty was playful after sex.

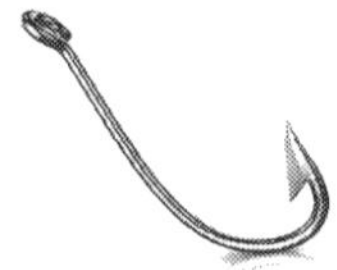

We washed up in the bathroom, and I tossed her a long sleeveless T-shirt to wear. It was perfect. The armholes hung down to her waist and anytime she'd move to one side or the other, it would swing wide and I could see one, or both, of her sexy breasts peek out.

I think when my mom asks me what I want for Christmas this year I'm going to ask for a Blake calendar. And a picture of her in that moment would be my July. I hoped I would get a chance at a good photo op for August and all the months thereafter, too.

Before the thought escaped me I asked, "Can I take a picture of you?"

She was twisting her hair back off her neck, the underneath still damp from sweat. "I don't think that is a good idea."

I smacked her ass on the way out of the bathroom. "Well I think it is a very good idea. Probably one of my best." I strolled my way to my phone that was still in the pocket of my shorts on the floor.

"Tell me how she got my number first," she said following me, barelegged, no panties, back into the bedroom area of the suite. "I need to know."

Oh, yeah. That. She made a good point for concern. Aly picked my phone up and had her way with it. I knew she went through my phone when I was in the shower. I had a weird feeling about it when I found it on the table, remembering that I'd tossed it on the bed. I didn't know exactly what had happened, but I could tell her what I knew for sure.

"I'd like to start with that girl. *That girl* is Aly. We dated for a while, if you remember when we met, I was breaking up with her? I've known her a long time. She works for Bay Brewing, too. Her father is the owner. Well, I'm sort of going to own part of it too, and so will she."

Blake sat down on the edge of the bed, listening and paying close attention.

"She was on the trip with me because her dad wanted her to get more experience in front of customers. That was why she was with me.

She checked us in and had my spare key. When I was in the shower she came in, found my phone and read our messages. That's how she got your number."

Her face looked contemplative.

"Well, it isn't my business really. I didn't like her contacting me. She wasn't very nice." I didn't want to ask her what was said. I wanted our night to stay upbeat and fun. I had a feeling that we'd only have a precious few hours.

"Don't worry about her. I talked to her about it. It won't happen again." I'd make sure of that.

"You know I can't be mad if you have a girlfriend. It wouldn't be fair," she said and her face brightened. "Hey, you might be polyamorous," she said very matter of factly, as she scooted her way to the head board of the king-sized bed. She patted the spot in front of her, her brown eyes looking luminous.

"I'm not polyamorous." A laugh sprang from my gut just saying the word. It was so out of the blue. I was anything, *but* polyamorous. "Why would you say that?" I laughed and stretched across the bed in front of her. She leaned forward on her elbows to talk to me. I could see down the front of the shirt.

My old tank was now my favorite article of clothing on the planet.

She bit her nail, one of her tells, "I don't know. I thought that might help." She thoughtfully ran the hand—the one she wasn't using as an appetizer—over my forehead and over my hair. She was always touching the mess on my head. If she only knew what it did to me.

Her body language said she was slipping back into a place where she wasn't comfortable with her thoughts. I didn't like it, so changed conversation lanes.

"Did you know that nail-biting is called onychophagia?" I asked, turning the conversation back to a neutral topic. I'd learned that my retention of useless knowledge really did serve a purpose. It relaxed this girl.

"I didn't know that, thank you. You're changing the subject. I wanted to know about your phone in exchange for some pictures. I think that needs wrapping up." Her blush spread over her cheeks and she looked down at her hands. She probably wanted to bite her nails, although there wasn't much left.

"Well, I told you everything I know about how she got your number. What else can I say?"

"Well, if you take dirty pictures of me, and anyone can just pick up your phone, then others will see them. Possibly send them to other people. It could be quite embarrassing." I laid back, crossways on the bed and she moved her legs so that they lay over my chest. I ran my hands up and down her skin. It was smooth, but not bare, more like a cat's tongue. It was more perfect than if they'd been perfectly shaved.

"You bring up another very good point. We wouldn't want that to happen. I suppose I'd have to install the locking feature on my phone." There. Problem solved. If only they would have all been that simple.

"Yes, I think you should." She looked at me with a face that read "anytime now."

I looked up and saw it sitting on the table next to her. "Hand it to me then."

She passed me the phone and I slid the slider over to activate it. I poked around until I found the right settings option. It was ready. All I needed was a four-digit pass code. I looked at the numbers and knew what it should be.

2-2-4-8.

B-A-I-T.

"Did you set it?" She leaned over on her elbow.

"Yep." I handed it to her. "It's locked. Like Fort Knox. No one's getting in that baby."

She took it, tapped it a few times and laughed, tossing it back onto my chest.

"That was easy." The woman got it on the first try. "Good guess."

"Good password." She made a production of fanning her hair out and she lay back on the pillows. "I'm ready for my close up, Mr. Moore."

I got close up indeed.

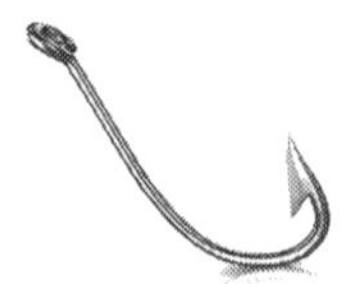

The next day was the fourth of July and I wanted to spend it with her. "What are your plans for tomorrow?" I asked as I prepared myself to leave the bed she was in and go to the other room.

"I don't know. I don't really have any. There are a few work things I could do, and I have to work a show on Saturday with my boss." She curled tighter into my side and nuzzled her face against my chest. "This feels good," she said softly. I could hear the sleep in her voice. She had every reason to be tired. I wasn't keeping count, but I'm pretty sure she had a handful of orgasms.

"I think you should spend the holiday with me," I said, as I ran my hand through her hair, root to tip over and over.

"That's right, it's the fourth." She looked up at me, her brown eyes looked almost golden up that close. "I don't know. Holidays are important."

"I'm very patriotic," I playfully assured her.

She deliberated. Her mouth twisted to the side, and her eyes looked out into space somewhere off to the left. "Well, okay then. Since you're very patriotic and I am too, then we should spend the day together. It just makes the best sense." Then she laid her head back down on my chest. One of her fingers traced a wide circle across the bridge of my sternum. Over my peck, around and back. It was probably a bull's-eye.

As soon as was sure that she'd fallen into a deep sleep, I snuck off to the other room.

I wanted to stay and sleep with her. I really did, but it made every morning I didn't wake up with her in my arms extra shitty. I hoped she'd understand.

A cruel reminder that she wasn't mine on a daily basis, well not in reality, was really getting to me. I was focused, though. There was something undeniable slowly pulling us together. I had to believe she felt it too and that it would all work out.

Nothing felt more right than when I was with her.

# FIFTEEN

## Blake

**Friday, July 4th, 2008**

NOTHING FELT QUITE AS perfect as falling asleep in Casey's arms. I slept like I hadn't in weeks. But waking up to find the spot next to me empty sucked.

I found my phone and sent a quick message to Reggie.

**Me: I'm fine. I'll see you later.**

I didn't need him worrying. I was shocked at how okay he was with my behavior in the first place. Any rational person would chastise me for my actions.

It was true, Reggie never had anything too positive to say about Grant. He wasn't ever mean or rude or blatantly said he didn't like him or that I should leave him, but it was pretty clear he wasn't impressed, in the least, by my boyfriend.

*Fiancé.*

Getting up to see what kind of shape I was in, I saw that there was a note written on the hotels stationary sitting on the bathroom counter.

Good morning,
honeybee.
I'm in room 811.
Come over when
you're up.
-Casey

I climbed back into the jeans and T-shirt I'd worn over the night before and washed my face in the sink. He'd left his toothbrush there, and so I took the liberty of borrowing it. My hair was a fine disaster and between my legs was gloriously tender. I felt incredible.

When I got to the room, which was right next door, I heard Casey talking on the phone as he approached the door to answer my knock.

"...Audrey, calm down. You can always drop the class if you don't like it." He opened the door and gave me a chaste kiss, and then held up a finger to tell me he would be another minute.

"Well, Dad can get over it. Take the classes you want. It's your life." Then he listened for a few minutes and walked over to the window to finish his call. All he was wearing was cargo shorts and they were hanging so low I would bet money he didn't have underwear on beneath of them.

There were two trays on the table and I could smell the coffee from where I stood. My stomach growled. I looked under both covers and they were the same. A stack of pancakes with whipped topping, strawberries and blueberries made to look like a flag.

He watched as I discovered the breakfast and put his hand over the receiver and said in a hushed voice, "See? Patriotic," as he pointed to himself. He then pretended to be serious as he whispered to me, "Blake, I eat those every morning."

I put my hand over my mouth and giggled.

"I love you, too, Audrey. Don't stress out. Go have some fun. Tell Morgan to call me... Okay. 'Bye." He ended the call and took a seat across from me at the table.

"I like these pancakes."

He said, "I thought you would. I like when it when you smile like that."

"Then keep making me."

And then he did.

We left our phones off and walked for hours. We ate hot dogs and stopped to watch street performers in front of The Bean in Millennium Park. We talked about our families and jobs. He bought us ridiculous Uncle Sam hats and we wore them the rest of the day.

We ate at a bar on The Pier and watched fireworks over Lake Michigan. We drank and laughed and kissed.

He was freedom and throwing caution to the wind. He was no work and all play.

We held hands on the sidewalk and in the cab as we rode back to my brother's building. When the car pulled up outside, he got out with me, walking me to the glass doors of the entrance.

"Today was a very good day," he told me. I agreed that it was.

"So now what?" After the day we'd had, I was even more confused and heavy-hearted parting with him. His face was tinted red from the sun and his eyes looked more like deep blue than I'd even seen.

His face changed from the easy-going, carefree Casey with the permanent grin, to a more mature-looking sober one.

"That's all up to you, honeybee. I'm free." He wrapped his arms loosely around me, low on my back and we swayed back and forth on the sidewalk holding a stare that was loaded. Loaded with 'should we's and 'shouldn't we's. Loaded with pleasure and reality.

We lived far apart.

He traveled more than not.

I was engaged to someone else and no matter which way I looked at it, I couldn't keep him for myself. It was too selfish.

"I think you like being free. It suits you," I told him.

"What suits you? What do you want?" Something in the timbre of his voice sounded like a truth. He really wanted to know where my head was. The trouble with that was I didn't have a clue.

"I don't know. I like talking to you and being with you, but—" Then he kissed me. His mouth cloaked mine with an unspoken urgency.

"Mmmm...No buts," he said against my lips. "Just leave it like that. You like talking to me and being with me. That's all I need right now. Let's leave it right there. Okay? No pressure."

Why was it when people said, "No pressure," it added an ocean's worth to the situation?

"Okay," I said.

"Okay," he said back. "It's settled. We're still friends." He placed his lips on my forehead and made a low humming sound, I closed my eyes and savored it.

Then he let me go.

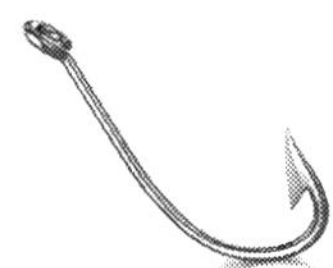

The next weeks were busy. I worked alongside Bridgett and followed her wherever she went. Since she ran the Seattle office, I was naturally paired up with her most of the time. I made friends with another new hire, Melanie, who worked out of the San Francisco branch. She and I were basically hired to do the same job.

Grant had contracted workers to do most of the major renovations, but he was adamant on doing what he could on his own at the house.

We set a date for the wedding, May 23rd of the next year. My mother proceeded to buy anything and everything that said the words "groom," "bride," or "wedding." I was thankful, though, since I was busy working, she told me she would handle everything. Wedding plans barely registered on my radar. Of course, it wasn't like it was swept under the rug. It was in every conversation I had with my family or Grant.

The wedding. The house.

The house. The wedding.

I almost felt like two different people.

The wedding and the house Blake, the work and the Casey Blake. It was only sometimes when the two met that my brain dissolved onto itself. Like talking to Reggie or Micah.

"I can't believe you're getting married," she said when I told her.

"I know, sometimes I don't even believe it myself." That was true. Work and Casey Blake didn't really act very affected by the upcoming nuptials either. I don't think that half of my brain really accepted it was happening.

"Cory and I are pregnant," she said, in the middle of our wedding conversation. She blurted it out like she'd being trying to hold it in for some time.

"Oh my God! When are you due?" I was shocked. I knew they were serious and that they'd moved in with each other, but I wasn't expecting a cart before a horse with them.

"I'm due at the end of April. With your wedding in May, I might still be fat, but you know I'll be up there with you. If that's what you want." The last sentence sounded weird off her tongue.

We never spoke about Casey and me. I hadn't told her a thing. I assumed that Casey and his brother spoke, though. She always seemed to hint or mention him. Even though I think her question was made to sound like, if she wasn't too fat she'd be there for my wedding. But it sounded a lot more like she didn't expect there to actually be one.

It didn't feel right hiding what was going on with Casey from Micah, but I wasn't really sure what to say. *We were friends…who sometimes fucked?*

We talked about how she was feeling and how it all came to be. She was in love with Cory and her, although nervous, excitement still sounded happy. When I spoke about my wedding and Grant, I tried to impersonate her enthusiasm, but I couldn't even convince myself.

Casey and I were in constant contact over those weeks and what led into months. I was starting to do shows on my own and he was traveling most of the time.

I'd missed him in at the beginning of August. He was in Seattle, but I'd been in San Francisco. It always seemed to work out like that. He came with Audrey and his dad to help her get situated at school. She'd chosen to go to Cornish, a great art focused college, against her father's best advice, but Casey said she was really happy to get away from California and that it would be good for her.

He told me one night he was glad she was in my city, because if she needed anything I could be there in a hurry for her. That made me feel pretty good.

We talked incessantly. I could tell you the local time in almost any stateside city by late September.

I knew that when I got married it would all have to stop, so I guess I was cramming as much Casey in as I could.

It didn't sound or seem fair to either Grant or Casey, but I didn't know how to stop. I couldn't imagine a world without Casey in it, but felt I needed to stay in the world with Grant as my center.

When we got too intense during phone conversations, or when things got over-heated, I'd ask to switch back to texting. He always sounded annoyed with it, but did it anyway.

We were, for all intents and purposes, friends.

We debated everything and he pissed me off. He told me that I was a poser because I was a gourmet-trained chef who liked Cheetos and canned cheese. He let it go after I called him a poor man's Sam Adams. In fact, he hung up on me that night.

I welcomed those nights. The ones where I laid in my bed and he told me how sea horses mate, or about all the theories he'd read on the never ending controversy of which came first: the chicken or the egg? I'd fall asleep on those nights, wherever I was, and I felt like I was home.

The other nights were more difficult for me. My nights with Grant.

From the outside, everything looked like a best-case scenario for a young couple and their happy future. Things were typical, calm, and I painted on the face of a woman starting a future with a perfect man.

I faked every orgasm Grant thought he gave me. Though our sex life was still active, it was just that. Active. Activated. Choreographed. I knew what he liked. I did it. He knew what I liked. He did it. It wasn't torture, and for him it was genuine. Grant was always sincere.

It was me.

After every fake climax, I'd pull myself into the bathroom and run water over my pale face and look at myself. I'd breathe and try to put all my thoughts back into their separate corners. Until, one especially overwhelming, or underwhelming, depending on how you looked at it, night I decided to bring my phone into the bathroom with me.

I texted Casey.

**Me: Tell me what you had for lunch.**

**Casey: I'm glad you asked, actually. I was going to tell you about it. I had haggis. It was totally disgusting and I'll never eat it again.**

I was happy that he replied quickly. All of the jumbled feelings and emotions I had rolling around in my head and stomach quieted and calmed. Things went back to the way they were. He still waited for me to contact him in the evenings, unless he knew I was out of town, even though I didn't ask him to anymore. Every time I send him something he was always right there. Just a send button away.

**Me: Haggis is disgusting. Why did you eat it?**

**Casey: Marc bet me I wouldn't. I won twenty bucks.**

**Me: Congratulations.**

**Casey: Thank you. What's up with you?**

**Me: I was just going to bed. I thought I'd say hi.**

**Casey: Hi LOL**

And I heard it. My generous memory let me actually hear his laugh. That was all I'd needed.

**Me: Goodnight.**

**Casey: I wish.**

*Me too.*

Smart phones were dangerous weapons. Casey's company, Bay Brewing, had a twitter account. I followed it. I set up an account of my own after I found theirs. I used the user name @BettyTRubble. I had a feeling that Casey was the person behind the account. It was to my benefit that there were pictures of him available to me whenever I wanted. Even though I let him take pictures of me when we were in Chicago, I didn't have any of him and I wasn't brave enough to ask him for any. So the twitter account, that I checked almost hourly, had to tide me over.

And it did. There were pictures of him smiling and laughing. Mostly doing work things and marketing, but it was all the same to me. Seeing his crazy wardrobe and hair whenever I wanted made me feel like I was a secret agent.

That probably made me a little bit of a stalker, but I didn't care.

# SIXTEEN

## Casey

**Friday, October 10th, 2008**

I DIDN'T REALLY GIVE a fuck if it made me a stalker. It was public knowledge and good for my business. Blake's company, Couture Dining Incorporated, knew what the hell they're doing.

I didn't want my first trade-show to be the first show we met up at. So, since CDI had an information-rich website—including pictures of Blake at trade shows, new restaurant openings and with new clients—I made a decision to follow their staunch social and marketing excellence.

Since, taking over thirty percent of Bay Brewing last month with the help of my mom, stalking Blake, and ultimately her boss's moves with their company, these trade shows proved to be good business and hopefully the traveling would lead to pleasure as well.

If I had anything to say about it, there would be a lot of pleasure.

We didn't talk on the phone often, okay we did, just not as much as I'd like. But we text every day about nothing and everything and I both loved and hated it. I was becoming stingy and sharing her was difficult.

I couldn't wait to see her face when she walked in. It was Friday and according to The Atlanta Food and Beverage Show's itinerary, she should be arriving to set up her booth anytime minute.

That was pretty much what the first day of the show entailed. Setting up display areas and signage, and then walking around and getting to meet the other vendors. It was great networking for Bay. Afterward, there would be a cocktail thing and a dinner.

It may have been a little overboard to call the organizer and have our tables placed across the aisle from each other. I could admit to that. But ask me if I cared. It'd been too long since I'd seen her face. I wouldn't be able to focus on work all weekend if I was wondering where she was and making up excuses to leave the booth to seek her out.

And Marcia, the event planner, was very receptive. Turns out her husband loves beer. Who would have thought? I may have walked an inappropriate tightrope to get my way, but I'd gotten it, so to hell with it.

I'd do what I had to do, and if that meant bribing a middle-aged woman with beer for a front-row seat to a weekend of, at very least, seeing her front and center, only fifteen feet away for a whole day, then I was guilty. I don't give a shit.

Since Bay only had a handful of employees—and we were currently swamped—I'd suckered Troy into joining me that weekend. He actually knew quite a bit about the company and the process, but really, all the people wanted at these shows was a nice-looking face and free beer. Not to sound like a chick, but he was a pretty good-looking guy and I had enough beer to last a week.

Troy had many jobs. He worked with my brother at Tinnitus Music, played in a few bands, and worked some nights in a recording studio. Sometimes he even bartended at The Front Row, a music venue back home.

I arrived early, knowing I'd want to be done setting up by the time she arrived. I even knew when her plane landed. If she took that morning's direct flight from Seattle to Atlanta and then came straight there, she should be walking in at any moment.

"I'll grab the ice in the morning. I'll just take this cart up stairs with me tonight," Troy said about filling up the sample and display tubs.

"Good idea. One trip."

"You say that like you're surprised that I'm good at this. I'm a musician, remember. I know how to gig."

"Gig?" I huffed a laugh, "When was your last *gig*?"

"Fuck you. It wasn't that long ago," I heard him say, and then I thought he called me a dick under his breath as he set up the signs behind the booth.

That's when I saw her walking through the double doors that lead into the massive convention room in the bottom floor of the hotel hosting the event. She was wheeling in two huge hard cases, probably full of their company's propaganda. She was prettier then I remembered.

She was luminescent. Her hair was pulled into a loose ponytail and pieces of it had fallen out, and she'd cut the front part again, which fell just above her eyes. She was wearing dark brown dress pants and an ivory, silk sleeveless, button-up shirt. So hot.

As I watched her sign in and talk to the folks at the front of the room who managed the registration, I pulled my phone out.

**Me: What are you doing right now? I want to tell you about what I'm looking at.**

I watched her startle and heard the sound of her phone from across the room. She was fantastically disheveled, and I couldn't help but laugh. She sprang into action looking for her cell. When she found it in the pocket of her jacket, which was threaded through the handles of her cases, she swiped her hand across the face to open the message.

She smiled and blushed.

The couple on the other side of the table gathered her registration forms and documents and set about putting them into the event folder that each vendor was given.

**Honeybee: I'm busy. I'll text you later.**

She smiled again, but didn't put the phone away. She was still holding it when I sent a message back.

**Me: Too busy for me now? Come on. I really want to tell you about this.**

"Dude, you're not doing shit. You better be naming a beer after me for this," Troy complained from behind me where he almost had the whole booth ready to go.

"Sure, I'll call it Man Bitch Ale," I replied, but I didn't take my eyes off the front of the room where she was standing.

"Who are you staring at?" Troy asked as he stood by be and followed my line of sight. Blake and Troy were both a Micah's graduation party, but Troy was too wasted that night to remember anything, let alone a girl who wasn't there for a whole hour before she left to get drunk by herself. "That girl? You're looking at the one at the registration table."

I didn't answer, I only watched as she finished with a message she was typing back to me.

**Honeybee: You're so needy. What are you looking at?**

**Me: I don't want to tell you now.**

**Honeybee: Good. I'm busy. Text later.**

**Me: I'm not texting you later.**

I liked playing that game. Even though the look on her face was one of annoyance and confusion, I reveled in the way telling her I wouldn't text her later visibly bothered her. She sucked her bottom lip in her mouth, pulling at the right side of it, and scowled at her phone. She still didn't notice me. One of the event workers escorted her to her booth.

Her focus was solely on her phone, and she didn't look up as she walked. She couldn't be browsing anything. It was damn near impossible to do that with one hand. And with her only one free hand, she hauled her cases behind her. She barely noticed that one was tipped on its side and she was full-on dragging it. Blake's shoulders were hunched forward, looking a little deflated. She kept her eyes locked to the same spot on the phone.

When she got to a spot where she had to make a turn to stay in the mostly unfilled aisles, I texted her once to prove a strange theory. I told myself, playing the devil's advocate, "She's not rereading your message, don't fucking flatter yourself."

**Me: Cheer up, Betty.**

Instantly, she released her lip.

I'd really missed her. How was it that I'd only spent a handful of hours with this girl and I missed her that much? It couldn't only be because she was sexy as hell in bed. It probably wasn't that she was ambitious and weird. I didn't know what, but it was something. And seeing her in front of me brought home how much I'd truly missed *her*.

I didn't think she'd try to text with one hand. I totally thought she'd wait, and then she'd see me before she would have time to type back. But she surprised me.

She stopped in the middle of the aisle about thirty feet away. She should have let go of the rolling suitcases, but she held onto them. And with one hand she sent a message.

**Honeybee: Dnt do tht.**

It flashed across my screen.

I held my phone out in front of me, higher than I normally would so that I wouldn't have to look away from her. I was enthralled. It had been so long since I'd seen her and my greedy eyes wanted to indulge as much as they could.

**Me: Do wht?**

She let go of both cases and they fell to the outside of the walkway around her legs. With both hands she typed.

**Honeybee: Don't play with me like that. We're friends. Remember? Don't be a jerk.**

**Me: Just friends?**

Still holding my phone up close to my face, keeping both in view, I saw the breath she pulled in. I prayed to myself that *that* was what lying to yourself looked like, before I read her reply.

**Honeybee: Yes.**

**Me: We'll see about that.**

I closed out of the message. I didn't know what she'd reply. I opened the camera app instead and waited for it to ready itself, taking the time to zoom in a little, and allowing the lens focus on her.

I said, a little louder than my speaking voice, "There comes trouble." I was so glad I'd had the forethought to take the picture, as her face was priceless. It was pure Blake.

Her eyes lifted to mine hearing my voice, like her ears were tuned to me from all those feet away. She didn't even need to scan for me. Her sharp gaze landed on me instantly. Then she did this thing where she sucked both of her lips in her mouth to keep from either screaming or smiling. I'd be happy with either; and knowing that it was one or the other made me want to do the same.

But I held my shit together and tried my best at being cool.

Then reality hit her and she realized that the person escorting her to the booth was picking up her cases and dragging them to the area right across from mine.

I was a fucking genius!

But she didn't know I was a genius. She thought it was something else. I could see the awe on her face at the realization we were right across from each other, in the same state, town, building and room as each other. It was awesome to watch.

When she finally started walking toward me, her hands out in front of her cream silk-covered breasts, phone still in hand, ponytail and bangs swishing from side to side, she asked, "Can you believe this?" Then she shook her head wildly and looked from one side of the aisle to the other. "What. The. Hell?" she said slowly and to herself.

"I saw you walk in. This is crazy, huh?" I smiled. "Looks like you're right across from us." I tried to make a "that's weird" face when I shook my head like she was, playing along. Then I couldn't resist and went to her.

There was a bounce in my step for many reasons. Our booth was finished; hers was not. I'd had Troy and she appeared alone.

Things were working out.

"Is this all of your stuff? Do you need some help?" I asked.

She said, "I'll have more tomorrow, this stuff is easy really. I'll have some food on the table and someone here to help. I came today to register and make sure everything got here." Then she looked at me in wonder. "How are you, like, here?"

"My company sent me. Thought it was good marketing or something. I do these shows all the time."

"You do?" I imagined the wheels in her head were spinning, trying to remember me talking about these shows, but I never had. She never asked what I was doing when we text. How was she to know that I'd been in over a dozen cities in the last few months? If I wasn't at a show I was scoping out bars, hotels, restaurants and talking to distribution houses about getting us into their retailers.

"Yeah, I haven't been in San Francisco more than four nights in probably the last two months. It's been wild. Why?"

"I don't know. I just...I don't know. I've been traveling a lot, too."

She huffed. “I guess we were bound to run into one another. Me with the food. You with the drink. Makes sense.”

I hated that she rationalized it. It was more fun when she thought it might be some cosmic force, but no. She was only befuddled because *she* hadn’t thought of it.

It was incredibly difficult to be in the same space as her and not have her in my arms. They ached to be holding her, my mouth was dying to kiss her, but I kept my distance. It was excruciating.

I said, “Let’s get a drink. Let me help you get this all set up first.” She only nodded and smiled.

She was right. She didn’t have much. Two, vertical signs like ours, and a cover for the table that had pictures of their client’s restaurants. She unpacked a few pamphlets and propped up a few things and that was it. She’d said that there would be more tomorrow.

That was true.

I’d seen from pictures online a small buffet and some of their favorite signature idea dishes. They displayed food with before and after menus. It was genius. Their company overhauled older, tired restaurants into new fresh versions of themselves. It was actually pretty fucking cool.

As soon as she finished tidying things up for the morning she asked, “Can we walk around first?”

“Sure,” I said.

“Then we’ll get drinks.”

“I said *a* drink,” I corrected, being innocuously argumentative.

She deadpanned, “I always overdo it when I’m with you. Why stop now?” Then laughed outright. “That was bad,” she said as she cackled. “I’m sorry. I’m sorry.”

I laughed, too, mostly at her laugh. It came straight out of her gut. Boisterous and loud.

My phone stole my attention away from her giggles. It was Aly. I silenced it and put it on vibrate. I didn’t have time to talk to her. Not when everything was working out so well.

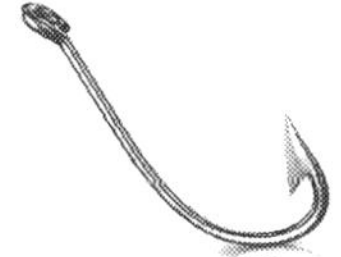

"So who is that guy with you? What does he do?" Blake asked me as we sat at the hotel bar in the early afternoon. We'd gone straight from the convention center to the restaurant in the hotel and bellied up to the bar. The hotel was full of other vendors and their inhabitants, making the bar loud and crowded, even for that early hour in the afternoon.

"He's an old friend. He doesn't actually work for Bay. He just doesn't have anything better going on and I got him to tag along. These things are better with backup."

We didn't order drinks when we'd ordered our food. I didn't because she didn't. It wasn't until Troy swung by our end of the bar, that he coerced us into getting real drinks. And by coerced, he really only said, "Hey. You guys need drinks." Then he lifted his half-empty Heineken in the air to be dramatic. "I'll buy first round," he said. It definitely wasn't *his* first round.

The best part about a bar being loud and over-populated when you were there with a girl, was when it was so loud that you had to lean in to talk. I stood at the very end of the bar, because there weren't any more seats open and I let Blake have the one on the end. I stood and ate around the end side and moved back and forth as the wait staff came to pick up their customer's drinks. They didn't seem to mind though, so I didn't see any reason to movc.

Blake ordered a BLT. She's a chef and she ordered a bacon, lettuce, and tomato sandwich. Classic.

"Hey, I like what I like," she said when I teased her about having a simple palate for a chef.

"Don't you want to see what that chef back there is really up to?"

"Nope. Not really," she admitted while taking her last bite. Around a full mouth she spat, "I come in peace." She tried to squelch herself from laughing at her own joke and a piece of bread flew from her mouth and landed on her plate. It was both disgusting and adorable.

When she finished swallowing and taking a drink of her beer, she said, "What's amazing about a BLT is that they're always good. The perfect ratio of meat to veggie to bread. It does the trick every time."

"Are you staying in this hotel?" I asked out of nowhere. All right, it wasn't out of nowhere. I'd been dying to know. I thought she would. I hoped she would, but I wasn't sure.

Even with my new flare for stalking, I recognized that would be too much.

Troy and I were staying there, but we had two rooms. It was part of his agreeing to come with me that he had to have his own room. Troy liked women and I didn't need to be around anything that might make me uncomfortable around possible clients and industry people the next day.

One time when we were in high school, he had sex with a girl on the floor of my bedroom. I knew he was a good dude, when he explained why he hadn't done it on the bed. "Dude, I didn't even know that girl. I wasn't about to mess up your shit. Besides the floor worked just fine." Then he gave a few air humps to the closest wall for good measure.

"I'm staying here. Isn't everyone?" she answered.

I didn't give a fuck about everyone else. My only concern was if she was sleeping there. "Yeah, I guess they probably are."

"Are you going to that thing tonight? That party thing?" Blake asked.

I didn't really want to.

What I wanted to do was take her upstairs and rip that fucking tease of a silk shirt off her. Every time the door opened, a breeze blew in and her goddamn nipples got hard. I damn near did, too. The way that silk hung tight to her breasts made me want to destroy it. I couldn't tell from her voice if she'd planned on going to the party or not. "Maybe for a little while. Best to get in and get out of those things," was all I could get out of her.

"Yeah, that's a good plan. Tomorrow will come early. I should probably have an early night," I said into her ear while leaning in and motioning to the bartender for another round. "We might as well enjoy the afternoon then," I added with my best good-boy smile.

My mouth being that close to her face, her skin, was driving me mad. It was the same as the last time we were together. Probably better.

Wait. Probably worse. Worse because I already knew what I wanted. I already knew what it was like to not have it. To not have her. And I felt the loss of her every night when we were only texting, "Goodnight," instead of kissing goodnight.

It was that thought that kept racking my mind.

That and... *You Fuck, you think about this girl every night while you jack your dick in the shower. You figured out a way to be around her again. Quit wasting your fucking time. Touch her. If she doesn't want you to, you'll know. Then you can stop.*

So I touched her, mostly to gauge her reaction. Well, that and because my arms were going to fall out of their sockets in protest, if I didn't. I ran my hand up the small of her back, and I felt the warmth of her body all the way to her shoulder. I left my arm possessively draped there.

The bartender brought our drinks.

Blake looked at my arm.

The hairs on her bare skin prickled and stood. I knew it was because of me. The fucking prick-teasing door hadn't opened in minutes. Her doe-like eyes glanced over to her shoulder where my fingers held onto her, bridging my body to hers.

Blake returned her eyes to mine and said, "Is this going to get harder or easier?" There was an honest curiosity in her face. Her eyes were wide and a little glassy after having four—really stout—draughts. Her cheeks were flushed and her breathing shallow.

She reacted to my nearness.

Her body was saying to mine, "Where were you all that time? I've been right here." But she was trying to not think with her body but with her head instead. Her head needed to shut-the-fuck-up.

I didn't hesitate to kiss her right there. The moment was just right. Before she could weigh the pros against the cons and therefore me against him. I was the con and we both knew it.

My lips met hers and she fell forward into my chest. Her arms wrapped underneath mine and latched onto each other behind me. She pulled me tight. I felt a sharp scrape against my skin as she tightened her grip.

As she kissed me she said, "Say easier, Casey. Tell me that if this happens, then it will be easier."

"I don't know." I told her. I didn't want to lie, but for me it was easy to be with her. There wasn't a thing in the world that would keep me away from her in that moment. Nothing else mattered. The dream I'd been having over these last few months was coming true and I wasn't about to analyze the why and how of it all. I wanted to *live* it. The hard part wouldn't come until Sunday.

Fucking Sunday.

Fuck only having a few stolen hours.

And to hell with it, while I'm fucking things up, fuck the motherfucking ring I felt digging into my back right now. I'd think about all of that later.

Right then the only thing I really wanted to fuck was my honeybee.

# SEVENTEEN

## Blake

**Friday, October 10, 2008**

THE ONLY THING I wanted was to be with the man who had his arms around me. It was the only thing I'd been able to focus on since the moment I saw him that afternoon.

What was it about that guy? He was like a bad penny. Always popping up. If he were a penny, I would have put him in my pocket and called him lucky.

It was only five or so, but I wanted my bed and I didn't want to go alone. I asked him warily, "Can we go to my room?"

He pulled away from my lips, but what I'd just asked him didn't seem to register. He looked distracted by his own thoughts.

"Hmmm?" He queried running his nose up the side of my neck audibly smelling me. "You smell the same. You taste the same," he said into my hair and he kissed my head.

"So do you. Did you hear what I said?"

He pulled away to look at my face, now that whatever he was thinking wasn't distracting him anymore.

His curly hair was longer than when I'd last seen him. His big fat curls messy and playful. They suited him. On anyone else they would have looked silly.

"Come up stairs with me," I repeated, but I didn't ask the second time. I was past requesting what I wanted.

A fire lit in his bright eyes and all humor left his features. "You know what will happen up there, Blake. I thought you only wanted to be friends."

"We just kissed in public. I think it's a little late for that. Let's call this what it is and not beat around the bush. I want you. You want me. We have some unexplainable attraction to each other. So, are you coming upstairs to fuck me or are we staying down here and getting shitfaced? It's your call." I wasn't planning on laying it all out there like that, but we didn't have time to be shy. It was like the universe was handing me my favorite drug. And I was past pleasantries.

It had been months since I felt him inside me. Months since my body felt like it did. Months since I wanted to touch more than be touched.

I explained, "This doesn't have to be some romantic thing. It's anatomical. You're body wants my body and mine wants yours."

"Is that all that wants me? What about your ring finger, honeybee? Who does that want?"

Shit. My engagement ring. Wasn't *that* twisted? I felt ashamed of my engagement ring. Shouldn't I feel guilty about the thing I'd just said and the invitation I'd given to a man who wasn't my fiancé? But still, it was this ring that caused me to feel wrong and for all the wrong reasons.

"Don't do that," I told him.

"Do what? I thought we were telling it like it is?" The hard set of his face wouldn't crack and I couldn't tell if he was teasing me or if he was serious. He looked serious.

"Maybe you're right. I shouldn't have asked. Forget it, friend." I shrugged his arm off my shoulders and took a drink of my beer. I was irritated. I felt petulant. I felt like throwing a tantrum.

He grabbed my chin and held it front and center, his voice was low when he said, "First, don't call me friend like it's a swear word. It's mean. Second, we're going up stairs and we might miss the whole fucking party. Third, you're going to take the ring off. It isn't fair to the guy to fuck me while you're wearing it and I don't want it scratching up my back. Aly will see it. Get your purse."

He pulled away from the bar, pulled a few twenties from his pocket and started for the lobby.

He had just said so many raw things that left my mind scrambled, but the one word I heard loud and clear was "Aly."

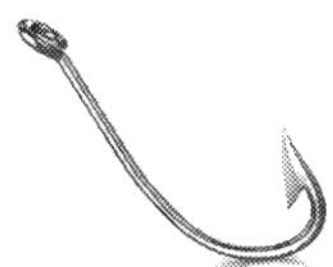

I met him at the elevators where he waited for me. Casey stood facing the stainless steel doors and didn't even look at me when I came to be by his side. He knew I was there, though, because as soon as I stopped on his left, he reached his long muscular arm out to press the up button and the door immediately opened.

We stepped inside.

"What floor, Blake?" he asked, but it didn't have even the slightest hint of sweetness that I was so used to.

"Eleven," I said on an exhale.

He pressed the button when I didn't make a move to do it myself, being that I was closer to the panel of numbers.

The joking fun Casey from earlier was gone. The Casey that wrote on mugs and sent me pictures of animals getting it on and crazy random facts, wasn't there anymore.

In place of him was a man who seemed taller, more rigid than my friend Casey from San Francisco. His posture changed from relaxed to guarded. His tone was one of a man about to take what he wanted. The change happened instantly at the bar after I called him friend. And I felt a little sick that my frustrated and shameful mouth was to blame for the switch.

His mind and silly personality drew me to him, but this new persona said no more fucking around and that ignited something deep within me.

The man I stepped onto the elevator with made me both boil with serious desire and want to run. His shoulders were set firmer, his spine straight. He changed into a different version of himself. I didn't want the old Casey to go, but in a way I'd pushed him into this. Playful Casey had a menacing air about him now that called to some part in my body that knew it deserved punishment.

I would try once to get back my friend, get back the smile I daydreamed about. If he didn't accept my plight, I would let him have it his way.

Or maybe he was just giving me my way. Only I knew that hindsight would tell me soon enough.

"You are my friend, Casey," I offered as soon as the blurry reflection in front of us mirrored a mercurial man and a nervous woman.

He didn't answer.

The elevator began to move with almost no sound. We were alone. Just me, Casey, and a tension that made me sweat.

I wanted to look up at him, but anxiety froze me, eyes straight ahead. My index finger toyed with a piece of skin that framed my thumbnail; I itched to bite it.

"Why don't you keep saying that, Blake? You're only trying to convince yourself." His unwavering timbre vibrated my bones and every molecule in my body heard his message.

*He didn't like being called my friend.*

The lift slowed its climb as it approached my floor not stopping to let anyone on or off on our ride up. When the doors opened the sun almost blinded me. The hallway in front of us was long and at the end of it was an all glass wall. Through it was the sun setting over downtown Atlanta, the flaming dusk setting precisely in the center of our view. He didn't hesitate to walk straight out of the lift and then he paused, waiting for me to do the same.

"Are you all right?" I asked.

His expression was blank, but I could see a hurricane brewing in his eyes. If I were being honest with myself, I would have admitted to feeling the tiniest bit of fear. The facts told me that I'd only met this man a handful of times and had some long-distance conversations with him. Yet there I was taking him to my room, even though he didn't seem familiar.

He wasn't drunk, neither was I.

I didn't know what was going to happen. It was adventurous and scary as hell. My instincts told me Casey wasn't malicious and that I wasn't in any real danger. It was thrilling. It was arousing. It was fascinating seeing a new side of him, even though I didn't like the reason for its appearance.

"What's your room number?"

"1128," I said and walked straight past him and into the sun.

He followed close behind and I, for once in my life, didn't have to dig for my room key. It was in the pocket of my jacket, which was slung over my purse. I slid it into the card reader and the green light flashed and the lock clicked.

The tension made everything more vivid. The beep of the lock. The smell of the recirculated air-conditioning that hit me in the face as soon as I stepped into the dark room. There were black-out curtains, which were closed, blocking out the fiery sunset behind them.

I could feel him just behind me.

I only made it in five or six feet before the sound of the door shutting caused me to jump. The darkness in the room seemed blacker than normal. Instantly I heard him kick off his shoes, then the tale-tell sound of a southward zipper. Pants hit the floor and spare change rolled out of a pocket. I made out the rustling of shirts pulling away from skin.

Then I felt his radiating heat, his breath on my neck, and my heart touched my insides, both front and back.

"Where are we doing this?" He sounded much cooler than the heat pouring off him felt. His hand reached around my middle and pulled me back into him. "You were right. My body wants your body. Do you feel that?" he asked as he dipped to grind his hips into my backside. "Take your clothes off."

There was no sweetness to the request. No tenderness in the sentiment. As my eyes adjusted to the darkness of the room, I saw a chair to my right and I went to it, pulling away from his touch. I didn't say a word, automatically doing as I was instructed.

Something about it felt fair. Felt right. I didn't deserve his kindness. I was a cheater. I was a liar. I was a bitch who called someone a friend to be spiteful.

I undressed and I'd never felt more naked—more exposed—despite being cloaked in darkness where he couldn't observe my body. I could barely see his naked form and he loomed like a brooding statue. He wasn't moving, and I couldn't even tell if he was watching me. I could only see his flesh in contrast to the pitch black in my hotel room.

"The ring, too." Systematically, I slid it off and it made a tinkling sound as the metal hit the top of the table next to the chair. He reacted to the sound like a runner would a starting block at a race. The second my ears registered it, I felt him. His bare skin against mine. I was malleable. He was solid and unyielding. His thighs hit me in the ass and they felt as hard as stone.

His hands found my hips and walked me forward until my knees hit the bed. Casey leaned in closer and said, “This is what you wanted, Blake. This is anatomical.” He turned me around then pressed me forward until my hands came out in front of me to steady myself on the bed.

“So that’s what you’re getting from me. This is only my body.” His hand again wrapped around my middle and cupped my sex. After rubbing back and forth over my tender, hypersensitive skin he said, “I suppose this *is* what you wanted, you’re already so wet.”

I hadn’t paid any attention. Was I really aroused? For the past ten minutes I’d been held hostage by my screaming mind, I didn’t even notice how his behavior was affecting me physically.

Just as he slipped a finger between my slick skin, I panted his name, “Casey?” He must have heard the alarm in my voice, too, because he eased up the pressure and stilled his hand.

“Yes,” he said evenly.

“Are you angry with me? I don’t want to do this when you’re mad. I don’t know you that well. I know we’ve met, hell we’ve already had sex. We send each other messages, but I’m a little scared.”

“You’re scared? Of what?” he asked. His voice was still level and calm but it didn’t sound as sharp as it had.

I admitted. “You. This. Do you want to hurt me? I don’t know you like this.”

Before he spoke, he took a deep breath as if to collect himself. “I don’t know me like this either.” His hand moved smooth strokes over my skin, in a more sensual way. “You drive me crazy,” he said as he stood me up and turned me back around, his other hand never pausing, gently kneading my breast.

Being face to face, I felt compelled to reach out for him. I wrapped my arms around his waist and reeled him in closer to me.

“You give off mixed signals. I’m always trying to read you,” he admitted. He sounded as frustrated as I was.

Heat spread to my outer limbs as a building need grew inside me. I didn't say anything.

He continued, "But see, I guess you like this too." He kissed my collarbone and sucked. "You call me a friend, then invite me up for more than friendly activities. You act like you only want something physical from me, yet when I don't speak to you and hide myself from you, you become submissive and turned on."

His mouth continued lower until he was kneeling in from of me, gripping my breast and softly biting at my nipple with hooded teeth. "Now, when I dial it back and touch you like I've been dreaming about, you practically melt in my hand," he said.

Both of my hands found his head and I ran my fingers through his curly hair and onto his scorching shoulders.

His voice had softened, but it was still laced with turmoil when he said, "I only want to give you what you want. You just have to tell me what that is." His mouth kissed my hipbone. Then Casey drew a deep breath through his nose. "You smell so fucking good."

Oh my God. I felt equal parts uncomfortable and worshiped at the same time. No one had ever shamelessly, and very obviously, inhaled me so, so intimately.

He slid a finger back into me, and pressed his tongue right over my clit, applying a masterful amount of pressure to it as his touch languidly relished me. "You taste so good, too."

My knees went weak and I held onto him. I felt them beginning to quake every so often from the nerves in my thighs short-circuiting from pleasure.

"So, Blake. What's it gonna be? Just my body?" He stopped everything abruptly, but I felt like I still might go off, if only he would blow across my incendiary flesh. That's all I needed to tip these sensations over the edge.

"Or do you want other parts of me, too. The *me* parts. The *Casey* parts. It's up to you, honeybee."

I didn't want to answer. Admitting things to him felt like a trap. One that I'd set for myself.

"I don't deserve all of those parts," I said out of breath. "It's not fair."

Casey's mouth pecked light kisses over me and then he gripped my hips on either side, lifting me onto the tall king-sized bed.

"It's fair if you really want them," he said as he bent down and spread my legs. I leaned back on my elbows, initially, but since I couldn't see him I let my head fall back and hang.

"I don't know what I want," I confessed.

An "mmm" sound came low and throaty from the man between my legs who was acting more and more like the Casey I knew. The Casey I'd started feeling something real for, even if I didn't know what that something was.

Between his seductive cajolery he spoke against me, "It's not the best possible answer for me, but I think that it's the truth. So, let's start small. Short-term." He braced himself over me and his face hovered close to mine. My legs spread open around him, desperate to surround his hips and pull him closer to me.

"What do you want from me this very second?" he asked.

"A kiss," I said, repeating his initial request in Chicago. We'd only kissed briefly in the bar, and I was aching to feel his lips on mine.

"I like that answer. I want that, too." Then he kissed me deeply. My toes curled from that kiss. Then he pulled away and continued, "And what else do you want from me right now? And don't say I don't know. It shuts me out. And if you do, I'll shut you out, too."

I needed a quick answer, so I said, "Touch me."

He chuckled at my cursory reply and tsked, "You can do better than that, college girl. Try more than a two word sentence. Tell me what you want."

*I wanted it all.*

# EIGHTEEN

## Casey

**Friday, October 10, 2008**

*I WANT ALL OF her.*

It altogether pissed me off when she said we we're *only* anatomical. I felt it deep in my gut, anatomically sick.

She racked my brain. We had messaged and talked on the phone. Would someone who basically had no guarantee of any physical gratification spend all of that time on the fucking phone?

No. Not any sane man anyway. And there I was on top of this beautiful woman, simply begging me to be physical with her. I was clearly thinking like a lunatic.

Don't get me wrong. It was about to get physical, but when she dissected the emotional part from whatever this was, it stung. Even when I gave her what she was asking for—just my body—she still reacted. And fuck if that hadn't turned me on. I wanted her to get mad. Protest. Argue. But she didn't. She merely adjusted herself accordingly.

I wondered if I'd ever know that girl.

It was so damn dim and I would have given anything to turn on the light. To see her. To watch her.

She pulled herself up, using the stability of my arm, which also was holding my weight. So I shifted to the side, following her lead. Taking my hand and running it over her stomach she begged, "Please, touch me here." Her hand was warm and it slid atop mine as I took over, granting her a request that weakened me.

"Please, Casey," she asked again, even though I was already palming her wet pussy.

I had to swallow whatever the hell the feeling was that tried to claw its way up my throat. Almost in a whisper, I said, "See that wasn't hard now was it, honeybee? What else?"

Her legs were still dangling off the high-top mattress, so she couldn't get enough leverage to lift into my hand like she wanted it. To say it wasn't gratifying making her try so hard and ask for it would have been a major fucking lie. And at the moment, she was loving every second.

My fingers steadily increased their pace and my mouth found her breast. I played gently with it and then decided to see if I could push her, make her even more frantic for me. Remembering how much it turned her on when I was being cooler and rougher I wondered if she'd like a little naughty along with her nice.

Maybe that was what she really wanted all along. I could give her that. Hopefully the prick who bought her the ring wasn't doing it for her. Maybe he couldn't satisfy her.

Maybe, Betty liked trouble *and* that. Whatever it was that I just did. I cataloged that piece of information under: "Honeybee Likes" in my mind. Maybe I knew more about her than I'd thought.

I kissed her perfect nipple and then bit it as I went from one to three fingers and rubbed the inside of her like it was a Jeanie's lamp. I heard the climax build as her heavy breathing and ahhhs escalated. Her hands latched onto me and her dull finger tips burrowed into my skin. In that moment I was a little relieved that she had onychophagia.

"Yes. There. God." She panted and I felt the inside of her milk my hand, trying to grab her orgasm and hold onto it. My body—the delivery vehicle. Best job ever.

As her grip weakened, I slid down her, placing my knees on the floor. My hands never left her and as she came down from her come-high, I paired her soaked pussy with my mouth. And it tasted like she'd sounded a few seconds ago. All sex and desire. She was just as sweet as

I remembered. Maybe more.

I couldn't fight the urge anymore and reached for the switch on the bedside table next to me. The light was dim, but still shocking in comparison to the darkness, which her eyes were adjusted to. I blinked a few times, trying to bring my focus back and when the haze cleared, I would have sworn she was a mirage.

Creamy flushed skin, legs spread for me, her center glistening from her release and the pinkest nose I'd ever seen. I wanted her to come in my mouth before I took her, but I had to taste her lips first. Seeing the look of ecstasy on her face was all it took. I climbed up the bed on my knees, as fast as I could, and grabbed her face with both hands and dove in.

When I finally pulled away she said, "You wanted a kiss, too."

"That's not all I want." I picked her up with one arm and dragged her up the bed so she was almost sitting up on the over-sized pillows against the headboard.

Then I returned to my previous mission.

She smiled and ran a lazy hand through my hair. I winked at her and smiled back.

"There's the Casey I know," she sang.

I placed kisses all around her naval and told her, "I have lots of Caseys. Pick the one you like."

I went to work on her tender flesh and in minutes she was coming again.

She either had a hair-trigger g-spot, or I knew her body instinctually, or I was just really good. I'd sort of hoped it was all three.

When she'd finished the second time she leaned forward and pulled me to her for another kiss. Kissing her with her wetness on my mouth was about all I could take. As she licked and playfully bit at my bottom lip, I sat down and she climbed onto my lap, straddling me. After two orgasms she was dripping wet and sank down with only minimal effort. Her body enveloped me.

We sat witness to each other as she rode me slowly. She was a sight. The sweat beaded down her neck. It ran across her chest to the dip between her breasts. The way her eyebrows subtly drew to each other when she felt me touch end of her. The flutter of her lashes. She was art in motion.

"You're so beautiful, Blake," I said, looking up into her eyes as she rose and fell with a hypnotizing rhythm. I brushed her hair back over her shoulders and pulled what was left of her ponytail out.

"I think you are, too," she said softly.

If I wasn't busy having sex—correction, being ridden expertly by a goddess—I would have put up more of a protest at being called beautiful, or almost being called that anyway, but I didn't have it in me.

Her speed picked up as she moaned and brought her forehead to my shoulder.

"Condoms," she urgently said, "We need a condom." But she continued to grind on me like it was her job.

*We need a condom?* Shit.

*God, she feels good around my cock.*

We hadn't used one before or ever talked about it, for that matter.

*Mother of God, that shit's tight.*

I supposed it was due to the fact that around her, my dick had a one-track mind. And the goddamned track was a one-way headed straight for her perfect pussy.

"Really? We never used one before," I reminded her.

She stilled. "I know," she panted as she kissed my shoulder. "That was stupid. I mean, I'm clean—"

I interrupted with, "I'm clean, too. Are you on birth control?" That was the last thing our fucked up arrangement needed.

"Yes, but I go for my shot next week. Better safe than sorry," she told me. "Is that okay?"

I whispered, "I have one, but it's all the way over there." I'd made it sound like it was all the way in China, but I didn't want to stop. She felt too good.

"Let's go there then. Unless you want to pull out."

That wasn't going to fucking happen. Not because I wouldn't, but because I couldn't.

"Okay." My hands under her thighs, I lifted her and scooted us to the end of the bed. "Hold on to me."

Her arms tightened around my neck and she linked her feet behind me. I walked the few steps to where my pants were on the floor. I knelt and laid her onto her back. She just watched me, her face dreamy and sex-drugged.

"Are you all right?" I asked, just to make sure.

She nodded. "I'll be better when you put your dick back in me."

*You dirty little thing, you.*

However, the naughty things she said didn't sound just right coupled with her innocent voice. The combination made it funny and I stifled a laugh.

"We're going to have to work on your dirty talk, honeybee."

She shrugged and watched with rapt attention as I rolled the condom onto my hard cock. I leaned forward and positioned myself at her entrance and said, "Want to stay down here?"

"I don't care. Please, just fuck me."

*All right, that was much better.*

In fact, it was fucking perfect. I didn't hesitate, pushing myself forward into her. I wasn't going to last very long. With every thrust she met me. My pace built and she dug into my ass, notifying me she was close again, too.

"Blake, I need you to come for me. I don't—" and before I could tell her why she threw her head back and said my name.

"Casey, oh. Oh, Casey." I lost myself. I pushed forcefully one last time and buried her down into the carpet with my hips, emptying into her.

"I needed that," I said out of breath.

She replied, as winded as I was, "Me, too."

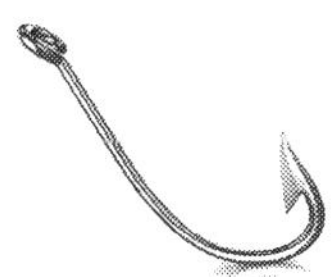

When we both had our bearings about us again, I helped her stand. I was curious. "I think we could still make the party if you want to go?"

Her face told me her answer, but she spoke anyway.

"I'd rather stay up here and order food. I don't feel like going down there anymore. You can go if you need to." The expression on her face told me she wanted me to stay, to be with her again, and to talk face to face.

I hadn't realized how much I missed actually being with her in the flesh, until then. It was incredible, watching every thought she had color her face with sincerity. She didn't hide her feelings, or she was just miserable doing it.

"Well, I'm not hungry right now, but that sounds like a good enough plan. I need to call Troy and see what he's up to. No doubt harassing someone I'll have to deal with tomorrow," I joked.

"He seems like a good guy. He's funny," she said thoughtfully. After pulling on a shirt from out of her suitcase, she found her band and started tying her hair back.

"He is a good dude. He's been our best friend pretty much all our lives. He actually works with Cory now at Tinnitus Music." I pulled my jeans back up and zipped my fly, after making sure my junk wasn't in the way.

"Like the instruments?" she asked. I was a little surprised that she knew of them.

"Yep. He makes drums." I went into her bathroom and washed my hands, running water over my face. When I came back into her room, she was lying lazily across her bed. I fished my phone from my pocket. Swiping it open and unlocking it, I'd seen that I'd missed a call from my mom, one from my brother, and a call and text from Troy.

**Troy: Dude, I'm with a chick. See you tomorrow.**

**Me: Sounds good.**

I'd call my family back later.

"I'm all yours," I said and plopped down next to her.

"Were you mad at me? Earlier?" she asked as she worried her lip.

I scooted back so I laid against the pillows at the headboard, as my hand habitually clawed through my hair.

"I wasn't mad," I said hoping it sounded honest. The truth was I *was* mad and for many reasons. I didn't like that she didn't want me for more than a fuck and I was mad that I lied about Aly seeing the marks. The only way I could cool my temper was to shut down a little. I wanted to scream and argue with her, but we'd only just seen each other after so long. If she only wanted a physical thing, then I was going to give it to her.

In the same way I wanted her to beg me for my body, I wanted her to beg for the rest of me, too. Fuck her boyfriend-fiancé, whatever. She didn't really want him anyway. She couldn't. Not the way she gravitated toward me.

It was the wrong thing to say—the thing about Aly—but I felt cornered. I'd felt wounded, and I'd reacted.

I decided to come clean about it.

"Hey, come here," I told her, and pulled her arm so that she'd curl into my side. "I didn't mean what I said earlier."

She looked up at me with those big doe eyes and looking a little worried she asked, "When you said what?"

"When I said that you needed to take off your ring so that I wouldn't get scratches. I just didn't want to look at it." She looked down at her bare hands.

"Why? You know I'm with someone and I know you're with Aly." She lowered her eyes as she spoke about her assumptions regarding Aly and me. I supposed that, to her, they weren't assumptions since I pretty much told her that we were together.

"I'm not with Aly."

"Casey, you don't have to lie to me about her. I have Grant and you have Aly. It's fair."

Well, it wasn't fair, because I kept turning Aly down. I hadn't been with anyone since the last time Blake and I were together. Only she couldn't have known that. I wasn't about to touch on that subject. I couldn't stand to hear about her and Grant. That door stayed closed.

"It's true. I was just being a prick. We didn't get back together. I work with her and I see her a lot, but not like a relationship. She doesn't particularly like the situation, but that's the way it is."

We sat there for a few long minutes, her body relaxed and then she said, "Good, I know that it shouldn't bother me and that it isn't my business, and we both know my situation, but it upset me. I'm sorry that I'm a hypocrite." I didn't know how to take that, but the idea of her being jealous was both awesome and, as she even pointed out, ironic to me.

If only things were as easy to sort out on her side of the bed. But I had to leave that alone for the time, too.

We watched something on the discovery channel about Navy SEALs, which I wanted to watch, while we ate room service. It felt normal. We talked about her new job, which I already knew a lot about because I'm a creepy stalker.

We'd pulled back the curtains when we sat at the table and ate shitty room service. Well, mine was shitty. I ordered a steak that was over-cooked and an undercooked baked potato. Blake ordered another BLT, citing you really could never go wrong with it.

We thumb wrestled for the remote and I only let her win the first time, since it was her room and I'd made her sit through a long documentary about the military. To be honest, I didn't watch much of it. I'd already seen it twice.

Since it was her turn, we watched the Food Network and she yelled at the television like it was a sporting event. "That's not real. It's not that easy," she screamed. She was more entertaining than the show.

Some hours later, lying on our bellies facing the TV, and after we'd ordered ice-cream for six, it seemed, her eyes began to get heavy with sleep. I brushed the hair away from her face and we studied each other for a while.

Her small hands played with my hair. Her finger traced my nose, eyebrows, and lips. She started to hum when she exhaled.

I needed to leave. I couldn't let myself sleep in the same bed with her again.

I didn't want to wake up with her in my arms unless she was mine. And according to the ring she slipped back on when I was in the bathroom, mine she was not.

I let her study me for a little while longer before saying, "I think I'm going to go."

She pouted and that alone almost changed my mind. But shit. There was only so much a man could take.

"No. Stay here." She smiled and raised her eyebrows suggestively, trying to persuade me to abandon my reasons instead of her.

I placed a kiss to her forehead and lifted myself off the bed in a push-up type of way, trying not to look into her eyes again. They would cause the dissolving of my will.

"I'll see you tomorrow. We can do something tomorrow night, too, if you want? I'll take you out." At that she thought. She liked that idea, but her excitement on her face was short lived.

"Okay, but you should just stay here tonight. You had that bad steak. What if you get sick? I know how serious food borne illness can be." Blake lifted up on one arm and placed the back side of her hand to my face alternating from side to side. "Yep. I was right. You feel hot."

She was so fucking adorable.

"I'm glad you think so, honeybee." I playfully said as I began to reverse, looking for my absentmindedly chucked shoes from earlier. "Like you said, we have an early morning and a long day."

Her temper peaked. She was still trying to keep her voice animated and light, but I heard the anger growing underneath. "No. Stop putting your shoes on. I'll let you sleep. I was just playing. Promise." She grew more resilient. "Casey Moore, get back on this bed with me," she demanded and reached out to pull me on top of her, but I tugged away.

"Just stop. I can't stay. Okay? I'll see you in the morning."

"You can't stay or you don't want to?" That made twice in one day that exact tone entered my ears.

"Calm down, Blake. I'll see you tomorrow. Goodnight," I said trying to qualm an escalating argument.

"Whatever. I need to call Grant anyway," she said under her breath, but I felt it sear right through my back. I tensed and stopped as I was about to turn the doorknob, letting myself out.

"I'll let that slide, because I did it to you earlier," I said. Then, I turned around to make sure she got the next part loud and clear. "Don't use your relationship with him as a weapon against me out of spite, Blake. I already fucking hate it enough."

I watched her cringe, scowl, and then soften in less time than it tooks to blink an eye. I couldn't be here for another minute longer.

"Goodnight," I repeated and shut the door gently on my way out.

Even though I'd been the one to make the choice, I'd be lonely in bed without her.

# NINETEEN

## Blake

**Saturday, October 11, 2008**

I WAS SO LONELY in that big bed after he left. I lay on my back, looking up at the ugly popcorn ceiling, thinking about everything. Again, my mind went to that pretend place where Casey was my boyfriend and then I fell into a wonderful sleep.

I dreamed that we were in a grocery store buying food and he kept filling the cart with paper towels. When I woke up remembering it, I thought to myself, *I'll need all of those paper towels to clean up the huge mess I was making.*

I dressed in a camel-colored, pleated skirt and a sleeveless black top, paired with some sensible black leather flats. I pinned my hair up in the back loosely and arranged my now longish bangs over to the side, to keep them out of my eyes. I wore my thick-framed, black glasses and minimal make up. This was a work event after all, not fashion week.

When I got to the convention center floor, I noted that Troy was already at the table across from mine and had everything ready to go. My help for the day was Melanie, and she was there, too. They were laughing at something when I walked up the aisle.

"Good morning, Melanie. How's it going?" I asked as I stowed my bag under a chair behind our tall signs.

"Good, so you know that guy?" she whispered with a blush across her cheeks. I could already see where that was headed. But they were both grown-ups, and really, who was I to question someone's behavior.

Melanie knew I was engaged.

She lived in San Francisco, same as the boys.

Who knew? She and Troy might actually hit it off. Melanie was just as crazy as what I'd seen out of Troy the night before. And she didn't have a problem hooking up at events, as I'd witnessed a few times over the past few months.

"Yeah, he's here with a guy I know. They live in San Francisco, too." I could tell Troy was listening to our conversation, so I said louder, for his benefit, "Isn't that right, Troy?"

"You're from San Francisco? That's cool," he answered and smiled at my colleague.

"Born and raised. Live in the Mission area," she replied, beaming.

We finished getting the pamphlets out and making sure the sample food was holding its temperature as the hustle and bustle of a trade show ensued all around us.

It was forty-five minutes later before Casey finally showed up. When my eyes found him he was talking to a lady by the door and handing her his business card. I watched as he leaned in and whispered something in her ear and then gave her a huge Casey smile. He looked back at her as he took his first steps away.

My gut lurched.

My head knew better. I had no business being anywhere near jealous of any woman he was with, but I was anyway.

I pretended to be looking at something with an early attendee, but I watched him out of the corner of my eye. He always looked so alive. Well, apart from the night we met, when he'd been aloof and dismissive initially, then attentive and affectionate. I'd only seen him a handful of times, but every time was the same. The way he wore his clothes like he didn't care, but still managed to look like he stepped out of a catalog had me captivated.

He walked to us, smiling and waving at others, looking like he didn't have a care in the world. He wore red jeans—yes, red jeans—and a black scoop neck T-shirt tucked in loosely behind his belt. He was sexy as hell. Wild curls sprang from his head and he was unshaven, I wanted to say, "fuck this show, let's go back upstairs." Or, "hell, fuck upstairs there's room under this table." He looked that good.

Of course, he was there to peddle beer. And I bet he did a damn fine job. Casey was naturally charismatic and always looked like he was up to something. It's one of the things I liked about him the most. His playfulness.

When he walked past me, he looked over the gentleman's shoulder whom I was talking to, and in a mocking way pouted his lip and shook his head feigning agreement with what I was saying. I had to cough to disguise my laugh.

I then heard my phone vibrate. After finishing up with my first real interested bystander, I glanced at it.

**Casey: This is going to be fun. I'm going to fuck with you all day.**

Shit. I didn't think that was an empty threat. It was going to be a major pain in the ass trying to concentrate on work with him standing right in front of me, but having been warned officially that he was deliberately trying to crack my professional exterior? I needed to have my game face on.

I managed to hold it together an hour later as he performed a rather vulgar oral pantomime, which took Melanie down cold. She had to excuse herself.

I didn't budge when Casey slipped a finger through his zipper and waggled it at me, I only responded with the most classy nose-itch/bird flip I could muster while still in business character.

**Me: I'm a little tougher than you think, Lou. Better quit while you're ahead.**

His table was busy when I sent the message. I did that intentionally to goad him. It didn't hurt that I pretended to take a picture of my boobs first. He watched, eyes bugged out and then his gaze darted to where his phone was, desperate to look when it signaled he had a new message.

*Point for me.*

When his line slowed down and he had a quick break to look, he only said over the aisle, "Real cute, Betty. We still on for tonight?"

I looked to Melanie, knowing that she was familiar with my relationship status, and said the only thing I could, "Only if Melanie and Troy go."

"Excuse me," Troy said to his customer. "I'm in," then he continued with his schpeal.

I looked to Melanie again and her smile said it all.

"Looks like we're going out," I said.

The one-up shenanigans continued through the afternoon, but stopped when I went to the bathroom to discard my panties. When I sauntered back, I conveniently stopped by his side of the aisle and dropped them at his feet.

No one except Troy could see them, since there was a table skirt, but I effectively made Casey loose his train of thought completely. When his customer left their booth, I watched as he picked them up and smelled them before pocketing my underwear in his red jeans. A few minutes after that I witnessed him adjusting his erection.

I think that's called a hat-trick.

We agreed to meet in the lobby at nine o'clock to go out in *Hot-lanta*. I changed into a little, army-green silk romper and paired it with my nude pumps after I took a quick shower, but opted to not rewash and dry my hair.

It saved me some time. I was secretly hoping that Casey would be in the lobby and as I rode the elevator down almost an hour before we had all agreed to meet. I was surprised. He'd had the same idea, because on the way down I got a text asking me if I wanted to get an early start.

The elevator pinged and he was sitting in a club chair facing the doors as I emerged only about ten feet away.

When the doors opened, catching his attention, he smiled just for me realizing that we had shared the same idea.

"Does a hobby horse have a wooden dick?" I rhetorically asked, returning his funny anecdote from months ago. I looked him over and he hadn't changed at all. Still wearing the same clothes he had all day. He sat laughing at me as I swayed my hips in my short romper and heals walking to him.

"Is Troy down here yet?"

"Nope. Just us." He grinned. As he usually did, he had a teasing gleam in his eye. He stood offering me an arm, "Shall we?"

I took it and we walked down the long marble hall to the bar on the other end of the main floor. In my heels, I was closer to his height.

"Are you wearing a onesie?" he asked, and bumped his ass into mine as we rounded the entry to the hotel bar. I looked down at my ensemble. It was a one-piece, but a onesie? Hardly.

"Are you wearing red jeans and trying to make fun of my clothing choices?"

"I am. These remind me of you." We chose two open seats at the bar. Neither of us indicating where we were headed, only intuitively knowing that was where we'd go. He didn't ask me what I'd drink. He simply ordered two vodka tonics.

"Care to elaborate, Mr. Kool-Aid?" I laughed pretty hard at my joke.

He didn't.

Casey leaned into me and said against my cheek. "Because, honeybee, when I make your pussy wet, your nose turns the color of these jeans. I'm hoping to compare the two later."

The seduction in his voice was promising and I knew he could deliver. My face heated and I prayed my nose wasn't glowing like his pants. I didn't have to wonder for long, because he placed a kiss on my nose and said, "Don't worry, it's only a little pink right now." Then he laughed as he paid for our cocktails.

We playfully flirted, which was fast becoming our native tongue. The bar was filling up as trade show attendees came down to unwind after a long day.

Casey and I consumed three drinks while we waited for Troy and Melanie and I secretly couldn't wait to get him back out on a dance floor. If I had my way, he'd be staying in my room that night, even if I had to tie him to the bed.

My phone rang. It was Grant. I saw Casey's face as he read the name that appeared on the screen. I looked to him. For approval? For assurance? For sympathy? I wasn't sure.

"Well, are you going to answer it? Better now than later," he said and flagged down the bartender. I slid the answer bar and accepted the call coming from my fiancé.

"Just a second, Grant. It's loud in here. I'm going to walk out into the lobby." I stood on shaky legs as I walked out into the open area, through the chatter of the lounge, and past Troy and Melanie. "I'll be right back," I quickly said to them as I passed.

"Hi there," I said to Grant, letting him know I could hear him, and I was far enough away from Casey's ears. I realized in that second that I walked away on Casey's behalf rather than mine. I had heard, loud and clear, what he said to me the previous night, about how it made him feel, and I didn't like the thought of making him uncomfortable. *That* was why I left.

All the while, I should have left out of fear or paranoia for Grant to hear him. Even though I thought about it, I didn't feel it.

"Hi. How's the trip?" Grants voice was bright and cheerful. It was quiet aside from him speaking, so I assumed he was at home.

"It's going really great actually. We got a few leads and made some really nice contacts. Melanie and I are about to go out dancing."

Half-truths. I could officially add those to my resume.

"That sounds fun. Take a cab. Don't walk." Concern coated his words.

"We will."

"And don't drink too much. It makes me nervous."

"I won't. Hey, what are you doing tonight anyway?" Better to change the subject than to let him dwell on me gallivanting around a city I wasn't all that familiar with.

"Just some paperwork. I'm at the office." When he should have been out having a good time with some friends, or even doing something at the house, there he was at his office doing paperwork. It bothered me, but mostly it made me feel bad for him. He was such a hard worker and played by every rule.

Yet, here I was, his fiancée, about to go out on the town with a man who, only minutes before, I'd fantasized about stripping naked and tying to my hotel bed.

Grant wouldn't ever do this to me. Never mind why I was doing it. I didn't even know all the reasons. How I could do this to *him* was the question rolling through my mind. If only I could work out exactly which *he* was fairing.

"You should call it a night. Go get a beer. What time is it there?" I looked at the time on my phone and did my fast zone calculations that I was so good at. "It's only almost five. Call Shane. I'm sure he'd like to get out of the house."

"I might." I looked through the glass wall into the bar and saw Casey staring at me, nodding his head at something Troy was telling him. He motioned a two to the bartender and then they all tipped back brown shots. Except for Casey, he did doubles back to back.

"Grant, is it okay if I call you in the morning? Melanie is waiting on me."

"Yeah, yeah. Sure. Have fun. Be careful. I love you."

Before I could say it back, I turned my body away from two prying eyes and replied, "I love you, too. See you tomorrow." I disconnected the call and headed for the ladies room. I needed a minute.

If flying from one part of the world to another, across time zones and datelines, gave one jet-lag, then what was it called when one's heart traveled from one man to another and then back in mere minutes?

I'd love to know.

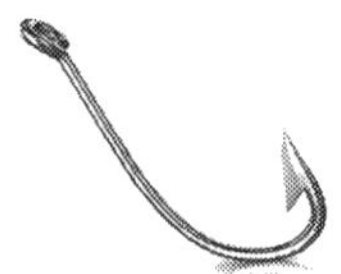

We went to a club named Taboo. Melanie had been there before. It was a little comforting having at least one person who knew their way around. If the name had anything to do with the atmosphere, I had a suspicion I was in for a real experience.

We stood in line outside for a while, but it was a beautiful, albeit humid, October southern night. There was a breeze that washed past every now and then. It was refreshing.

Troy and Melanie hit it off great. Although, I wasn't really getting a flirty kind of vibe from them. It was more of a kindred spirits thing.

They talked about his job at Tinnitus and how she'd dated a few musicians. They even knew a few of the same people back in their hometown. I saw them exchange numbers earlier and I thought it was kind of cool.

"So how do you guys know each other?" Melanie asked as we got closer to the club's roped off doors.

Casey spoke first, "Her best friend from college is in a relationship with my brother." The answer was true. Half true. He neglected to add the part about where we had a few one-night stands, communicate almost daily, and we fucked on my hotel floor the night before. But who was really paying that close of attention?

I still had a sour feeling in the pit of my stomach. I couldn't quite call it guilt, because I couldn't truthfully admit—even to myself—that I regretted being with Casey. Whatever it was, it made me feel anxious. All I wanted to do was get another drink and lose myself on the dance floor with him.

Casey hadn't touched me since Troy and Melanie showed up in the lounge and I was eager to feel his hands on my skin, even though it was risky. But I wasn't worried about Melanie. She was a love-the-one-you're-with kind of girl and my desire made me reckless.

Taboo was precisely that. A variety of people were inside the club, and for club hours we were pretty early. Having had a few more drinks at the hotel, it was only a little after ten when we finally gained admittance.

They played house music and the layout was totally bizarre. When first we walked in, there was a glass wall separating us from a dance floor that was elevated about waist high. Upon looking up, through steel beams, I could see the underside of a glass second floor where people had started to dance as well. Strobe and ultraviolet lighting made everything look aggressive and otherworldly.

Melanie and I decided to find a table while the guys got our drinks. We selected a secluded spot in the back where you could see both dance floors and we didn't have to scream to talk.

"So what's the real story with you and Casey?" Melanie asked as soon as we were seated on a circular white couch with a small coffee height, glass table, which glowed bright red from within.

"I don't know what you're asking me? His twin brother and Micah are dating. You remember me talking about her, right? I met Casey when I was in San Francisco for her graduation last spring." I answered as casually as I could manage.

If one tells a half-truth at nine o'clock and another at ten thirty, do they cancel each other out? Or make one complete true story? Even I wasn't believing my liar's logic.

I was thankful that Casey and Troy were walking toward us just then, with two shots and two beers apiece.

"Good spot, ladies. Let's have some fun," Troy said as he placed his handful of drinks on the low table and came to sit by me. It felt strange, but I pretended like it was no big deal. All the while, my skin was screaming for Casey.

"Should we toast?" asked Melanie over the thumping music. Then, answering her own question, she lifted one of the clear shots above her head. We all followed suit and soon there were four arms stretched upward, toward the center of the seating area.

"We'll all make one," she instructed. "I'll go first. Here's to meeting new friends and replacing the shitty ones."

"Here's to finding someone to lay on top of me later," Troy said and we all laughed.

"Here's to brave men who wear red pants," I said, because I couldn't think of anything good.

We all looked at Casey and he smiled weakly, "Here's to the bait."

His eyes were fixed on mine and then he raised his shot a little higher signaling for everyone to drink. It was tequila. No lime. No salt. And consequently, no feeling left in my throat. It was like fire all the way down into my stomach.

"I'm going to hit the ladies room and then I'm going to dance upstairs. Meet back here in a while?" asked Melanie and we all nodded our agreement.

When she left I sat in my seat next to Troy feeling two things. Casey's eyes burning through me and the liquor burning through my already murky judgment. I wanted him, but didn't know what to do or say.

Then Troy asked me, "Do you like to dance, Blake?" A smile crept from east to west across his cleanly shaved face. My gut reaction was to look at Casey and gauge his reaction to this, but I focused my eyes on the beer in front of me. I leaned forward to grasp it just as Troy slipped an arm around the back of my seat.

"She isn't dancing with you, man," said Casey from across the table.

"She's not? How about you let her make up her own mind, *man.*"

"She's mine, Troy," said Casey a little louder than necessary. I presume it was the alcohol making him so quick tempered. I wasn't looking forward to a repeat of last night. Or maybe I was.

"She is?" I didn't know what had gotten into Troy. He hadn't behaved like this earlier or last night. He'd only been fun and, more often than not, a source of comic relief.

"She is tonight," Casey deadpanned.

His sudden claim to me made me feel hot and also a little nervous. But before the situation could escalate, I moved around the circular seat to him and extended my arm.

"I want to dance with you," was all I needed to say. What I'd said was one-hundred percent true. Apparently, I *was* capable of honesty. Sometimes.

He didn't hesitate, and even gave me a Casey smile, as he walked me to the lower dance floor. When he found a place that suited him, he turned to face me, still holding my little hand in his big one.

"What was that about?" I asked as our bodies cinched together.

"Don't worry about it. He's being a...a Troy." His lack of a better word made me giggle a little and could feel some of the tension roll off his body. My hands snaked up around his shoulder and he brought one of his around low on my waist. The other hung fluidly at his side.

"I liked your toast," I told him.

He leaned and looked down at me so that we could talk face to face over the lyric-less music. He started moving us to a hypnotic beat and said, "I thought you would."

My hand, on its own accord, rose into his hair, my heels giving me an advantage I didn't usually have. I splayed my fingers wide and clutched him.

Then I kissed him.

I couldn't hear his moan, but I felt it. Through his shirt, which was already beginning to cling from sweat, and through mine, which was doing the same, I felt his chest vibrate with a low rumble. His tongue teased at my lips and I opened my mouth without thought or concern.

The one hand around my waist soon became two.

We grinded against each other for what felt like hours. Song after song we moved our bodies together like we shared a person. I thought back to the first night we danced and how it felt just like that.

Real. Hot. Genuine. Easy.

He was right. I was his. In that space and time, my body was the property of Casey Moore.

# TWENTY

## Casey

**Saturday, October 11, 2008**

I TOLD TROY SHE was mine, but the truth was, I belonged to Blake. She could toss me out anytime she wanted, but I couldn't do the same to her.

Her taking that call earlier did things to me. It made me livid and jealous and made me realize, again, that she wasn't mine.

It wasn't a good time to talk about it, but I needed to relieve some of this tension I was drowning in. The music was loud, so bent down closer to her and I spoke into her ear.

"What are we doing, Blake?"

I felt her smile against my cheek. "I think we're dancing."

"You know what I mean."

She pulled away and met my eyes with hers. They looked so big, magnified by the shading and makeup I wasn't used to seeing her wear.

"You know what we're doing. We're having fun." She smiled, but it slid off her face when I didn't smile back.

"What am to you?"

"Casey?" She looked worried. But I didn't care. I wanted something. I wanted her to say something to me to let me know that what I was feeling wasn't fucking insane.

"Fucking tell me the truth. You can lie to everyone else, but right here, right now, just tell *me* what this is?" My mouth overloaded how I wanted that to come out. Immediately, she grew rigid in my arms. I'd made her uncomfortable, but I was uncomfortable, too. And maybe for the first time she would actually deal with it.

I knew that she'd just frozen up and left me. She was in my arms, but I'd pushed her into a corner that Blake couldn't handle.

"We fuck, Casey. We talk on the phone and we fuck. Is that what you want me to say?" Our bodies were pulling apart, mostly hers from mine.

"A really long one-night stand, huh?" I joked sardonically.

"Yep," she shouted over the music, I could see her temper beginning to surface like mine. She continued, "That's what men like you want isn't it, Casey? Fuck and run?"

She was trying to rile me up.

Falsely I admitted, "Fuck and run sounds kind of nice right about now."

"I couldn't agree more," she deadpanned.

I scanned the club, for what I needed, and saw what I was looking for. "Well, I don't want to waste any more of your time." I grabbed her hand and practically pulled her through the mob of bodies that congregated on the dance floor.

Walking us down a long hall, I turned every door handle as we passed them. She didn't put up any resistance. When one turned, I peeked my head in, didn't hear anything and then pulled us both inside. I moved her so she was wall and I locked the door.

It was dark. There wasn't even enough light for my eyes to adjust. That was fine though. I was making a point. And if I had to watch her face as I did it I would have surely backed out.

I unbuttoned the sexy-as-fuck green number she was wearing and batted her hands away when they came up to my chest.

"Stop," I said quietly, making sure to keep as much emotion out of my voice as possible. I didn't want to frighten her. I wanted her to know exactly what she was asking for when she'd suggested this. When she made this something that it wasn't—at least for me, it wasn't.

With all of the buttons released, I pushed the straps off her shoulders and the whole thing fell to her feet. I felt her try to push her body against mine, but I backed away. I flipped her small frame and she faced the wall. She trembled under my hands.

"Blake, are you scared?" I had to know. Yes. I wanted to give her a taste of her own medicine, but I didn't want to cross a line. She didn't answer. So I leaned into her and pressed my forehead into the back of her hair. "I don't want to hurt you. You make me crazy. I want you to know how I feel." Her ass pushed into my cock and I realized she wasn't shaking out of fright. It was lust. Maybe this really was what she wanted.

So be it.

"You want me to fuck you like this, don't you? You've been begging for it all weekend." I had to admit, the fact that she was responding to this made me feel powerful and mighty. Like I actually called the shots for a second.

"Say it. Tell me to fuck you, Blake," I growled as I pressed myself hard into the back of her. Her thong-parted ass cheeks felt like they were ten degrees hotter than my hand. I was still fully clothed and decided I would remain that way.

I unlatched my belt, one button, and unzipped my fly. I pulled myself free and ran the length of myself down her delicate ass. I slipped my hand from behind between her legs and found her soaked-through panties. When my hand met her pussy, she whimpered, "Please, Casey."

I moved the silk aside and pushed two fingers deep inside of her. Her sharp inhale told me she wasn't expecting it. It was thrilling.

"Not what I want to hear." I moved them in and out and stroked her already clenching core. Then I pulled them from her, leaving her panting and circling her hips in my absence.

"Fuck me," she said, but it was so quiet that I could have missed it if the room wasn't so still and I wasn't so focused on her body.

"Louder, I don't think you mean it." I moved in closer to her, pressing her to the wall with my hip and rocked my hips to tease her. My hands found her breasts full and her nipples hard. I squeezed them both at the same time and she bucked.

"Fuck me," she said, but she was still holding back. My hips began rocking into her, mimicking the motions I so badly wanted to act out. I put my mouth on her neck and sucked, making sure not for too long or in the same place.

"Please, Casey." Her frustration was evident in her plea. "Fuck me!"

Those were the magic words and she shouted them in earnest.

She panted, "Fuck. Me. Just fuck me."

I kicked her legs farther apart with my left foot and clutched one of her ass cheeks while I positioned myself at her opening. Then plunged in.

I didn't wait for her to relish in the sensation too long though. Partly because my dick was about to explode from the scene that was playing out, and also because I needed to fuck her as bad as she wanted me to. But most of all, I wanted to make my point.

I slammed into her over and over. She came and then came again on a fast loop. She met me with every thrust. Saying my name and screaming, knowing that no one was going to hear her. Her voice filled my head and my world was consumed with her. I didn't let up. I was merciless. Pushing into her that last time, I heaved my cock with punishing force and came harder than knew I was possible. My screams harmonized with hers.

For good measure, I surged forward one last time before I pulled myself out. I reached into my pocket and pulled out a fifty-dollar bill.

"Use this to get back to the hotel." I slipped it under her hand that was still plastered against the wall. Blake's breathing was labored and I'm sure she was still in that twilight head-space between sex and thereafter.

I kissed her shoulder.

"This is a fuck and run. Now you know the difference, honeybee."

I slammed the door when I left.

I fought my instincts and didn't go back to make sure she was okay. I hoped I'd opened her eyes to how she was falsely labeling what we were. I didn't know what the exact term for *us* was, but I knew fucking and running wasn't what we'd been doing. And now she would, too.

I met Troy at the bar and told him I was leaving. He decided to stay.

"Blake's still here. But I'm out."

He shook his head mockingly at me.

"This was her call, Troy. I've got to go. Make sure she gets back to the hotel. Would you?"

"Oh, I'll make sure all right," he said like a snake, but I knew he wasn't.

"If you weren't my best friend…" I pointed at him, adrenaline coursed wildly through my veins from the lesson—I hoped—I gave the girl who I'd rather be leaving with.

"What? If I weren't your best friend I wouldn't have to watch you do this? I wouldn't see how she's got you so twisted up? Yeah, if I weren't your best friend I'd probably have a fat lip right now. But I am you best friend and I'd rather have the fat lip than feel how you're going to when this all falls apart." Troy got in my face, chest swelled and eyes dilated.

I didn't want to fight him. I was already in a war with myself.

I turned and left.

I went back to the hotel and changed rooms. I didn't want to see her. I turned off my phone.

I needed space. I needed time to think.

I needed to wrap my head around the one fact that I hadn't let myself think about the whole weekend. The thing that was making this paralyzing pain sharper in my chest.

She was fucking engaged and she never even mentioned it to me. She was going to marry *him*.

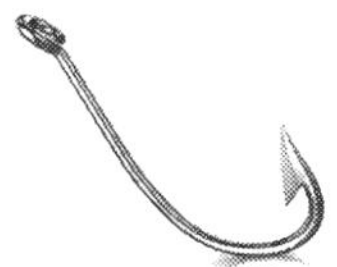

I left the next morning and went to the airport for no good reason. My flight didn't leave for four more hours. I sat there and watched the planes come and go. My mind was a labyrinth.

*If I go this way what will happen? If I do that will it even make a difference?*

I wasn't getting anywhere no matter which way I spun it. She was with him and I still wanted her.

I powered up my phone after having it off after the club. I needed to make sure Troy knew I was already there.

**Honeybee: I get it. I'm sorry.**

**Honeybee: You didn't answer your door so I guess you're asleep. See me in the morning? Please?**

**Honeybee: I said I was sorry. I meant it. You're being a little dramatic, Lou.**

**Honeybee: My flight leaves in an hour. I'm in the lobby.**

**Honeybee: This hurts. Stop it.**

That was the one that got me. I think her plane left at eight that morning, ours didn't take off until two. She was long gone.

**Me: Why didn't you tell me you were engaged? When did it happen?**

I got a coffee and put my ear buds in, she was still in the air somewhere over Colorado I was guessing. I sat there for a few more hours. I tried not to think.

I just listened. But I'll be damned if every single song I heard didn't sound like it was written specifically for what was running through my mind. Fast songs, the slower more melodic ones, they all related.

Was that how my life was going to be from now on? Could I even take what she had to give me at face value anymore?

Did I even have a choice?

Later that night, I finally started to make some kind of peace with it all.

Something fowl had died in my refrigerator while I'd been on the road and I'd spend the better part of the evening aggressively cleaning out the putrid appliance. When I was walking in from taking the trash out my phone rang.

It was her.

I looked at the ceiling for the answers, but then I realized they weren't there. They were on the other end of that call. I connected the call, but my voice didn't kick in in the normal way it should.

"Casey? You there?" she asked not knowing if the call had gone through.

I walked to my recliner, sat down and leaned back. "Yeah. I'm here."

"I didn't think you'd answer. I'm really sorry." That was all good and well, but her apology didn't fix anything.

"What do you have to be sorry for, Blake?" I ran my hand through my hair and sighed in exasperation. "The whole thing sucks."

"I know." Her voice cracked, something I hadn't heard before. "For me, too. I don't know what I'm doing anymore."

"When did you get engaged? How long ago?"

"July," she said quietly. "The day Aly messaged me and told me I was a nobody." She sounded liked she'd been scolded for stealing cookies and was trying to plead her case.

My head pounded.

My eyes shut and tightened.

The day Aly messaged her? Wait. I'd seen her after that.

"I saw you in July." My voice was cool, my emotions were anything but. It had to be a coincidence. The two couldn't be connected. "Why didn't you say something then?"

"I don't know," she bellowed through the receiver.

I couldn't hold in my frustration any more. "Yes, you do. Why? Why didn't you tell me?"

"I didn't want it to stop. I didn't want you to, I don't know, ignore me." She sighed.

"What do you want? Because you're confusing the fuck out of me."

The line was quiet, but I could hear her moving on the other end. It sounded like she was tapping something. It was the only tip I had that told me she was still there.

Tap-tap-tap.

Tap-tap-tap.

"I told you. I don't know," she said.

Again it sounded like the truth, but what did I know about her truths? What did I know about her at all?

I knew her nose lit up when she was turned on. I knew she had a temper to rival the one I was growing into. I knew that every time I was around her she consumed me. I was back at square fucking one.

"Are you really going to marry him?" I had to know. If she was, then what was all of this for?

She sniffed. "Do you want this to end, Casey? I know it's messed up and that I'm messed up. But for now, can't we just have fun? I don't know what I want."

"Then why did you tell him yes?" I'd lost my temper.

"Because! I did! You had a girlfriend. We had a one-night stand, for Pete's sake. I've been with Grant a long time. He had just bought me a damn house! That day, when Aly said those things, I didn't know what to think. She obviously knew we were talking. I didn't know what to believe, then Grant took me to the house and proposed. It seemed like the right thing to do at the time." Her voice had escalated to shouting, but then it lowered again when she continued. "But now…now I don't know."

It *was* messed up. She was right. If I would have just dead-bolted my hotel door. If I would have told Marc that I wanted to take the trip alone. If she would have called me like she said she would and told me about what happened.

If.

If.

If.

IF!

Still, she wasn't married yet and she was talking to me. And she didn't know what she wanted. There was still hope. Still a chance that maybe she wanted me. We still had time.

"It's okay."

"It's not okay, Casey."

"It will be. We don't have to talk about that. Not now."

"We don't?" She sounded hopeful, relieved.

"Well, you're not off the hook yet, honeybee."

She mock-laughed, a small nervous chuckle vibrated through the phone. Then Blake said, "I feel awful."

"I don't." I kind of did. I shouldn't have lied, little and white as it was, but I wanted her to talk to me. The sex part was crazy hot, and her body made my rational thinking quite the opposite, but there was just something about her. Her wit. Her charm. Her.

And to actually tell the fucking truth he was a fool. What kind of man, who had a girl like *my* Blake, wouldn't feel the need to light her up, to get her eyes shining like I'd seen? If he wasn't doing that, and clearly he wasn't, otherwise what was she getting from me? You know? Like why the hell didn't he spend every moment playing and kissing and fucking showing this girl a good time?

Was mediocre really all what she wanted? We had more than that, didn't we?

I knew what she wanted. She wanted a thrill.

I was her thrill. I wasn't her boyfriend, and I wasn't her fiancé. I was a spark. Something that excited her; something that made her bones hum with life. And if that was the kind of thing she wanted—because I sure as hell did—then I'd give it to her.

I'd show her. She'd see it, eventually.

I didn't know about marriage or houses or even how a real relationship worked.

But I was positive that I wanted her the same fucking way people wanted summer in February and how dogs want their bellies rubbed. *Naturally*. Lighting her up came naturally to me.

We spoke for a little longer, after pausing for the dust to settle, and it was almost like nothing had happened. We argued and laughed. She told me that she didn't like the old Star Wars as much as the new Star Wars and so I hung up on her.

She called right back just to hang up on me.

I called her back and we talked for another two hours. I told her about the time I flipped a golf cart my junior year in high school, after I drank too much, and broke my collarbone.

She told me about how her best friend from high school, Kari, had a ferret who bit her every time she tried to enter her friend's bedroom. It got so bad that she wouldn't go over there anymore.

So her friend had to come over to her house to hang out. It didn't sound so interesting until she got to the part where her friend and her oldest brother started dating and eventually got married. She'd began the story with, "Want to hear the story about how a ferret got my brother married?"

Who could say no to that?

Before I got off of the phone with her that night, I said, "I want to do this, if you want to do this."

She yawned and said, "I want to do this."

Then we hung up for real.

## Tuesday, November 4th, 2008

**Me: I'm coming to Seattle to see Audrey. She's homesick and I set up a few meetings?**

**Honeybee: When?**

**Me: Next weekend through the beginning of the week.**

**Honeybee: I'll be in town.**

**Me: I'll be in you.**

*Delete.*

**Me: Maybe we can meet up?**

**Honeybee: Sure.**

Audrey was homesick, for her sister, not for me.

Sure, she loved me, but Audrey and our younger sister Morgan were almost inseparable. Since Audrey left for school, Morgan had begged me to take her for the weekend to see her and I had a few new customers in the city I could visit, so it worked out.

It had also been a while since I'd seen Blake and I wanted to.

Like really wanted to.

We'd re-implemented the she'll text me first in the evenings policy.

I hated it. I hated thinking about it and sometimes when I was in a particularly dicky mood about it I'd text her back that I was busy and that *I'd* text *her* later.

I always felt like I'd shown her.

Then I'd realized that what I really wanted was to talk to her and that I was the one postponing it. Then I'd give in, twenty minutes later, and text her back.

I couldn't help it.

## Monday, November 10th, 2008

**Honeybee: What is a four-letter word for idle or proud? How was your day?**

**Me: Good. Signed contracts with two wineries today. Wine drinkers like beer, I guess.**

**Honeybee: It's for their husbands. If there is beer then the guy will go. You're saving marriages, Lou. Bravo.**

I guessed that would be good for my karma, since I was doing my damnedest to prevent one.

**Me: Makes sense. How was your day?**

**Honeybee: I made the best tartar sauce on the planet. So, not bad.**

**Me: Vain.**

**Honeybee: Okay, maybe not the best tartar sauce, but it was good. Everyone liked it.**

**Me: No. Your word. It's VAIN.**

**Honeybee: Oh. Good. I was like 'my sauce rocks, fucker.'**

**Me: LOL. Your sauce rocks.**

## Friday, November 14th, 2008

**Me: Picking up Morgan and catching a plane. Text me later?**

**Honeybee: Safe travels.**

Morgan was so excited. It was crazy how different my two younger sisters were and how much they loved each other. Morgan, Ms. Optimism Fix The World, and Audrey, Ms. I Can Paint A New, Prettier World, couldn't have been less alike. Where Morgan followed the rules, Audrey followed her heart. A scholar and an artist, and two best friends.

Sure, they each had their own best friends, but for the most part they were so close. They rarely fought, which we all thought was strange. Cory and I fought like the north and south in high school at times.

On the flight, Morgan told me about how many of her classes were weighted how she'd actually graduate in December, but that she'd still walk with her class in March.

"I'll start college this winter actually."

"Are you serious? No break?"

"I just had a break in the summer and there will be Christmas break in between. It won't really change anything, I'll still live at home with Mom and Dad. I'll just go to City College for classes instead of Balboa High. It'll give me a jump start for my freshman year," she explained.

My little, baby sister was about to start college. That was weird. "Will you leave after that?" I should have encouraged her to go out into the world, like I had Audrey, but Morgan was the baby. I selfishly wanted her to stay at Dad and Carmen's for another few years.

She shrugged.

"I haven't decided. I might just stay in the Bay. Go to UCSF. It's ridiculous to pay for out of state college when I have amazing schools in my backyard. I can live at home and save even more money. I could volunteer more that way."

I looked at my little sister like she was a tap-dancing pigeon. She laughed at my expression as we were touching down in Seattle.

"It's called growing up, Casey. I want to be a responsible adult." Her face was so genuine and proud. It was amazing watching these two girls turn into such cool young women. Audrey was at art school, passionate and driven by her every feeling.

Morgan was motivated by her conscience.

"Have a little fun, too. Okay? You're making me look bad," I teased as I helped her get her carry-on out of the over-hear compartment.

"I will, Casey."

As we walked through SeaTac to find Audrey, who was meeting us there, I powered my phone back up.

**Honeybee: I'm at the Hotel Max.**

**Me: What? I thought you were in town?**

Morgan was planning on staying with Audrey and I was going to get a room near campus. In my head, I imagined that I'd see Blake. Get a coffee or take a walk or something. It sucked to think that I'd missed her.

Missing her was a full-time job.

**Honeybee: I am. I'm at the Hotel Max. It's near Cornish.**

Oh, shit. I was wrong. She hadn't left. She'd got a room.

"Yes!" I shouted as we walked from our terminal to baggage claim. I even did the fist-pump victory move, usually only reserved for scoring in sports. But it finally felt like I'd won something. She took a step toward me, and on her turf nonetheless. There was finally a point on the *us* side of the scoreboard and that was one less for *them.*

"What is that all about?" Morgan said, rubber-necking to see her brother acting like a fool in the airport. Her curly, blonde ponytail swinging as she teetered between watching where we were going, for the both of us, and looking at me for a clue as to what was so awesome.

"I'm meeting up with...my friend," I answered her finally.

Her face looked skeptical, but she smiled. "Must be some friend."

**Me: I'm going to have dinner with the girls then I'll be there. What room?**

**Honeybee: 1002**

Dinner could not have gone any damn slower. I loved my sisters, but they were in their own world talking about people I didn't know and things I didn't much care about. Well, I might have if I didn't know that a woman I'd been dreaming about was waiting for me only minutes away. In a hotel room.

I don't know why Blake did it, but I wasn't about to question it.

# TWENTY-ONE

## Blake

**Friday, November 14, 2008**

I ASKED MYSELF OVER and over, what the hell was I doing?

My logic was simple. My family was at early holiday party, which I'd bailed out of days before. And Grant would be working late. He said earlier he was going home after his last showing and that he wanted to work on the house the next day. He was expecting me to be there, too.

We only had one night. But we still had *one whole night.*

He wouldn't even know I was gone. Still, inviting Casey to my apartment seemed wrong on so many levels. I doubted that anyone would just stop by. That would've been weird. I was already having a hard time thinking about him when I shouldn't be. When I *really* shouldn't be. I didn't need a constant reminder of him in my home.

A hotel was a better plan. It was safe. It should have felt wrong and dirty, but it felt right and I was excited to see him. It had been a while.

I paced the room.

He'd sent a text when he landed and had planned to eat dinner with his sisters. That was kind of sweet, I thought. He was a great brother. He talked with his sisters all the time and if they called when we were on the phone, he always switched over to get their calls instead of letting it go to voicemail.

I don't really know what about that made me like him more, but it did.

I had to leave my brothers voicemails all of the time. They could learn a thing or two from Casey. When I thought about it, I never really had to leave Casey voicemails either. That made me smile. He made people feel important.

I checked my face in the mirror. Where that morning I looked run down, at that moment I appeared awake and alert. I felt excited and nervous but in a good way. Every time I thought I heard a sound at the door I felt a flutter inside me that sent tingles, like little air bubbles, through my veins.

Then it was the real thing. It was him.

After he knocked again, I peeked through the peephole to see him standing in front of it with a Cheshire cat-like smile. His hands were behind his back and his hair was the perfect mess. His tall slim figure was wearing jeans, chucks, and a loose, black and white striped V-neck T-shirt. He looked edible.

I opened the door too fast and allowed what little coolness I had, run right out of the room like when I was a child on a hot summer day waiting for my dad to get home.

"Hi." I laughed and stepped back for him to come in. He grinned and came inside. It was a little awkward, and a lot not awkward at the same time.

"Hi," he said, but he looked like he was hiding something.

"What's behind your back?"

"Oh, this?" he rhetorically asked as he brought a brown paper sack out between us. I had the urge to grab it. "It's nothing."

"What is it?" I made a move to steal it, but he saw me and swiped it away.

"Punchy tonight, are we?" He laughed.

"I'm going to punch *you*, now what's in the bag?" I said as I stealthily began to walk circles around him.

"Well, Audrey was telling Morgan about this place downtown that had the best cheesecake. So..."

"Oh. God. Tell me it's cheesecake." I'm not a sweets kind of girl, unless you count chocolate, ice cream, and cheesecake. Then I'm a fiend. And if it was the place I was thinking of, then I was going to melt there on the spot.

"It's cheesecake. Well, it's a few cheesecakes actually." His face remained stoic and demure.

Cheesecakes from downtown that could fit into that little bag? I knew exactly where they were from.

"They're already closed. It's after eight. How did you get them?" I asked. Don't ask me how I know that The Confectional closes at six. It isn't like I'd ever been there a little too late and nearly cried or anything.

"I have connections. And I think I remember a particular day when my favorite girl didn't get her dessert."

I watched his eyes roll up and to the right. He was adorable in that moment. My heart swelled watching him play with me in real-life, just has he had all these weeks on the phone. It was like getting-paid-on-your-day-off good.

Casey continued, "The menus you ordered from that one place—the Prick Printers, I think you called them—came in all wrong and you said that you should have been an accountant instead. Remember?"

I did remember and more interesting was that he remembered, too.

"I remember. All I wanted was—"

"Quadruple Chocolate," he interrupted, answering for me. "And I didn't get you one."

Cruel. It was so cruel to bring up the best, most delicious chocolate heaven for your mouth and not bring one. The Turncoat he was.

"You didn't?"

"Nope." Then, the most evil grin spread like fire across his face. He was incandescent and ornery. "I got you two."

I thought I was dreaming. Right here before me was a sinfully sexy man who brought me ecstasy on a platter.

"I think I need to sit down." I was humoring him and trying to be funny, but in all actuality, the concept of him thinking to bring this made my knees weak.

"Yeah, your nose is looking a little pink." He laughed, breaking the pretend concerned character he was trying to pull off.

"What did you get for you?" The possibilities were endless.

In a voice almost as rich and smooth as the dessert in the bag, he crooned, "I didn't. I thought it would be more fun to convince you to give me one of yours."

This man.

Laughter shot out of me, erupted really. He was so serious and trying his best to be debonair. It was too much. Or maybe it was one of those moments where your happiness escapes through your mouth like a bank robber sprinting for a getaway car. And I fell back on the bed in a fit of ridiculous laughter, holding my stomach.

"Oh, that's good!" I hollered. "You're so full of shit!"

"What?" He looked hurt. "I thought it was a good idea."

After I sorted myself out and my laughter wound down to simmering giggle, I asked, "So, what on Earth do you think you could possibly do to merit one of those?" In his distraction, Casey deep in thought, I was finally able to snatch the paper sack away from him.

Sweet Jesus. They were really in the bag.

Maybe I wasn't giving him enough credit. I made a snap decision to up the ante. He didn't know how good the Quadruple Chocolate cheesecakes were. Otherwise, he wouldn't have made such an elementary offer.

"Okay, but first you have to take a bite." His face twisted not understanding what I meant.

"I win already?" he asked.

"No way. Not even close. I want you to know what you're fighting for."

"Oh, I know what I'm fighting for." His words played into my hand, but they hung heavily in the charged air between us. He walked to me on the bed as I unceremoniously unwrapped one of the treats he'd brought.

He could have that one, the one with the piece missing. That was, if he earned it.

With the fork that I found at the bottom of the bag, I sank it deep into the cheesecake. My mouth watered.

"Come here," I said. He leaned over and put his hands behind his back and opened his mouth wide for a taste.

"Ahhh," he sang.

Putty. This man was putty.

"Close your eyes." He followed my instruction well.

As he waited for the chocolate, my body committed a crime. I stole his bite. The forkful of smooth, creamy dessert almost melted on my tongue.

I moaned.

He peeked.

I smiled, because I was caught.

I only had one option. Kiss him with it still in my mouth.

I lunged up to his mouth and paused right before our lips made contact. This wasn't some normal cheesecake, this was crack. After he got a taste, I was certain he'd do anything for more. It was going to be beautiful torture.

Our mouths collided. A low growl came from his chest and he steadied himself against my shoulders and pried our mouths apart.

"You're in deep shit," he said and licked his lips.

Then his tongue. Then his lips again.

I was lost. I couldn't even answer.

"I'm getting that cake, honeybee," he said as he took the bag, the cake and the fork from my hands and lap. He placed it on the bedside table. "I might even want both pieces now."

My shoulders shook as my chuckle tumbled out. "You've got a lot of work to do."

"Maybe even overtime," he added like the Devil.

"Maybe. You better get shakin'. I plan on having both of my cakes and eating them in front of you."

He ripped his shirt over his body and threw it across the room, not even caring enough to see that it landed on the wall sconce by the television.

My cheeks hurt from smiling.

He kicked off his shoes.

"You look good, by the way," he said as he undressed himself. Tossing socks and shoes anywhere they landed. His jeans came off and then he was just a man in boxers grinning ear to ear.

"Thanks, so do you."

"Are you ready for this?" he asked, but it sounded more like a warning. The smile from his mouth was gone—he had put his game face on—but it was still present in his eyes.

He sunk a knee into the top of the feather bed and like a lion teasing his prey he waited for the right moment. Then he took my body by storm, stripping me of every stich I wore.

A better woman than me could say she resisted, but I couldn't. I'm not that good of a woman. I gave my body to him. He kissed my legs and my stomach. He did things to me with his fingers that made the levity of the earlier moment transform into meditation. Every muscle I possessed flexed at one time or another, of their own free will, and at times I thought were odd.

His tongue slid up the center of me and he hungrily sucked at the most divine spot. He was merciless and voracious for me. It was then that the fibers of my lower back tensed and my spine arched, offering my breasts to the open air between me and the ceiling.

As he slid into me from behind—after rolling me over and then lifting me to my knees, his front against my back—he said my name. My hands balled and made fists with my fingers as I clutched his hair behind me.

My legs quaked. His hands wrapped around my waist and held me possessively as together we bent over. My face laid flat against the sheet. His breathing and mine synced to rhythm of our movements. Back and forth, push and pull, became the tide that the moon in my very being orbited.

He rolled me over and pulled me to the end of the tall mattress. Casey spread his legs so that our bodies could align at the right height. He moved my legs to his shoulders and began a measured pace.

He pulled the left side of his bottom lip into his mouth and then kissed my ankle, never taking his eyes off me.

"How do you feel this good?"

At first I assumed I'd only thought the words. It wasn't until he replied, "I have motivation. That's how," did I even know that I wasn't mute after all.

"Motivation?" I panted. He deepened the pressure upon every push inside my body. His hips ground, swirled, and then struck again. It drove me mad.

Then something changed in his eyes. It was like his lustful bones and muscles and tempered skin were in the driver's seat, but his head chose to take the bus.

Our eyes met and did the speaking for us. They said everything our mouths wouldn't.

He looked exquisite and torn.

"What are you thinking about?" I whispered, like it was a secret and I didn't want anyone else to hear.

"I'm thinking about how every second that I'm not buried inside you, I think about this. And then I think, here I am, and it's still not enough."

He bent forward and paired our lips, my legs falling to the sides of him. His hands swept under my head as he kissed me.

Our faces contorted. Not the erotic faces you'd want to see. But they were honest and didn't hide how they felt. I wished I were more like my orgasm face. It was the most honest of all my faces. Only with Casey though. Only with him.

We climaxed like that. Our releases finally caught up with us and rushed into our bodies as if it was but one crest and we shared it. My brow furrowed and my mouth fell open.

No sounds left our mouths.

No breaths took leave of our chests.

Everything stopped except a handful of pulsing muscles that met at the center of us.

It was neon darkness at zero decibels. Everything, and also just this one tiny, precious thing at the same time.

When both of our bodies gave up and the throb between us subsided, he inched his way up onto the bed and dragged me up with him. Then he collapsed on top of my chest.

I lay there and ran my fingers through his hair. It was sweaty in the back and it felt cool against my hot fingertips. As I breathed, a hum began in my throat that I neither agreed to nor protested.

It was the most peaceful moment.

He looked up at me and said, "I really want that cheesecake." He then took my relaxing nipple into his mouth, re-energizing the sensitive tip, and it tightened again with his new attention.

I didn't know where it came from, surely my actual self would have went for the cheesecake, but at the moment I wanted to indulge myself with him. *He* was my guilty pleasure. Cheesecake wasn't even on my radar.

I convinced him to take a shower with me. By convince, I mean, I got up walked into the bathroom and hooked my finger at him saying,

"We need to wash up before we eat."

While I washed my hair, he kissed my neck.

I looked for the evidence of his broken collarbone, and found a small knot still present where I'd seen it before. I washed his back with my bare hands. It was the cleanest back in history.

I couldn't stop touching him.

He washed between my legs and said, "God, I want to feel you bare. I don't want anything in between us." His unfiltered words again took me by surprise, but when he put it like that, I had to agree. In our situation, we could have tolerated a few less obstacles.

We christened the shower in the Hotel Max with as much enthusiasm as we had the bed minutes earlier.

"So, how about this Quadruple Chocolate cheesecake?" Casey asked.

I'd forgotten about the cheesecake.

"You deserve both pieces," I said with gratitude. "But I'll give you the bigger one instead."

We ate it on the bed wearing over-sized bath towels and watched Food Network. He told me about his sisters and the meetings he lined up for that Monday and Tuesday. He said he hadn't even rented a room yet and I told him that was good because he could have that one.

He still had a hang-up about sleeping together.

He walked me down to the front drive of the hotel when my cab came.

I told him we were even for the room because of the cheesecake and he laughed as he kissed me into the taxi.

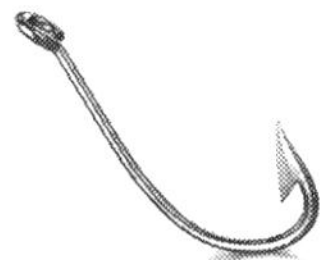

I spent the next day picking out plumbing fixtures with my mother as Grant tore the bathroom in the new house a part. Casey and I text back and forth all day. He told me that he actually went back to The Confectional and got more mini-cakes and that I was right about how good they were.

When my mother remarked on how much I was texting Grant and that he probably wasn't getting much done, I just laughed. An omission I supposed. When we got back to the house and after we measured a few windows for blinds, Grant called out to me and asked to grab his phone from the car. My mom didn't say anything, but I saw an expression cross her face that I didn't recognize before, then she went back to what she was doing.

I met Casey at a breakfast place by his hotel on Tuesday morning. He had a meeting and then an early afternoon flight.

We talked and laughed, like we always did.

He was charming and charismatic, like he always was.

He rubbed his foot against my ankle under table and *that* was new.

We made arrangements to meet up in cities when we could, which wouldn't be all that difficult. And when we could, we would attend the same events.

We met in Tucson a few weeks later, and Minneapolis the week after that. We shared leads and I found myself asking my customers about their beer selection and Casey recommended me to more than a few places he visited.

Those weeks flew by on the road. It was the days in between trips that seemed to drag on and on.

**Me: Why is wool so scratchy?**

**Casey: Is this a joke or are you really asking?**

**Me: Asking.**

**Casey: I don't know, it sucks. You know it's like sixty-five here today, so I wouldn't know. California is better than Washington.**

**Me: Wool isn't everything.**

**Casey: I have beer?**

**Me: You always have beer. I can't move.**

**Casey: Come on. You miss me.**

**Me: I miss your big cock.**

This was something new for us. It wasn't a few weeks after Casey was in Seattle before we tried to sext or have phone sex, as they say, I was really terrible at it though. He always sounded sexy and in character, where I was even more awkward that I was in real life.

**Casey: My cock only gets one adjective?**

**Me: I miss your cock. There. Better?**

**Casey: No. My massive, cunt-hungry, pussy-pleasing cock is offended.**

**Me: You are a sick man.**

**Casey: You'll get there. You just have to keep practicing. Now. You were saying... you miss my cock?**

I missed all of him, but that felt even dirtier to admit.

# TWENTY-TWO

## Casey

**Friday, November 14, 2008**

I HAVE TO ADMIT, honeybee is terrible at sending dirty messages. The other day I asked her for a dirty picture and she send me a picture of her upper thigh. Her thigh.

It's a great thigh, but come on. What did she expect?

I replied with my elbow. I may have overreacted.

She knew her proclivity for being verbal wasn't the best. Especially in a fabricated situation like being on the phone. It was so weird, because in person, she was a siren. She said the right things, her body moved like a diamond stylus needle on vintage vinyl, flawlessly teasing me. Her needy voice was seductive and her scent could drive me mad. Her taste? God, I could go on forever.

But her dirty phone talk was funny. Maybe it was the frustration I could hear in it, whereas when we were in person, I didn't allow her to get that worked up. I couldn't. I wanted her just as bad, probably more, than she wanted me.

"Are you touching yourself?" I asked the night before the night before Christmas. The holidays were shaping up to be shitty. There wasn't very many shows planned then. When most people just wanted to spend time with their families, I wanted her to be with me.

That's what I told myself, I that I wanted her away from her family and to be somewhere with me. Deep down, I knew that wasn't true at all. What I wanted was to be sharing those holidays together with *our* families.

Maybe we would have spent Thanksgiving here and she could have met my mom, Dad and Carmen, and the girls. We'd have Thanksgiving dinner with my mom and Cory, and Micah now, too, since they were expecting.

My mom would want her to cook, fearing that her dinner wouldn't be worthy in front of a trained chef. Blake would gush over the food. My mom was a great cook and Blake loves food. She was probably one of the least picky eaters I'd ever met.

Then we'd go to my Dad's and play games with the girls and eat crappy pie that they'd made themselves. Special for the holiday. The girls would love Blake and ask all sorts of questions. Carmen would pretend to be cool like her for my father's sake.

My dad would probably be more in love with Blake than I was.

She'd play cards with us. Probably drink too much, but still win every hand. She had those kinds of powers. Her ability to will things her way potent. I was no stronger than a deck of cards.

In my fantasy, that really wasn't a fantasy at all, we'd spend Christmas with her family up north. I'd try my damnedest to make her Dad and older brother like me. I'd bring them all cases of beer, which was the key to making friends—if Bay's profit margin had anything to say about it.

I'd court her mother every chance I'd got. I'd compliment her telling her that she should be proud of such an independent daughter. I'd tell her that she'd get along with my mother, and pray that they would.

Reggie and I would talk about travel and cars. I'd ask to take his car for a ride the next time I was in Chicago. He'd surprise me and say yeah.

We'd watch movies and fall asleep early.

In this alternate universe, I'd sleep on the couch to solidify my respect for her dad and their home. Of course, as soon as I was certain they were asleep, I'd sneak up to her room and find her in the hall sneaking down to me.

We'd kiss in the light of a snowman nightlight and the twinkle of their Christmas tree. She'd walk me back down to the basement and we'd try our damnedest at being quiet. And we'd fail.

She'd go back upstairs after telling me that that Christmas had been her favorite.

These were the kinds of perverted thoughts I had. Not just ones of her spread eagle and touching herself for me, like I asked her to do on the phone that night before the Christmas Eve that wasn't our first.

She'd do everything I'd asked.

She'd push a finger into herself under my direction and I'd watch her beautiful hip raise to meet it. The look in her eyes begging me to do it myself.

*Okay. Maybe I thought about that shit, too.*

I guess that's how those dirty phone calls started.

That's right. It *was* usually me starting the explicit dialog. Just like that night.

After she'd told me she was, in fact, touching herself, I gave her things to do that I was positive she liked. I told her exactly how to do them and listened to her breathing. We both knew she wasn't the best at the dialog part. She said, "Keep talking to me. I'm so close."

Listening to her labored inhales and exhales, I stroked myself and told her all of the ways I wished my hands were taking care of her.

When she'd said, "Ahhh, yes," I knew she was finding her release and mine was on the way. My eyes shut tight and I pulled a long breath, through my teeth, as my hand squeezed my cock. The sensation of cool air over my teeth sent a shiver down my spine and propelled my orgasm into present tense.

"Did you just come?" She lightly laughed on the other end, having listened to my release as hers subsided.

"Yeah," I laughed, too. "Is there a problem with that?"

"No. I'm surprised, is all. I didn't really say much." Her tone was half shy, half sorry.

"It doesn't take much, honeybee." I laughed. "You did plenty. Trust me."

We talked a little longer than normal. Neither of us had to work the next day, but we'd be spending time with our families for the next few days and wouldn't have many opportunities to connect.

"Okay, I'm falling asleep," she growled through another yawn.

Even over the phone, hearing her yawn made me do the same.

"Good night. I'll talk to you soon. Okay?" My eyes were heavy, too.

"I wish things were different," she said. I heard the sleepiness in her voice and wondered if she was completely lucid, or if she was half-way awake and half-way asleep.

Did she want me to offer her an alternative? Was that what she wanted? Did she still see me as the fuck-and-run guy, only worthy a good time in bed? I wanted more with her, but did she want more from me? Maybe she didn't think I was capable of that?

What the fuck was she thinking when she said she wishes *things* were different?

I should have asked her which *things*, but I didn't.

"I do, too. Let's work on that."

"I'm going to marry him and—" she whispered and then her voice trailed off.

"Don't," I said, and then I pressed the end button. I wanted to talk to her more, since it was one of the few times we actually talked about what was happening. But then I didn't want to hear what else she was going to say. I wasn't ready for her to say no. I wasn't ready for her to tell me that this wasn't going to pan out. That I was going to be the one left hanging.

But reality told me I was.

She was going to marry him. I had to figure out how to change that.

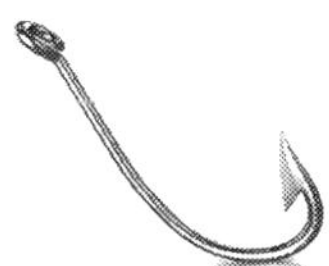

Christmas went by fast, and then it was 2009.

Troy didn't have much of a family, so he spent the holidays with us. Since Micah's family lived so far away, she was there, too.

New Year's Day found all four of us lounging around my apartment, watching movies and eating ourselves sick. Micah made every appetizer known to man, even though she could barely eat any of them, having a rather nasty case of morning sickness that seemed to last and last. Her doctor said it should phase itself out, and even though she didn't complain, we could all tell she hadn't felt that great.

"I fucking love these mushroom things, Micah. I think I've ate twenty of them."

"That's funny. They're Bla—" Then she cut herself off. "Everyone loves them." It was no mystery that she and Blake talked often. I'd witnessed it on both ends. Blake and I were together when Micah had called her excited about the first time she felt the baby kick.

When my brother called me on the other line about five minutes later, I left the room to hear the same news. Although baby Moore was a surprise, they both seemed very pleased and thrilled about it. It was interesting that neither of them felt rushed to get married because of it, though. Agreeing that the baby and the marriage, if there were to be one, would be totally separate—not a cause and effect type of thing.

"It's okay. You don't have to pretend like she doesn't exist. Not for my benefit anyway," I stated. It wasn't as if I called Cory or Troy about what was going on with Blake and me, but when she came up, I talked about it. I never went into a lot of detail, probably because I didn't think Blake would feel comfortable with it, but I didn't have anything to hide.

Micah sat up a little straighter on the couch and leaned into the crook of Cory's arm, pausing the movie. That wasn't a good sign. Yeah, I didn't mind talking about it, but that was totally different than being interrogated about it and that's exactly what it looked like was happening.

"All right, then tell me. What's going on with you two?" she asked. There wasn't any accusation in her voice, evidence of her neutrality.

I wasn't sure what Blake had said, if anything, but I didn't want to pretend like it was nothing either. Unsure of what to say, I replied to her question with one of my own.

"You talk to Blake, if you want to know what's going on you can ask *her*."

Then my curiosity piqued. I tried to play off my interest by popping another heavenly stuffed mushroom into my mouth and talking despite it being full. I asked, "What does she say?"

Micah and Cory shared a knowing look between them and then Cory looked to Troy. It seemed that maybe they'd all had this conversation. Only it was the first time they'd had it with me.

"What?" I asked looking at all of them in sequence. None of them looked like they wanted to go first. "Jesus, what? If you have something to say, then say it. Or ask. Shit. Someone say something."

"What are you *really* doing, Casey?" My brother spoke up. Trying not to rattle my cage, his voice was moderately toned. He was using caution. He straightened and leaned forward and steepled his hands in front of himself. "What do you guys have going on?"

I took a few calming breaths, suddenly feeling defensive, and finished the last mushroom on my small plate. I remember thinking that I wished I'd had a few more to buy myself more time.

"Listen, Blake and I are friends," I said, *hating* that I used the one word that made me cringe when it came from her mouth. "I don't know why you guys are making such a big deal out of it."

"Bullshit," Troy said under his breath, but intentionally loud enough for all of us to hear it.

"Bullshit? What the hell? You don't know what you're talking about."

I hated that I was denying anything more than friendship and I felt my pulse beginning to quicken. I was frustrated with them, but I was downright livid with myself more for making light of what I really felt.

Troy interjected, "Then why are you getting all shitty about it, dude? I was in Atlanta. I'm not stupid. If that was you two being friends, then I'm doing it all wrong." He was being a dick. Someone needed to show him how a real friend would act in that very situation. Show him that friends didn't like it when their private business was being judged.

My brother butted in, "Casey, I've seen you on the phone with her, or when you get a text, we're not blind. Tell us what's going on so that we get it." Micah leaned in toward me, too. It felt like a confess-your-sins kind of conversation.

"What? We talk, we message each other…"

"You hook up in different cities on business trips," Troy spouted.

My head snapped and I stood, feeling like I needed to get at least a leg up on the scene playing out, but when I stood up I still didn't have it in me to totally lie about it.

"So?" I looked to the couch at my brother and Micah, and they waited patiently for me to go on. I saw concern on both of their faces, which mollified my growing anxiety. "So we meet up," I said to them. "We see each other out on the road sometimes. It gets lonely out there and we get along."

Troy, the prick, coughed. "So you're just fucking?" he asked.

I turned my speech to him. He looked evil with the red filter through which I was seeing him.

"No were not *just* fucking! If it's any of your business, we talk almost every day. Does that sound like *just* fucking? We talk about how our days went. We eat. We drink. We talk about you guys. We make fun of each other. We fight. And, yes, sometimes we fuck. And it's awesome. But it's not *just* fucking, you asshole."

"Okay, great," Cory added. "Then you like her. Great. But there's one little problem with that. She's engaged." He looked to Micah for support. The nod of her head was permission enough for him to continue. "Where's that going to leave you in May when she gets married? I mean seriously, have you two talked about that? What then? You call it off?" He leaned back again and I sat back down in the recliner.

"I don't know."

"I know she cares about you," Micah said. "She does. But then when I ask her about the wedding she acts like everything is normal. Like she's just planning a wedding. I think she's really going to marry him, Casey." She sounded apprehensive and like she was as worried for Blake's sake as mine.

Hearing Micah say that Blake was going to marry *him* made me glad I'd stopped at twenty mushrooms. My stomach churned. She was going to marry him. Something I'd known was a fact, yet somehow never actually thought would happen. I supposed in a way, I'd told myself it was impossible.

Micah might as well have said that they'd found Hoffa's body. That he'd been beaten and murdered and brought up from the bottom of some river somewhere. Something everyone knew, but never actually expected would come to pass.

She said quietly, "We're worried about you."

Worried about *me*? Feeling the room shift, I looked to Troy. His head was down, focused on the Mountain Bike magazine in front of him on the coffee table, but he nodded that he'd agreed with what Micah had said. So did my brother's expression.

“Thanks, but no thanks,” I said. “I love you guys, but I can take care of this. I’m fine. Maybe you were right and we *are* just fucking. If she gets married, then she gets married. I’m cool. Okay?” I said in triplicate making eye contact with them each individually.

“Okay,” they repeated back punctuating our conversation as finished.

I lied to them, but the truth hurt worse.

The reality of it hit like brass knuckles against my skull. Except it wasn’t brass knuckles, it was the truth. And it wasn’t my skull it pulverized. It was my stupid heart.

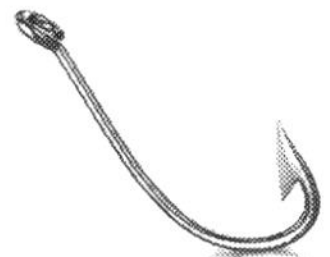

January’s known for being cold, and although I didn’t feel cold toward Blake outwardly, the mercury inside me dropped in general. I was irritable. We hadn’t seen each other since before Christmas and it made me antsy.

Every time I tried to arrange something for us, she was busy.

What Micah said started to peck away at me. So did what Troy had.

*She is going to marry him.*

*You’re just fucking.*

Even though I didn’t believe either of them, I couldn’t hide from the reality that it was anyone’s game.

I went on a trip at the end of January to Lake Tahoe and it sucked.

I fucking missed her.

The meeting went well with the resort, they had actually been the ones to request it, and I sealed the deal on Friday night. With two days left in the cabin, I did *a lot* of thinking. A lot of coffee. A lot of Baileys and a lot of trying to figure out what the actual fuck was I going to do if she got married.

**Honeybee: How’s Tahoe. Touristville?**

**Me: I won’t know. I haven’t left this hot tub in two days.**

**Honeybee: Sounds awful. You probably look like a California Raisin.**

I was peacefully intoxicated and feeling bold upon receiving her upbeat text. She was right as rain and I was wallowing like a fool.

The clock read ten thirty. We were still in the same time zone.

**Me: So Grant went home then?**

The Baileys in me was a curious bastard.

**Honeybee: No. And what's that supposed to mean?**

**Me: It doesn't mean anything. You text so I guess he left. You probably wore him out. You're good at that.**

I should have deleted it, but I should have done a lot of things that I didn't. And way too fucking many things that I did.

**Honeybee: Someone's drunk.**

That's *my* Blake, fiery and fierce.

**Me: Yeah I'm drunk. We're both doing things were good at.**

**Honeybee: I think I'll just talk to you tomorrow.**

**Me: No you won't. We'll speak tomorrow probably. But we never say anything.**

**Honeybee: What do you want me to say? I feel like saying goodnight.**

**Me: Fine. Goodnight.**

But she wouldn't let it end there. She hated giving me the last word.

**Honeybee: Why don't you drop the attitude? You're being mean.**

**Me: Sorry. What persona would you like, Betty?**

**Me: Angry likes to fuck hard? Or maybe it's easy-going, don't-give-a-fuck about anything? Take your pick.**

**Me: Well.**

**Me: Tell me. I'll be that one. Just. Tell. Me.**

She didn't answer for a long time. I put my phone down feeling like I'd really pissed her off this time. She probably wouldn't call the next day, probably not for a few days now. The exact opposite of what I'd wanted.

I dipped down below the water and screamed into the humming of the jets.

When I came back up I heard the sound of it ringing, but I slipped reaching for the towel and it went to voicemail. Almost immediately I heard the chime of a new recording.

It was Blake.

"Hey, it's me." I heard a dog park in the background and knew she was outside her apartment, I'd heard the same dog bark his ass off many times. "Listen, I didn't want to fight with you tonight." She paused and I looked at my phone to make sure that wasn't the end of the message.

Finally she started talking again.

"I'm sorry. And you're right. I'm not being fair. I want to meet up with you. Email me your next few weeks." She sighed heavily. "I miss you. I hope you're all right. Take some ibuprofen and drink some water. Call me tomorrow if you want. 'Bye."

Damn right she wasn't being fair. Fair would be breaking it off with that guy she likes to cheat on and giving this damn thing with me a real shot.

# TWENTY-THREE

## Blake

**Saturday, February 14, 2009**

THE WEEKEND WASN'T GOING to make anything better, but I had to give it a shot.

I was shaking. Running the razor up my soapy leg. I'd been nervous all day.

It had to be the last time, but I wanted to make it count. I knew how twisted that was. Finish on top, as they say. After tonight I'd go back to being the adoring fiancée.

I'd be faithful.

And if that was my last night with Casey, I'd need to make it count. I wanted to remember every second.

After my legs were smooth and everything else was in order. I put my face under the hot stream of water coming from the showerhead. I thought about the shower we took in Seattle. About how his hands roamed my body and touched me everywhere a man could touch a woman. My hand ran down to my core, feeling my trimmed hair.

*God I want to feel you bare. I don't want anything in between us.*

His words echoed through my mind and I reached for the soap and the razor. I'd gone down to naked skin before, but it was a very, very long time ago. I thought it was probably in college.

I took my time, doing a thorough job. When I was finished my skin felt new and sensitive. Like the hair had been hiding me from wondrous sensations. I ran my fingers over myself and anticipated Casey's doing the same.

After I had dried myself and applied his favorite-smelling lotion, I blow dried my hair, then stained my cheeks and lips and darkened my eyes and lashes.

I pulled a black garter up each leg. I wasn't going to be wearing much, but I wanted to enjoy him taking his time removing them. I pulled the black, thigh-high stocking up my calves and fastened them to the garters with the clips that hung from ice-blue bows. I slipped my legs through the black silk underwear and prepared myself for the icing on the cake. The set that I'd ordered, and was currently dressing in, came with a corset.

It was black with ice-blue ribbons matching the bows on the garters and panties. It laced up the front. I'd looked at the ones that laced from behind, but they looked like a nightmare. I'd already have a struggle getting into one I could watch myself lace.

When the last hook and eye was latched, I straightened it and pulled. Instantly my chest looked bigger, fuller and heaved from the already very low-cut fabric that held my breasts. I ran my hands up the sides, feeling the rigid and straight boning, and yet I felt so comfortable and held together.

I pulled on the blue silk robe that completed the ensemble and went out into the main room to find the shoes and start a fire. I plugged my phone into the suite's speakers and got out the champagne, putting it on ice in a bucket on the coffee table in the main room. I brought a plate of cheese and fruit to the table and then I went back to the kitchenette for the last piece.

The courage. The kind from a bottle. I had ordered a small decanter and placed it on the table as well. I was going to need a few shots if I ever had a prayer of pulling this off. Seduction wasn't my forte. But he deserved it.

I usually felt so awkward and clumsy during sex. Well. Not with Casey.

With him I felt worshiped and desired. He acted like he craved me in the way he moaned from kissing my neck sometimes. It made me feel special. Made me feel sexy and wanton.

I arranged the extra pillows and blankets, that I'd ordered up, and they looked so inviting there on the floor in the center of the room.

I'd given it some thought on my plane ride here this morning. I wanted the night to be unforgettable. It was already unforgivable.

I downed two shots. Back to back. The cognac tasted sweet and bold. The taste lingered on my tongue.

I left the robe on. I wanted him to open me like an expensive gift. I wanted to watch his eyes up close when he saw what I was hiding underneath.

I'd told him to be there at eight and it was five to when he knocked. I'd left him a key—as was customary for us at hotels then—knowing he would use it if I didn't answer.

I rose to my feet, with an extra four inches added from the Brian Atwood heels which Reggie bought me for Christmas. How was I to know they'd come in so handy when I'd sent him a joking picture in a text message version of a fairy-tale princess's Christmas list?

As I stood there preparing myself, my heartbeat didn't exactly feel fast; it just felt strong. A powerful pulsing that reverberated throughout my whole body.

The door handle clicked.

I'd turned the lights out, only a few recessed lights over the bar area and the fireplace remained lighting the room. It was tastefully amber and dim. The backlighting behind his body from the bright hallway, when he opened the door, gave me a chill.

He wore a perfectly tailored suit and looked so masculine in profile. It fit to his tight body in magical ways. His hair was tamed back with that miracle product he used to make it look controlled, and in the light, I could see the front was beginning its rebellion, loosening and falling forward more than it should.

He looked like a king. King Casey.

He closed the door gently and pocketed his hand into his slacks making the fabric taught over his already visible bulge.

I licked my lips.

I wanted another shot, but I didn't dare move.

His blue eyes glittered from the lick of the flames behind me.

The song changed. I recognized it within the first few chords. The single guitar. The arpeggio. *Slow Dancing in a Burning Room.*

I swallowed. Eyeing him standing there, looking at me, the beautiful confusion of it all made my mouth water.

His eyes wandered over me like a search light, both warning and guiding my body home.

He walked toward me and I started forward to meet him halfway, but he held a hand up and stopped where he was when we were still feet apart.

"You look like my wildest dream." His perfect hand still hung in the air. "Let me look you at you little more. This memory has to last me long time, honeybee." He pandered his time. I watched him examine every detail of me. I thought I'd feel self-conscious, but the opposite happened.

I was proud, and having him take the time to look at every one of the things I'd done to get his attention felt so gratifying. I had prayed that at least one would capture his interest.

The corners of his lips quirked when his eyes shifted focus down toward my garter clips. He faked coolness by biting his bottom lip, but he didn't fool me.

Finally, he said, "Come here."

My right leg, my left leg and I, we all went to him together. My entire body working on its own. It was so easy.

"Wait, one more thing," he interjected. Then did the international sign for spin-it-a-around, his smile bleeding through every feature on his face. His eyes looked like neon in the darkness.

I did a slow twirl, looking over my shoulder on my way back around. I batted my eyes to get a reaction.

"You look like the definition of temptation." His eyes squinted and he pantomimed a come-here head nod. God, his claws were sunk so deep into me. If I looked like temptation, he looked precisely capable of charming-the-pants-off the Queen of England.

With my shoes, the height brought my eyes to his lips, my favorite latitude on planet Earth.

He ran a hand over my hair and pushed it behind my shoulder. "I can almost taste you, you smell that good," he said, hushed. "You did all of this for me?"

"I did." I was fixated on his mouth. I wanted to put my lips on him. I wanted to touch and undress him, but this was his show and I was only too happy letting him run it. The energy coming off him was palpable.

"Do you know how hard I am? I don't know if you considered my lack of restraint when it comes to you this close to me." His hands grazed way down my arms. "What is all of this?"

"I wanted to do something for you." I looked up at him through my lashes. "I want to make you happy. I want to be your Valentine." I took a deep breath, the anticipation of his body hot against mine at the forefront of my thoughts. "Open me."

Ten fingers rushed my face and his lips crushed mine. Then he lifted me into the air. Eye to eye. Mouth to mouth. His arms wrapped around me and held me close. Mine went straight into his hair, my fingers spreading to get a grip on my unavoidable man.

"You taste like the night we met," I heard him say.

He walked us farther into the room, me in his arms, our mouths tasting one another, his tongue circling mine to a beat unheard before.

I let my head fall to his neck and I opened my mouth to wet him with kisses, inhaling his scent—earthy and masculine and something sweet and only him.

The music changed again, but at that time, I couldn't tell you what the song was.

When my feet touched the floor again, his hands were urgent. He undid the bow where my robe tied in the front and he pushed the silk off my shoulders. The fabric easily slid off me.

The look in his eyes was feral. "Look at you. You're trying to kill me, aren't you?" He teased as his hands found my breasts and cupped me. Like he couldn't decide what he wanted to touch, he roamed me. Over the tight trussed-up corset, around to my ass, and back in quick succession.

"I've missed you. I know I'm not good to you and I'm sorry," I said, not knowing where the words were coming from.

With a finger over my mouth he said, "Shhh. I'm a big boy. I can handle it."

He was right. He did handle it, but what I didn't know was how. I could barely manage.

He continued, "You're *my* Valentine. Tonight you're mine. Understand me? Even your thoughts." He caressed my cheek. "Don't think about anything but me. That's what I want. I'm going to take everything you're wearing off. I'm going to touch every inch of you with my mouth. And I'm not going to pretend this is just a fling tonight, like I've done every time. For one night, I want you to pretend like it's me you're promised to," his thumbs ran over my lips, "Mine to care for and adore. Say yes to *me*. Even if it is only for tonight. Please?"

His words came honest. I knew he didn't always say what he felt, because of me. Because I fought my feelings hard and so, battled his as well.

I'd said the most honest sentence I had, "Then I'm yours." And with all my damned heart, I wished the words were true. He had never offered me more, and I didn't think he ever would.

He took his time unwrapping me. I luxuriated in the feeling of his hands on me and my body followed his gentle direction. When the corset was gone and I stood there in my panties, my hands began wandering him. I couldn't help want to touch his body the way he had been mine.

My nimble fingers undid the button on his coat and he shrugged out of it. My hands untucked his pressed dress shirt and began the climb of buttons separating him from me. I pulled it open and found him, like always, well defined and muscular. His stomach cut with lean muscles that flexed under my hands. His chest strong and firm. The long ridge of his collarbone, my favorite meal.

I didn't bother with removing his shirt. Having even the slightest access to him was enough for me.

In my panties, stockings, and shoes I bent down to my knees with one thing in mind. I wanted to taste, to touch, and to have all of him. To please *only* him.

I kissed along the top edge of his dress pants, undoing his belt, and pulling it through its loops. Then, I tossed it away. The zipper went the way zippers do in these situations, and to my wonderful surprise, he wasn't wearing anything underneath. I smiled at my discovery. It looked like he had finally made a decision about his undergarments.

My mouth continued to water.

His skin, too, was bare. But unknown to him, so was I.

My fingers circled underneath his length and pulled him out. I ran both of my hands under his pants to his ass and pulled them down farther to expose his scrotum, taught and collected tightly against him. Everything about him was beautiful.

I took him into my mouth and felt him flex inside me, growing even fuller. The taste of him was so intoxicating. His skin was like catnip and the more I had of it the more I needed. I looked up at him to see him watching me in wonder, his jaw ticking and every glorious muscle from my face to his was in full view.

I moaned around his cock, the sight of him like this stealing the remnant of every wayward thought from my head. It was only him and me. This night *was* for us.

I moved to a slow beat, enjoying every twitch, every breath he took while I pleasured him. He stood anchored in his spot. He brushed my hair back away from me, threaded his fingers through it, and pushed himself deep inside me before he pulled out of me and urgently pulled me up his decadent body. He kissed me, still holding my head in his hands with my hair. It was rough and his chest rose and fell in time with mine.

"Go lay down over there, Blake. I want to play with my Valentines' gift." A shiver ran through me. He released my hair and I backed up without looking at where I was going. My body on autopilot, I did what I was told.

I felt brazen and daring. I felt like I was living a fantasy. I leaned back on my elbows and drew my legs up then parted them like I'd dreamt of doing so many nights on the phone.

He came to crouch next to me and took stock of the table's offerings.

"May I have a drink, honeybee? Good choice with the cognac. If I didn't know better, I'd say you were sentimental." His voice was rich with sensuality, but his eyes were alight with happiness. He was going to play with me. I was his toy tonight. *His* toy.

He fixed himself a drink. Two pieces of ice clanked in the glass, then two fingers of the sweet liquor followed. He brought the short glass to his lips and hummed his pleasure at the taste.

I was on fire and the anticipation of him touching me was thrumming through my veins.

His shirt was open and his pants, although still undone in the front were pulled back up.

The runaway lock of hair, which had broken formation from the rest, was gathering company from us running our hands through it.

While I'd been studying him, I hadn't paid attention to my wandering hand that was now rubbing my breast. My mouth was open and I was nearly panting.

After he drank down half of the glass, he touched my leg at the knee and leisurely ran his fingers up the skin to my thigh. His barely there touch wasn't enough.

I wanted more. I needed more.

I spread my legs farther for him and unabashedly ran my hand to my sex. I rubbed myself over my panties trying to satisfy a need that was blazing deep inside me. His eyes watched me touch myself and I saw that his desire matched mine. The usually cool and easy-going Casey, was again gone, and in his place was the take-control lover I dreamed about nearly every night.

On his knees he climbed closer to me, between my legs, and his hand met mine.

"I want you, Casey."

He replied, with a firm demanding voice, "Say it again."

"I want *you*."

Maybe it was the ambiance and romantic mood of the room. Maybe I felt so free because it was, decidedly, my last time with him.

That singular thought made me panic and I had to remind myself why. I had to recite in my head, *Because you're marrying another man. Because Casey only likes chasing you. Because he doesn't want the same things you do. He doesn't want a family. He doesn't want a home. He likes traveling and being carefree.*

And it was those exact things that made me believe I had to leave him and made my heart retch to let him go. Because he would never offer me anything different and I could no longer live with the desperate yearning I had for him, that was entwined with my deeper desires for home, future, and stability.

Then he caught me and halted the runaway train that was my thoughts.

"I told you, honeybee. No thinking like that."

Had I said all that out loud? Or was it possible my thoughts were loud enough to hear.

Still, even though my mind was playing chess with itself, my body and heart never strayed. They belonged to him.

"Then kiss me. Distract me."

He reached for the table and his glass, emptying it in his mouth and I watched as he downed every last drop, including the ice. Returning the empty glass to the table, his eyes found mine and I saw a hint of mischief.

He dipped his head to my neck. The sensation was hot, but I could feel the coolness of the ice at the same time. He kissed my chest and when he took my nipple into his mouth the ice across my warm flesh sent a rush of need straight through me. I bucked my hips trying to find the pressure and friction I craved, but he backed away and down my body, taking his ice with him.

When he got to the elastic at the top of my panties he stopped and looked up at me.

"You're so beautiful, Blake. Your body was made for me." He kissed above the little blue bow on my panties. He said, low and sultry, "Your smell haunts me." He dipped his head lower and breathed me in, his eyes flickering as he inhaled. "I crave the taste of you, like a man starved."

Sitting up a little, he grasped both sides of the thin string that circled my hips on both sides of the expensive lingerie bottoms.

Then they were gone.

He caressed me with his stare. His eyes took in my bared flesh and he prayed, "Mercy."

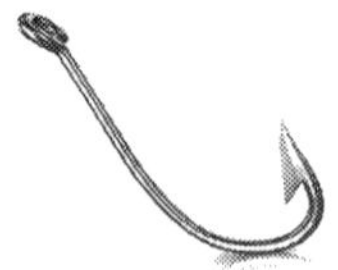

We laughed and had sex and then laughed some more. We stayed up longer than the moon and watched the sun rise over Aspen out of my terrace door. He stayed curled up and the blankets.

When I got up to re-fill my glass he said, "Sensuous."

I looked at him perplexed. It was a strange time for a complement.

"Excuse me?" I retorted.

"Since-you-was-up, get me one too." Then he handed me his glass. "And more ice, please."

We drank all thc cognac, ate all the food.

We were tired, but because we hadn't gone to bed, Casey stayed with me.

Whenever I'd start to fall asleep he'd remind my body what it wanted more.

Him.

I had to fly out that afternoon and since all of my hopes and prayers were denied, and feet upon feet of snow didn't fall over night, making my voyage home safe and undelayed, I'd have to just come out with it and let him go.

I looked at my nails, they'd been bigger messes than that, and I willed myself not to bite them. I didn't want to show him any of my trepidation. If I was going to end this, I had to seem sure.

I allowed myself more minutes, chickening out every time I began to speak.

My back against his chest, his back against the bed. Both of us still on the floor.

"We had a good time, didn't we?" I said as so many memories flashed through my mind.

He jostled me and held me tighter, readjusting his hands around my stomach.

"Don't," he said and kissed my hair. My heart agreed with him. It didn't want this to end either.

"I have to. I'm getting married," I said, my voice small, but I thankfully I still sounded resolute despite the sharp pain I felt in my chest.

"Why? Don't marry him." His mouth met my head again, but he didn't kiss me. He simply put his lips there.

"I have to Casey. This isn't right."

He shifted and I steeled myself; it wasn't going to end well. I'd known for months that this was coming. Those months went so fast. I'd give anything to have a few more. To relive all of them again.

"What's not right about it? Name one thing," he argued.

"It's not real. This isn't real life." I scrambled off his lap, pulling one of the covers with me and facing him. I felt exposed and my feelings for him burned me from the inside out.

His head fell back onto the bed and I watched his pulse thump through the flesh on his exposed neck.

"How did this get so out of hand, honeybee? It isn't real because you won't let it be. Why? Is it because I don't have money? Because I hate to break it to you, but I'm doing just fine. You want a house? I'll get you a house. What else? What else!?" He looked up and shook his hands at me. Then stood, not bothering to cover himself up.

"You know that's not what this is about."

"No, I don't. I don't know shit about what this is about. You never tell me. I'm always guessing and I'm tired of it. Tell me how I get you."

I wished I knew. If there was some magic time eraser I would have waved it around and taken me back to school in San Francisco, before I'd met Grant.

I'd meet Casey first instead and I'd love him the way he deserved. Entirely. Without conditions. And I wouldn't feel so sad to see him so sad, because he wouldn't have to be.

"You won't get me, Casey. Besides, you can do better than this. Look at us. All we do is fight." He could do better, but I didn't ever want to know about it. I planned on making a clean break.

It was better that way. Better for him. I wouldn't be stringing him along. And I wouldn't be cheating on my fiancé who, also could do better than me. It was all I could do to make it right.

The tiny piece of my heart that *was* noble, the same sliver stamped with Casey's name, reminded the rest of me it wasn't any way to treat either of them.

He said, "Maybe I like fighting with you. Ever think of that? Maybe I like doing everything with you."

He pulled his pants on and found his shirt. Then, after a minute to reflect, he turned to me. "You know you're right. This isn't fair. But you're wrong though, too. I do *get* you. I have all of the parts he doesn't want or give a shit about. And if you can't see *that*, then fuck it. Fuck all of it!" he shouted.

I was glad I didn't wait any longer than I already had. I was going to be a mess when he left. I'd need some time before I had to board a plane and away from him for probably the last time. I could already feel pieces of me pulling apart and dying.

I stayed where I was on the floor while he got ready to go. He surprised me and came to me before he left. Leaning over, that beautiful man kissed my forehead.

"If you really want to marry him, then don't call me anymore, honeybee. If this is what you want, then so be it. For the record, I know it's a big fucking mistake. You're going to realize it, too. One day. Don't fucking call me then, either."

I clenched my teeth to keep from screaming that I'd changed my mind. Which was a lie because I never really wanted to do this in the first place.

"You never offered me an alternative," I whispered.

His lips pursed one more time against my skin, and paused as if savoring me.

My eyes shut tight. I only had to hold onto my emotions for a little while longer. I'd made it that far without breaking down.

I watched him walk out the door.

Sobs retched out of me the second I knew he was really gone. I would hear the slam of that door for the rest of my life.

So many times I'd prayed he would choose to stay.

# TWENTY-FOUR

## Casey

**Sunday, April 26, 2009**

I SLAMMED THE DOOR on her, again, when I should have stayed and fought. I should have fought harder for her, for me, for us. But she wasn't on our side.

*She wasn't on our side.*

There was no use.

That winter seemed to take forever and I stayed gone a lot. I was working, building our brand, and I was doing well professionally.

Personally, I was sucking big-time.

It was easy to avoid people when you were out of town five days out of seven. I talked to my family on the phone regularly, but I hadn't seen them much since the holidays.

But it was finally April, and I was hoping that with spring shit would start clicking again, because for the last two months it seemed like nothing had.

I didn't go around Micah or Cory much, they were laying kind a low too, but they had a much cooler reason. They were preparing for parenthood. My mom had told me that she went with them to get strollers and baby things a few weeks back and that Cory was a nervous wreck. She made fun of him and said that our dad had been the same way.

"You'll make a good daddy, too, one of these days. I hope I get to see it, baby-boy." She laughed on the other end of the line, again poking fun at me for not having a steady girlfriend. Even though, I knew she knew something, because after Micah's baby shower—an event I made sure to be out of the state for—she told me that Micah's best friend had chatted her ear off and that she was a pretty girl. Then, she'd said, "Oh, Casey," which was mom-speak for *what did you do?*

I didn't tell her. Not then. I didn't talk to anyone about it. No one would say what I wanted to hear and no one would want to hear what I had to say. So I saved us all a big fucking headache and kept my mouth shut.

That April morning, I'd picked my suitcase up off the luggage carousel and started for the front of the airport. I'd been gone for days and all I really wanted was a hot shower and my bed. That was the last time I was taking a red-eye on a Saturday night.

I hadn't slept well on the plane. I thought about Blake and wondered where she had been traveling. Or if she had at all. I wasn't allowing myself to check up on her through their website anymore. It wasn't a sane thing to do. Even I could see that.

How did she get me so worked up? And why in the hell did I keep chasing her? She'd told me—I don't know how many times and in about twice as many ways—that she wouldn't leave him. I'd only wished I fucking knew why.

I powered up my phone and the damn thing went crazy. It was nine thirty on a Sunday morning. All of the missed calls were from Micah. All of the texts were from her, too.

Terror rose in me. That many calls from Micah was wrong, and the fact that my family hadn't tried to reach me led me to believe it was something to do with Blake.

Before I could let my imagination wander too far, my phone rang in my hand. It was Micah.

I answered like there was nothing wrong, I thought that maybe if I believed it hard enough it would be true, "Good morning, Micah."

"Like hell it is! Oooo... Can you find your brother for me? Where are you? Are you in town? Oooo... Hold on." She pulled the phone away from her mouth and swore like I'd never heard her before. She had a mouth on her.

"Hey, Mic. Are you all right? I don't know where Cory is. I just got off a plane. What's going on?"

As I stepped up to the curb, a cab pulled right up in front of me. I didn't bother with putting my things in the trunk, tossing them inside and shutting the door.

"Um... I think I'm fine. Oooo..." She was sort of panting and moaning. I wasn't a fool.

She was in labor.

"Hey, where are you. Where's Cory?" My mind tried to figure out why she'd be calling me.

"I don't know where the hell he is. That's why I'm... Oooo... calling you. Oooo... Oooo... Can you find him for me? Ahhh... please, Casey." She started to cry, I could tell she was panicking and in a lot of pain.

"Hey, I'm not far. I'm going to pick you up and we'll go to the hospital. I'll find him."

"Oooo... okay. Hurry." She huffed and hung up.

"Hey, can you get me to 595 Holley Avenue, just South of San Bruno? Fast?" I told him and pulled a few twenties out of my wallet. It was very likely that he'd be driving us to the hospital and he was in for a hell of a trip. I wanted him to know I had money.

He had us there in no time, taking side streets to avoid the busier ones.

When I went inside I found Micah squatting in her kitchen.

"Oooo..." she breathed when she saw me. "Did you find him? Oooo... should I wait here for him?" Her cheeks were streaked with tears.

Where in the fuck was my brother?

"No I haven't found him yet, Momma. I called Dad and Troy. They're going to find him for us. Do you know where he was going?"

"A bike ride. He was going riding. Oooo... he's been acting funny. I think he was going to clear his... OOOOoooo... Oooo... head."

I helped her up and started us for the doors. She was waddling from side to side uncomfortably, moaning and wincing with every step.

"Wait. Casey, get my bag. It's on my bed."

"Okay, just stay right here." I moved her hands to the doorframe and said, "Hold onto this. I'll be right back."

I shot into their bedroom and on the way I saw all of their new furniture and it really hit me. My brother was about to be a dad.

I bet he *was* freaking out.

When I got back to her she had her head hung and her hips swayed back and forth, like she was rocking herself.

"Are you okay? Shit. You're not okay. You're in fucking labor! Let's get you to the hospital. Cory will meet us there," I said, waiting for her to go.

"Just a second," she said on a rather windy exhale. "Oooo... just a second." I stood there, anxiously. We needed to go that very second.

I didn't know much about childbirth, but if watching the Discovery Channel taught me anything thing, it was when a woman was ready to go, she was ready to go. And Micah was looking like she was already halfway there.

In the cab, I text my dad and Troy about him going for a bike ride and I held her hand. She almost broke every one of my fingers.

"I left my phone on the counter. Shit. Oooo... I need you to call Blake. She wants to fly here."

If this wasn't a rock and a hard place. Here this poor woman was about to pass something the size of a small Thanksgiving turkey and she wanted me to call the one person who I'd been trying to *not* call every second of every minute of every hour of every day.

So I created a diversion, I hoped that by the time the contraction that hit her right after she'd requested for me to call Blake she'd have forgotten. Cory could call her when he showed up.

"Let's wait until Cory gets here, you probably have a whole list of people to call. I don't want to spoil his good news."

"Oooo... Where is he?!" she wailed.

That driver deserved a gold medal in cab driving. He had us to the hospital in a blink. He pulled us right up to the emergency door and even helped by grabbing our bags out as I ran inside to get Micah a wheel chair.

"Um, hey. I need some help out there. My brother's girlfriend is having a baby. Like soon," I said, as I walked to the ER desk. The middle-aged woman, who I'd spoken to, wasted no time. She sprang into action, moving around the counter grabbing a chair on her way.

We ran back out to the curbside, where the cabby was counting out loud with Micah.

"Four. Three. Two. One. Oooo," they said in unison. It might have actually been funny, if I weren't close to having a fucking heart attack.

"Hello, there. Looks like we'll be having a baby today," said the nurse. "I'm Nancy, now let's get you inside." She had Micah put her hands around her neck and she pivoted her around so that she could sit in the chair.

As we walked inside she shouted, "Marie! Call OB and tell them I'm bringing them one." She kept talking to Micah as she pushed her down the hall. "Honey, what's your name and who is your doctor?"

"I'm Micah Cruuuuuuuse. Ahhh. Oooo. And my OB/GYN is Dr. Wolfe. Oooo...," Micah said through gritted teeth. She was sweating and her short hair was all over the place. I felt so bad, yet I didn't know what the hell I should do.

"And this is your boyfriend's brother, right?" she asked. I didn't think that was so much for her to aid in her check-in process as much as it was to take her mind off what was happening.

"Mm-hmm," Micah answered.

"Well, brother, where is this baby's daddy?" Nancy asked me.

"He'll be here shortly," I said, taking my phone out of my pocket to see if I had missed something in all the commotion.

The nurse wheeled her on and on, but as we turned down the last hall and went through the last set of doors, I could tell we're were in the right place. I heard screaming from both women and infants. We walked down the pink hallway and another nurse thanked Nancy and they switched off.

"Good luck, honey. And congratulations," the sweet ER nurse told her as she walked away from her and back toward me and the way out.

She grabbed my arm and whisper-yelled in my ear, "You better find that dad. Fast."

"Yes, ma'am," I said and smiled at her.

By the time I was walking to the room they'd wheeled a miserable Micah into, my phone went off.

It was Troy.

"Hey, you find him?" I asked, before I knocked on the door.

"Yeah, he's on Angel Island riding with Joey. I got a hold of him. They're going to try to see if they can get a ride back somehow. Cory is freaking out. They're going to take the 12:25 ferry." But even if they could catch the ferry back, to the city from Angel Island, it would still be some time before he would get there.

"Does Joey have a phone on him?" I asked.

"Yeah, I just talked to them."

"Okay, I'll talk to you later."

I dialed Joey's phone and Cory answered it on the first ring, "Hey, are you with her?"

My brother was frantic, I could tell by how loud he was. Cory wasn't a guy who yelled a lot, but neither was I normally.

*Only when it came to her.*

"Yeah, I'm with her. We're at Seton. She's okay. They've got her in a room."

"Okay, good. God. I'm freaking out. How's she doing?" His panic turned into concern.

"She's fine. She's breathing funny, just like she's supposed to. Do you want to talk to her?" I asked as I gently rapped on the door. I heard the nurse tell me I could come in and so I let myself inside.

The room was nicer than I'd ever expected. It sure as fuck was nicer than any I'd been in. Micah was changed into a gown already and they were getting her information and setting her up in their system.

I walked over to the bed, where she looked pretty much the same. Sweaty. In a lot of pain. And terrified.

"Cory is on the phone do you want to talk to him?" I asked.

"Oooo... Yes! Oooo...," she panted.

I gave her the phone and relief washed over her face. I don't know what he was telling her but she closed her eyes. Tears falling down her flushed cheeks.

"Just get here as fast as you can. Please. I need you," she told him. "I will. I love you, too," she added before she handed the phone back to me.

"Hello?" I said into it not knowing if he'd hung up on not.

"Hey, you take care of her until I get there. Whatever she wants. You got me? You take care of her. We're getting the 12:25 ferry. I'll be there in an hour," he instructed.

"I've got this. She'll be fine. I swear."

After I ended the call with Cory I made sure that she didn't need anything. She didn't need anything except Cory.

The nurses had attached all sorts of gadgets to her and had monitors gauging all kinds of things. After she was checked and they told her that she was already dilated to five centimeters and something else—something about a face—another doctor came in and gave her an epidural.

They said that she still had a little time to go and that she should try to relax. That epidural thing was magic. Almost instantly she looked better.

I thought about how glad I was that Cory didn't have to see her the other way. It wasn't that great.

"So, now will you call Blake?" she asked. I couldn't distract her and her contractions were at bay, so I was kind of fucked.

"Really, Micah. I'll do anything for you right now. Just, please, don't ask me to call her. You can use my phone." I handed it to her, but she didn't reach for it.

"Nope, I need you to call her. Tell her I'm here and that I'm fine. Tell her that the baby is coming and that she needs to get her ass on a plane." Then the bitch smiled. "Please."

I shook my head at her, knowing what she was up to. "You're evil. Seriously though, I don't think she wants to hear from me."

"I think she does." Micah said.

"What the hell? On New Year's you basically said to leave her alone. Now, I'm leaving her alone and you're telling me to call her. I don't get it," I confessed.

"I don't know. She hasn't been the same lately. Maybe we were wrong," she said as she situated herself a little better on the bed pushing her body up with her arms, her legs no longer cooperative.

She added, "I guess I thought that you two were just having a fling. But now you're both so…so meh. You know. I saw how happy you were and I could hear it in her voice, too. Maybe I should have told you to fight for her."

I looked at her eyes, and they were focused on mine. Her short pixy hair was still in disarray, but since she wasn't in as much agony, she sort of looked cute. Big belly, silly gown. I'd really grown to love this girl and I was happy she was the one my brother had found. She was perfect for him.

That's what a relationship was supposed to look like. Not like what

Blake and I were.

"She's still getting married, Mic. I don't think I can change that."

"Try," she said.

*Try.*

I looked at the face of my cell phone, knowing I hadn't deleted her number. It was right there in my hand. Every time I picked up the phone to give in and apologize, but mostly to hear her voice again, I'd remember it was there and I'd have to fight myself not to call.

I looked back up into earnest blue eyes and she said, "Call her."

It sounded so simple. I pressed the button the on the side of my phone and it lit up. I tapped in the passcode that I still couldn't stand to change.

2-2-4-8.

B-A-I-T.

I found Honeybee's number, which was arbitrary, because I knew it like the back of my dick.

I gave Micah one last look. She rubbed her belly and looked hopefully at me.

"Here goes nothing," I said.

As soon as I hit the green button, excitement exploded inside me, but I had to be cool. I was all fucking lit up inside with the thought of hearing her voice. Even if I didn't know if she'd be as happy to hear mine.

I'd missed her so much more than I realized.

# TWENTY-FIVE

## Blake

**Sunday, April 26, 2009**

I REALIZED THAT I missed him more when I was completely alone. When I was with other people, I could almost pretend like it never happened. Until something that he would like popped up. Sometimes it was a song, or a joke, or a beer I had with dinner in some city I wish we were in together.

In that moment, alone in the shower washing the conditioner from my hair, my thoughts went back to him.

They were vaporized when I heard Grant knock on the door. I heard it open and he said into the steamy bathroom, "Hey, Blake, some Casey keeps calling your phone. Do you want me to answer it? It seems important, she's called three times."

Time froze. I didn't say anything. Then Grant repeated, "Blake!"

"Yeah, I mean no. Don't answer it. Can you bring it to me? I'm getting out."

Obediently, he went to retrieve my cell.

Casey was calling me. During the middle of the day. This was unprecedented. Maybe he wanted me. Maybe he wanted more than just a fling.

We hadn't spoken since Aspen and it had been over two months. I'd totally let go of the hope that he'd really wanted more than what we were.

*Grant said she.*

I pulled a towel off the rack in my bathroom and wrapped my hair up first. Then I wrapped the larger one around my body and grabbed the phone that Grant handed me through a half-closed door.

I sat on the toilet lid. I thought that maybe I'd imagined what Grant had said. Maybe my overactive imagination just wanted to hear it was him, and so that was what it chose to hear. It had been doing that a lot. His name was everywhere. Television. Movies. KC and the Sunshine Band. Kansas City was the worst. Everything was Casey this Casey that. Yeah it was spelled KC, but it read the same to me.

I saw his beer in restaurants and hotels when I traveled, having been referred by him. Even after everything.

I heard it in a store one time and then I shouted it, too. I couldn't help myself. Heard a man shout it and then I repeated it, yelling at the top of my lungs. It was his friend's name. I think they might have been partners. And I looked really foolish.

I heard it in my dreams, too. That made waking up a real bitch.

Then there it was written in Helvetica Neue in my shaky hands.

Casey.

"Hello," I said, calmly. Even though I wasn't.

"Hi."

I was him. My heart raced and my vision blurred, my eyes fluttered closed on the other end and I felt the urge to laugh. I sat there in the john and waited for him to talk again. Speaking had been stricken from my resume.

"Blake, are you there?" he asked.

"Yeah," I answered. "How are you?"

*How are you?* That was the stupidest question I could have asked and I definitely didn't want the answer.

If he was bad, I was worse.

If he was great, it would have killed me.

"I'm here," he said. "Sorry to call. I know it's… Whatever, listen, Micah is at the hospital. She wanted me to call you and let you know that the baby is on its way." His voice gave nothing away. Flat. He just spoke. I couldn't tell how he felt at all. That kind of really sucked, because I was dying to know how he was. At least then I might know how I was.

Of course he was calling me for that. The baby.

He wasn't calling me for me. Or for him. It was for the baby. I desperately tried to swallow the disappointment.

"Right. Is she okay?" I asked.

"She's doing fine. She is in labor, but she's doing great so far. She thought that you would want to know."

Still, I couldn't get a read on him. It was like we were merely acquaintances. Maybe that was what we were.

"Good. I'll get a flight. I was going to be in town this week anyway. Which hospital?" My voice was all over the place. I sounded like a pubescent boy. Squeaking through my awkward swallowing and around my heaving lungs. Through all of it, though, I still wanted to burst out laughing.

I had stayed away from him and him from me. We were following the rules. The unspoken moral code of a person in a relationship, and a person who liked living out of a suitcase.

He abided by them.

It was daily recovery and nightly withdrawal. Which was odd because he'd only ever spent one night with me. Yet, that's always when I thought of him the most.

"We're at Senton."

"All right." Then I laughed. Maybe it was a nervous thing, maybe my body was happy and reacted by chuckling at the worst possible minute to spite me. "Sorry." I coughed.

"What's so funny?" he asked.

"I don't know. I just felt like laughing."

"You're so weird," I heard him say softly, like he thought it out loud. I heard it though. Humor. Candor. It was small, but I could smell it like blood in the water.

"Weird because I'm laughing?" I cracked.

"Yes. This is totally supposed to be awkward and uncomfortable and you're ruining it for me."

Then I cackled. Laughter poured out of me and I folded over with joy. He was laughing, too.

"Seriously, Blake. This is weird. Stop laughing. It's fucked up. We're in a fight."

In a fight, like when my brothers would lock me in my room? Like when Kari used to borrow my clothes and then not return them in high school? In a fight suggested it was only for now. That eventually we wouldn't be in a fight.

We were in a fight and that sounded like the best news I'd heard in months.

"What are we fighting about?" I asked out of morbid curiosity. It had been way too long since I'd taken a dip in the vast, open mind that was Casey.

"Because you're stubborn and I'm a pussy." He laughed outright. I heard Micah bark a laugh in the background. I hadn't realized that she was there. We'd usually been alone when we were on the phone in the past. I'd assumed he was in the waiting room or somewhere else.

"Was that Micah? Can I talk to her?" My dearest friend was in labor and I'd just heard her laugh. That didn't add up.

"Blake, I'm having a baby. Get your ass here," she told me.

"I'll be there as soon as I can. Are you doing okay? You sound great for being in labor," I admitted. It wasn't at all what I'd expected to hear.

"I'm fine. They gave me an epidural. Be glad you weren't here earlier. I was a mess. That shit hurt for real. Shit," she said. "It's still feels like hell, but much better. I wish Cory was here already."

"Where's Cory?" I asked, a little taken back that he wasn't with her. He'd been all over her night and day for the last few months. Every time we talked he was there. Even though their voices were different, they still sounded similar, and I love calling her and listening to Cory talk to her while we were on the phone.

"I made him get out this morning. He was driving me nuts! He was on a bike ride. So Casey brought me here. He's supposed to be here in a few minutes. It's so crazy. He's been under my skin lately and now that he was finally doing something, that's when this baby decided to show up." She laughed a little and I heard a little moan slide out.

"Well, good luck. I'll be there as fast as I can. I love you. Just focus and get tough."

She growled at me through the receiver. "I'm tough."

"Okay, here's Casey again," she said and passed me back.

"Hey," he said. There wasn't really anything else for us to talk about.

"Hey, okay. So I'm going to call the airlines and see if I can get my ticket moved up. Should be there some time later today or this evening, if it all works out."

"Sounds good."

"Casey?" I said before hanging up.

He let out a long sigh. "Yeah."

"Can you please text me if anything happens? Do you mind?" It was baby time, and I was dying to know what gender it was and all of the details.

"Sure. I'll text you. Will that be okay?" I heard the hint of sarcasm.

"Yes. Grant's not coming with me. Besides, Micah is having a baby." That sounded like a good excuse.

"Okay, I'll let you know."

"Thanks. 'Bye," I said and ended the call.

I'd become a whirlwind. I was used to traveling, so I already had a full second set of toiletries that never even left my bags. I threw clothes in my suitcase, packing for about a week. I was supposed to make a trip there this week for work anyway.

I packed up my laptop and chargers and put last minute things in my carry-on.

Grant was actually kind of excited for me. When I came out of the bathroom, I'd screamed, "Micah's having the baby." Yes, I was over-the-moon thrilled about that, but I think what really had my blood racing was that I was about to see Casey.

Grant offered to drive me to the airport so that I could call and make arrangements to at least get on standby. As it turned out, I wasn't going to have to wait that long. The customer service person was able to get me on a flight that afternoon and I'd be at the hospital in hours.

I got a coffee and took a seat in the terminal at which I was to board said flight.

I looked through social media on my phone and coincidentally found my way over to the Bay Beer Twitter page. Like always, there were pictures of the staff back at the brewery, as well as all the new things that had just started happening for them. Beer enthusiasts were taking pictures with their pints and tagging Bay Brewing.

They were doing really, really well. I thumbed through their photos, like I always seemed to do, and found one of Casey. It was a newer one. He still looked as handsome as ever. He had his hair trimmed, but not cut. So it wasn't as wild as I'd seen it could get. He wore faded jeans, a Rolling Stones T-shirt, and a fitted gray sports coat. He looked good in anything.

It had been about an hour and a half since we'd spoken, and sitting there I got my first message from him in far too long.

**Casey: Cory got here. They said she was going to start pushing soon and kicked me out. Probably won't be that long.**

**Me: Thanks for the update.**

**Casey: I said I would let you know.**

**Me: I know.**

**Me: Are we still fighting? I think it's obvious that I didn't know.**

**Casey: Didn't know? We haven't talked since February. Didn't you notice?**

**Me: Yes I noticed. So who won?**

He didn't answer right away, and in that time, they'd called for boarding. I watched my phone diligently. I knew I'd have to turn it off soon, but I was enjoying the communication with him too much to miss his message.

It wasn't until I had my carry-on stowed and my seat belt secured before I received one back.

**Casey: Can we see each other?**

The correct answer was no. In true Blake fashion, I didn't get it right.

**Me: I hope so.**

**Casey: Not for sex. I just want to see you.**

**Me: Will you be at the hospital?**

**Casey: I don't know. Text me when you land.**

**Me: Okay.**

It was stupid and I knew it. I shouldn't want to see him or talk to him or any of the other nine thousand things that I wanted to do.

I powered my phone back up when we were told it was safe.

**Casey: We have a boy!! Foster Eugene Moore 7lbs, 2oz Bald as a door knob.**

**Casey: Hurry up.**

**Casey: Serious, don't planes go faster than this? I don't remember it taking this long.**

**Casey: I'm going to meet you at baggage claim.**

My heart raced. He was going to be there. Or he was there. I checked the time on the last message. It had been about thirty minutes, there was a good chance he was there and waiting for me already. The person next to me couldn't move fast enough. I needed off that plane.

I had been preparing for my wedding.

I had been readying a house to be a home.

I had all of these things to be excited about, yet it was knowing that a goofy, vagabond gypsy of a man was waiting for me. For that I was truly excited.

As soon as I was free of the small seats, I flung open the latch and grabbed my bag. All of my courteous traveler manners had escaped me. I didn't let people go first. I didn't speak my pleasantries to the flight staff as I exited. I was going to see Casey.

I ran down the ramp to the terminal, I was familiar enough with San Francisco International to know which way to head.

Then there he was. Sunglasses on his head. Curls casually laying how they did. He wore colorful striped long shorts and a blue, zip-up Bay Brewing hoodie. It wasn't a sexy look on anyone but him. As I got closer, our eyes met.

I was heaving my carry-on and my bag and I felt like I weighed three hundred pounds. I couldn't move fast enough.

He walked slowly toward me with a fantastic smile.

"Did you know that the end of *What's Up Doc* with Barbra Streisand and Ryan O'Neal was filmed almost right where we're standing?" he said like we'd just seen each other the day before.

I dropped my bag and wrapped myself around him.

Not at first, but after a few seconds, I felt him hug me back. He smelled like him. My lungs had an infinite amount of space and I feared I'd suck his shirt straight up my nose. I felt relieved. Then when he adjusted his hold and latched onto me tighter, kissing the top of my head, I felt home.

"I hate missing you," I said into his chest.

"Then stop missing me," he said.

"I don't know how. Don't you miss me?" I looked up at him. His face was scruffy, but trimmed and magnificent.

"Not any more than usual."

He let me hold onto him a little longer, then he braced my shoulders and pulled away. The worst feeling in the world was Casey letting me go. I thought, I didn't even remember kissing Grant when he dropped me off. Maybe, I hadn't.

He picked up my bag and I followed him out. When we got to a car, he hit the key-fob and the horn startled me.

"Is this yours?" I asked.

"No, it's Morgan's. I stole it to pick you up."

Wow. Morgan had a car. She was sixteen already? When we'd first me she was only fifteen, but I supposed it had almost been a year ago. A whole year. Then I tried to remember what day it was when Casey and I first met.

"You're quiet," he said, as we pulled into traffic. The knowledge that this was the first time I'd ever ridden, with him driving, in the car buzzed through my mind, as I desperately tried to remember when we'd met.

"I'm trying to remember something," I said deep in thought.

"Like what," he said, switching lanes and accelerating.

"What day we met," I said before I could lie.

"May 23rd," he said rather speedily.

"May 23[rd]," I repeated. My head spun. Why hadn't I realized that before?

"Yeah, are you telling me you don't remember?" He sounded a little offended. His face was scrunched together and he pulled his sunglasses over his eyes.

"No, I remember I just didn't know the date."

Why had I done that? It felt so wrong and for all of the wrong reasons. When I should have felt guilty for marrying someone on the exact one-year anniversary of my unfaithfulness, I was disgusted that I was marrying Grant on the anniversary of my first night with Casey.

I was the worst.

"Oh, what does it matter?" he said.

I choked a little, that remark had stung, but he didn't know why. He had no reason to feel obtuse about it, like I did.

"It's my wedding date."

His jaw ticked. And he deflated back into the seat, pressing harder on the gas petal.

"Congratulations," he said and we didn't speak again for rest of the drive.

We didn't joke.

We didn't laugh.

I was trapped in my head, and he was trapped in my heart. We were both trapped in that little silver hybrid.

He pulled right up to the curb, but didn't get out. I sat and waited for him to say something. Minutes ticked away, until he put the car in park.

"Say something," I said.

He turned toward me and gave me a weak smile.

"I don't know what you want me to say. I don't know what you want me to do," he shouted. "I hate this. I hate that you're marrying him. I hate it, Blake! It. Fucking. Sucks. You. Fucking. Suck."

"I *suck*!?" I yelled back. Our voices booming in the small space. "Yeah, you know what? I know I suck. I fucked up. I fucked it *all* up. What did you want me to do?" I asked, trying to lower my voice so that the people walking around outside of the entrance didn't hear.

"I wanted you to tell me you wanted me. Me, Blake. Me!" He hit the steering wheel. "But you never did. You never would. You never will. And I don't know why."

"What? Where is this coming from? You never wanted a relationship." I stopped myself before adding *you just wanted to fuck.* I remembered how he set me straight the last time I'd accused him of wanting to fuck-and-run.

"How do you know? I never had the option," he said, the timbre of his words softer.

"You did, too," I said under my breath.

He looked at me, but I couldn't see his eyes.

"Take these motherfuckers off!" I lunged at his glasses and threw them on the dash. Under there was a storm brewing. Green and blue clashing. "There. Now, look at me."

"I don't know what I should have done differently. I don't know where I misled you. Or why you'd think that I wouldn't. I don't talk to anyone like I talk to you. I don't laugh with anyone like I laugh with you. I don't..." he scrambled for the right word, "God! I haven't had sex with anyone since you. Don't you know that? Don't you know I wanted you?"

"Wanted."

"I still want you. I always want you. But you want whatever it is that you get from him more. So, it is what it is. Or was. Or what-the-fuck-ever." He faced front again. "Micah is waiting for you. Visiting hours are almost over."

"I think you suck, too," I added, knowing that the right time to say that had passed, but it had to be said.

We sat there again.

"Let me get my bags out."

"I'll take them to Cory and Micah's. Just go."

There really wasn't much more to say. Or there was but we were both too bull-headed to do it. Bull-headed or scared.

So, I left.

The discussion was over.

# TWENTY-SIX

## Casey

**Sunday, April 26, 2009**

SO, I LEFT.

And then I left again. I didn't have to work, but I couldn't be in town. I wouldn't be able to hide from her. I was sure we'd run into each other at the hospital. I'd called Cory that night as I re-packed a fresh bag and told him I was leaving.

"Why don't you finally stick around and fight for her," he'd said.

"She doesn't want me to."

"How does she know? I don't think she knows what she wants because you've never shown her what she could have. Man, you chased this girl all over the country for the last year, but you never came out and told her what you really wanted. What was she supposed to think? For a year, you pretended like it was okay she was with this other dude, and now it's not. That's convenient."

"I've got to go," I told him. I knew on some level that he was right, but fuck him for saying it after it was too damn late.

"You do that. Come see your Godson when you get home. And your mom. You can't run all the time."

His words were spot on. *Run*. That was what I was doing, but I honestly didn't know how to stay.

He was irritated at me and had every right to be. I didn't know what else to do.

I flew to St. Louis. It was the next flight out when I arrived back at the airport for the third time that day.

I drank a belly full at the Adam's Mark. The bar was big and full. There had been a Cardinals game and I was surprised that for midnight on a Sunday night it was still that busy. They had won and the place looked like Times Square on New Year's Eve.

I didn't go home that week. I was supposed to have a few days off, but I spent them in St. Louis walking around downtown and sitting on a barstool wherever I found one.

Days went by, I jumped back into my regular routine.

Work.

Sleep.

Dream.

Blake.

Then I did it all over and over again.

Money rolled in, I was officially a partner in the company. The new building was up and running, and I was keeping them busy writing new deals with clients and increasing the shipments with customers we'd already won over.

As May 23rd crept closer and closer, I battled with myself.

On May 3rd, I decided it was bullshit. I hated her and at least she wasn't marrying me with her cheating ass. Then, I rationalized that I knew better.

On May 4th, I Googled *How To Stop A Wedding.* That was interesting reading.

I went back and forth, over and over in my head.

Text her. Call her. I did none of those things.

On May 11th, I decided I had to lay it all out there. Had to give it one last shot. Otherwise I was never going to climb out of this funk.

On May 22nd, I rented a car, figuring that by the time I got to her, I'd know what to say.

# TWENTY-SEVEN

## Blake

**Saturday, May 23, 2009**

I DIDN'T KNOW WHAT to say or think. Everything felt surreal.

I woke up at my mom and dad's house, the morning of my wedding, and simply went through the motions.

My mother was already in the shower. It was five a.m. I only had Micah and a few cousins standing up with me as bridesmaids. My mother having taken the helm of the wedding ship shortly after it began, took it upon herself to nominate them. I went along and asked. They said yes. Everyone was happy.

We were all getting ready here at nine.

Micah and Cory drove up with Deb, Casey and Cory's mom. She came to help them with Foster since he was still so tiny. I told Micah that it was silly for her to come all this way after just having him, but she wouldn't hear of it.

They were staying at a hotel nearby, which I think made both Micah and Cory feel much better.

My dad asked, "Blake, what's on your mind?" as I drank my first cup of coffee in my pajamas.

"Oh, stuff," I said, blowing air across the hot mug.

"Anything you want to run by your old dad?" he said, reading the paper.

"I don't think so," I told him, taking a seat next to him, grabbing the entertainment section.

"It's your wedding, Blake. It's perfectly normal to feel nervous or anxious," he offered. "You got some cold feet?"

"I don't know. I don't know if they were ever really all that warm," I admitted.

My father put his paper down, folded it, and placed his mug down on top.

"Talk," he said.

I took a few breaths, tried to organize my thoughts so that I didn't sound like a maniac. Like the selfish little bitch I was. Then, I told the truth.

"I don't know if this is right. I don't know if Grant is the one." My eyes started to burn and I rubbed them, trying to pass off the action for early morning grogginess.

"Why not? Don't you love him?"

"I do. But sometimes it feels like it's missing something."

"Like what?" he asked sympathetically.

"Like me." My fucking lip started to quiver, so I hid it by taking a drink.

"Well, I hate to break it to you, baby doll, but today is your wedding day. It would be devastating if you weren't there."

"I'm not saying that."

"I think I know what you're saying. So, hear me out. You don't feel like yourself when you're with Grant? Is that it? Like you're someone else?"

"Yes. What does that mean?" I took another sip.

"Do you *ever* feel like you're yourself, Blake? Or is it only around him?"

It was pathetic. My dad probably thought I was having some sort of stress-induced psychotic break. When in reality, I was freaking out because deep down I didn't want to marry Grant.

"Can I tell you a secret?" I whispered.

He nodded, giving me his full attention.

"I've not been totally faithful to Grant. I know it's bad, and before you think I'm terrible, just know that I feel so bad about it. But, Daddy, if I loved him the way I should then I wouldn't have done that, right?"

"Is it over with the other guy?" he asked.

"I think so. I broke it off. Lots of times. I knew it was wrong, but dad—" I didn't know where to go from there.

"Do you love him?" he asked.

"I don't know." Then I noticed that tears were already falling. "I never let myself think like that. You know. I never let myself think that that was even a possibility. But Daddy, I'm me with him."

"Shhh, don't cry. Is it that boy with the hair?" he asked and it surprised me. How did he remember that?

"Yeah, how did you know?"

"Baby, dads know. You got to tell me though. Right now. Are you going to get married today? I'm behind you. Whatever you decide. But Grant is a good man. He loves you. He wants to take care of you and make a life together. Are those things you want? Because as a dad, that's a pretty good son-in-law package. I don't know this other guy. I'm sorry. I wish I had met him, and then I might be a better judge. But anyone who could let my little girl go is a fool. And he doesn't deserve you. Come here."

I went to him and cried on his shoulder. I sat on my dad's lap feeling the truth in what he'd said. He walked away from me so many times. Grant never would.

If I left Grant and went with Casey today, I might be heartbroken again by the end of the week. I had no way of knowing.

It was time for me to grow up.

It was time for me to finally do the right thing.

# TWENTY-EIGHT

## Casey

**Saturday, May 23, 2009**

I DROVE NINETY DOWN the interstate toward her house. It finally felt like I was doing the right thing.

I knew her parents' names from conversations with Blake and it didn't take much to find their address on my phone. I also called Micah and begged to know where she would be. So there was also that.

My foot heavy on the throttle, the rental car ran wide open.

I couldn't take it. My adrenaline was amplified in my blood. My bones were aching with a need to see her one last time before she was his. Till death do them part.

Well fuck that.

I wanted them to part now.

At very least, if I got there and saw her happy with my own eyes I could go. If it was true, then it just was.

But I knew in my gut it wasn't true.

Not as true as us.

I exited the freeway and rounded the corners a little faster than I should have. The back end of the car slid and the tires squalled at me at every turn. I was reckless, what did I have to lose besides *everything*.

I was more afraid of wrecking my heart than I was of wrecking the fucking two-hundred-dollar-a-day rental.

I pulled in down the street from their house, the drive way was full of cars. As I began my walk up the cement stairs leading to her parent's front door, I saw a long black limo coming down the street.

I changed course.

I ran around the back side of the house, between the bushes and the brick of her parents' home. I didn't stop to think if she was in the back. My instincts knew I'd find her there.

Around the corner was a small patio and a large French door. It was cracked. I heard two voices.

One was hers.

Blake was in there.

"Are you ready, sweetheart? The limo is pulling up," said a woman.

"Yeah, okay," Blake said. Her voice sounded pained. She didn't sound like my honeybee. She didn't sound like Betty. "I need a few minutes. I'll get my things together and I'll be right out. You can send everyone to the limo. I'll be right there, Mom."

"All right, but I'll wait by the door for you. I'll help you down in your dress."

I waited until I heard her mother's heels clip-clop away from her. My heart raced. I felt like I'd been shot up with pure adrenaline. The vein in my neck throbbed almost audibly.

I walked to the door slowly, not wanting her to be frightened or scream.

"Blake?" I said quietly as moved into the open doorframe.

I startled her, but she covered her mouth. Her eyes instantly filled with tears. Her mouth was open behind her hand and she sobbed. Her eyes overflowed, it was like they held back an ocean and her eyes fissured, leaking behind her lids.

"Shhh," I said shaking my head. My stomach lurched at the poor sight in front of me. As I crouched before her in her white gown, I felt all of the pain that this whole thing had caused her.

She knew. She felt it as much as I did.

Her chest heaved silently, stifled by her perfectly manicured hand. She wore false nails. I don't know why that struck me and resonated, but it did. Blake bit her nails. If she was nervous, she bit them. When she was anxious, bored, troubled, she mauled her fingers until they were a mess. Slapping some false shield over one of her personality traits—something so telling about who she was and what she was thinking—made me think irrationally.

She was uncomfortable.

She was a mess, but she didn't have her nails to show it.

Fake nails, for a fake wedding. At least to me, it all seemed fake.

"Don't do this, honeybee. Look at yourself," I urged her. "You don't have to do this to yourself. You don't look like a woman about to get married. You look devastated. Please, stop crying. Talk to me." I rubbed my hands soothingly up and down her thighs, trying to give her some comfort.

Her hand fell away and her eyes clouded over, an eerie stillness came over her face. She took a few breaths, holding a hand out in front of my face. Palm-side out. But she didn't look into my eyes. She hadn't since I crouched in front of her.

"Stop. Just stop." She hiccupped and sniffed. "Why are you here, Casey?"

I didn't answer. Surely she knew damn well why I was there.

"Why don't you ever just leave me alone?" Her voice broke as she whispered a scream, "Leave. Me. Alone."

"No. Talk to me." I hadn't expected her to be so angry, so livid. I guess I hadn't thought about it all the way through. There were things that I still had to know. "Why him? Why not me?" My hands found my hair and I pulled it in frustration.

"You know why," she said with heated venom, reminiscent of the Blake I was used to. But then it iced over just as fast when she continued, "Don't act like this was something that it wasn't."

"Not *wasn't*," I shouted, a little louder than I should have. Then softened, "*Is. It still is.*"

"This isn't a fucking love story, Casey. This is life." She huffs, then choked back a sob. I try to think of something to say to that. Then she continued, "We met in a bar and we had a one-night-stand."

I was grinding my teeth. My jaw ticked hearing her blasé description of a night that meant so much to me.

I defended, "One-night stand? Woman, there's nothing about that night that was ever going to be just a one-night stand." I shook her leg, and my teeth set to clench again. "Now. Call. This. Shit. Off!"

A fleeting spark danced across her brown eyes. "It's too late." Her words gentled. "We can't do this anymore. I can't take it. It's too hard. I'm too tired. Please, leave me alone. Just go, Casey." Her stupid mouth must have made her heart mad, because the hands that had been hanging loosely at her sides were now balled into fists.

Then she shoved me back with them. At first weakly, then she came at me again.

I stood up, taking her with me grabbing her with my hands. My shaky fingers wrapping easily around her small wrists.

Her nostrils flared and her breasts rose and fell in fast succession. The white lace of her dress raised and lowered with each hit of air her lungs stole from the room. She stared at me. Her eyes clear and so resolute.

"Fine," I let her go. "Hit me. Blake, kick me out! You've always been good at that. Go ahead. Get mad. That's all you, but you're not fighting me." I stepped back feeling my own temper rear its head again. Like a tidal wave every time my mouth moved, I couldn't hold any of it back anymore.

What was the point?

"You're. Fighting. You," I said slowly. And I punctuated it with my finger in her chest. Not hard enough to move her, but enough for her to feel me and know I was going to fight back. "You fucking love me. *Not him*!" I shouted.

"It's too much!" she yelled. "Oh, God what have I done?"

"It's not too late. Make this stop. Be mine. Be all mine." She came to me, a ray of hope shot up my spine, making me stand taller.

She wrapped her arms around my waist so tightly, crashing her cheek to my chest. "I'll always be yours. I can't help it. But it can't. I can't stop all of this now."

I arched my back, and cupped her cheeks angling them up at me and spoke as calmly as I possibly could, the emotion of this whole thing finally hitting me in the stomach. "Yes, you can. I'm right here. Call someone. Call Reggie." I leaned down to her face. "Please tell them. Tell them that you're calling it off."

I reached for my phone in my pocket. "You can," I urged.

She looked at it in my open hand and then back to my eyes. It was like watching my heart get hit around a court during a live or die tennis match. Love serving love.

"Call your dad, Blake. Tell him you choose me. *Choose me*." I trembled under the weight of my phone. "Fuck it. I'll call him myself. You want me to fight for you? That's what you want?" Her eyes over flowed again, her lip quivered before she steadied it with her teeth. "Because I'm two fucking seconds away from picking you up and carrying you out of here. Fuck everyone else. I want you. *I* love *you.*"

She pulled back, stepping on the train of her dress and almost stumbling before catching herself. "Don't. Don't." She was the one pointing at me now. "Don't you say that. Not now! How could you? How could you love me? I'm marrying Grant." Her body was covered in lace and her face wore regret.

"You're not marrying him. Not today," I stated.

"Yes, I am." She straightened, her stubborn will rebounding. "Why now do you want me so badly? You didn't care before. Now that I'm getting married, all of the sudden you *love* me?!" Her voice escalated. "You're making me crazy!"

"I always wanted you. I've loved you the whole time. It's you! Why don't you love me? Huh?" My shoulders hunched forward, I wasn't cut out for fighting like that, and I liked it more when we were fighting about sleeping in the same room and not answering messages. I didn't like this. It felt different.

It felt final.

My voice lowered as I tried to calm myself, but my fist shook, in front of me, in her direction.

"What is it that you get from him that you won't let me give you?"

She fell back down on the chair she was sitting on, her hands held together on her lap. She looked up at me and said, "Forever, Casey. He'll give me his forever."

"I'll give you more than that."

"You say that, but we did…we met in a bar. I'm just a game. You only want the chase. You'd leave me."

"I wouldn't." Thinking back over our history, I realized, she had every right to think that. And I fucking hated it.

"Grant won't leave me. I can't picture a life with you where you won't get sick of this, of me. You'll get bored." She sighed like she had let something out that she'd been struggling to hold on to.

I looked at my feet. I'd worn nice clothes, in the event that I was watching a wedding I wished never happened. I looked at those fucking black dress shoes.

I said, "You're so wrong. I love you so much that I hate you. You're so fucking blind. You're a fool." I wrung my hands.

"Yeah, well fuck you." And she meant it. She'd never said that to me. She was either doing her best to make me leave, or she was testing my fight. "See? This is how it is, Casey. This is how it ends. Just like I always knew it would."

In a rush I lifted her by her arms and I kissed her. If that was it, I was getting one last taste.

When I'd poured everything I had into that one kiss, I felt her tremble and melt into it. Then she went rigid and shut me out.

"Oh, this isn't the end, you liar. You can kick me out of this house. You can try to avoid me all you want. But I'm in here." I touched her head and stepped back, still holding tight to one arm. "And I'm in here," I place my hand over her heart.

"Casey."

There it was, my final argument. I didn't hold back, terrified it still wouldn't be enough.

"The scared part of you might marry him today. But the brave fighter in here—she's *mine*. She always will be. Love doesn't give a fuck about a piece of paper. When are you going to realize that this isn't *just* love? There isn't even a word for this." My hand moved from her heart to mine, and I pressed my palm into myself. "Blake, I know you better than you give me credit for. So straighten up your white gown, fix your makeup and hair and put on a happy, phony forever face. I hope that you have to pretend it's me to walk down the aisle. I hope every time you blink tears away today you see me."

She turns her head and coughed another sob. "Casey."

"Look at me." When she hesitated. I repeated, "Look at me, Blake. Remember this face." It was then I felt the hot sting of tears and the cool dampness on my cheek and I swiped at the with a shaky hand and said, "Remember what this looks like. This is what you've done today. You go. Marry him. Make everyone happy except you, but don't think you're going to cry on my shoulder about it later.

"You feared rejection, Blake? Well get a good look. This is what it looks like, honeybee." I felt my chest ache and tear under my clothes. My blood ran cold. And she still didn't say anything.

"I could beg you not to do this all day, but it won't matter. *You* set this date." It happened to be the same day as the expiration of my heart.

I let her go. When my fingertips left her skin I felt disconnected, from her and myself.

She didn't say anything, her eyes looked glassy again like when I came in. "I hope you're fucking miserable, too," I said.

I walked to the door, then turned back, "Congratu-fucking-lations. You were waiting for me to leave you? To hurt you? You *just* beat me to it."

She flinched.

Her voice was ragged and breathy. "I wish I'd never met you."

I laughed at that. "Well at least we can agree on something, honey-bee."

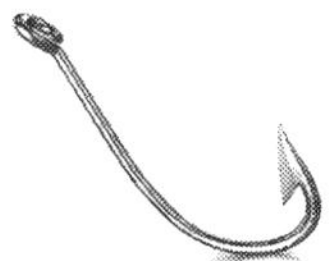

I walked to the car. I drove away. But my body was numb. On autopilot, I drove to the address that I'd memorized from the invitation on my brother's refrigerator.

*We met in a bar.*

So fucking what! What did that have to do with anything?

*I'd leave her. Get bored.*

That wouldn't happen. Not now. Not after all this time.

She was more scared of me leaving her than being in a marriage that was just *good*. What a cop-out.

My mind rattled on and on. I thought of a million other things I should have said and then ten different ways I could have said them. I kept seeing the look on her face and I had to come to the reality of it possibly being there, etched in my mind, forever.

I hoped she *did* remember what my face looked like that day, but then again, what would that fix? Nothing. Nothing is fixed if I don't get to be with her.

No right. No wrong. No Blake.

I pulled up to the park where the ceremony would take place. There were signs everywhere that said Warren-Kelly Wedding with big ass arrows pointing the way. There was no good reason for me to go. But when I decided to drive to her house, I knew I would have to if things didn't go my way.

And they didn't, so there I was.

I parked farther away than I needed to and chose to walk through the grass. If my brother saw me he'd freak out, but at that point, what could anyone really do to me?

Chairs lined a sidewalk that led to a large fountain. The sidewalk circled the squirting sculpture and forked off into more paths each a third of the way around.

The seats were full and there was a buzz about the gathered crowd. The wedding was to start at one and it was now half-past. No one seemed too concerned, but there was an anxious weight to the air. Maybe it was just me, holding out for hope that she wouldn't show up.

I saw my brother sitting a few rows back from the front. The bridesmaids weren't there yet, and neither were Blake or her mother. They couldn't be that far behind me, I thought. I took a seat in the corner in the very back off to the wide side, away from the aisle.

It felt like a funeral. Maybe it was my black fucking shoes.

I watched Cory looking at his phone and then I saw him give a thumbs-up to someone. A few minutes later, I heard the crunch of tires on the chip-graveled road behind me. It stopped just past some bushes and then I heard doors open.

I had to keep reminding myself that I needed to watch.

After that day, I wasn't going to chase her anymore. I'd hoped that the reason would be because she'd let me catch her, but the reality of it was she pulled herself from the chase.

*I wish I'd never met you.*

I needed a drink.

Giggling and shushing. Hushed whispers at my six. I didn't dare turn around to see. I kept my head down and waited.

My chin on my chest I pretended to be invisible.

Violins played.

My inner guy told me that I was being stupid. That no woman was worth this.

Bridesmaids walked. I watched them out of my periphery.

Reggie and probably Blake's other brother, Shane, walked to the back of the seats to collect their mother.

Violins played.

She walked down, arm in arm with them to the first row, and sat. Two other people walked by, probably his parents; they sat on the other side. I kept my head toward the grass and only looked up with my sunglass-covered eyes.

The violins stopped.

Everyone turned and stood.

Violins played the wedding march, the saddest song I'd ever heard.

I didn't stand. I literally couldn't stand for that. I forced my heavy head to turn and I looked past the people in my row.

Flashes of her laughing at me, leaning in with her eyes closed and her mouth puckered for a kiss, and her flushed-pink nose…they all taunted me. The smell of her, taste of her, feel of her all at once hit so strongly that it crippled me.

Violins fucking played.

They walked by. It was so fast. I didn't know what I was hoping for. Maybe she'd be looking for me. Maybe she'd turn around and run. But they simply walked past row after row until I couldn't see them through the standing guests anymore.

It got very quiet and everyone sat, putting the vision of my wildest fantasy and my worst nightmare in front of me all at once.

The priest spoke loud enough for all to hear. We were gathered there that day by God. Good, maybe he would share some of the blame.

I felt sick.

Catholic ceremony. Stand-up. Sit-down. Peace be with us all. Peace wasn't with me. That was one thing I would forever be holding. For someone else I guessed.

They gifted each other metal rings.

They said the Lord's Prayer.

And then violins played.

They were pronounced husband and wife. He kissed his bride. My

Betty. My Honeybee. She kissed me goodbye.

The sun was bright. What a terrible day for a wedding.

I stood too soon. I couldn't stay a minute longer. The couple parted from their inaugural kiss as his and hers. Her hair and veil blew as a breeze passed me and touched her. She looked straight at me.

I took one last look at her. I kissed the palm-side of my fingers, as she watched me standing there like a fool. The luck of it was that I was in the back and everyone was looking at them. Her face froze on mine.

Grant smiled at his parents.

She stayed still in her spot as he started to walk them forward and the opposite way down the aisle. But in her distraction, she paused. He noticed and looked at her and followed her gaze to me. He whispered something in her ear, shaking her concentration and breaking her connection with me.

She shook her head, rattling her thoughts. She turned to him.

My brother caught it, too. His head looked over his shoulder and directly at me. It was a look of shock and then pity.

My feet were steadfast and moved without my telling them to. Into the car. Onto the road.

I heard my cell phone ring. I suspected it was Cory and let it ring to voicemail. I'd text him later.

I drove south. Toward home.

I stopped for gas in a small town hours later and refilled the rental. I didn't even have a real tie to the vehicle I was escaping with. Escaping. That's what it felt like.

I thought the further I got, the more miles I put between us, that the pain I felt in every cell would dull. It didn't.

I could still hear the violins.

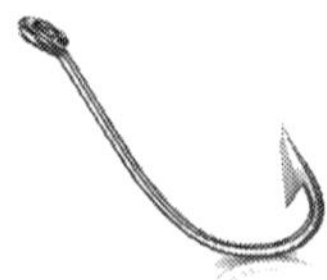

"Casey, it's me. I don't know where you went. Shit. Why did you come? Why did you do that?" I listened to Cory's voicemail. He sighed then went on, "I know you were there. Dammit. Just…just call me when you get this. Text me or something. Let me know where you are. I'm sorry. I love you, brother." Then he hung up.

I'd driven straight back to San Francisco. I didn't arrive in town until around six thirty in the morning. When I walked into my apartment, the sun was coming up and I was thankful to be so tired. My eyes gave in and I fell asleep the second my head hit the couch.

When I awoke around three that afternoon, I listened to my voicemail from Cory again and read the texts he'd sent.

**Cory: Would you text me already? Where are you?**

**Cory: Are you okay? You're pissing me off.**

**Cory: TEXT ME!**

If I could feel anything, I would have felt bad for freaking him out.

I had the rental picked up and I headed to the bar. Hindsight would show that the Hook, Line and Sinker was a terrible choice. It was only early afternoon, but I had a lot of things to drown and I needed to get started.

**Me: Home.**

There I'd sent a message to Cory.

Then I sent a message to Nate asking if he was working tonight. It was a Sunday and I knew he worked every other one.

Nate was working at HLS and I was glad. I had every intention of drinking until I was kicked out, and at least I could talk him into serving me past when everyone else would cut me off.

"Hey," I said to him as I walked in. He sized me up, not saying anything. There were only a few others in the bar playing darts and two were shooting pool. No one sat at the bar.

I chose the stool in front of where he was stocking bottles and changing out the nozzles on the liquor. He had most of the bottles on the bar so he could clean the glass shelves and mirrored wall behind them. He still didn't say anything, but he examined me pretty closely.

He reached under the wooden bar and pulled out a double-shot glass, sliding it to me. I stopped it with my hand.

"Troy or Cory coming?" he asked.

"Nope." My eyes landed on the bottle of Remy Martin and I

thought how fucking appropriate. Without a second thought to the glass, I opened the bottle and tipped it back. It was strong and it burned going down. Accustomed to the taste, Remy being a once upon a time friend of mine, he bit me back when I rushed him down my throat.

It was raining, fitting, and I'd really dressed up for my night out. Flip flops, brown tattered cargo shorts, white T-shirt, and a zip-up Bay hoodie. I showered quickly, but didn't shave. I didn't even look at my hair and let it dry like it was. I'm sure I looked really fucking mental. I was a book worthy of being judged by my cover.

"Looks like I'll need another bottle of Remy for the shelf, you just bought that one." He chuckled, not having a care in the world, and joked like the world wasn't on fire. I supposed his wasn't, but there was enough smolder coming off me that he could at least tone down his chipper fucking tone. "You're the only guy that drinks that stuff anyway."

I hadn't drunk it here since that first night. I looked at him squinting. "Same bottle?"

"Same bottle," he said, walking to the back room for its replacement. It was still mostly full. I both hated it and loved it at the same time. I didn't want to empty it. It was pitifully ironic.

When he returned with the new Remy bottle and a few others, he sat them down on the bar in front of me.

"Can I get a glass of ice?"

He threw about five cubes into a Glenciarn glass and handed it to me. I said, "Play some music, would ya? Something louder than these violins in my head."

I walked myself, the glass, and both bottles of Remy Martin to the booth in the back. After emptying my hands of my chosen mind eraser, I unscrewed the light bulb a quarter turn so that it went out, burning my numb fingers, my reflexes already slow, so the pain didn't hurt. Maybe I'd hit my deductible on pain.

Nate turned music on and what a good man. The beginning riff to *Bulls on Parade* pumped through the speaker that sat right behind that very booth.

I opened the new bottle, poured the amber cure over the ice and swirled it.

I looked at the old bottle. It was short, round and clear. I ran my thumb over the staff wielding sitar and hours passed.

Nate left me to it, not bothering me much, only coming over to switch out my glass with a fresh one with ice. He brought me a glass of water the last time. I'd slowly drunk a giant's share. I sipped the room temperature cognac and swallowed memories and fantasies alike.

My head in one hand, my finger circled the rim of the glass, I was officially Hemmingway drunk.

"You look like you need a friend," said a sympathetic woman's voice.

*Aly.*

I didn't respond. My eyes were hot and when I looked up to see her they felt dry for having stared at the same spot on the table for hours.

She sat opposite of me and looked around the room.

"It's hopping in here," she said sarcastically. "I can't believe I almost missed this party."

"I'm not in the mood, Aly," I croaked and took the last drink within my glass, immediately reaching to refill it.

"Oh, I'd say you look like you are in a mood. A bad one, too." I looked at her blankly, trying to show her this wasn't a good time to play an angel. I was still missing the devil.

"Listen. I don't know who called you to come down here. I'd rather they hadn't." I heard my words run together, my head lulled a bit. My drinks were gaining on me and they caught up to me all at once. Maybe I hadn't noticed since I hadn't spoken or been forced into logical thought for a while. It was almost peaceful letting my mind sink to the bottom of the glass.

"Nate called your brother. Cory called me."

"How cute. You have a Casey's Drunk calling tree." I patronized her and slapped the table.

She jumped.

I pulled my hood up over my head and yelled at Nate, "Thanks!"

He lifted his head from the draught he was topping then flipped me off and went back to the beer.

"Casey, don't be a dick. They're worried about you." She reached her hand across the table and it touched me.

I recoiled. "Don't. Hey, I got myself into this. I wonder if everyone will throw me a I-Told-You-So Party. Yeah, that'd be awesome. I can get all of these *Poor Casey, you knew this was going to happen*, and *what did you expect* talks out of the way all in one shot. Well, did you guys ever think that I *didn't* think this was going to happen? Did ya? I WAS WRONG!"

Nate made quick time to the table and shoved me over on the bench, backing me up against the wall.

"Listen. You don't have to yell at her. We get it, man. This shit sucks. But this is life. You made a choice and shit didn't turn out. You've got tonight to get ripped. Sit here all fucking night until you pass out. Be my guest. All the time you need. Tonight. That's life, man. Wake up!"

"I don't want to wake up," I growled back like a rabid dog.

"That's your choice. This shit will lose you a lot more than some girl."

"The girl, Nate. The. Girl." I slumped, brought my thumb and index finger to the bridge of my nose and took a breath. "I'm drunk. Just let me be drunk. Please?"

He raised his hands in surrender. "Sure, no problem. I'll get you some more ice. He stood to return to the bar, grabbing my empty glass. "Don't yell at her again." He pointed to Aly with the hand that held the glass and gave me a threatening look. "Got it?"

He didn't wait for me to answer. We both knew it wasn't really a question.

Aly didn't say anything. Her eyes looked red, but she smiled at me. It was more toothy than sincere.

"Just. Leave."

Was everything from then out going to be make believe?

# TWENTY-NINE

## Blake

**Sunday, May 24, 2009**

THE WHOLE THING FELT like dress-up from when I was a child. Make believe. I was the bride and Grant was the groom and we got married and we were going to live happily ever after. Everyone else believed it, why didn't I?

I saw Casey at the wedding. I was glad that my mother gave me a Valium when she found me like she had still sitting in the chair.

She'd heard everything. So, I didn't feel the need to tell her anything more. She kissed my forehead and simply asked, "Are you ready to go?"

I said no, but got up anyway. I loved her for not asking more about it.

The wedding breezed by. The reception did the same. We danced. I drank and then I drank a little more. Micah took care of me while she was there, but she left a little after ten, and I couldn't blame her. They had little Foster to take care of.

The night went on and on.

Finally, we went to the hotel and Grant put me to bed. He took care of me.

"Thank you," I said as he pulled my shoes off and pulled the covers up over my dress.

"You're welcome Mrs. Kelly."

Then I puked.

We flew to St. Bart's the next afternoon. I was well and truly hungover and Grant was delicate with me. I wore my sunglasses and admittedly was zero fun.

When we arrived on the island I'd asked him if we could rest up the first night and he agreed. It was the first night of our honeymoon, the second day of my marriage, and I would have given anything to be anywhere else.

"I'm sorry, Grant. This can't be that much fun for you," I told him on the second day we were there.

"It's okay. I just want you to feel better. Maybe we can do some stuff tomorrow. Go out. See the island a little. Maybe do some snorkeling or something. To be honest, it's been kind of nice not doing anything." He sat at the opposite end of the couch and rubbed my feet as I lay there watching television.

"Okay. I'll be better tomorrow. I promise." Then I pretended to fall asleep until I actually did.

The next morning, I woke up and felt much better everywhere except in my chest. I expected the pain that had taken up residence there wasn't from overindulging at our party.

I decided to take a walk and clear my mind. Get my head straight.

I wrote Grant a note letting him know where I'd gone, grabbed the hotel's stationery and pen, and left.

My crazy mind concocted this crazy notion that if I wrote everything down and threw it into the ocean that I could let it go. I think some old tribe somewhere used to do that with dead people. They'd set them free. That was my plan.

I desperately needed to do that the memories of Casey and the part of my heart he lived in. I kept replaying over and over the things that he'd said to me before the wedding.

He told me that he loved me. He told me that I was his. Deep down, I knew that was the truth. But, why hadn't he told me sooner? Why hadn't he offered permanent before? He told me he got me, so surely he should have known that was what I wanted all along.

I sat there on the sand, popping all of the stupid fake nails off my fingers. My nails weren't pretty, but at least they weren't fake.

I thought about the word fake and how it applied not only to the nails I wore, but the wife I already was. I didn't want to be a fake wife. A fake anything.

Clarity came to me on the beach as I wrestled cheap acrylics and bit at dried glue.

Then I wrote. I wrote everything that I hadn't ever let myself admit. Pen to paper my secrets leaked out.

I must have been gone for hours. When I returned to the room, Grant was getting out of the shower. He was attractive and fit. He looked every bit the put-together, perfectly groomed, and shaved blond man who I'd known for so long.

"So you're feeling better then, Betty?" he asked and I could have died. Had he literally just called me Betty? I didn't know what to do.

I laughed, and said, "What?"

I stuffed the letter that I didn't have the heart to throw into the ocean, into an envelope and then into the front compartment of my luggage, while I waited for him to clarify or prove that I really had lost my mind.

"Betty. You signed the note this morning with Betty. Is that something new?" He grinned.

"Oh, that," I said. I'd signed a letter to my husband with a pet name I used with *him.* That was a new low for me. "I was playing around. You know. Seeing if you were paying attention." I acquiesced.

He sauntered toward me with nothing on but a towel.

"Well, I like it. Betty. I think it suits you."

Every time he said it my body reacted. Some twisted sensory thing misfiring inside my libido.

"You don't have to call me that. It was just a joke." I felt embarrassed, and honestly it felt so wrong.

"I could call you Mrs. Kelly," he said, as he wrapped his arms around me and kissed my neck.

"Well, I am Mrs. Kelly," I told him. "So, maybe we try out Betty while we're here." It was so immoral, but hearing it made nerves react and my blood flow like it hadn't in so very long.

"Betty it is then," he said.

We made love and he called me Betty throughout. I would deal with the shame of it later. At the moment, I was enjoying the memory.

When he said it as he came, surprisingly I did too. I didn't have to fake it. I just had to fake who gave it to me.

I didn't pretend to be Betty. I was her. My brand of wrong started with imagining he was Casey and ended with me biting my cheek to keep from letting Grant know.

In the mornings, before Grant woke up, I'd go into the town. I'd shop around and it was nice. Grant did a lot of work after he woke up on most days, so he barely noticed I wasn't there. I bought two bronze ships that reminded me of Casey and me. Always passing, never headed in the same direction. That was the problem. We never had the same goal.

In an island off the coast of somewhere sunny, I changed my direction.

Everything was all wrong. Up was down. Left was right. Only a few days before, I'd made vows to this man. And on the beach one morning, I made vows to myself to undo them.

I had but one goal. If it wasn't too late.

# THIRTY

## Casey

**Monday, May 25, 2009**

MY MAIN GOAL WAS letting her go. And a few days after May twenty-fucking-third, something entirely different stole my focus.

I walked into my mom's house and found her lying on the couch, something that I couldn't ever remember seeing her do. She was napping. In the middle of the day.

I went to her and sat down on the hardwood floor.

I shook her gently.

"Hey, Mom. It's me. Are you okay?" I asked as I sat on the floor beside her. She looked sick, and not at all like the last time I'd seen her. When was that? A month ago? The hospital when Foster was born?

She looked a little thinner then, but not really ill. She hadn't mentioned anything when we talked on the phone.

She stirred and her eyes fluttered open.

"Hi there, baby boy," she said. Her eyes looked puffy, probably from sleep, but they also looked a little sad.

"What's wrong? Mom, you look like you don't feel very well." I didn't want to make her feel bad if she wasn't that sick by saying so, but she didn't look herself.

"I don't," she admitted and leaned up on one arm. She ran her free hand through my hair. "Have I told you how proud I am of you?" It was a somber question, not a happy one.

"Yeah, you have." The hair on the back of my neck stood up, my instincts screamed that something was really fucking wrong. "What's going on? You're freaking me out."

"There is nothing to freak out about. And there's nothing you can do. I'm sick," she admitted, but my intuition told me there was more.

She wasn't sick-sick. My mom was never sick. She grew damn near everything she ate. She was fit. My mom was healthy.

"What kind of sick?" I felt like I already knew the answer.

"Well, right now I'm tired more than anything. Spending a few days on the road with a newborn can really drag it out of you. I don't know how I did it with two of you at the same time." She chuckled and I watched what seemed like happy memories skirt past in her pretty blue eyes.

"And?" I asked knowing she was stalling.

Finally, she drew a breath and said, "And I'm dying." One lonely tear fell out of the corner of her eye.

"No, you just have the flu or something. Don't be like that. Come on. I'll make you something to eat." This wasn't happening. Did I not have control of anything? I wasn't going to accept it. She couldn't die. I needed her.

"Oh, honey. I have cancer. Lots of cancer in fact. You name a place in your old mom and it's there."

*Cancer.*

"What? No. No. No." I shook my head while I ran my trembling hands over my face, trying to scrub the words she'd just hit me with away. "No. You're lying. Don't say this. No. No." My voice cracked and my ears rang.

It didn't make sense at all. My dad who ate trash and smoked cigars should have cancer. I love him, but for fuck's sake, that seemed more believable.

"Are you sure?"

She laughed and swiped at the other tears that fell out chasing the first. "I'm sure."

"When did you find out?"

"About a year ago, I've actually made it a lot longer than they thought I would."

*A fucking year!?*

"Why? Why didn't you tell me? Are you going through treatments? I could have been here. Why didn't you tell me?" I had to make a major effort not to yell at my sick mother. But I was so mad.

"Because, Casey, all I wanted was for you to be happy. I'm no fool. I know you've been chasing that girl. Micah told me all about it. And don't you get mad at her, either. I wanted you to follow your heart and that meant chasing your dream for the brewery and seeing what was possible with Blake. I knew about her wedding. You didn't have much time, honey. I couldn't get in the way."

"Get in the way? You're my mom. I should have been here. And Blake didn't want me. I was being stupid. It was all for nothing. I didn't get her and I missed out on being here for you. Were you alone?"

"No, sweetheart. Cory and Micah know and your dad. I told them not to tell you," she said without shame. "I wanted you to at least get a fair shot. I wanted you to find *your* happiness. And, baby, you were so close."

I stood up, panic, fear, anger. Every terrible emotion I'd ever felt hit me.

"I'm going outside for a minute. I'll be right back."

I walked outside and then I kept walking. When I made it to the end of her property that butted up against the woods, I screamed. I swore. I damned everything I could think of.

Myself. Blake. My mom. Dad. Cory. Micah. Cancer. Lies. That fucking bar. My job. Everything was to blame.

How could they not fucking tell me? They let me pursue some girl who would never want me, and as a result, stopped me from spending time with my mom who did want me. How the fuck could they have done that to me? Do they think I am that selfish that I wouldn't care about my own mother?

But what would I do if my dying mother asked me to mind my own business and keep her secret? I'd have done whatever she'd asked. As the minutes ticked by, I realized it wasn't their fault.

I sat out there for probably close to three hours working and re-working everything over in my head. How could I fix this?

All I knew was that I wouldn't leave my mom. Not now. Not when she'd put herself before me, and what she wanted *for* me.

It was settled.

# THIRTY-ONE

## Blake

**Saturday, July 4th, 2009**

"IT'S SETTLED. JUST DO it." I told the tattoo guy.

"I don't feel good about this, not shaving your hair back here." He told me again for the thousandth time.

I was getting a tattoo at the nape of my neck, slightly under my hair line—although, part of it was actually in some of the hair. That was where we didn't agree. I didn't want to shave it. That would look weird. He told me the issues and I thought I could manage.

Yeah, yeah. Infection.

Yeah, yeah. It could get in the way.

He was tattooing one simple character. A symbol really. So I didn't see the need.

"I've signed all of your waivers, now do it." I had had enough of his ninny-picking. I'd thought that tattoo artists were supposed to be reckless and wild. This guy sounded more like my mom.

When it was finished, I went back to my hotel room. I was staying in Las Vegas for a few days working on a restaurant overhaul in the Bellagio. It was going smoothly and I was happy to see this project finally taking shape.

I began traveling with the ships, for no other reason that they made me feel better. When I would think about all the times and talks I'd had with Casey, I'd take them out.

The two were similar, certainly a pair, but they weren't identical. One was a little taller and I thought it was more masculine. So, symbolically, it was Casey's ship. The other was leaner and looked more feminine.

I started modifying the Casey ship on my last trip. I painted the belly of the ship red and laughed the whole time remembering those ridiculous pants.

There was a band that went from the stern to the bow and I painted that white with liquid paper. I wrote The Lou on it with a fine-tip Sharpie.

That night I decided to work on a new part of my custom Casey ship, it needed some lime green, like the sunglasses he wore to the coffee shop the morning after we'd met.

A paper clip would do the trick.

I unwound the metal and reshaped it into a pair of aviators, which by my own admission, looked crooked and wonky, but I had to go with what I had. I saw the lime green nail polish in a shop a while back and picked it up. I pained the metal and hooked it to the mast in the front and the one in the back.

Then I ordered up a bottle of champagne and toasted to how crazy I'd managed to become in my twenty-five short years.

I was certifiable.

## Saturday, September 12th, 2009

I thought about reaching out to him every day, but I didn't.

I ran into Audrey, the eldest of Casey's younger sisters, whom I'd met twice, once at Micah's shower and then again at the hospital when Foster was born. And we had coffee.

She'd returned to Seattle already in her sophomore year of art school.

"You don't have to tell me anything, but I know you and my brother had something going on," she admitted, and was sort of warning me where her line of questioned was headed. "What happened?"

I looked at her, her wild curly hair that reminded me so much of her brother's, only lighter, and tried to answer with only my expression. I tried to give her a *let's not go there* look, but evidently it looked more like *maybe you should beg*.

"Please, Blake. I won't say anything to anyone, I'm just curious. I mean, I've never even seen you two together, I only know bits and pieces from overhearing my brothers talk, and from what Morgan has told me. I want your side. No judging. Promise."

She was sincere. And Casey had been right. She was a romantic. It was so unfortunate that our story wasn't a romance instead of a comedic tragedy. I would have enjoyed telling her that story more.

I drew in a long breath and decided that, maybe talking to someone who knew him—and sort of knew me—might help. It could be cleansing.

After I married Grant, I never spoke to Micah about it or Casey again. I don't think either of us knew what to say. It would probably sound something like, "How nice. Your baby's godparents had a secret affair and now they won't speak." Totally normal.

I warned Audrey right off that it wasn't really my place to tell her any of what I was about to say, and that it was a little weird to be chatting about Casey, especially with Casey's younger sister. But she waved me off and said, "Just fucking get on with it already."

She was a lot like him. No wonder I felt at ease spilling my guts.

"You may not like me after you know everything," I said.

"Blake, I told you, no judgments. Mistakes are mistakes. I'm sure you only did what you thought was right. Now tell me."

I started from the beginning. And I spared no detail. She laughed and so did I. When I thought I might cry, she did, and I fought the tears back.

We drank about six cups of coffee apiece before it was all said and done. She was holding my hand as I slowly spoke about my wedding and how we'd fought right before it.

She really didn't judge me. She listened with more understanding than I would expect from an eighteen-year-old. It was cathartic to release the story from within my heart. I didn't feel less sad, just a little lighter.

We'd be friends.

We didn't speak every day, but it was probably once a week.

Her classes started at Cornish and she was very focused on her work. She was talented in all things artistic and interested in learning everything about all of them.

Photography. Painting. Sculpture. Design. She was always talking about someone else's art like she loved it as much as her own.

I was packing a bag to head out the next day when I got a message from Audrey.

**Audrey: I was asked not to call you, but he needs you. I know that he does. His mom died last week.**

My hand covered my mouth as in shock and sadness squeezed the air from me. I had to go to him.

I'd wasted so much time, waiting for the right time to set my plan in motion. Afraid as usual.

I couldn't call.

I couldn't text.

I had to go to him.

But first, I cried.

# THIRTY-TWO

## Casey

**Friday, October 16, 2009**

CRYING ISN'T A WEAKNESS. That's one lesson my mother taught me that I will never forget. Yeah, I was a man and I didn't enjoy it. I hated it in fact. I prided myself on being able to push my feelings back, when able, and be tough when I had to be. But there are moments that shit sucks. Pain hurts. And men cry.

We buried her on Sunday.

Sunday night I drank myself sick.

Monday felt like I was living in hell.

Monday night I drank myself sick.

My phone battery had died days earlier and I wasn't conscious enough to care. I'd been staying at my mom's house the past few months. We still had a lot of paperwork to sort through, and thank God my dad was being helpful.

He'd been more than supportive to a woman who was his ex-wife over the past few months. Hell, even Carmen helped. Audrey flew back for the funeral, but then had to leave on Monday to get back to class.

Since I was sleeping through my days and drinking through my nights, I hadn't had much contact with anyone. But they brought food by and left me notes on the counter. The food went in the refrigerator, and the notes went nowhere.

It wasn't until the following Friday when I actually got up at a respectable time. I called into work to see how everything was going and I was happy to hear that everyone had pulled together and that even Marc had been coming in to help. It made me feel at peace knowing that everything in my life wasn't going to shit.

I still had my job.

I could still have Aly if I'd wanted her, but I was a beggar now, and I didn't have the luxury of being choosey.

I didn't have the two women who meant the most to me.

I sat on my mother's back patio and drank a whole pot of coffee black, out of a Styrofoam cup—which before I would have hated—but, I went for easy and it was on the counter.

People bring you shit like that when you're grieving. Paper plates. Casseroles. Dish soap. Trash bags. But it's all shit.

A month ago I wouldn't have even considered drinking coffee out of this shitty disposable cup, but what did it matter right now? I didn't taste it. It wasn't good. It just was.

I watched the garden for a long time that morning. Her plants looked overgrown and their yields were falling off and rotting. It looked depressing. And I couldn't stand another depressing thing at that moment.

I went into the basement and found my mom's gardening tools and decided to do something about it.

My mom would have shit if she saw the waste happening in her yard. Her body having gone to waste on her, she knew what it felt like. Cancer was like that. It kills your life, not just your body.

Knowing what she would have liked to see, I got my shit together and readied myself for some time in the dirt.

First I picked the ripe fruits and vegetables. There was so much. I'd never be able to eat it all. I'd need to talk to Cory and see if he knew who she gave it to. Maybe she donated it. I made a mental note to look into that.

Then I dug out the undergrowth and weeded around everything that belonged there. It was relaxing and for the first time in the past week, I didn't feel so far away from my mom. Not that I hadn't ever been away from her, because God knows, up until she finally told me, I had been jet-setting. Chasing a girl who didn't want me. Or didn't want me enough.

This distance was different. She was no longer a phone call or text away. And that fucking sucked.

I'm a man, but in that garden, I finally cried. I cried because a good woman was robbed of her old age. And I'd been robbed, too. I thought of things I'd never even let myself consider. She wouldn't dance with me at my wedding. She wouldn't be there when my kids were born or teach them how to tell which strawberries were ready to be picked.

She was gone.

All the while, in the garden, I kept looking at that fucking shed.

*"Casey, honey don't you think it would look nice painted red?"* she'd say every so often.

I understood the translation of her mother's speak. What she meant was, *"Casey, paint the damn shed red for your mom. Wouldn't ya?"* I never did.

And she was right.

Kneeling in that garden cursing God and doctors that Friday, I realized a few very important things. Sometimes you know what the answer is before you hear the question and my mom's fucking shed needed painting red.

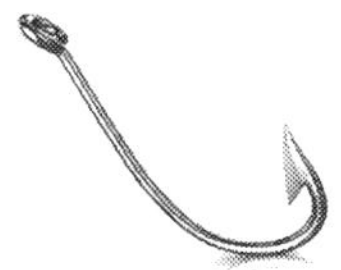

I didn't come into the house until it was dark that night. Then, I actually warmed up some of the casserole stuff that had moved into the refrigerator. It turned out, there's a reason people bring food like that. It was good and it would keep.

I took a shower and slept in my old bedroom. It was the first night in many that I dosed off rather than passed out.

I woke up feeling better than I had. Not great, but I'd take any improvement for what it was. It was barely after dark when I went to bed and, consequently, I was up with the sun.

I drove to the hardware store and bought red paint and other supplies that I thought I might need to get the job done.

I dragged out the old stereo from the basement to the shed and set it up. I'd need some tunes for my job. I turned on a modern-rock station and let it set my pace.

The wood was bare, but it was in pretty decent shape. I probably should have done more in terms of preparation, but I was focused solely on making the damn thing red.

The shed wasn't too far from the house, only a hundred feet or so, and I began on the side that faced it. The back side met up to the tree line, so who would care if by the time I got to the back, my handiwork was less than stellar? I relented that if I could singularly paint an entire fifteen by thirty foot shed, I didn't really care how perfect it looked.

I trimmed around the big door and decided I would get white paint the next day and do the trim, if I finished the entire structure that day.

The morning was hot, but I didn't stop. I pulled my shirt over my head and ran it across my almost bare scalp to remove some of the sweat. I tucked it into the back of my tattered cargo shorts and continued.

At about two, I went inside and grabbed some water and a handful of strawberries.

I continued to paint. My mind went where it usually did on standby.

*Blake.*

I hadn't spoken to her since our fight before her wedding. Before I watched her stroll down the aisle and begged God that she'd stop and leave.

Chalk that up to another unanswered prayer.

I was too far away to see her face or hear her voice as she said her half of the vows, but I couldn't tempt myself by going that close. It would have been too difficult to not make a scene or object, like in the movies.

I surrendered and let it happen. As if I'd had any control over it at all.

The thought still made me a little sick.

Then, like my wandering memory liked to do, it tortured me with flashbacks of her and me together. Random glimpses of happiness and pleasure which only felt like anguish and pain in hindsight.

The way her hair would stick to her face when we were both covered in sweat.

Her laugh and the way she hummed before she fell asleep.

Her pink nose. Her smell. Her taste. Her.

"Looks like you've been busy."

I really was losing my mind, because I started hearing her voice. It was like she was speaking to me. My arm burned as I rolled the paint high on the last of the exterior shed walls. I'd just started the final side and the blisters I'd given my hands were raw.

I could feel the heat radiating off my shoulders from the hours in the sun. I was thirsty and thoroughly tired.

That had to be why my mind had finally cracked. Her voice was only a figment of my imagination a reprieve my consciousness gifted to sooth me.

"Casey?"

There it was again. The sound was almost clear enough and bright enough to believe. I ignored it. I wouldn't let myself turn around only to learn I really was going mad. Then I felt a cool hand on my leg, as I stood on the lean-to ladder resting against the almost red building.

The fingers stayed in place and I felt my eyes close. Either I was certifiable or it was real. I was afraid to find out which. I held my breath as fought my mind to tell me the truth.

Was I fooling myself?

Was it really her?

Had I brought her out of the thin air by concentrating on her so hard?

Then she said, "Hey."

I finally allowed myself to look down at my leg. There was a hand. And it belonged to my honeybee. She was really there. On the ground at my mom's house.

I rested my head against my arm and tried to calm my breath. I didn't know what to say. Excitement at the thought of seeing her ran quickly through my veins. Then, I realized seeing her now would be one more memory I'd have to hide from later.

"What do you want, Blake?" I sounded tired and beaten.

She didn't answer, only retracting her touch from my leg.

I was past the point of tip-toing around her feelings. She didn't mind stomping all over mine in her wedding shoes.

One shaky foot after another, I climbed down off the wooden ladder.

"I don't want anything, Casey," she answered softly.

"From me, you never do." Stepping away from the last rung, I dipped down to grab the last water bottle I'd brought down with me. I took a long drink, tipping the bottle back, and I got my first good look of her, that I'd had in months.

Her hair was the same, but she looked thinner and more tired than the Blake of my memory. When I'd got my fill of water, I poured the last little bit over my face, dropping the bottle onto the ground when it was empty.

I ran my hands back and forth over my buzzed hair and the water came off the short strands in a mist that felt good on my hot, sunburned shoulders.

"I just wanted to come and see how you're doing since...," she paused not knowing how to word the obvious, "...well to see how you're doing." She looked over the paint job avoiding my eyes. "This looks nice."

I didn't have any fight in me, not at that moment. "It does," I said, and walked a few feet away to the shade and sat down on the long grass.

It needed a mow.

I brought my knees up and leaned back on my aching arms.

"Look, Blake. I'm not in the mood for your shit right now. If you came here to play the concerned lover, or *friend*, save it. I don't want to hear it."

My abrasive words bounced off her and she finally met my eyes again.

"I *am* concerned." She twirled a finger into the hem of her T-shirt and I saw her other fingers shake from where I sat. My ability to read her body still present as ever.

"Okay." I raised my eyebrows when I said it to tell her, with my face, that I was losing my patience.

Neither of us said anything as she stood there in the sun, beads of sweat beginning to form on her forehead.

It was a standoff and it was going anywhere. I had to break the silence, move this forward. To where I wasn't sure. "You could have sent a card or whatever. You didn't need to come here."

Her voice steady and sure she said, “Yes. Yes, I did.”

“Why?” I drew out the word on a long exhale.

She looked to me and then to the pail of cherry red color, then back again. I was lost as to what she was thinking. I could see something growing braver behind her eyes. She went to the unused pack of paint-brushes and chose the widest one. She held it up as if to ask if she could do something with it.

I shrugged.

She walked to the paint and slowly dipped the long horse-hair brush deep into it, lifting it when it was thoroughly coated. She looked to the wall, silently questioning if it was still okay.

Again, I shrugged. The whole thing was like a weird dream. Maybe the sun got to me and it *was* one. Maybe I was laying on the ground unconscious and it was all a fabrication of my subconscious. My vision blurred as I thought about the likelihood of that being possible. I stared off into the woods to the side of the barn.

Blake saying, “Because of this,” broke my spell. When I gazed back at her I saw that in letters about two feet in height, she’d wrote the word *BAIT*.

It stole my breath and it felt like my heart ripped more in a new place and healed in another. My shoulders fell forward, the weight of them more than I could hold up anymore. I leaned up and brought my dirty arms to my dirty knees, tucking my head in the hole it created.

I didn’t know what to do.

I was sad. She could make me happy. Then she’d kill me all over again.

Blake came to me and knelt so that we faced each other on the grass. She didn’t touch me, but if I knew her as well as I thought I did, she wanted to.

“Look at me, Casey. We need to talk. We need to be honest.”

“Honest?” I was always honest with her. It was her who couldn’t be honest with herself, let alone me, or that husband of hers. “Haven’t we already had this conversation before? Like fifty times? I don’t need to hear it again. You didn’t have to come all the way here to remind me that you don’t want me. That you made your choice. I don’t want to fight with you anymore.”

She bumped my knee, “Oh come on. You miss fighting with me.”

She lifted her hand and showed me a gapped pinch about an inch wide, "Just a little?"

"You know what I mean. This isn't a good time for this. For what we do. I can't." I sounded exhausted.

She scooted closer and threaded a leg underneath mine and wrapped her other leg around my back. She turned my face to meet hers. "Well, I miss it. I miss it a lot. I miss you."

"I miss you, too, but—"

She cut me off. "But now isn't the time to worry about that. We'll sort all of that out later. Whatever you decide I'll agree to." Her voice, coaxing and smooth, felt like a balm on my soul. "Right now, you need a bath. You need to let me feed you. And I'm going to take care of you." Her smile was warm and I didn't have the heart to refuse her. I couldn't have refused her anyway, because I desperately need this. So much.

As we walked up through my mother's terraced garden onto the concrete patio behind the house, I asked her, "How did you know I was down there? I was behind the shed."

She laced her fingers with mine and said, "I could hear your music when I got out of the car out front. So, I followed my ears."

"And how did you know I was here at this house?" My phone had been dead.

"Audrey told me," she said, then turned to face me. "Why didn't you want them to call me? Why didn't anyone tell me?" The hurt on her face was as plain as day. I always knew that when she finally learned about what had happened, that she'd feel terrible I didn't want her to know.

"I asked them not to tell you." It was the wrong thing to do, but knowing that my mother hadn't told me about her condition because she didn't want me to stop pursuing Blake still ripped at my insides. My mom wanted me to win her, even if we'd lose precious time together.

"Why would you do that? You know I would have been here for you."

"It's complicated," was the only thing I could honestly say. She took it for what it was worth and gave my hand a squeeze. Feeling her hand in mine really did help.

It didn't give me my mom back and it didn't give me back the time I wasted chasing her to spend with my sick mother, but it felt good.

She was right. I didn't have to have everything figured out right now. I just needed to feel something better. I'd worry about the rest when she would eventually leave me again. I wondered who would be here for me then.

The house was pretty much a mess. The last week hadn't been that great and cleaning wasn't on my to-do list. There were dishes in the sink. A bag of beer bottles stashed next to the trash can. Papers scattered all over the counter and plants from the funeral were dying all over the place.

"Wow," she said in awe at the mess I'd let get out of hand. When I looked down to see her expression, she wiped it away and replaced it with one that was more nonchalant than anything, "It's not that bad," she finally added with a small smile.

Her eyes darted around to the fresh vegetables and fruit I'd brought in from the garden. I saw a plan forming.

"Okay," she said. "Since you're already dirty take a few of these," she said as she handed me a half dozen ears of corn and continued, "and go outside and shuck them. Make sure to get all the silk off." She turned me back around and pushed me toward the large French doors with both hands in the middle of my back.

When I got to the table and unloaded, she'd already run inside and grabbed me a bottle of beer from the refrigerator. I looked at it and questioned if drinking was a good idea.

She must have seen the words on my lips, because she said to my unspoken statement, "You're only having a few. And I'm having some, too." She turned and went back into my mom's house. I watched the sway of her hips and felt a peace wash over me like I'd never known.

This is what it would be like if she would have chosen me. We'd never done anything domestic like this. She was a chef and she'd never cooked for me. We'd spent all of our shared time in other cities, in hotels.

I wondered if I would have shown her that I wanted this, if she would have wanted it with me, too.

Maybe it was the sun still getting to me—even though by then it was already tucked behind the timber—but it felt like a rogue puzzle piece had finally locked into place.

I had blame in what had happened between us, or what consequently didn't happen, too.

I'm sure it was probably too late. But for the first time in what felt like months under water, I took a long breath and started to regroup.

I finished cleaning the corn meticulously, not wanting to disappoint a chef with my negligent work. I picked up the ears and bundled them in my battered hands. The sun was almost completely set and the kitchen lights lit up the back of the house.

Before I got to the doors I stopped.

She looked like a dream. My favorite dream. She looked like my home.

She'd done a fast, but thorough job picking up the trash and emptying the sink of week-old dishes. She was in her element. She'd put my mom's apron on.

Seeing that, my eyes grew hot and burned. I couldn't move. She'd even folded the middle up around where it tied so that it wasn't too long. Just like my mom did.

My honeybee was in my kitchen cutting up carrots and peppers and god only knew what else to make food for us. Places inside me melded back together, and I physically felt my heart beating again. Part of me felt wary, but I was too damn tired to feel anything at that moment. I just needed to take it in and enjoy it. Surrender to this unexpected gift.

My fight for her wasn't over. As long as both of us could keep finding our way back to each other, it might never be. In that moment, I didn't care about her marriage with Grant. It didn't matter who she chose to *marry*. It mattered that we had something that you couldn't put down on paper. Something you couldn't choose, but was chosen by. Something bigger than merely changing your last name. What we had was only for us. It was indefinable.

We were both slaves to it.

# THIRTY-THREE

## Blake

**Saturday, October 17, 2009**

I'M A SLAVE TO this pull that Casey's heart has on mine. I'd thought that not seeing him in so long would dull it. It never did. If it wasn't love, then it was something equally unconditional.

When my eyes fell on him earlier that day, I almost didn't recognize him. His face looked hollow and lackluster where it used to glow and shine.

He'd cut off his beautifully wild hair, and in place was a short buzzed replacement. I can't say that it didn't look good, but it didn't look as good as his curly locks did. I missed them. I missed the way they would automatically wrap around my fingers like they were holding me close. The way they moved when he was animated.

But it was his eyes that were the most changed. The light that was there had dimmed. I felt bad for thinking it, but I hoped it was because of his mother's passing and not because of me.

I'd tried to call his phone, but then I absolutely couldn't take not hearing from him anymore. So I called Bridgett to see if I could work out of the San Francisco office for a while.

It worked out well for us both, since Melanie was on a month-long trip to Costa Rica and they were a little short staffed while she was away.

Grant didn't like it when I let him know I was going to be gone for a month, but he eased up when I told him I would come home for a long weekend in the middle. It wasn't like we were going to see each other that much anyway.

We never did.

I busied myself cleaning while Casey removed the husks from the fresh corn outside. I'd taken the trash out to the bin that I'd seen on the side of the house out front when I arrived. I loaded the dishwasher and tried to make some order of the counter space. The whole house wasn't a colossal mess; it was concentrated into one central place. The kitchen.

I'd looked in the cupboards and found some vegetable stock and decided a light vegetable soup would do just fine. There were some chicken breasts in the freezer and I had them thawing in the empty sink.

I could tell that it was a kitchen that got used a lot.

It was a home. It even felt like one to *me*.

Grant and I had renovated an entire house, but it didn't have a feeling like this place did. It didn't have any of the natural charm. It didn't have the notched wood in the pantry marking every inch of two boy's lives. It didn't have the calendar with birthdays and anniversaries scribbled down months in advance.

My heart was heavy for Casey, and Cory, too. But Casey mostly. Cory was starting his own family and he had Micah, who no doubt would be supporting and caring after he'd lost his mother. But Casey seemed to be alone.

I didn't have time to think about those things. It wasn't the best time to talk to him about how I'd made such a terrible mistake. And how if only he could give me some time, I was going to ask Grant for a divorce.

But I couldn't do it right away. We'd only been married a few months. But crying on your honeymoon behind big black sunglasses, and saying it was just a bad hangover wasn't normal newlywed behavior. It had instantly felt wrong. It felt like an injustice, to both me, Casey and Grant.

I loved Grant. I cared for him a lot. But I never felt as powerfully consumed by him as I did by Casey. Sadly, it took seeing the grass on the other side of the fence to prove to myself it was greener.

But all of these thoughts were for another time. Another day. I prayed Casey would allow us to have them. Even though, he didn't owe me anything.

I heard him at the door just as the broth was beginning to boil with the potatoes I'd quickly cut up. So I wiped my hands on the apron I'd found hanging in the pantry, and went to open the door for him.

"All done?"

"Yep, probably not as good as you would have done, but to be fair I'm not a chef."

"This is very true."

"It looks better in here."

I looked around and agreed. It did.

"It wasn't that bad, I told you," I repeated, even though my initial reaction was shock when we came inside earlier.

"Whatever, it was bad. Thank you. It even smells better in here. What is on the stove?" He talked as he walked over to the pot that was perched atop the six-burner range. Like I'd said, his mom's kitchen was pretty amazing.

He still didn't have a shirt on and I could see how the sun had scorched him badly. "Just a quick soup and some chicken, then we'll take a bath. Wash your hands and sit down." I took the corn, rinsed it, and then stood them on their ends, running a sharp blade down the long sides scalping the cob. "Need another beer?"

"Yeah, I'll take one, but I can get it. Are you ready?"

"Sensuous," I said playing his game from our former life.

He chuckled and it was music to my ears. He seemed different than when I'd first showed up. Hopefully, he decided not to hate my guts like I deserved. I'd made a decision before I even got on a plane to California that even if he hated me I would help him somehow. I had to. So, now with the change in his attitude, it seemed like things might be all right. And all right was better, because we were at least in the same room. Fighting or otherwise. If we did fight, it would be because he was right and I had been so very wrong.

I couldn't concentrate on that in that moment though. I just needed to be there. For him.

He opened the cold bottle of honey-brown lager and placed it where my empty stood. After discarding the old one, he took a sip and sat across from me, watching as I cooked. We were both quiet, but there wasn't the monstrous tension from before.

With us, sometimes it was like dipping your foot into a very hot bath, you had to go in slowly or it would scald you. We were readjusting. Something we actually *were* good at.

He cleared his throat and asked, "So you're in town for work?" as he traced imaginary circles on the counter top not meeting my gaze.

"Well sort of," I answered. "Do you know where there's a colander?"

He pointed to above my head behind me and I turned to locate it. It was nestled atop the cabinet, along with some matching handmade, I guessed, pottery bowls. They were beautiful. The paint was blue and it faded into a teal green color at the bottom. They looked like they were fired when they were still wet, because each had unique drippings down the sides.

I turned around, but knew that it would be a stretch. I wasn't super short, but it was up way high.

I'd met Deb a few times and she wasn't taller than me. I assumed there was a footstool or a step ladder close by, but when I didn't find one with one glance around, I decided to make a go of it and pray I didn't drop his mother's beautiful colander.

I got as close to the cabinet as I could and firmly grounded my left hand on the counter top, stretching my right arm as high as it would go while pushing myself up as high as I could with the other. Two hands startled me when I felt them wrap around my hips and lift me into the air like I was but a feather.

Casey steadily held me up high so that I could clutch the dish with both of my hands and held me there until I said, "Got it."

His body was close to mine and I felt his hot skin through my T-shirt on my way back down to the floor. My body reacted like it always had with him. I grew warm and tingly, and my panties were beginning to dampen. That was familiar.

I felt my lungs beg for more air and I had to cough to clear passage for the influx of oxygen they demanded.

Casey must have taken that as a sign that I was good to go, but he didn't move away completely. Left were his hands, still firmly holding me by the waist.

The air in the room was humid, from both the boiling stock and from us. Of course, he was sunburned and I was merely hot by association.

Finally I made a move to the side and around him, smiling as I turned, "Thanks."

I collected my cut-up veggies and ran them under the water in the garden sink on the island. "I love this kitchen," I said, trying to break the silence and distract myself from his nearness.

Getting frisky in a kitchen was one thing, but getting frisky while cooking was dangerous, and we were already dangerous enough together.

I turned the soup down and let it simmer as the chicken baked in the oven. We drank beers and walked around the family room that was open to the kitchen.

We'd stopped in front of pictures and I'd try to guess who was who, only getting it right about half the time. Casey and Cory were easy to tell apart for me, with their different styles and looks, but when there were children, it was almost impossible to know the difference. They were both very cute boys. It's funny how life makes you look different.

Then we stopped at one on the mantle that wasn't that old. It was Casey, his mom, and Cory at Foster's birth. I wasn't able to make it in time for his arrival, but both Casey and his mom were there.

The look on her face was perfect. The boys were both looking into the camera for the photo, but Deb didn't take her eyes off her grandson. Her mouth was open, smiling wide and you could almost hear her cooing at the infant. The picture was priceless.

"She liked having lots of pictures of you guys around," I said facing him.

"She liked the real thing more." He shrugged and started back toward the kitchen saying, "So did I."

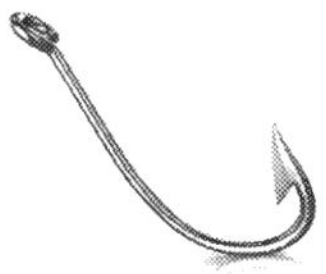

The soup was good and the conversation came back. He had his moments. I'm sure that was normal.

It killed me he was in pain. That he was suffering. I needed to show him I was here for him. Yeah, showing up was nice. And making dinner was a thoughtful and necessary gesture, but I'm sure many people had done those things for him over the past few days. I needed to give him what no one else could.

Selfishly, I hoped no one else was.

"Thanks for helping me clean up," I said as I handed him the last dish. We'd hand-washed the few we'd used, deciding it was easier to clean them in the sink.

"Thanks for dinner."

Things between us had been very cool in comparison to what we were used to in our past. Before, when we'd see each other, he'd be inside me within hours. At the very least, we'd touch each other reconnecting for our time apart, almost instantly. That day was different.

It didn't feel forced, it simply felt slower. And that was okay considering our circumstances.

His mother had just died.

I was about to cheat on my husband, instead of my boyfriend or fiancé. Like it was any worse, but my actions were about to lead me into commandment breaking territory. Thank God himself that I wasn't religious enough to feel His guilt, too.

But enough time had passed and I longed to touch and rediscover him.

"You need a bath, you're getting smelly, Lou." The use of my old pet name for him brought some of the old twinkle into his iridescent eyes.

"You know what, Betty? I, too, could have *sworn* I smelled something. It smelled like recirculated air. Maybe you're the one who's smelling up the place."

It was wonderful to have him playing with me. For us, sarcastic banter was as common as arguing. But that night, I was determined the keep the conversation like that. Easy, friendly, and sweet.

Perhaps, I needed it, too. Maybe even more.

"Well what are we going to do about it, both of us smelling so damn awful like we do?"

"I suppose we should take that bath." A rascally smirk spread across his face. I was proud to help put it there.

"We'll this is your place and you need it more, you should go first. I'll go get my bag from the car and—" before I could finish he'd wrapped me up in his arms and pulled me to his bare chest.

"You're not going anywhere. Except the bath tub with me."

"But my stuff," I queried. I had my luggage in my rental car that was parked in Casey's drive.

"Well, I guess that's tough shit," he sweetly whispered into my hair above my ear. Then he lifted me off my feet and carried me down the long hall that led to the west side of the house.

He walked us into a large room, which I would think was the master bedroom of the house. "Is this your room?"

"Yeah, it was my mom and dad's when we were kids, but when they divorced, she moved into the spare room on the other side of the house, closer to our rooms. She said that she liked the view out to the back better and it has its own door to the patio."

"Oh, this is big." I blushed after realizing the double entendre.

"This room was the spare room for a long time. I moved my stuff in here, but when she was sick, I felt better sleeping down on the other hall, in my old room."

That made my heart ache, so I placed a soft kiss to his neck. His breath hissed through his teeth and he stopped walking until I lifted my lips away.

Then he walked us into an impressive bathroom. It was as excellently furnished as the incredible kitchen was. Everything was white. The large soaker tub, white quartz double vanities, and a white-tiled floor. Everything else was chrome or glass. There was a giant walk-in shower on the opposite side from of tub and there was even a towel warmer.

I was impressed. I bet she had people wanting to visit all the time for the lavish spare bathroom alone.

He sat on the edge of the tub, I still straddled him, and he reached behind us turning on the oversized faucet. When his eyes met mine again I found the same smolder there that I remembered.

"Lift your arms. Unless you want to take a soak with your clothes on. And that's okay. You *are* a married woman now," he said in a joking voice, but it soured me.

Instantly, the thoughts in my head spun. They were familiar, too. The jabs.

I focused on a place on the wall, but I still raised my arms as he'd instructed. My body always did do exactly what he commanded of it. Some things never changed.

He took my shirt off but didn't let his eyes roam my flesh, instead they searched mine looking for the extra script to my inner dialog. He read me well.

"Hey, honeybee." His voice was laced with remorse. "I'm sorry. I'm sorry." He cupped my cheeks and rained kisses all over my face. Repeating, "I'm sorry." Over and over. I felt the shift in his apology. It intensified with his mouth on me.

When he pulled away, his eyes full of emotion, he took a long look into mine. He looked uncertain, which probably mirrored me.

"I'm sorry, too." I felt a buildup of tears begin to seep from my eyes. "I'm sorry for a lot of things," I whispered and looked down at his chest.

Casey lifted my head, with shaky hands that were still at the sides of my face, and took a lengthy uneven breath.

"We've both said things, done things, and made mistakes," he admitted.

He kissed my nose, then pulled back far enough to stare straight into me. "It doesn't mean that they were true, that we wanted to or that we won't do it again. We have right now, honeybee, and as bad as we are—we're good too. You're here. For *me*. I know you are. That means something. It means a lot."

Hot tears streamed down my cheeks now, and with the outpouring of them I felt like I wanted to bare my soul.

"I don't want to be married to him." Then I sobbed. "I'm staying in California for a while. I don't want to go back, but I have to." My chest constricted at the thought.

The water in the tub filled and began to lap at my feet that dangled in the basin. He stood, holding me and then turned to sit me on the edge. Casey, kneeling before me, ran a gentle hand down my shoulder and my back, stopping at the latch on the back of my bra. When it was unfastened, he slid the straps down my sides and then pulled it away, tossing it to the floor where my shirt laid.

"Stand up," he said. "Let's get in this tub and we'll figure it out."

When our clothes were removed and we were situated inside the large porcelain tub, facing each other again, I almost felt like I could do it. I almost felt like I could say the words.

I wanted him. Not Grant.

I wanted to be Casey's wife.

I wanted all of it. This house. His kids. A life here. But I didn't know how to do either, how to make it all happen *or* even say the words.

Instead, I asked him something that had been haunting me for over a year. "Why didn't you ever sleep with me? Why didn't you ever just stay?" My voice was low and somber, but my question sort of was, too. It always bothered me that he never wanted to wake up with me in his arms.

He reached for a large cup that was positioned on the tub shelf beside us and filled it with warm water. He poured its contents over my head, wetting my hair.

"I never *wanted* to leave, Blake. I had to."

"But why?"

As he sunk the cup again to refill, he paused his work to think about what he was about to say.

"Because it hurt too much to wake up with you and then not wake up with you. Does that make any sense?"

His answer did make sense. I remembered that first morning and I ached to feel that with him again. That morning was a gift, and had I known how dear and precious it was, I would have paid attention to every single small detail and laid there with him for hours.

"I understand. I'm sorry I did this to you. To us." This time I looked back at him, giving him the focus he deserved. Sometimes I felt like I was looking at him, but not allowing myself to see him. It was much too hard not seeing him when I needed to most.

"Will you sleep with me tonight?" I didn't mean to sound as desperate as I did; it just came out that way.

He looked torn. Then poured the water over my head.

"Are you really going to stay here?" he asked. I took the cup from him and repeated what he'd done to me, pouring the water over his practically bare head.

"I want to, if that's all right. I know you're going through a lot. I don't want to be something else to add to your stress. I'll be in San Francisco for a little while. Maybe a month. I don't know about every night, but I know I want to stay tonight."

Truth.

"What does Grant think about you staying here for so long? Did you have a fight?"

We didn't have a fight, we rarely did, and I'd left before it was possible. If I would have waited for him to get home from work and told him face to face about my trip, I wouldn't have been able to get here as fast.

So I only sent him an email, which was normally how we communicated during the day.

Yes. I emailed my husband that I was leaving for a month. It was cold, heartless even. It felt disgusting, but I did it. Guilt ate at me as I typed it, but ease replaced it when he sent one back like it was the customary way to do that sort of thing.

I got his reply when I was waiting to board the plane. He wasn't happy about me being gone for so long, but I was often gone for weeks. He asked me if I could come back, for a weekend, in the middle of my trip and I agreed. That seemed to be enough for him and he replied to travel safe and be careful.

I never felt like he missed me. Not the way Casey did.

Every time I saw Casey after a long break, his face would split into a wide open smile, his teeth were so perfect and bright, and he'd come to me like he couldn't wait another minute for me to walk all the way to him. That always felt so good.

"No, we didn't fight. We never really do."

How weird was that? Something that should have been a good thing in a relationship was such a bad thing for our marriage. There was never a fight. No passion. No desperation. It just was.

"Not like we do," I said and tried to smile.

"We do know how to fight, don't we? It's becoming a second language fighting with you. Over and over and over. I think by now we're almost fluent."

I dipped the cup under and tipped the whole thing on him, more on his face than on his head.

"I miss your hair, Casey. I don't like it this short." I couldn't help myself and I inched closer to him. Wrapping my legs around his waist and rising up higher on his lap. His hands found my backside and pulled me even closer. I could feel him growing hard between us. My hands moved over his short hair and my thumbs ironed out the fine red wrinkles on his forehead that the sun had made and time had creased.

I touched his face and lips.

"I miss your mouth." And then I kissed him chastely on the side where his lips met in the corner. "I miss the way your eyes undress me the moment you see me." I dotted kisses along his jaw to his ear, feeling him harden even more under my lap, his hands firming their grip on my ass. I said into his ear, "I miss the way your breath feels in my ear. I want you, Casey. I always want *you*."

His mouth moved around my face to find its mate and they devoured each other. Nothing in the moment was rushed. We had no place to go. We were where we needed to be.

I rose up and felt him at my entrance and without a guiding hand, I sat myself on him and didn't stop until he was all of the way inside me.

Nothing felt like Casey Moore.

"I miss you, too," he said over and over like a mantra as I rose and fell slowly over top of him. He wrapped his arms around me tightly and kissed me everywhere his mouth could find.

"I hate it when you're gone. I hate when I can't talk to you. I hate thinking about you with him. It's killing me. It's killing me not being the one who gets to have you. Stay, Blake. Be mine."

He spoke loving words in my ears and told me how much he needed me. We moved so slow that the water barely lapped in the tub, taking our time. Savoring the sensations.

As we got closer he brought a hand between us and touched me the way only he did. His thumb dancing delicately over the sensitive spot he was so familiar with. He stroked it like a flint catching my body on fire.

"Tell me you're mine, honeybee, and I'll let you come."

My orgasm was on the precipice of ignition, so I had no other choice. "I'm yours. I've always been yours, Casey. Please." I begged, craving my time-denied release. "I'll say whatever you want."

His thumb slowed and moved away from the epicenter of my building climax. "No, Blake. I don't want you to just say it. I need you to mean it."

My body was wanton and throbbing for its orgasm. I ground myself onto him and moaned my truth, "I always want you. *Only you.*"

Our mouths met feverishly, out teeth hitting together as we feasted on one another.

He relieved me, bringing his hand back to my screaming body, and in less than three or four deft strokes we were coming. I stilled and let the feeling of him emptying inside me claim all of my senses.

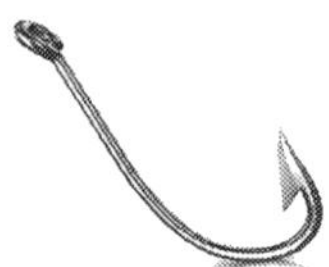

I didn't have my bag, and therefore I had no clean clothes in the house to put on. When we left the confines of the tub, when the water grew cool and shivers peaked on both of our flesh, I wrapped myself in a large towel and stood there like I was waiting for further instruction.

"Did you mean what you said?" I asked as I watched him rummage through the cabinet under the sink.

Absentmindedly, he replied, "Yeah." Finally popping his head out, holding a new toothbrush out to me.

"You did?" I retorted, knowing he wasn't paying attention to my question.

His face looked befuddled, as if he didn't follow.

"You just answered yeah. I don't think you heard me." I quirked an eyebrow at him. He looked so calm and almost like the easy-going man I knew months and months ago.

"I heard you. You asked if I meant what I said and the answer is easy. Yes. I don't know what you were talking about." He stood and smiled wrapping his arms around my shoulders, while I gripped the toothbrush in between our bodies. "The thing you don't understand is that I've meant everything I've said tonight." He kissed the top of my head. "Now brush your teeth. It's time for bed, Betty. I hope you're not tired."

I prayed that it was real. All of it.

The wicked grin on his face made my heart beat double time.

I stood beside him at the sink. Even though there were two, we shared. He already turned the water on and was dispelling the paste to his brush. He looked at me expectantly in the mirror and offered me a squeeze. I pointed the head of the new toothbrush at him and he gave it a stripe across the bristles. We brushed our teeth smiling like it was the most normal of activities.

He also found a comb and brought it with him into the bedroom. We walked to the end of the bed and it was like we didn't know what to do. We'd been in beds together plenty of times, but that time, I was nervous. It felt poles apart from before.

"What side of the bed do you sleep on?" I asked him, a little shyly.

"Are you serious?" He looked at me like I was being audacious. "It doesn't matter to me. I've been dreaming of sleeping all night with you for so long that I don't give a fuck if you sleep side to side at the end of the damn thing."

I giggled. It really was irrelevant, because I didn't care either.

"This is a bit weird, isn't it?" I asked. My pulse was racing. I heard what he'd said earlier and I wasn't sure what this would mean. I wanted it, but I didn't want to do more damage to him than good. Of all things, this is what I stopped to consider. All of the things I've done to this man, and that was the thing that caused me to pause. I felt silly.

"It's new. We've never got in bed knowing that neither of us were going to run." He laughed and pointed at me with the comb. "You're not running, are you?"

"Not planning on it," I said sarcastically. The truth was I really wasn't planning on it, but my plans always seemed to change.

"Well, then. Get up there, Betty. Make yourself at home." He still wasn't wearing any clothes, just a towel and my eyes wandered over his skin. He'd lost a little weight, which only made his muscles seem more prominent. The lines in his back were strong and defined as he began walking to the closet.

He returned with a pair of boxers and a T-shirt.

"Are those for me?"

"One of them is. Which one do you want?" He was being playful and it was nourishment for my heart. So, I chose the least likely of the pair.

"I'll take the boxers."

His face lit up like a Christmas tree. "That's my girl."

He handed me the plaid boxers, which were way too big and didn't want to stay up after I pulled them up my legs. I let my towel fall, going topless.

Casey threw the shirt on and dropped his towel. He clapped his big hands together, and then rubbed them conspiratorially. "Now this is a sleepover!"

He smacked my ass as I climbed onto the four-poster bed and I crawled my way to the center. He followed and scooted behind me. He unraveled the towel, which was holding my wet hair up, and let the cool locks hit my shoulders and back. It gave me chills. He pulled at me and wedged my ass between his legs.

After leaning over to the bedside table, he threw the remote control onto my lap, telling me, "Find something good." Then he moved my hair to the side and kissed the nape of my neck, finding a surprise there.

"You got ink?! Let me see." I held my locks up for him to examine hoping he'd like it. I'd got the tattoo on a whim, praying that one day he'd see it and knowing that if he never did, I'd still have a reminder of him with me forever.

"It's a hook. You got a hook tattoo?" he softly said, so close to my skin that gooseflesh appeared down my arms and legs.

"I did. Do you like it?" I didn't know what he would think of it. After I'd got it, I badly wanted to send him a picture.

"It's beautiful. Perfect." he added and kissed it. The hook was thin and delicate, centered barely under my hairline. I'd had the artist draw the thinnest of strings that tied at the eye of the J-shaped piece of metal. I'd instructed him to hide a C and an M in the line and to have it wrap the throat and shank. Yes, I'd studied hooks. To anyone else it would have looked like an unassuming hook and string, but to me it was a secret tribute to the man I deeply missed.

"It's your initials hidden in the string," I said.

He kissed my neck once more and then said, "Thank you, honeybee," like I'd given him something precious. Casey's simple words were full of meaning and the swallow I heard after he spoke didn't go unnoticed.

I channel surfed, passing sports and sitcoms alike. I wondered if he had any of the good channels. It was getting late and I'd just about lay money that I could find something we'd both enjoy. Then I stumbled onto a skin-flick and tossed the remote aside, after turning the sound down.

I felt the comb slide smoothly through my hair, which I was sure would be littered with rats and tangles from the many rushed knotted ponytails I'd hastily thrown up throughout the day's travels.

Over and over, he dragged the comb through my wet hair running a hand behind it, almost like he was petting me. I watched the naked couple on the television touch each other and felt both relaxation and desire seep into my pores.

When I'd tired of not seeing him after minutes of viewing the erotic movie, I caught the comb behind me and captured his hand. I turned where I sat partway and found his eyes, hooded and glazed over.

"Do you always watch porn topless at slumber parties, or is this new?"

"It's been a while," I said coyly. I released his hand and placed mine on his leg. He licked his lips, and on its own, my tongue came out to wet mine. "I'm usually completely naked."

"Your dirty talk is improving. Tell me more," he said bringing a hand around me grabbing a free breast.

"I've been doing some reading on it," I said, trying to keep the smile out of my voice, which has always been my problem. "Studies show that men love it when you tell them how wet you are."

His breath caught and he held it, nodding his head slowly. He closed his eyes like he was soaking in my words, then muttered under his breathe. "Finally, a study I can get behind. What else do *they* say?"

"*They* encourage the use of genital slang." I turned towards him fully and away from his grip on my chest.

He leaned back and I crawled up his body, keeping my legs between his. My arms holding my weight above him. His hands found my sides and held me there.

"*They* also say to ask for things that you want—to beg if necessary—and to repeat your lover's name." My voice was husky and low. Watching him swallow hard almost made me lose it, but I stayed the course. Holding back all the humor from my face, as best I could.

He asked weakly, "Have you tried any of *their* theories?"

"Not yet. I've been waiting."

"I think now would be a good time. Education is very important."

I took a breath and lowered my mouth to his ear. I licked the lobe and said as seductively as I possibly could, "Casey?"

He exhaled a long rumbling, "Hmm?"

"Can you feel how wet my pussy is? Please?"

That was all it took. In one fast move he lifted me and rolled us over. Kicking my legs apart, he masterfully switched our positions.

I was in Heaven.

# THIRTY-FOUR

## Casey

**Sunday, October 18, 2009**

HAD I DIED AND gone to Heaven? Or maybe it was my mom showing me what it was like.

Only hours before, I had been sulking and brooding. Painting a damn shed. Then Blake appeared out of nowhere, painted Bait in red on the wall, took care of me and made me eat, washed me in the tub with her two small hands, and then there I was in bed with her, about to sleep with her, really sleep with her, for the first time in over a year.

Oh, and she'd just asked me if I could, please, see if her pussy was wet.

Well, you bet your sweet fucking ass I could. I'd never been surer of anything. She was ready for me, but I'd make damn sure she knew exactly how wet I could make her.

I gazed down at her, with my weight on my arms, the same way she had, and turned the tables. "I like your research."

I couldn't take it any longer and leaned down to kiss her smiling lips. I paused before our mouths met and watched her close her eyes. It was one of those rare and sublime moments. I'd trade my soul for a picture of her like that, frozen in time. Her hair splayed over the white pillowcase under her head. In *my* bed. Her lips pursed ready for mine. She looked peaceful waiting for me.

All for me.

"Look at me, honeybee." And her eyes fluttered open and met my gaze. She grinned unabashedly and wrapped her arms around me causing my balance to wane, and I fell atop of her. I heard a contented laugh come from her and crushed my mouth to hers. Her tongue didn't hesitate, meeting me and running itself over mine.

I felt her hips grind against my naked lower half. I felt her readiness soak through the boxers, but I wanted to make her beg for real, like her bullshit research had mentioned. My lips left hers and ran across her clavicle.

I retreated lower, kissing my way down to her navel and I circled it, leaving a wet trail every step of the way. I skimmed my hands up the inside of the loose shorts and found her dripping and so ready for me. But she'd have to wait.

I wanted her just as bad, the head of my hard cock sneaking up the front of my shirt. But if this relationship had taught me anything, it was patience. And I could hold out for a little longer if it meant hearing her desperate for only me.

I parted her damp flesh and ran my thumb from her clit to her entrance. Her back arched, her body invited me to come inside. I felt her clitoris delicately bead and throb under my touch and knew she would come undone with little more than what I was already doing.

But I wasn't leaving her tonight. I had nowhere to go. I was taking my time with her. It would be such sweet torture the likes of which she'd never had to deal with.

In the past, I'd been too rushed to be with her. So needy to make her come, almost trying to prove to her that I could. But I knew I could. She'd come to me, skin marked with my letters, because I needed her. To sate my needs and confirm her own.

I continued the mild assault with my thumb. I skirted my fingers over her opening, promising to go in, to bring her the release she craved, but I didn't. Instead, I removed my hand and watched her face and body grieve its loss of me. I reveled in that power.

I slowly removed my shirt and her boxers, pulling them down her legs inch by inch, letting the fabric graze her love-slick skin. Her nose was that beautiful shade of pink that haunted my dreams.

I led her leg to the side of my face with my left hand and found my cock with the other. I kissed her ankle and rubbed myself, making a show of it.

She writhed. Her pouty mouth shaped into an "O" as she watched. She could only take so much. I watched as her hand slowly crept to her center and began its own sensual mission, her long middle finger finding the spot and running over it in time with my strokes.

Just as I saw her head start to dip back into the pillow and her eyes start to close—sure signs that she was getting close to her peak—I moved her hand and stilled my own.

"Not yet, honeybee. You have to wait." She didn't argue, only nodding her compliance, biting her lip. She was breathing hard and I watched as she tried to rein in her desire. "You're not ready yet."

"I *am* ready, Casey. I'm ready *now*." Her voice sounded seductively deprived.

I lowered myself to kiss directly on the bare flesh above her pink pussy. *Pussy*. If she said that word, then I'd have no choice but to cave. I'd probably cave anyway, because this power I had over her was heady. It always was.

Blake in the throes of passion was always a precious sight, but Blake being submissive and obeying my will was nirvana. Not often over our history had we played with the roles much, always too rushed to take our time. Although, there were times in the heat of an argument, she'd yield to me when she knew her body had sided with mine. That time in Atlanta, she would have done anything I told her even though she was a little afraid.

Thinking about her like that only served to chip away at my tenacity and so I continued my onslaught.

I licked at her swollen skin and sank my rigid tongue through her, diving in, giving it one long taste.

"You taste so sweet, honeybee," I said against her skin in between kisses.

She was bare, precisely how I'd liked. Smooth and silky. Nothing to hide her away from me.

What I'd said wasn't all for show to drive her crazy. I'd done my research, too. Certified by the University of Blake. She'd always reacted to me telling her how much I loved her pussy.

She wasn't that vocal, but let me tell you something real about what true amazing was. The way Blake smelled, felt, tasted, and looked when she'd clench up tight in the face of a climax. Amazing. I'd prayed almost every day that I was the only man who'd ever *really* seen it.

So, I didn't continue with my worship. She'd tip over the edge too soon. I only gave her enough to reinforce my torture.

"Touch me," she panted. "Please, Casey. Please."

So the begging *was* a dick-wagger. She was right. My cock twitched hearing her say my name. *Who was I really torturing?* If I made it five more minutes, then I'd have been lucky.

Her hands found my head, void of the hair, which she loved to touch. I couldn't deny that feeling her skin on my skin wasn't a new sensation I liked. I loved hearing her say she'd missed my hair, knowing the reason I cut the shit off was because I couldn't stop feeling her hands run through it in my sleep.

She embraced me and pulled my head in closer to her center, attempting to give herself relief.

I reached for her hands with one of mine and held them together above my head, tight to her flat belly.

"Don't you get it yet?" I whimpered, in between wide licks up her cleft. "I've got you. Right now, your mine. Let me keep you for a few more minutes. Even if it is just on this ledge."

It was then I slipped a finger past my mouth and slid it into her and she moaned. Still not fighting the hold that I had on her hands.

"Casey, I need you. I need yoooouu," she groaned, losing control of her body. "Please. Make love to me. Please, I can't take it any longer."

*Yes, my sweet honeybee, that is exactly what I'm going to do.*
*Make. Love. To. You.*

I climbed up the bed, released her hands and they went straight to my back. Her grip sinking into my muscles, her fingers fitting perfectly between my ribs.

So in tune with her, I didn't even waste the thought on guiding myself into her. My body was educated in hers. Her body was searching for mine between us. Squirming up with her pelvis, her greedy sex found me.

We could find each other with our hands tied behind our backs.

I pushed into her and she came apart the very second my hips rocked into hers.

*My God*, I thought.

Then my lips said, "My God."

All complex thoughts were gone.

She quaked and seized around me and I felt a slickness that could boost any man's ego ten-fold. Yes, in fact she did come and I could *feel* it.

I ground against her as she rode me from the bottom through her pleasure. Then a carnal male drive took over and consideration was simply a thing of ten minutes ago.

My fists balled the sheets under the pillow she laid on, and my other hand held her hip as I set a punishing rhythm, losing any precious control I thought I had.

Her hands were everywhere, gripping my back and grasping my shoulders like she couldn't get a good enough hold on me. My hand slid under her ass and lifted her to an angle that sent fire up my spine.

"Ah, I want you to come again, Blake. Can you do that for me?" I hissed air through my teeth, feeling my back starting to tense and my ab muscles beginning an all too familiar twitch. "I want to come inside you while you're screaming my name."

Her center clenched and then I brought my hand between us and ran my hand over her quickly, parting my fingers around where we met. She came off the bed, her arms around me tight and the force pushed me back onto my heels.

My words and my ejaculation came at the same time.

"God, you're here. Ah, fuck, Blake. Fuck, Blake!" We held on to each other so tight, chest to chest, hanging on for dear life.

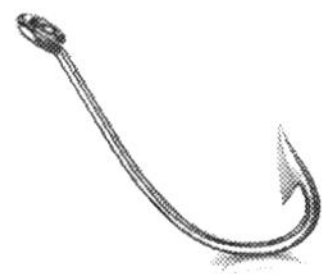

I lay there that night, with the whole world in my arms. Biting my tongue to keep from telling her how much I loved her again. It was all I had, but it never felt like enough. I thought about it and came to the conclusion that that was what love was. Never having enough of something. Always wanting more. Being greedy with your heart.

The wind blew in through the long, sheer curtains from the north and it ran across the flowers in the garden out back. The scent reminded me of why she was here. Reminded me of what I'd lost.

Blake had fallen asleep merely minutes after we came after the third round, which ended only a few minutes prior. It was almost light outside. She lay on her belly in the crook of my arm with one of hers stretched across my chest. I rubbed my hand up and down her side, her skin was velvet on my battered palms.

Every so often she'd startle, but only waking enough to squeeze me, letting herself know I was still here—I thought–and then she'd fall back into her slumber. It filled me with hope.

I watched the curtain move in the wind and it finally lulled me to sleep.

I was visited by the reoccurring dream I had often about Blake's wedding. In my dream, I stood at the altar with her and Grant.

It changed though. Sometimes I'm the priest. Sometimes I say their vows with them, like a third party. But it was always the three of us standing there. In this particular version, the priest asked Blake to kiss her husband and she kissed me.

When I woke up the next morning I didn't feel the dread I usually did. I felt like maybe she was going to pick me. As my eyes blinked open, the first thing I saw was the small tattoo she'd had done on the back of her neck.

She was rolled away from me and slept peacefully. Her side rose and fell like the tide. After we'd exhausted ourselves physically and emotionally last night, she'd swept her hair up into a messy bun on top of her head. Still held up with the elastic, her hair was just so that I could see the ink through the few wispy pieces that had slipped from the hold of the hair tie overnight.

The hook wasn't very big. I wondered how they'd even made the lines so fine and faint. It was delicate and not very noticeable at all. My initials stuck out—at least to me—plain as day. Knowing that she'd marked her beautiful skin with my brand did something inside me.

It made that possessive voice, which I always tried not to pay attention to, louder.

*She is yours and her skin bares the mark that proves it.*

Instinctively, I pulled her warm body flush against mine and I held her like that until she began to stir, waking up. Her body relaxed into mine and fit into every void my body left for hers. Her ass tucked into my hips, my legs were traced with her legs, one of her feet slipped in between my calves. The soft cool skin of her shoulders and back perfectly paired with the hot skin on my chest.

I had one arm under her and her head lay on it, her fingers woven into mine where they met. My free arm wrapped around her flat stomach, my hand almost reaching from one side to the other of her.

I felt her belly rumble. She was hungry and she'd lost a lot of weight since I'd last seen her body. Her hipbones were sharp, the definition of her ribs showed, her clavicle more distinct. She didn't look unhealthy, but for someone who worshiped food the way she did, it was a clear message she'd been going through something, too.

The thought of her being hungry, or ill, after recently losing my mother the way we did, lurched at my gut.

She needed to eat.

I said softly in her ear, "Good morning, Betty." I put my lips on her shoulder and left them there. "Let me make you breakfast."

She laughed a little, "What are *you* going to make *me*?"

"Pop-tarts."

She stretched her arms above her head, and in her stretch her ass pressed deliciously into me. "What kind?" she said through a wake-up yawn.

"What does it matter? A Pop-tart is a Pop-tart."

"So not true. Some Pop-Tarts are good, some aren't." She rolled to face me. "So what kind do you have?"

"Maple and Strawberry, I think."

"Okay, I'll let you make me breakfast then. I'll brew the coffee." And she grinned.

"This is something new now, isn't it?"

Her eyes looked thoughtful. "This feels all new. A new day." I grabbed her by the ass and lifted her to my stomach to lie on top of me.

"I like new days when they start like this." I paired our foreheads. And she closed her eyes.

"Me, too."

We made Pop-Tarts and coffee and sat outside. Blake cut up a melon that I'd brought in from the garden. It was a little foreign and a lot more natural than I thought it should be. Even after all of this time and everything, we still knew how to be Casey and Blake.

We remembered how to talk to each other. In a matter of an hour, it didn't even feel like we'd been apart.

I charged my phone and called my family to let them know I was still alive. They all sort of got the hint that I needed some space after I'd told my sister Morgan to, "leave me the fuck alone for a while."

It was rude and so I apologized when I finally reached her.

"I'm sorry I snapped at you the other day, Morg," I said before we got off the phone. "I wanted some space, but I'm glad you wanted to be here for me."

"It's okay. I know it's hard. I just love you so much and I hate seeing you unhappy." She started crying. "I don't want you to be alone." Her heart was so big, so tender. My baby sister lived to help others.

"Hey now, don't cry. I'm not alone." I looked at Blake on the patio through the big window, she was smelling one of the flowers. I didn't feel alone anyway.

"You're not. Who's there, Aly? Troy?" She sounded hopeful.

I couldn't lie to her. It wasn't my style. "Blake's here."

"Casey, she's married!"

"I know," I said. I knew that more than anybody.

"So what is she doing there?" She never seemed to like Blake and whenever her name came up she acted offended. Morgan's morality and sense of right and wrong was like a compass. Everything was simply good or bad to her. Which was a bad way to be, but Morgan was good to her core.

"She came to see me. Don't be like that Morgan, you might be smart, but you don't know everything."

"I know what you looked like after her wedding. I know you love her and she married someone else. Those seem to be valid reasons for me to dislike her. How would you feel if someone treated me that way?" She told me once that she wanted to be a nurse, but she was more equipped to be a lawyer.

"I'd tell you to think for yourself and be happy. This isn't your business. I love you, and thanks for your concern, but she makes me feel better. You don't get it. *You* only know the *story*, Morg. I've lived it."

She sighed on the other end. "I love you, too. Stop talking to me like I'm a little girl."

"You are a little girl." I laughed. "To me."

"Whatever. I've got to go. Please, be careful and be good to yourself. Can you meet me for lunch next week?"

"I will. I'll talk to you later."

"Okay. And Casey?" she said as an afterthought, "I'm glad she makes you feel better, it's about time she did."

How is it that my younger, my least experienced sibling, was wiser than all of us?

The day wasted away. We watched television. We had sex on the half wall of the stone patio. We made food and listened to music. We took a walk down to the shed. The red "Bait" still written on the back wall facing away from the property.

"This really is something, isn't it?" she said that night as we looked at the sky, even though it was nearly starless. We watched the clouds pass between us and the moon. It felt a little symbolic.

"I think so."

She rolled over and looked at me, all business. "I like it."

"I know."

"I want this," she said in exasperation, falling back against the blanket looking up again. "I want this!" She screamed into the night.

What it must be like in her shoes. I'd spent the better part of the past year, or more, trying to figure that out. Listening to her cry out for what she really wanted, lying there beside me, and hearing it was that. There. With me. It breathed life into my person.

"Then take it," I said.

"I'm trying. I want a divorce. I don't love him like—" and she paused, but I heard the full sentence. She'd never told me she loved me. And I'd only told her in a fight.

She asked, "Can you give me a little more time?" Her voice was barely a whisper.

"I can try, if you *mean* that."

"I mean it."

"How long is a little time?"

"I don't know. I just got married. My parents—" she paused again, leaving another dangling sentence in the damp night air.

"Just say it, honeybee. We passed polite a long time ago."

"I don't want my parents to hate you. I don't want them to hate me, either. I just married Grant. They've known him a long time and they're so close. They won't understand all of this." She rolled in my direction. "I need to start talking to them. I can talk to my dad. I just can't spring it on them. I need to give it time. Maybe a year."

Another year? Fucking hell. But what was one more at that point? It would take me more than that to get over her, which was fact.

I thought about what she was offering. She wanted me to wait. More. A year. A year wouldn't be so bad as long as we still had communication. Without that, I'd smother in my head. She asked me for time to ease out of a marriage that looked great on paper, but shitty on the wall.

We could at least count on Reggie to be on our side. He never liked Grant to begin with, according to Blake.

But could I patiently wait while she went back to him?

I answered the best I could, the only answer I ever had for her. "You know I can't say no. That's what this is all about. I can't say no to anything you ask of me, and you can never say yes to me in return."

"I say yes to you more than you know." Blake sat up and hugged her knees. "I say yes to you on the inside."

That made sense. It was fucked up and nobody else could possibly get what she meant, but to me, that was real.

"Don't make me wait too long. Please, Blake. Not a year," I pleaded.

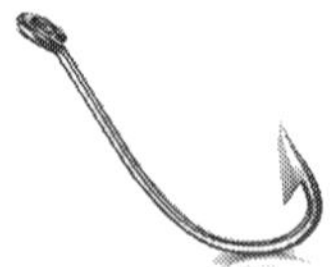

She didn't go to work on Monday. I showed her how I made my first homebrews in the basement and we decided that someday she'd make one of her own.

We talked about things we'd never discussed before. Things that were listed under the category of *Future*. Each moment felt almost fictional.

She worked on Tuesday and the rest of the week. Things moved. The cogs of life started to turn.

We even had Cory, Micah and Foster over on the weekend.

If I was going to win a life like the one I was pretending was real, then the wait would be worth it.

It was perfect. I felt relief like I'd never known. Having Blake around morning and night, being able to touch or kiss her on cue of any whim I had to do so, was fucking life changing. It was like that time she let me sample the cheesecake, giving me just a taste so that I knew what I was fighting for.

*This life. This was what I was fighting for.*

The only difference was this time *she* was the one who had to do all the fighting. Maybe she was reminding herself how much she loved the cheesecake, too.

In those two weeks, we thrived. I hadn't seen her bite at her nails once. She was *my* Blake, and it suited her so well.

# THIRTY-FIVE

## Blake

**Thursday, November 5, 2009**

THE NEW SLEEPING ARRANGEMENT with Casey suited me fine.

Waking up with his arms around me felt like the way waking up should be. The most horrific part was realizing that all along he was right. It would be too hard to wake up with him not there.

I had promised Grant I would come home for a weekend and it seemed that Casey's and my time was on fast forward right to that day. Both Casey and I knew it was coming. I'd told him the night before over dinner, that even though I didn't want to leave, I had to.

He got quiet for a while, but he didn't fight me. Maybe we were all fought-out by then.

"I hate it," he said. "I hate you going back to him. Every cell in my body says no."

"It won't be for long."

He leaned forward and ran his hands over his head, and I noticed how much it had grown in only the past few weeks. He was frustrated and I physically watched as he denied himself telling me not to go.

"I'll be back on Monday."

He looked out into the setting sun. "Monday then."

The next day he said he was going to go for a bike ride while I waited for the cab. He didn't want to watch me leave.

I left a note for him in the bed that we'd shared for fourteen nights in a row. I also left my ships.

Lou,
These are my ships. Please keep a close eye on them. Although they sail apart at times, they always find their way back.
Two ships in the night, one heart in their ocean. I'm trying to get them on the same course for us.
Trust me.

YOUR, Betty

As I sat in the porch swing waiting on the car, a little silver, hybrid pulled into the drive next to Casey's black Lexus RX.

It was Morgan. Just what I needed. She didn't like me much, Audrey had alluded to that fact.

"Hello, Morgan," I said politely as I watched the yellow cab turn down the lane and begin that way. I stood to ready the bag I was taking back with me for the weekend.

"Hi, Blake. Is Casey here?"

I started down the sidewalk, knowing that one of us would have to step aside. Even though I was years older than her—she was inches above me, tall like her brothers—we both stopped feet apart, at an impasse.

"He's on a bike ride."

"Does he know you're leaving?" she asked as she noticed the cab pulling up behind hers.

"God, yes. He knows I'm leaving. It's only for a few days."

She smiled, but it lacked authenticity. "Good. He seems a little better on the phone. I came to see if he wanted to go get some lunch, since I got out of class early."

"I'm sure he would like that. He won't be long. You should wait for him." I smiled and tried to show her what a real one looked like. He always talked about how Morgan was a sweet girl, but to me she seemed a little short.

"I think I will," she said and stepped to the side so I could pass with my small suitcase that I was rolling behind me.

"Thanks," I said as I walked toward the taxi. "Morgan?"

She turned back to me and popped her hip and tilted her pretty blonde head. "Blake."

"When Casey is hurting, I'm hurting too. I just want you to know that."

"Good, then stop hurting *yourself* and come back." Then she gave me a genuine smile. "Please."

There she was. There was the sweet sister Casey had told me about.

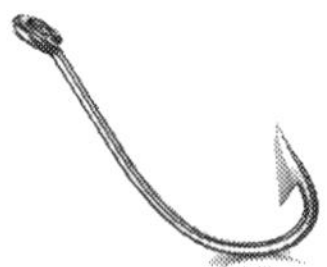

When I got home, I was surprised to find that Grant was already there. Quite surprised really.

Go figure, on the day I was initiating the demise of my marriage, by speaking my mind and being honest with him and myself, he'd be there like a perfect husband.

That's how I'd decided to go about it anyway. Honesty was supposed to be the best policy, or some shit like that. I was going to be truthful. See what happened.

There he sat, in our house, the house he gave me that never was a home. It isn't a home if you don't feel like yourself when you're in it.

"Hi there, you," he said when I walked in and dropped my bag.

"Hi. I didn't think you'd be here," I said quietly.

"I haven't seen you in two weeks. Of course, I'd be here. I missed you." He smiled at me and I forced a smile back, acknowledging inwardly that it probably looked like Morgan's.

I hadn't called much, but he didn't either. I could only guess he'd been busy and assumed I had been, too.

The San Francisco office was busy, there were many projects in the planning stages, but honestly I could have done most of the work I added to my plate from Seattle.

I'd only been in that house, with him, for minutes and I already felt drained.

He was home. Like he should have been.

That night went slowly and also faster than I'd hoped. I was staring bedtime in the face. I tried to fake being asleep on the couch while we were watching something on CNN. On another night it would have naturally put me to sleep. But on that night, my adrenaline was off the charts and my heart raced like a frightened bunny.

Still, I closed my eyes and laid my head back like I would if I really was tired. And deep down I was tired. Just not the sleepy kind. I was tired of pretending. Tired of all of it.

I wasn't shown mercy.

I managed to fall asleep, but I woke up in Grant's arms as he carried me to our bed.

Dread washed over me like it had before.

I felt it. My intuition knew that I was about to have sex with my husband and my soul knew it was about to be unfaithful to its mate.

Like time and like again, being with Grant made me think about Casey with another woman. Aly. That was a game my mind loved to play with me.

Grant's lips on me. Her lips on him.

Grant removing my shirt. Her breast in Casey's mouth.

My stomach lurched. My moaning, again, misinterpreted for desire.

Then, my thoughts of Casey saved me. He came to me through my senses. I was able to pretend it was his fingers caressing me, his body entering mine.

It was a fuzzy view, but I fought like hell to see it as my husband touched me in all of the ways he'd thought I'd loved.

My defenses knew what to do and propelled my body into action. I knew what he liked, too. I needed him to come for my thread-bare sanity to return.

"Call me, Betty," I begged, needing that extra push to aid my show.

"Betty," he panted in my ear on cue. "I missed you so much, Betty."

It was erroneous. I was abysmal. In those moments I hated myself, but I'd decided to tell the truth. So I said the truth, but I wasn't speaking it to Grant. I was talking to Casey, my words falling on the sheets of my husband's bed.

"I missed you, too," I said and I swallowed the lump in my throat.

"I'm going to come," he admitted like he always did.

"Yes, please," I said, knowing it was almost over. I pinched my eyes tight and pictured Casey's face giving me his best smile, I mentally held tight to it as Grant cried, "Betty!" into the pillow beside my head.

When I was sure that he was asleep, I got up and retrieved my phone and went outside to send a message to Casey. On my way, I grabbed my favorite mug, the one that originally said, "Lou likes trouble" and filled it with cold water from the tap in the door of the brand new stainless steel refrigerator.

I sat on the concrete stoop just outside the back door.

**Me: Remember the mug you bought the morning after we met?**

**Casey: The yellow one or the striped one?**

He replied almost immediately and oxygen reentered my bloodstream.

**Me: The yellow one. I still have it.**

I bit at my thumbnail waiting for him to reply.

**Casey: It's a good mug. Is it Monday yet?**

**Me: Almost.**

**Casey: I want you here. I can't sleep.**

**Me: I can't either.**

A feeling in my gut knew that I had to stay in Seattle. The right thing for Casey was for me to stay and get this marriage ended as fast as possible.

I wanted him, but I wanted him in a permanent way. I didn't want to go back for another two wonderful weeks and then have to leave him all over again. It wasn't fair.

But I couldn't tell him in a message. I pressed the call function and his line rang.

"Honeybee?" he said as an answer.

I could feel the agony for both of us and I hadn't even said hi back yet. I sat there actively reminding myself to breathe in and out. Preparing my throat for the ugly words that were about to pass through it.

In the long run, this was the best way. *The only way.* This would cause the least amount of damage for us, if we really did have a future.

I was done with yanking him around.

"I don't think I can comeback on Monday."

"What?" he shouted on the other end. My eyes screwed shut. That one word brought home exactly what was coming and my heart broke hearing the distress in his voice. I wished it wasn't me who'd always made him sound that way.

"Blake, don't even start with this shit. You're coming back," he demanded.

"I want to, Casey, so bad, but I need to do this right. I can't keep going back and forth. It's not fair to anyone and it's making me crazy. I don't want to hurt anyone, but I keep hurting us. I just don't want to hurt any more people than I have to. I can't come back to you until this is done."

"So, fine! Make it done by Monday. Even better." I heard something smash, it sounded like a bottle. "I knew you were going to do this."

"Listen to me before you get mad. Please." I felt my pulse everywhere. Was there ever a more shitty situation?

"Mad?! Is that what you think this is?" he asked.

There I was hurting him again. How could I even make this right, make this all up to everyone.

I rushed to add, "It will make me do this faster if I have to leave you alone. Does that make sense?"

Reminding him of how I felt about being without him had to work in my favor. It was all I had left.

"So what? You want to quit talking again?" He huffed a sardonic laugh. "No fucking way, Blake. I shouldn't have let you go."

"It's a means to an end. Don't you see that?"

"So no talking again, until this is over?" his voice calmed, but not in a good way. "Damn you, Blake. God damn it!"

I begged, "Please, Casey. Please trust me."

"Trust you?" he repeated, like hearing it back would make me grasp exactly how outrageous I sounded. Like I didn't already know.

"Trust. Me." I stood and nervously paced, my index finger taking a mauling.

"Promise. Honeybee, promise me you're telling the truth."

"I'm telling you the truth, but I will *not* promise. I've already made promises. And I've broken every single one of them. My promises aren't worth much these days."

We were both silent, like my fresh tears, for empty minutes.

"Then what?" He sounded so defeated. "What can you give me? How do I know? Fuck! How do I know this is real this time?"

"Because. Because it's true. I want you. I need you. And I want to really be yours. It's true." The pitch of my voice, while trying to keep my volume down, only came out squeaky and shrill.

"Don't take too long," he said. "You said a year the other night? So here it is. Your year. I hope, God I pray, that it doesn't take that long. And if not talking to you helps you move this shit along, so fucking be it. Don't call me. Don't text. Honeybee, my trust in you has an expiration date now. So do whatever the hell it is you think you have to do to make this right." He let out a resigned breath. "God, I can't believe this."

"I'll miss you so bad."

"Sometimes it feels like I started missing you the moment we met. I hate this."

He didn't say anything for a little while. I listened as his breathing slowed and I think he made his peace with my plan, at least enough to agree to it. Then he said, "Hurry back to me," and hung up.

I didn't get a chance to say goodbye. Maybe that was his intention.

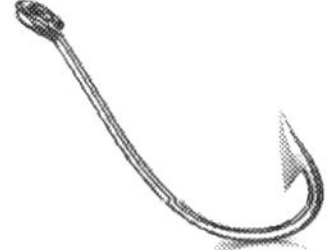

Days passed.

Weeks fell away.

I made good on my word. When Grant worked late, I told him what I thought about it. Or what I should have thought about it if I wasn't hell bent on getting out of our marriage.

I'd confided in my father again on Thanksgiving while he was having a cigar, frying a turkey, and quite frankly ruining a beautiful bird.

He got me good and drunk, too. I thought that maybe he knew I needed to talk and it was no secret that a little hooch was good way to go about it.

Grant went to his parents, but I didn't, choosing to spend our first Thanksgiving with my folks and apart from my husband. Yeah, that might have been a flag for my old man.

He was understanding, but surprisingly sided with both Casey and me. Telling me that I was dumb for putting him through all of that again, but he commended me for not running away simply because I wanted to.

He told me I was a smart girl and that he had my back.

I slept on their couch and flipped my mom off when she tried to wake me up at two in the morning to go shopping with her. Shane, who still lived there, wasn't so lucky.

It had been almost a month without him. Something that, sadly, I'd been through before. Too many times.

I'd spoke to Micah a lot, I told her the truth, too. She was supportive, but pretty much warned me that if I didn't get my shit together, and in so, that if I hurt Casey again, she would be the one whooping my ass.

I thought that was fair.

Micah and Cory decided to get married, which was kind of like an engagement, but in their own weird way, and they'd set the date for New Year's Eve. Only about a month away.

I tried not to ask her about Casey, I didn't want her to think that the only reason I called was to get the latest on my Godson and my year-plus-long one-night stand.

Even still, she always made a point to mention what he'd been doing. I was grateful to have a friend like her.

Reggie called me every day.

"You know you can come visit me anytime you want to get away, Blake. It would be nice to have you here. I could use a distraction myself," he'd said during one of our evening chats. He sounded stressed and I hoped everything was okay. I hoped Nora was there for him.

"You're busy, you don't need your mess of a sister there cramping your style, but I love you for inviting me," I told him. Honestly, being in Chicago would only remind me of Casey, not that I could escape him anyway.

I'd been spending more time in the office, not travelling because I felt like that was just avoiding my home situation and ultimately my goal. Micah had told me that Casey had been travelling almost nonstop, but that he called to check in every few days no matter where he was.

Time passed in black and white.

I spent more time with Shane than probably ever. His mood suited me. It probably wasn't healthy feeding his depression with my shitty vibes, but I did it anyway.

We went to movies and barely talked. Sometimes we'd finish the night in a bar, while my husband worked.

Christmas came, but I wasn't into it. Instead of buying presents for family and friends, I gave them all gift cards. I only bought actual presents for Foster, and sent them to California in a big brown box.

I probably would have tried to ship myself if UPS would have had one big enough.

I was miserable and certain Grant could feel it. He wasn't a prick, or a bad husband. I often felt bad for him. Consequently, I wasn't being cruel or mean, but showing him *me* and how I was really feeling was starting to register with him.

I was counting down the days.

Grant wasn't really showing an ounce of concern for our demise, and only validated that I'd made the wrong decision by marrying him. It was like Reggie was right. Had I married a robot? Was he not upset that our marriage was a sham? He he ever have extreme emotions about anything?

My body was there same as always.

But I was finally able to admit that my heart and mind was with Casey.

# THIRTY-SIX

## Casey

**Thursday, December 24, 2009**

IT WAS LIKE MY mind was somewhere else.

I was traveling all the time, trying to make the days seem like minutes and the minutes go by as fast as possible. There was no end.

I didn't sleep well.

I didn't eat like I should. I was on a mission. Hold my breath until she came back. Tolerate life without her.

Everyday my fingers itched to send messages to her. Sometimes they typed them anyway.

**Me: Stop this. Please just get here.**

Delete.

**Me: I hate not talking to you.**

Delete.

**Me: How was your day?**

Delete.

**Me: I'm sorry I left you in Atlanta. I should have taken you back to the hotel and showed you how badly I wanted you for**

**my own.**

Delete.

**Me: I love you.**

Delete.

It was Christmas Eve. Lou and Betty were 0 and 2 for the holidays.

I spent most of the afternoon with my family, promising to come back the next day. Everyone was in full wedding mode preparing for Cory and Micah's big day the next week. The idea of another wedding repulsed me.

Carmen really stepped up. Since Micah's family lived far away and our mother was gone, she took Micah under her wing and did everything to assure that this family would have something to look forward to and be proud of.

God, I missed my mom and I was sure Cory felt the same way. With the wedding approaching, probably more.

I spent the afternoon with Foster. He was my kind of man.

He didn't ask questions.

He didn't look at me like I was something to be pitied.

He didn't mind that I opened my second beer only twenty minutes after my first.

I found presents address to him from Auntie Blake under the tree, and without asking anyone, I helped him open them.

She'd sent him baby toys and clothes and a book. The thing that caught my eye was he title, *The Invisible String.* I stared to read it and put my wingman out cold. I didn't get to finish because Micah took the baby and I'd look like a fool reading a children's book about loving someone from far away all by myself. He gave him a rain check.

Instead, after his mother shut down our party, I continued to drink and pretend to be interested in what everyone was talking about. Only chiming in when absolutely necessary.

I was glad Troy was there. He drank with me and if my memory served me right, he put my consumption to shame that night and my sister Audrey had to drive him home.

By nine o'clock I was calling a car to come and pick me up. It was just as well. I probably wouldn't feel like driving in the morning and I'd need another to come pick me up from my house.

I would sleep alone and most likely dream about Grant's wedding to the woman I loved for the millionth goddamned time. But least I'd get to see her. *How pathetic*.

When I got back to the house, my house, my mom's house, the last place I'd seen Blake, I started a fire and docked my iPhone, playing Christmas music as I watched the flames lick the pecan wood I'd brought inside for the mild winter.

I did what I did every night.

I brooded.

I thought about her.

With him.

Were they having a merry Christmas? Exchanging presents and playing board games with their families? Where they arguing and going to bed angry?

God, what I would have given to be going to bed angry next to her.

I was nine sheets past three sheets to the wind. I'd had my fill of drink, but I was still up. Sleep avoided me like two north magnets those days.

My head sagged onto my chest until I heard a familiar voice, and it lifted itself to confirm who I was hearing.

*Aly*.

She was here in my living room.

"Casey?" she said, inquiring to see if I was awake. I hadn't moved, only tuned my ears into her presence.

She came to me where I sat in the chair that faced the fire, which was nearly out by then, and crouched down in front of me.

My eyes didn't want to look. I'll admit. It wasn't my finest moment. I'd stared so long at the burning wood that my eyes were dry and they watered when I shut them to ignore that she was there.

I didn't ask her to come. In fact, I'd done everything in my power to avoid her.

I never wanted to be a person who made someone feel less than worthy. I knew how she felt about me, but that still didn't make me feel anything for her.

Yet, she was the one who was there. I needed Blake, but instead I had Aly. I hated that I knew how it would play out. I hated predicting the next few hours, but I was so damn lonely.

I craved Blake's touch, but I could have Aly's.

I was in misery.

Aly was a pacifier. It was wrong, but I was weak.

When she moved her hands to the tops of my legs, I turned my head away from her again. I wanted to resist, but then I thought of Blake nestled warm in her bed next to her husband.

I had been *faithful* to a woman who didn't know the definition of it. A woman I loved all the more for her crimes, because she committed them with me.

Aly's hands wandered without my protest to halting their curiosity. We'd been together in our past. In my life pre-Blake. She wasn't completely foreign.

I was tired of fighting. I was tired of being alone.

I stood and took her hand. My feet weren't steady and my steps showed her exactly how much I'd consumed. She went with me anyway.

I took her to my old room. The one opposite the house from the bed Blake and I'd shared. Even with the haze that the alcohol provided, I was lucid enough not to bring her there.

She was gentle with me as I stood there and let her take my clothes off. I still didn't look at her, though. There was a nasty taste in my mouth as hers moved over my skin. It did nothing to excite me. I was limp. Numb to her.

"Casey, let me make you feel good," she whispered in my ear as she took my length in her hand and massaged me, persuading my body to agree to her plight. "She's not here. She left you," she said, and if she'd only known that it wasn't helping her cause, she probably wouldn't have mentioned it.

"She's comin' back," I slurred. She walked me backward to the bed and I sat on the edge when my knees hit the mattress.

She straddled me. My hands stayed next to my body, they didn't embrace her. They were powerless, too.

It wasn't until she said, "I know you love her. She isn't here, though. I can be her tonight. Please, love me like you love her. Just for tonight. Let me be her."

My vision cleared and I finally made eye contact with her. I saw an honesty there. No strings. The woman who was caring for me in this moment wanted to be here. I wanted to give my love to Blake, but she was gone.

"I've been drinking," I told her in defeat. Even if I did want to participate, now that we were there, I couldn't see how I would be able.

"Shhh. It's okay." She breathed into my hair, it had grown out a little and she ran her fingers through it in a way that reminded me of my honeybee. Two hands ran up the back of my head, scoring my scalp. I let my eyes close and gave in.

She reached between us and even to my surprise I was hard, not to my full potential, but enough to get the job done. That was good enough for her.

She took her shirt and bra off. I leaned back on my elbows and watched a girl that I didn't love mount and ride me like her life depended on it. My dick reacted like dicks do. It took what it was offered and I watched with lazy eyes as she fucked me.

She didn't hold back and she required very little from me. As she grew closer to her climax she leaned into my face and kissed me. I closed my eyes again and thought of Blake. Images of her riding me and saying my name flooded my intoxicated mind.

I remembered Blake saying, *"Then kiss me. Distract me."*

The thought of her moved my lips into motion and I let myself feel the pleasure that Aly gave me. It felt wrong, but so did everything else.

"You can have me, Casey," she panted. "I'm all yours. I can make you happy."

Her words filled my ears and in a moment of spontaneous sobriety I flipped us over. This clarity brought home exactly what I was doing, but my body was already doing it and I couldn't stop. It only knew to take what it needed. It was hungry for intimacy.

For nearly two years it had been only Blake. I hadn't been with another woman. There, in my childhood bedroom, I was fucking a girl who wanted me and dreaming of a girl who I couldn't have *yet*—according to her.

My hips thrust and I looked away from Aly. I focused on the shelf on the wall.

My childhood trophies. I pounded into her roughly, finding my sea legs in the process.

She moaned my name and told me how good I made her feel. She came and writhed under me. I fucked her until I came so hard that I had to grind my teeth to keep from screaming another woman's name.

I pushed into her harder than I knew I should. She took it. She took all of it.

"Ahhh!" I yelled as my dick pumped, angrily.

When I was finished I fell back to the bed, to the side of where she laid. "You can stay if you want to, but you can't sleep with me. I can get up and move to another room or you can. It's up to you."

"I'll stay here," she said out of breath. "And that's a nice tattoo."

"What's nice about it?" I said bitterly and left the room.

By the time I awoke, alone in my bed the next morning, she was gone.

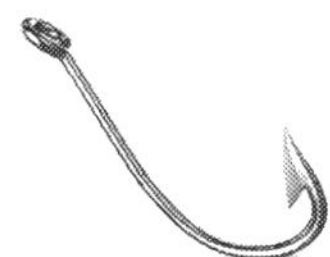

The next week was go here. Do this. Be here at this time.

Cory and Micah decided to throw a huge New Year's Eve party and say their vows in front of their guests instead of having a full-fledged wedding. For that, I was thankful.

Honestly, I knew that Blake was going to be there and even though I'd pledged not to talk to her or communicate with her, until she'd ended things properly with her husband, I couldn't wait to see her.

I was aware that Grant was coming with her on this trip. I didn't like it, but I was curious to watch them together. I wanted to see first-hand. I wanted to see them with each other. Were they flirty? Or were they merely casual and friendly? I needed to know.

It was Friday and my stepmother had arranged a rehearsal dinner of sorts at the golf club my dad belonged to. I showed up a little late, but I showed up. At some point in the afternoon, I'd lost my balls and considered calling in sick to my brother's wedding.

That simply wasn't an option.

So I took a shower and cleaned up as best I could. If I couldn't have her, I'd do my best to make her see what she was missing. It was cruel, but I didn't give a shit.

I was past giving a shit.

I wanted my girl.

I wanted my honeybee.

The banquet hall was full when I walked in. Music played, although I didn't know what fucking kind it was. It sounded like standards, but then as I waited on my first drink I thought I heard the singer croon, "How do you want it?" wasn't that a TuPac song? I'd have to ask Cory about the music later.

Then I heard her laughter from across the room. God help me, I missed that laugh.

I turned my back and leaned against the solid cherry bar.

She was wearing a fitted black dress and she had a tiny little colorful thing on her head. It was half mini-veil, half hat. It was kind of weird. I'd seen women where them in magazines, but never in person. It covered the left side of her head, the side that was closest to me. She looked so beautiful, smiling and talking.

A guy came to the bar and ordered a Rum and Coke and a Remy Martin on ice.

*Remy Martin on ice. It had to be for her.*

My attention turned to him. It *was* him. I recognized him. I was standing next to Grant.

I took inventory of the man. I'd seen him at their wedding, but only in profile, and definitely not this close. He was dressed sharply in a three-piece suit. He had all-American written all over. Freshly cut dark blond hair, a clean shave, and smelled like cologne.

I hated that fucking rat-bastard.

We shared a brief look as the bartender fixed his drinks.

"Hello," he said.

I only nodded. I had to keep my mouth shut.

Then I saw Audrey making her way through the crowd.

"Casey! Isn't this nice?" she asked as she sidled up next to me, linking her arm in mine. "You're sitting next to me," she said.

I watched Grant's face turn from nonchalance into recognition. His head sharply cocked and his ears drew back like a dog on alert.

"You're name is Casey?" he asked coolly.

I don't know what you would call it, but my machismo swelled, the fact that hearing my name startled and shocked this man meant something. I didn't know what, but it was something.

I gave him my biggest, most cocky smile. "I'm Casey," then I offered him my hand to shake.

He looked dumbfounded and like he was computing something. Blake's brother was right. He sort of resembled a robot.

*Be-boop. Be-boop. I'm in love with your wife. Compute that, asswad.*

"I'm Grant Kelly, it's nice to meet you," he said, but it didn't sound like the truth. I had a feeling like he'd heard my name over the course of the last few years and that I wasn't what he was expecting.

"Enjoy the party," I said and then walked off to take my seat with my sister.

I sat at our family's table. Blake and Grant sat at Micah's. Their backs were to us and I was glad. I could feel the pull of my body towards Blake's, but I knew better.

I played the part of happy brother as well as Blake played the part of happy wife.

Appearances were everything. My family knew. All of them, I think. We weren't much for keeping secrets. But they played their parts, too.

It was the one thing I could be thankful for.

# THIRTY-SEVEN

## Blake

**Wednesday, December 30, 2009**

I WAS THANKFUL THAT we were interrupted by speeches when Grant got back to the table from getting us drinks.

"I just met Casey," he said as he scooted his chair in and unfolded his napkin over his lap. He draped an arm around my chair. My mind scrambled. I'd been sick with worry all day knowing they were going to be in the same room as each other. "You should introduce us more. Later perhaps?" Grant said quietly to me as Mr. Moore addressed, and spoke about Cory and Micah, on their behalf, to the guests at the dinner.

This was stress.

Having my husband and my lover in the same room. Having the man I wanted and the one that I was with talking was beyond what I could handle.

"Sure," I said, clearing my throat. "He's Cory's brother." Like being Cory's brother meant something to Grant.

Food was served.

My palms were sweaty. I willed myself not to bite at my nails.

Music was played.

We mingled a little, but I felt eyes on me from every angle. From

Audrey who only smiled at me, to Morgan who smiled, but not for my benefit. It was the first time that real paranoia gripped me.

Then there was the pull Casey had on me. It was exhausting knowing he was in the same room, but I couldn't turn around and look. Every move I made felt like it was both right and wrong.

I didn't have to search for him, I knew right where he was. At least I'd never get caught looking for him, because my body was synced to his.

"Can we say a quick goodbye to Micah and head back to the hotel? I'm getting tired," I said to Grant. It was still a revelation, him being here. It didn't even register on my radar that he would want to come. The last time I'd invited him to join me in San Francisco was when Casey and I first met. That seemed like such a long time ago. He'd made the decision only a few weeks ago after I'd returned from a quick trip to Cincinnati.

"Sure," he said and kissed my forehead. "Do you see her?"

My eyes scanned for her and Cory and I found them with Casey and Audrey. By the time I found them, Grant had already started us in their direction. When we got to them it was Grant who extended a hand first to Cory.

"Thanks for having us tonight. It was nice to see you again. Micah, you look beautiful and very happy." He kissed her cheek.

"Thank you," she said. No one made eye contact with me.

I leaned in to hug Cory, "Good luck tomorrow," I said, and then I hugged Micah. Hard. I wanted to cry.

I wanted comfort from somewhere, from someone. *I wanted to hug Casey.* The saint that she was let me hug her until I was ready to let go.

"Are you okay?" she asked into my hair before I pulled away.

"I don't know. I'm just really tired," I confessed and wiped the tear, which slid out without my permission, with the back of my hand. "I'm so happy for you." I gave her the biggest smile I had and laughed a little when a few more tears slipped off my cheeks.

When I left Micah's arms, I felt Grant pull me into his side.

"Weddings make Blake emotional. Don't they, baby?" Grant asked as he rubbed my upper arm in quick strokes and gave me a little shake. "Her eyes were swollen for days after ours."

I looked up at him and he was looking at Casey, who was looking at me. It was the first time all night that I allowed my brown eyes to indulge in the blue of Casey's.

He looked so handsome. A little rough around the edges, but his hair had grown out a little on the top and it was trimmed neatly on the sides. His face was covered in a light beard. The top two buttons on his steel gray dress shirt were open and the tiny sight of his body underneath made my mouth water and my body flush.

"Time to go," Grant whispered into my ear. All this time, all of these days and nights, minutes and months, I'd never been in this place. Never had Grant been in my ear while I was looking at Casey like that. A chill ran up the back of my neck.

I thought that this might be it. The second I break free and say no to Grant and yes to myself. To Casey. To the possibility of perfection. To risk giving everything to Casey, to give him more than the mere fraction of myself that I possessed.

In my silent panic, time slowed. I watched Casey's eyelashes dip and touch over his cheeks. My pulse thrummed in my ears. A peaceful broken smile became his face.

I chanced a look at my husband, he turned our bodies to leave and began walking us away from them. From *him*.

If I would have had the strength, I could have resisted the backward look over my shoulder. I wouldn't have seen the look on his face. I wouldn't have watched the scrap of faith in me pass past his lips in a whoosh.

I wouldn't have seen his balled fists shoot up in the air, as he looked up and turned his back to us as well.

My heels clicked against the marble as we walked to the doors in the front of the country club.

Grant talked in the car.

"The food was good," he said.

"Everyone seemed very nice," he said.

"They're a great couple," he said.

"It reminded me of our wedding," he said.

"For some reason I thought Casey was a woman," he said turning my blood to ice. I remember him assuming that when he'd called the day Foster was born. I didn't react.

I listened and smiled when I should.

My mind split. I'd perfected the multi-tasked conversation. I was waiting for him to ask something about the tension back at the dinner, so I paid close attention to what he said with one hemisphere of my brain. But on the far side of my mind, I screamed in frustration and I wailed in agony.

I imagined going to Casey. Letting go of Grant and running to him before, rewriting the last minutes we were at the rehearsal.

In that car ride, I accepted that the love I had for Casey, which lived like a parasite in my heart, was the biggest part of me. It lived in every cell. My mitochondria duplicated it and spread our secrets upon generations within me.

I had no choice and the sad truth of that realization was, that if I had had a choice, I'd probably fuck that up, too.

# THIRTY-EIGHT

## Casey

**Wednesday, December 30, 2009**

WE ALL MADE CHOICES. I made the choice *not* to put my fist through the wall behind me as they walked out of the club's banquet hall.

The look on her face told me what I wanted it to. She didn't hide it very well. The fact was that she wasn't able to pretend, even with him standing right there, that she didn't want me. Her body couldn't lie to mine.

I'd stared holes in the back of her head all night.

I'd prayed for the second when she couldn't take it anymore. Still, the stubborn woman never looked. I watched as she shifted uncomfortably in her seat, under the scrutiny of my gaze. I watched how my simply being in a room with her turned her inside out.

One look was all it took.

She left with him. I couldn't watch that.

If she needed motivation to make the decision, I was going to help her.

I was taking Aly to the wedding.

She asked for a year.

I'd already waited long enought. I was done waiting. I wanted her now. I sent her a message, even though we'd said we wouldn't. I was done with that, too.

**Me: Hang-in there, honeybee. It's going to get rough.**

I sent her that message for a few reasons. I guessed her phone was probably off and that she'd see it before bed and so I'd, most likely, be the last thing she'd think about. And also to let her know that I wasn't waiting for her to text me anymore.

The rules had changed.

Plus, I wanted to let her know it was almost over. I wasn't blind to her pain. When it came to her, I could see past my own despair.

I was going to fight.

I was going to drag her through hell.

I was going to make her so uncomfortable that we'd have a resolution by this time the next night. Either she was going to hate me and or the inside of her.

A heart marked with my name.

"Have I ever told you how good-looking you are, brother?" I said to Cory as we stood at the bar. The Hook Line and Sinker looked better than it ever had.

Every table was covered in black linens and had large trees made out of sculpted wire lit from the inside with tiny lights. It was a great spot for a wedding and the perfect spot for a hell of a good party.

It was a good place to meet in a bar. It was the best place to meet in a bar. It's where *we* met in a bar. It might have been the wrong time, but it was definitely the right place. And here we were again. I relished in fated-like, ironic feel it all had.

"Yes, you have. And like I've told you before, you're right." Cory retorted. "Seriously, though. You look better than I expected you to. You doing okay?"

"I'm doing great. To the New Year," I raised my glass to him and he brought his to mine.

"To the New Year." We each took a long drink.

He added, "I see you brought Aly."

I looked at my feet. I knew what it appeared like to my family. It looked like a sign that I was trying to get back at her, but that wasn't it at all. I was just plain old trying to *get* her.

Aly was just another nudge.

It was wrong for me to do that to Aly, but who was keeping track of my mistakes those days? Sure as hell wasn't me.

"I did," I said.

"She cares about you."

"She does." My mood wasn't set to explain mode at the moment. "Are you ready to say those vows? Not going to run?" I teased and changed the topic.

"I'm ready," he said as he straightened his posture. "You know, I know how lucky I am. I see you and whatever it is that you and Blake have and it's painful to watch sometimes," he said and then thoughtfully added, "But I also know you and you wouldn't be doing this if it wasn't worth it. I've seen you pretty torn up over this girl in the past. But something's different tonight." He scratched his chin and laughed. "You look like you're going to war."

"Maybe I am," I deadpanned.

"Good." He bounced on his heels and leaned in to say conspiratorially, "Just remember this is our wedding. If you upset my wife tonight, we'll have a problem. Do what you gotta do," he said as he walked off to a waiting Micah.

The evening started with cocktails. Blake wore a black dress that I had a history with. If she was giving me clues, too, I was getting them loud and clear.

I didn't hesitate to walk right over to them. They were talking to Micah's mom and stepdad.

"Happy New Year," I bellowed as I came to a stop on Blake's side. Everyone responded wishing me a Happy New Year, too.

"So are you ready to stand up there with me Blake?" I asked, interrupting the conversation they were having and starting a new one of my own choosing.

Blake replied, “Um, up where?”

Grant’s hand slid around her waist and pulled her in closer.

Good. The fucker knew what my intentions were. He might not know his bride very well, but he sure as hell had me pegged right.

“The altar.” I paused watching her eyes go wide with shock. “You know? Best man? Maid of honor? We’re at a wedding? Any of this ringing a bell? I love that dress by the way.” I slipped that last bit in there as Micah’s stepdad said something to Grant.

“Have you seen my date?” I asked as Grant’s attention returned to the conversation happening between his wife and me.

“Your date?” Grant asked. “The blonde you came in with?”

“Yeah, Aly. Have you seen her?”

“No.” Blake answered in short. “I hadn’t.” Her reaction couldn’t have been better. Her nostrils flared and she took a deep breath. It was perfect; she looked like she was going to war, too.

Cory’s term for it was spot-on. We were going to war. Except, I was going to show her, finally, that we were on the same side. We wanted the same goal.

“Well, if you do, would you tell her I’m looking for her? Something funny just happened and I wanted to tell her about it. Well, anyway, I’ll see you up there,” and I pointed to the stage that had been changed into the semblance of an altar, where my brother and her best friend were going to take their vows.

I immediately found Aly and kissed her playfully on her neck. I didn’t look to see if Blake was watching. I hoped Grant was watching, too.

I made my way to the acoustic musicians who were playing for us that night. They were friends of Cory’s through work, but I’d met most of them before. I asked them if they knew a few of my favorites and then I made a request.

When it came time for them to say their vows, I stood opposite of Blake on the stage. Grant sat behind her, so he couldn’t see her face, but he sure as hell didn’t look away from mine.

Cory and Micah made promises to each other and to Foster, who was already at home in bed. They pledged forever and happiness and working out their future problems. Together.

Her gaze didn't leave mine.

I licked my lips and watched pink slash her cheeks and nose. That pink fucking nose.

I pretended to be itching and tapped my nose as she studied me.

*That's right, honeybee, you don't fool me. You never have.*

The ceremony ended.

Dinner was served, the music began, and first dances were had. Our sisters danced with Cory when Micah's stepdad danced with her for dance that was traditionally reserved for mothers and sons, fathers and daughters. They were good girls.

For an acoustic band, they were a lively group. Blake spent a lot of time with Micah out on the dance floor. Grant and I met again at the bar.

"So, you're twins, huh?" he questioned.

"Yep," I said.

"I think Blake and I are going to start trying for some kids. She was saying a few months ago that twins would be fun." His face was ambivalent, and a forced kind of friendly. "She loves Foster. I learned tonight that you're his Godfather. I hadn't realized. Hell, before yesterday I thought you were a woman." He laughed and took the shot, which I hadn't noticed, from behind his beer glass.

"A woman, huh?" I humored him. "Why would you think that?"

"Oh, I suppose it was just a misunderstanding." He held a one up to Nate behind the bar asking for another shot. Grant gave me a questioning look as to ask if I wanted one, too. I nodded.

Nate poured them in front of us and we half-faced each other.

"Care to make a toast, Casey?"

Before he could make the toast I said, "Here's to misunderstandings." He huffed and then tipped the liquor back, slapping the glass on the bar with a loud pop.

I watched him walk back to their table and take a seat, another drink in hand.

When I heard the beginning of D'Yer M'ker, the first song that we'd ever danced to in the very spot she was standing, I knew it was time for my next move.

Blake's body went rigid when she realized what song was playing.

She looked like a statue in the middle of the dance floor as I led Aly into my arms and began dancing to the song with her.

She was either going to hate me or crack. The warrior I'd seen on stage a little bit ago didn't seem as strong.

Holding Aly in my arms, my feet led me to face Blake and I mouthed the word "Bait."

# THIRTY-NINE

## Blake

**Thursday, December 31, 2009**

WHEN MY FEET FINALLY moved, they took me to the ladies room. I sat in the stall for minutes trying to calm my pulse and get a grip. He was only trying to get under my skin.

It was working.

I hated the thought of him dancing with her. That particular song was simply the icing on the cake.

He'd been like that all night. At every opportunity, he was talking to us, to me, to Grant.

*He loves this dress.*

*This place.*

I watched them have a shot together at the bar, right after my husband had already had three. Still, Grant hadn't said anything or gave me the impression he was angry with me. He seemed pensive, like he was working something out. I knew what he was piecing together.

I wasn't in control of the situation anymore. The only thing I could do was hang in there, like his text said last night.

Was it a warning he'd sent? I'd taken it as a show of support.

I pulled out my phone and replied to it.

**Me: Are you trying to hurt me?**

I washed my hands and looked at myself in the mirror. My nose really was pink. Stupid nose.

Then Aly came into the room, not paying any attention, digging through her purse. When she was all the way in the room, and heard me pulling the paper towel out of the dispenser, she stopped, an evil smile crossed her face.

It was not what I needed at that moment.

When I saw her come in with Casey earlier, I almost lost the ability to walk. I did lose the ability to talk and stopped midsentence while speaking to Micah's mom.

And there she was again.

I took a long steadying breath. The look on her face told me she was going to enjoy a conversation with me. I'd thought it best to get out of there as soon as possible.

"Leaving so soon? I was hoping to talk to you," she said coyly and walked herself to the counter, setting her purse down, continuing her search for whatever. I was gathering up my clutch to leave when she caught my gaze in the mirror.

"Your husband seems like a very nice guy," she said as she found and lifted her lip gloss out of her big bag. Her fingers unscrewed the lid and then her eyes found mine again. "He and Casey sure do get along. Maybe we could all go out sometime? You know, when you're in town." She began applying the scarlet color to her pouty mouth.

"I don't think so," I replied and then turned to head for the door.

"I don't think you *think* at all." She snapped and faced me when I had almost made it around her. "Do you?" Her voice sounded saccharine sweet, but her tone was anything but.

I stated, "Not tonight, Aly. You don't know what you're talking about."

"Oh, I know exactly what I'm talking about. Exactly, what *were* you thinking when decided to cheat on your boyfriend-wait-fiancé-wait-husband? What *were* you thinking when you came here after Casey's mother died and then just left him like you did every other time? What were you thinking when you brought your husband here?" Her voice had risen and she was just shy of yelling at me. Yelling things that I knew way-fucking-more about than she ever would.

She had good points, but it wasn't her business no matter how much she thought it was.

I collected myself and made sure my voice was calm when I spoke, "It would do you good to stay out of it. And while we're on the subject of why *we* do what *we* do, why do you want a man who clearly doesn't want you? Hmmm?"

Her hand collided with my cheek. The slap was hard and loud and it echoed off the marble walls. I was shocked. I always thought she was rude and manipulative, but I never thought she would be ballsy enough to hit me.

The bitch slapped me. I had been bitch-slapped in every sense.

All the while, I stood there processing what had just happened, she went back to applying her gloss. She finished and put it back into her bag.

"It's ironic, you know? That you asked me that. I ask Casey the same question. Why do you want her, if she doesn't want you back?" She stepped to me and surprisingly I stood my ground, even seconds after being hit. She continued, "The answer is simple. I love him like he loves you. So, go on and keep tearing him down. I'll be here every single time you do to build him back up. Just like I was the other night." She laughed again. "He always did know how to make me come harder than anyone else." Then she left the small room, but her words hung in the air as if they were in little, comic strip word bubbles.

As I feebly tried to calm myself, I thought about how this mess, our mess, had affected so many people. I hated Aly, but replaying the things she said to me I almost had to respect how much she really cared about Casey.

At least she had good taste.

Then, a flood of jealously washed those thoughts away.

*He fucked her?*

*He brought her here that night.*

*He danced with her.*

My head fizzed with doubt and anger and—even though it wasn't mine to have—betrayal bobbed its way to the very top.

I didn't know how much more I could take.

I needed to leave.

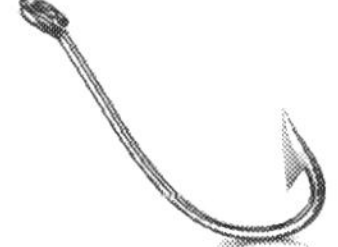

When I finally had my bearings, I found myself walking out into the bustling bar. I needed to find Grant and when I did he was, again, talking to Casey. I couldn't imagine what they'd have to talk about or why they kept finding each other. My stomach rolled like it had since the plane wheels left Washington State.

Their bodies both looked tense. Each man stood full-chested like roosters about ready to fight. I'd never seen Grant behave that way. He didn't give anything away the night before or that morning. I thought that maybe it was all in my head. Then I saw them there, almost chest to chest.

Something wasn't right. Something big was about to happen. The energy in the room popped and crackled. I had no choice but to throw myself at the mercy of the situation. The air was charged exactly like the air before a summer storm.

I slowly made my way to them. Listening to my heels catch on the uneven wood floor of the bar that changed my life. I diverted my eyes to the ground and took my place next to my husband.

"I think it's time to leave," I said and both men looked at me. I still couldn't make my mind up about who to look at, or maybe I had and thought better of it, so I continued to stare at my shoes.

"I was just talking to Casey. I didn't know you guys knew each other this well," said Grant. He had drunk more tonight than I'd seen him drink—well, ever. His voice held an edge to it that I wasn't acquainted with.

I chanced a look up at him, his eyes were glassy and blood shot.

"He's Cory's brother. I've known him since Micah and Cory started dating." It sounded like an excuse, even to me. My head and heart were at odds and it made me sound like a robot not knowing how to use my voice, not wanting to say the wrong thing with the wrong tone to the wrong man. I thought it was trivial how, in that moment, I was the one who sounded like an emotionless recording. My hands fidgeted and my hips rocked back and forth. My nerves were shot.

"*And* we share a godson, Blake, I'm Cory's brother and godfather to Foster, your godson. It feels like there's more to it though. Don't you think?" His face had hardened in the time I was in the bathroom with Aly.

Casey's inelastic posture didn't wear the same on him as his suave easygoing one did. His body was tense and uncomfortable, appearing as if it itched in all the wrong places. His words felt like wool against my two-faced heart. I felt his irritation and reciprocated it.

Grant was just the opposite. Loose. Fluid and his body moved in ebbs and flows and his face swayed with his head that looked back and forth between Casey and me.

"My wife," Grant said, the sound of his f fizzed like the air being let out of a tire, "wants to leave. With *me*." He grabbed onto my arm and spun me much faster than I was prepared for. Grant wasn't a hands-on kind of guy. This included all handy actions. Ass grabbing. Tickling. Petting. Pulling. He was always in control of his person. But not then.

His hand squeezed my arm right below my shoulder. The difference in height, and the force of his hold, brought me up on my tiptoes.

I whimpered. And I heard a gasp from around the room, it was another one of those moments in between songs where the volume on life gets cranked up to deafening decibels. I turned to find all of them watching. They all had been waiting. They'd all earned this show. Audrey's hand covered her mouth, but everyone else stood very still.

My eyes swelled with molten tears. I did everything in my power to not look into Casey's hard stare. Again, my willpower wasn't enough.

Much more sober than my husband, in every way, Casey's nose flared and a wicked smile parted his lips and his teeth bared. I'd been wrong. It wasn't a smile. It was more of a snarl and my free hand reached out to him.

It was the most freeing feeling, a cool breeze swept over my mind.

I stayed my feet into the floor and resisted Grant's pull toward the exit.

"No!" Casey shouted, having seen my hesitance. "I don't think she wants to go yet."

My husband turned and faced him.

I wrenched my arm free and went to stand in between them choosing to face Casey as he advanced. I was introduced to a vein in his forehead that I'd never seen before. He looked almost homicidal.

Grant's chest heaved as he stood behind me, snaking an arm around my waist, maybe to steady himself, maybe to hold on to me. "You don't know her! You don't fucking know what she thinks," Grant yelled.

I tried desperately to make Casey's eyes meet mine, but they bore into the man behind me. "Grant, you need to calm down. We're at my brother's wedding." His voice was firm and more rational than he had to be feeling. I'd heard this shouting voice before. I'd heard him yell and scream over much less.

My body reacted to this voice. But when didn't my body react to Casey?

Then he added, "And I don't recommend you put your hands on her like that again."

"I wouldn't hurt Blake." That was the truth. He really wouldn't, the Grant I knew wouldn't.

"I know you wouldn't, because I would know."

There it was.

"Stop, Casey." I breathed, my words were discreet. "Please."

He looked down to me.

I saw flashes of my life with Casey fire off in my mind. The laughing. The playing. The sex. The want.

He said, "This is our chance, honeybee. Do it."

"Don't look at her like that!" Grant snarled, interrupting the publicly private conversation Casey and I were having. "Take your fucking eyes off her. Let's. Go." Grant tried to turn me again and I moved with him.

"My eyes are the only thing I haven't taken off her," Casey said, not far enough under his breath.

We heard.

"Liar!" Grant spun and lunged for Casey.

He lost his footing and grabbed for Casey, snagging Casey's shirt, his momentum sent him past his target and Grant fell to the bar floor.

I looked up at Aly, who stood next to Nate at the bar. Nate held a hand up to Cory, who was ready to step in, telling him to hold off.

Grant laid there, the fall jolting his clarity some. He shook his head, having landed pretty hard.

Casey looking down at him. Only feet from these two men, my hands covered my ears as if I was trying to teleport away from there. I quickly realized that this place, this bar, Hook Line and Sinker, really loved to fuck with my life.

Grant made an attempt to stand up and, for some reason, Casey leaned down to help him. It was the most peculiar of things. Something flitted across Grant's face. He blinked slowly, over and over, fixated on one spot.

"Betty," he said and the air sucked from my lungs. "Your tattoo says Betty," said Grant pulling his hand free of the charity he'd been offered. "Betty. BETTY!"

Grant got up and hurriedly walked past me without even looking, knocking onto a few chairs as he passed. I didn't know exactly what had just happened.

When I looked back at Casey, his shirt was spread and the buttons ripped off like I'd seen it many times. One side was untucked and it was flapped open. Across his chest in a script that almost looked like a ribbon, it read, "Betty. Mine."

His body language changed. He, too, looked betrayed.

He said, "I guess he knows Betty, too. I didn't even have to tell him. You did."

He snickered and strode past me.

One door. Two men. Three minutes and I simply stood there.

Maybe it was longer.

The music started back up. The hustle and bustle resumed.

I couldn't turn around.

I had to go forward.

I saw Casey talking to a driver across the street and then get into the back of one of the cars Cory and Micah hired to get their guests safely into their beds.

I kept walking. I walk past the unmoving car, predicting that he'd roll down the window and say something.

He didn't. The car pulled away as I made it to the other side of the street.

I stayed the course. Keeping my word that I wouldn't go to him until I could be all his and he could be mine.

I needed to hit the situation head on. And head on took me straight into the hotel's elevator. I went up one floor higher, and to the opposite side of the building from the room where I'd let the proverbial cat get killed by curiosity, less than two years prior.

The argument we played out was new to Grant, but not to me. It was almost line-by-line of one of the many variations I'd rehearsed in my head over and over throughout the past few years.

This was the one where he asked me if it was true and I couldn't say anything.

He pleaded, "Just say it isn't true and then it isn't!"

The truth blurred. The lies blurred.

"I'm sorry," I said, and watched him drink a bottle of water, while packing his clothes.

"Why? Why, Blake. Why?" He'd said the word nothing short of ninety times.

"I wish I knew." Hello truth.

"How long?" he asked and stopped his packing to watch me with complete focus.

"So long," I confessed.

"So long?" He began packing once more, going into the bathroom and collecting his shaving kit and deodorant, not stowing them like he normally would. Instead of dutifully securing them in the mesh pocket under the lid of his suitcase, he just threw them in.

He repeated, "So long" over and over in place of his previous "why" in which he recited in various tones, trying each one out until he found a contrite-sounding one that he liked.

"Where are you going?" I asked.

He looked up. "Do you care?"

"Of course I do." Of course I do or otherwise I wouldn't have strung you along for so long. So damn long.

"God. What didn't I do right?" he asked, his voice sounding more like himself. More like the Grant I married.

"You did everything right," I said.

"Well, I guess not," he said, as he heaved the luggage off the bed. Pulling out the handle, it got stuck on its way to its full height, and he yanked it.

If it weren't such a bitch of a conversation, it would have been funny.

But it was and we didn't laugh.

He took a deep breath, his blond hair looking more disheveled than I ever remembered.

His voice was even and measured, which was par for Grant, and said, "I'm leaving. I'm calling the airline on the way. I'm getting on stand-by and I'm going home."

There it was.

When he made it to the door, he stopped. He unzipped the front pocket of his leather bag and tossed out a folded piece of paper. It landed on the floor. He looked at me one last time; then bowed his head and sighed. "I found this in your suit case a few weeks ago. I want you to come home, Blake. We can figure this out. Please, come home. But only if you want to."

He didn't even fight for me, not that I expected him to. He left.

I didn't have to unfold the paper to know what it was. I'd waited for that moment for so long.

# FORTY

## Casey

**Thursday, December 31, 2009**

I'D WAITED FOR SO long for something like that to happen. When you're sleeping with a wife who doesn't share your last name, you always think of how it will all play out. It was usually more dramatic in my head.

In my head, we'd duke it out and I kick his fucking ass. Blake would run to me and I'd kiss her like at the end of an action movie.

It wasn't like that at all by comparison. If it hadn't been at my brother's wedding, I would have levelled him. At least that was what I told myself. My adrenaline still surged through my blood.

I paced on the other side of the street, the driver asking me where I needed to go. I told him, "Back in time."

He said more than asked, "That bad?" A quick understanding and camaraderie linked us. I discerned that he'd been there before with only one nod of his head.

"I don't know if I should leave," I said. Then, I saw her come out of the bar, she looked like a lost person. She saw me, and her arms dropped to her sides.

She didn't smile. If she would have smiled at me, I would have been one thousand percent sure she was taking steps toward me, but instead as she got closer, she felt farther away. I stepped to the door of the stretch-sedan and he followed my eyes and then my cue, like a natural wing man. I had the driver, who told me his name was Andy, leave. We didn't get to the next block before I told him to head back.

I had him stop us just short of the doors so I could watch if anyone were to leave. I needed to see them walk out together. I needed to nail this coffin shut, my new tattoo was becoming a memorial. A tribute to love lost. Time and time again.

Betty.

Mine.

His. Always his.

I didn't know her.

He didn't know her.

I waited. Andy turned on the radio.

We waited some more.

Grant came out, raised his arm and almost immediately flagged down a taxi. He never looked behind himself to see if she was coming. Not once.

He got in and he drove away. Alone.

My heart sprinted.

Then, after a little more time, I saw her come off the elevator through the large glass windows. She had her suitcases. She was leaving, too. She looked around.

Was she looking for me? Had she really done it?

Her steps were rushed across the marble floor and she skidded to a stop in front of the doors to get through the glass turnstiles.

"Pull up, Andy. Please?" I asked.

He put the car in drive and crept ahead a few dozen feet so that my window was centered with the hotel doors. I rolled it down and looked out from my seat, waiting for her to see me. I knew she would.

And when she did her face eased, but her lip quivered and her shoulders sagged. Like she'd been holding everything together until that exact moment.

I got out and went to her. Her hands dropped the bags and wrapped around me. She clung to me so tightly and she cried. She didn't say anything, she just sobbed into my chest. I ran my hand across her back and let her do it.

When she calmed some, I lifted her chin to see puffy eyes and tear-streaked cheeks.

"Come on," I said. "Let's get in the car." I lowered to pick up her bags and carried them in one hand. Wrapping the other around her shoulder, I tucked her into my side.

Andy got out of the car and popped the trunk, taking her things from me and stowing them in the back. I opened the door and let her get in first then followed. I looked back at Andy and asked, "Can you give us a minute?"

He nodded and walked inside the hotel. Then I closed the door with us hidden away inside.

We sat facing each other, neither she nor I knew what to say. So we did what came easy, that with which reconnected us on an elemental level.

Our mouths touched, and after not touching for far too long, it seemed like a dam was finally opened. Our bodies let everything both physical and verbal go.

My hands pulled her onto my lap. I was elated. I said, "I can't believe this."

"I miss you so much," she said back. Her hands unfastened my belt buckle and she leaned back to expose me, not wasting any time. She was almost frantic.

Between kisses, I apologized for everything. For never standing up for us, even to her. For hurting her. For letting her go.

She moved her panties aside, brought my fingers to her mouth and licked them, preparing them to touch her and make sure she was ready.

She ran her hand over the words written on my chest and kissed them like they were the top of a baby's head. Tenderly. Her eyes closed tighter with every peck.

My dampened fingers found her already slick and wet for me. She lifted up and then sat down on me. My hands found her ass under the dress, which she had hiked up around her waist.

The moment she took all of me, I felt complete. She was here. She was with me. She *was* mine.

"Casey," she said as she began to ride me.

I tasted her neck and laved at her skin. Although I was already buried inside her, I felt my dick get harder still. Her scent made me harder. Her sounds made me harder. The sight of her rosy nose, as she arched her back and let her head fall away from me, soaking up the pleasure made me harder yet.

I felt the beginnings of her orgasm every time she came down on me, her muscles kneading me rhythmically. Her compressions growing fevered with intensity.

"Fuck me," she moaned.

I held her in my arms and turned us, laying her down against the seat, but I didn't let go of her. My body operated on instinct, thrusting into her. Her hands wrapped around my upper arms and she met me swell for swell.

"You're mine, Blake." I panted, everything felt urgent all at once. My words and my body claimed her.

"Yes, I'm coming. I'm coming," she confessed.

That made two of us.

"Ahhh. Fuck. Ahhh. Fuuuuuck!" I screamed and we shouted together, but our bodies kept moving. Pulsing again and again at different times, grasping onto our orgasms.

I sat her back up and leaned her against my chest.

Finally, she said, "Being with you makes it harder to be without you."

"You're not without me, honeybee. It's over. We made it."

Her head lifted and her brown eyes searched mine.

"I have to go to the airport," she said.

She had to go to the airport? The airport? To leave?

"No. You're not leaving this time," I told her. "I'm not letting you." That's just the way it was.

"I have to. I want this. I have to finish this. I have to make us right." She explained with the same thing she'd said before. Her manicured eyebrows arched and she looked at me for understanding, but she wasn't going to find it. As far as I was concerned, it had ended.

I clarified, maybe all of the events of the night had become too much to process, "We are right. He's gone. You're going to stay."

"I can't just leave it like that!"

"Yes, you can," I argued. She shuffled off me and pulled down her dress so that her legs were covered.

"I want you. Do you believe that?" she questioned.

"I think *you* believe that." I zipped up my pants and did up my buckle. "You have got to be out of your beautiful fucking mind if you think I'm letting you go back to him."

"You know I have to go back. I have to deal with this."

"Why the fuck do you do this to yourself? Why do you do this to me? Don't you understand how bad this hurts? Fuck!" My temper was back, but this time it was on the defense.

"This hurts me, too!" she shouted. She was in fight mode, just like me. Always fighting on the same side of the argument, but at the same time against each other. "You hurt me, too!" She yelled again.

"Not like this. I don't hurt you like this. He knows about Betty!" That last part fell out with everything else, but it hurt all the same.

"Did you fuck Aly?" she asked point blank.

"Yes, do you fuck Grant? Your husband?" I fired back.

"Yes, and you know what? You're going to love this—I made him call me Betty. Just. So. I. Could. Come."

"You're a real piece of work. You know that, right?" I scolded. "I don't even know why I fight with you anymore. I never win."

I rolled down the window and whistled loud enough to get Andy's attention. He was chatting with the valet near the door.

He walked out and I said, "We're going to the airport."

He tipped his hat and got in the driver's seat.

There was no point in arguing. Everything had been said.

When we arrived at the departure terminal, I watched her hand touch, let go, and then touch the door handle again. I saw the hesitation, but there wasn't anything that I had left to give.

Blake looked at me, there were no tears in her eyes and she smiled.

"Casey, I love you so much that it ruins me. It cripples me and wrecks my sanity. But, I do, I love you so much that it blinds me to right and wrong. But I'm not free. I can't give you my heart until it's mine. But you can bet your life on it, I will."

I turned my head and looked away. Her words were both acid and salve on my shredded heart. I was so tired.

Time would tell.

She got out of the car, and Andy helped with her bags.

I thought that she'd already walked off, that was the only reason I stole a look in the direction of the doors. But she hadn't, she was pulling something out of her bag. She knocked on the window, and I reached her direction, pressing the button of it to descend.

She tossed a piece of paper into the car and walked away.

Like a masochist, I watched her go.

When she was deep inside the doors and I couldn't see her through the people walking around anymore, I pulled out my phone.

I read a message that she'd sent earlier.

**Honeybee: Are you trying to hurt me?**

I looked at the time. It was midnight on the dot. Another New Year, another new day.

**Me: Our pain and our love are one and the same. I'll wait for you. Probably, forever if that's what it takes.**

Delete.

**Me: Happy 2010. Goodbye.**

**…The Bait**

# EPILOGUE

*To you,*

*I'm sitting here this morning making wishes on waves.*

*I'm on my honeymoon, yet I can only think of you. Of us. I wish I could talk to you right now, but we both know I never say the things that I should. Or maybe I do, but just to the wrong people.*

*I've used the excuse that we met in a bar, and that we were only a one-night stand, but you know me. It turns out that I'm a liar. Because the truth is, we've met lots of places. And no matter how hard I fought not to, I fell in love with you every single time.*

*I made a mistake when I said my wedding vows, because my heart had already promised them all to you. And you deserve someone who isn't afraid to tell the whole world how sacred a feeling it is being loved by you.*

*I wish that someday that someone is me. The whole me. All of the parts of me. Because you're the only one who's ever seen them and it's a crime that I've made you feel like they weren't yours all along.*

*You asked me once what parts of you I wanted. I'm selfish because I want them all. I want to find new parts of you and plant flags with my name on them.*

*If the saying "you hurt the ones you love the most" is true, then I wish I could love you less so that loving me wasn't so hard.*

*We fight. And we fight hard. I've only just realized that we were on the same side. And I'm rooting for us.*

*I don't know how I'm going to do it, and it might take me the rest of my life, but I'll see to it that you and that bait of yours catch this fish.*

*But most of all, you precious man, I wish you knew that I'm here, wishing for you.*

*Your honeybee,*

*Your Blake,*

*Yours only, always.*

# ACKNOWLEDGEMENTS

To my readers, my love for you has no boundaries or borders—it goes everywhere.

To the Mo Stash, you girls are the most fun cheerleaders I've ever met. I LOVE YOU SO MUCH.

To the blogs that drop everything for me at the drop of a hat. Bare Naked Words, The Never-ending Book Basket, Back Off My Books, Mixed Emotions Book Blog, Two Unruly Girls with a Romance Book Buzz and so many others that I hate myself for leaving out.

To Wendy and Claire, there are no bigger hearts than yours. Anywhere.

To my beta and proofreaders, Aly, Megan, Elizabeth, Michelle, Wendy, Tara, Jordan, Sandie, Laura, Sandra and Alexis this book is better because of you. Thank you.

To Laurel, your sweet heart and kindness make me want to be a better girl. So, you're stuck with me. When are you moving?

To Aly, you boss me around and I like it. You're my backbone. You say no when I want you to say yes. You make me look at things from the best possible angles, twisted as they might be.

To Erin, I can only hope to be as cool you when I grow up. Maybe we'll set off the airport metal detectors together one day.

To Natalie, I get emotional thinking about how much I love you. That's not healthy. You've been cheering these two characters on for over a year now. Part of my heart belongs to you—it's the weird part that no one else wants. Never leave me.

To my husband, you let me pass go AND collect $200 by taking the steering wheel of our home while I wrote this book. I love you so much. Forever and ever and probably the time life comes around, too. Kindred spirits we are. I'm chasing my dreams and I learned how from you. Fifty-fife cents, my love.

# ABOUT THE AUTHOR

M. Mabie lives in Illinois with her husband. She loves reading and writing romance. She cares about politics but will not discuss them in public. She uses the same fork at every meal, watches Wayne's World while cleaning, and lets her dog sleep on her head. M. Mabie has never been accused of being tight lipped or shy. In fact, if you listen very closely, you can probably hear her flapping her gums.

You're encouraged to contact M. Mabie about her future works, as well as this one.


http://www.mmabie.com
http://www.facebook.com/AuthorMMabie
http://www.twitter.com/AuthorMMabie

Made in the USA
Charleston, SC
10 August 2015